# Praise for the Women of Hope Series

## *FOR SUCH A TIME AS THIS*

"[A]n engaging tale of duty, romance, family, and love....I'll be eager to see what character Ms. Aiken chooses next to feature in this exciting new series."

—Serena Chase, USAToday.com

"FOR SUCH A TIME AS THIS offers readers all of the elements they love in one beautifully-written Esther-themed tale. Highly recommended!"

—Janice Hanna Thompson, author of
*Love Finds You in Daisy, Oklahoma*

"Courageous and level-headed, Olivia is a heroine readers will love, and Aiken does a masterful job of evoking life in a small Oregon town in the 1870s. Readers won't want to miss this first book in Aiken's Women of Hope series."

—Marta Perry, author of the *Pleasant Valley* Amish books

"The suspense writer in me loved the thread of mystery she skillfully wove into the plot. This book should come with a warning: Before you start to read, make sure you don't have anything else to do for the next several hours because you WON'T want to put this book down. Eagerly awaiting the sequel!"

—Lynette Eason, best-selling, award-winning
author of the Women of Justice Series

"Aiken in FOR SUCH A TIME AS THIS has created a well-crafted story with humor and characters you will care about."

—Margaret Daley, author of *Saving Hope* in the
Men of the Texas Rangers Series

# *REMEMBER ME WHEN*

# Also by Ginny Aiken

*For Such a Time as This*

# REMEMBER ME WHEN

A WOMEN *of* HOPE NOVEL

# GINNY AIKEN

FaithWords

New York • Boston • Nashville

FaithWords
Hachette Book Group
237 Park Avenue
New York, NY 10017

www.faithwords.com

Printed in the United States of America

RRD-C

First Edition: June 2013
10 9 8 7 6 5 4 3 2 1

FaithWords is a division of Hachette Book Group, Inc.
The FaithWords name and logo are trademarks of Hachette Book Group, Inc.

Library of Congress Cataloging-in-Publication Data

Aiken, Ginny.
  Remember me when : a women of hope novel / Ginny Aiken. — First edition.
     pages cm
  Summary: "Trapped in an abusive marriage, Faith Nolan finds the courage to defy her husband to help others. When her actions result in a false charge of murder, she finds the support she needs in Nathan Bartlett." —Provided by the publisher.
  ISBN 978-0-89296-847-3 (pbk.) — ISBN 978-1-4555-1811-1 (ebook)
1. Married people—Fiction. 2. Husbands—Crimes against—Fiction.
3. Oregon—History—19th century—Fiction. I. Title.
  PS3551.I339R46 2013
  813'.54—dc23

                                                      2012045481

*This one is dedicated to the memory of my mother, Olga Reyes, who went home to our Lord and Savior when I was in the weeds of writing it. She loved my books—thanks, Mom!—and even at my age, she kept after me to make sure I worked diligently on them; she always remained a teacher, decades after she retired. I imagine her these days holding class somewhere close to the Throne of Glory, surrounded by a gaggle of kids. Miss you, Mom.*

...the souls of thine enemies, them shall
he sling out, as out of the middle of a sling.

—1 Samuel 25:29

# Chapter 1

*Hope County, Oregon—1880*

With ease gained from experience, Faith Nolan measured then snipped a length of cord off the ball under the counter. She tied it around the neat, brown paper–wrapped package, and looked up at her new customer. "Will that be all, Mr. Purcell?"

The quiet man nodded. "Yep."

She handed him the totaled bill, then looked up to see who'd come into the general store. Inside the door stood Captain Curtis Roberts, the commanding officer at the nearby fort. She gave the polite Army man a nod in greeting, which was returned with a kind smile. He began to wander the store, but she caught him sending a glance her way although his back remained turned to her and her customer.

Mr. Purcell's lean cheeks turned ruddy above his brown beard. His gaze dropped to the counter. He shifted, shrugged, cleared his throat. "It's like this, Missus Nolan. We haven't been paid yet, since us new fellas just started working for Mr. Bartlett. But these days...why, it's mighty cold, ma'am, an' I'm needing warm und—er...well, you know."

From the corner where the captain stood studying cooking pots, Faith heard the sound of a choked chuckle. She smiled. So she wasn't the only one. It never failed to surprise her when the brawny lumberjacks turned shy around her, the person who actually sold them the unmentionables. "Yes, Mr. Purcell. You need your winter undergarments."

Relief bloomed over his weather-beaten face. "Yes, ma'am! Well, see...I've been wondering if you'd have mercy on me and be so kind as to put the sum on an account. I'll be good for it once Mr. Bartlett pays us next week."

The man, who'd only uttered two or three words since he'd entered the store, in discomfort seemed unable to stop the chatter. Faith glanced over her shoulder, leaned over the counter to look out the front window, and listened for a moment. She again checked the bill, a reasonably small one, then, with a cheery smile, said, "Yes, Mr. Purcell. We can do that—"

"No, we can't!" Roger roared from behind Faith.

Panic shot through her. Her heart pounded. Her hands chilled. Where had he come from? She'd checked to see if her husband was anywhere near only a few minutes ago, and she hadn't seen—or heard—a thing. "He's—"

"New around here," Roger said, spitting the words out as though they were something foul he'd tasted. "I heard."

Faith clasped her hands tight to hide the trembling.

The crisp rap of boot heels told her the captain was approaching. Oh, dear. How humiliating for such a gentleman to observe this dreadful moment.

Roger snorted. "And we don't know if he's gonna jist run with the merchandise and never come back."

"But, Roger, he's said he's working for Mr. Bartlett—"

"That don't make no never mind. You know the rules, Faith Nolan, and you better follow them."

Out the corners of her eyes she saw uniform-clad legs reach the corner of the counter. "Might I be of assistance?" Captain Roberts asked.

"Nothing to help," Roger muttered in dismissal. "It's all just between my missus and me."

When Faith realized Roger's words had served to turn the captain's attention back on her, she wished she could fade into the background. Instead, however, she felt frozen, caught in the Army man's fixed stare. Then she noticed what had caught his gaze. The large, angry bruise above her wrist, visible since she'd pushed her sleeves a bit up her arms as she worked, was not something one could miss.

Her gaze flew to his face. She saw pity painted there.

Shame seared her. A blush burned all the way up her neck and cheeks. She shoved her sleeves down, tugged them as far as they would go. In as firm a voice as she could summon, she said, "I...um...sorry, Roger. It won't happen again. I'll finish up here—"

"No, you won't be finishing up nothing." He glared at her. "I'll handle this, seeing as you can't do a single, blamed thing right. Go on. Git on out of here, woman."

Faith sucked in a ragged breath on her way to the back storage room, the weight of three stares heavy on her already burdened shoulders. It was setting up to be a long, difficult night. *Oh, Father, don't abandon me now—*

"He will be good for it next week," Nathan Bartlett, owner of the logging camp up the mountain, said from just inside the front door. Faith paused to listen. "I'll be making my payroll as I always do. You can extend him credit, Nolan. You know I keep a tight rein on my men, and I don't cotton with workers who can't—or won't—keep their word. He said he'd pay next week, and I expect him to do so."

From the relative shelter of the back doorway, Faith looked from Mr. Bartlett to her beefy husband and back. Few ever stood up to Roger. He was a large man, more burly and heavyset than tall, but powerful and cursed with a legendary temper. It took little to arouse it to full steam. To cross him was to jolt it awake.

The lumberman didn't look in the least intimidated. She wished she had that strength, that assurance.

Then again, Mr. Bartlett was tall, very tall indeed, one of the tallest men she'd ever seen, she reckoned, and he had the broad shoulders and powerful, muscular build to go along with his height. She, on the other hand, while tall for a woman, was built on a small frame.

Her husband narrowed his mud-brown eyes. For a moment, she feared he would argue with Mr. Bartlett, who had always been kind and polite to her whenever he'd come into the general store. But a quick look at the lumberman— silent, expectant, immovable—allowed her to ease her taut posture. It didn't look as though Mr. Bartlett would put up with any of Roger's tomfoolery any more than he did welchers.

Faith worried her bottom lip between her teeth. Without the logging camp's business, the Nolans' livelihood would be threatened. The bulk of their business came from Mr. Bartlett and the men at the camp.

Under Mr. Bartlett's unyielding gaze, Roger flinched. He patted back his thinning, gray-brown hair, tightened his lips, and jutted out his jowl-wreathed chin. "Fine, but if he don't pay me next week, I'll come after you for the cash, Bartlett. Understood?"

Instead of answering the belligerent question, Mr. Bartlett turned to his new employee. "What do you say, Purcell? Do you give Mr. Nolan your word? Will you pay him next week?"

The new logger nodded. "Yessir, Mr. Bartlett. I told the lady I'd be paying next week, and I will. I'm no shirker, sir."

His boss turned back to Roger. "Satisfied, Nolan? He's given you his word."

Roger hesitated once more, his fists clenched behind the counter where the men couldn't see them. Faith's stomach clamped tighter.

"I also," Mr. Bartlett said, stepping closer to Roger, his features more rigid and inflexible than even the mountain where he'd set up his camp, "give you my word. If Purcell here should fail to pay what he owes, you can come after me. I'll make good on the debt—you know I always do."

Faith blushed, thinking Roger had never dealt as honorably with the logger in return.

"And will *you* be having enough to cover?" Roger asked "It strikes me you been hiring men left and right and building some flumes and spending, spending, spending. I know my account ain't but a drop in a rainstorm to ya, but I still need paying."

With a look toward his new employee, the lumberman gave a jerk of his head toward the door.

Mr. Purcell hurried out, brown parcel under his arm.

Mr. Bartlett turned his flinty gaze toward Roger again. "Have I ever failed to pay?"

A muscle bunched in her husband's fleshy cheeks. "You ain't yet—but I always say there's a time for everything."

"Not for this," the logger countered. "I'm good for Purcell's bill. And for mine, as well. Which brings me back to my own business. I came about those things that were missing from my last order. I hadn't heard from you yet, but surely they've come in by now."

The muscle twitched again, making the jowl quiver, and Roger shot a warning glare at Faith. She shrank farther into the storeroom, but still left the door ajar to allow herself the chance to see what would happen next. The outcome of the confrontation would give her a good idea what she could expect later that night.

Her husband turned back to the lumberman. "Uh... there's been a holdup with the order. Not all I ordered's come in yet, and your other supplies were in what...ah... didn't show up. You'll have to wait till the next shipment."

Mr. Bartlett crossed his arms, and Faith again noted how solid he was. His broad chest and powerful arms reminded her of the trunks of some of the trees he harvested from the forest around them.

He'd always struck her as one who tolerated no nonsense, and Roger's blatant lie was nothing if not pure nonsense. With deliberate movements, Mr. Bartlett uncrossed his arms and approached the counter, his boots tapping an ominous beat against the store's wooden floor, his face in a tight frown. "I paid you, Nolan. In cash." He placed his hands on the counter, leaning right up into Roger's face. "My men work hard, and they need their food. You're my one and only source, seeing as you're the one with the mules to make it safely up the trail to the camp. No food means my men are in danger during the winter. Food, Nolan. We're talking about basic food. That, at least, shouldn't be too hard to get brought in through Bountiful. The equipment can always wait. Food can't."

Red in the face, Roger shrugged, leashed rage smoldering in his eyes. "I jist know what I know. I ordered your stuff, and it ain't here. I don't have your food or more of them other supplies. I can't do nothing about it. I s'pose you'll jist have to wait 'til the next shipment comes in. Maybe your missing stuff'll be in with that order."

Frustration narrowed Mr. Bartlett's eyes and bracketed both sides of his mouth. He blew out a gust of a sigh, shoved his sun-gold-shot hair off his forehead, and straightened. "You see that you let me know as soon as it does get here. I'll be waiting to hear."

"Sure thing." Roger made his tone careless. "I'll let you know."

Yes, Roger would let Mr. Bartlett know when his order arrived...when he felt like it. If he couldn't make an advantageous trade with someone with deeper pockets. Or a more attractive exchange.

As he had done the day before.

Faith had no idea who'd benefited from Mr. Bartlett's shipment, she only knew it had arrived two days earlier, and yesterday, when she'd gone to check the delivery against the original list, she'd found the corner of the back room where they always kept the camp's order empty again.

"None of your business," Roger had said when she'd asked, his voice a rough snarl. "It ain't here. I s'pose I'll git him stuff soon enough."

When Mr. Bartlett headed for the front door, Faith hurried to the stove. She needed to have a meal ready for when Roger closed up the store, or his temper would know no bounds. After a handful of muffled statements from Captain Roberts, she heard the door open and close. She sliced potatoes faster, skillfully missing her fingers in the process, even though the trembling hadn't abated much.

It surprised her, however, when her husband didn't immediately show up in their living quarters behind the store. Could he have left with the Army man? She supposed it didn't matter. She chose to appreciate the blessed silence that reigned in the building.

When the old brass cowbell on the front door jangled, Faith glanced up, craning her neck to peer through the doorway into the store. Theo Nolan, Roger's younger brother, stomped in, a sour look on his face, a box in his arms. Glass clinked with his every step, and Faith didn't know whether to cringe or relax. The two brothers would soon open one of the whiskey bottles in the box. She hoped they'd drink themselves into a stupor. Otherwise, Faith's evening would become, instead of merely dreadful, dangerous.

"You sss-shtupid cow!" Roger bellowed later that night, as soon as Theo staggered off to his room. Each one of Roger's steps brought him closer to Faith. "How many times do I…do I hafta tell ya? No credit! Them loggers…you give 'em a shh-chance, they'll rob me blind. You worthless thing, you. Dunno why I ever thought marrying up with you made any sss-sense."

The sour stench of the spirits Roger had swigged in the company of his brother smacked Faith's senses well before his fleshy palm struck her cheek. Her head jerked sideways. Her cheek stung hot. Tears scalded her eyes. Shame burned through her.

Her instinctive urge to defend herself surged, but with three years of experience behind her, she smothered it. The last time she'd fought back, Roger had come at her with redoubled rage. She'd spent days with her arm in a protective sling and both eyes puffed nearly shut.

"Do I hafta…um…hafta pound it into ya? No credit, you hear?"

Hand on her stinging cheek, she nodded. Panting, she met his gaze. "Ye—yes. I hear."

With a satisfied smirk, he reeled around and wove his way to the large brown-upholstered armchair he favored. He collapsed with a grunt and a belch. "Now, sss-see here, you lazy pig. Where's my supper? Don't tell me y'ain't made me nothing to eat yet."

Faith shook her head. "You know I wouldn't do that, Roger. Supper's ready. Let me dish up."

Anger roiled inside her, hot, impotent anger. *He* was questioning why he'd married *her*? She had yet to do anything untoward. She'd never done anything to hurt her husband. He, on the other hand, hurt her in a multitude of ways on a daily basis. Why had she ever thought marriage to Roger Nolan would solve anything?

She ladled a large serving of mutton stew from the kettle on the Excelsior iron stove into a deep bowl, then put three golden biscuits, split and buttered, on a small plate. She set it all on the solid oak kitchen table, and slid the honey pot closer to his place.

"It's ready," she said in a voice firmer than she felt inside. She poured a glass of milk, her husband's preferred drink with meals.

In seconds, he tucked in, shoveling the food into his mouth as fast as he could.

Faith shuddered. She returned to the stove, served her portion, and set the food aside. She'd eat after Roger finished. It was better that way.

She turned to the broad shelf where she kept her enameled steel washbasin, poured in steaming water from the ever-present hot kettle, cooled it with some from the bucket by the back door, and began to clean up. As she scrubbed at a scorched spot in the bottom of the iron kettle where she'd made the stew, she thought about how different Roger had seemed when they'd met.

Three years ago, she'd found herself utterly alone when her parents died during a raid by a band of rogue Nez Percé Indians. At the time the attack happened, she'd been at Metcalf's General Store in Bountiful, picking up supplies, and had been spared her family's fate. The killers had burned the homestead after doing in both Mama and Papa. They'd also taken their second horse, the cow, chickens, and the flock of sheep.

She'd been devastated.

And she'd had nowhere to go.

Each of the families in Bountiful had offered to take her in, but she hadn't been able to stomach the notion of charity, much less their pity. Nor had she wanted to become anyone's unpaid servant.

Two bachelors had come with offers of marriage. One had been a young ranch hand from another sheep operation near her family's land. The thought of going back to where the devastation had occurred had turned Faith's stomach, and since she'd had no feelings for the fellow, it had been easy to turn him down.

She'd thought Roger Nolan, the plump, well-to-do owner of the small general store up the mountain near the logging camp, would be a better choice. He'd struck her as settled and able to provide a decent living for them and the family she hoped she would someday have. He'd been polite, well-dressed, and soft-spoken, and he'd promised not to push her into anything she wasn't ready for.

She'd believed him. Surely the Lord would in time bless them with an abiding affection for each other. And so, in spite of Reverend Alton's qualms, she'd gone ahead and married Roger Nolan.

What a bitter mistake that had been.

Roger had a true talent to change on a whim. He should have joined a performing group. By now, she'd come to know any number of Roger Nolans.

Not only did he have that ability to change personality, but he'd also lied when she'd asked him if he was prone to drinking spirits. He'd assured her he was as dry as Hope County's dirt these past few years of drought.

As for not pushing her into anything she wasn't ready for...well, he'd assaulted her on their wedding night and every night since when he didn't drink himself into an unconscious stupor.

She glanced over her shoulder, and saw that Roger had finished his meal and returned to his armchair, a bottle of whiskey on the small table beside the chair. She cleared the table quickly. When done, she turned away from Roger to mask the bitter tears that stung her eyes. He took advantage of any opportunity, and he saw her tears as pure weakness. He'd come after her, seemingly for the sheer pleasure of asserting his dominance.

Sure, he controlled every aspect of their lives. But he couldn't touch her heart. She'd encased her feelings in a steel box.

And despite all he did, she sheltered still-smoldering embers of trust in her heavenly Father. Mama and Papa had lived with blessed assurance of His goodness, mercy, and love, and they'd passed it to Faith. She held on—weakly these days, true, but she still did—to God's promises. Her one personal possession, beyond the clothes on her back and the change hanging on the peg in the bedroom, was Mama's old, leather-bound Bible. She started each morning at the kitchen table with that battered but treasured book open before her, a cup of coffee by her hand, tears in her eyes, pleas for mercy on her lips.

She'd thought of leaving...oh, at least ten times a day. But where would she go? What would she do?

If she ran, she'd wind up right back where she'd been the day her parents died. And this time, she'd be a runaway married woman.

*For better...for worse...'til death do you part...*

A rumbling snore tore into her thoughts. She glanced at Roger, noticed the bottle, its contents far lower than they'd been the last time she'd checked. Once again, he'd drunk himself into oblivion.

*Thank you, Lord.*

She couldn't believe she'd reached the point of gratitude for unbridled drinking, but it was only in times like these that she found a few hours of peace. During those moments, she heard no ugly words, submitted to no unreasonable demands, endured no pain for her slightest infraction of Roger's multitude of rules. She dried her hands on the length of towel she kept hung on a hook to the far side of the stove.

No. She'd given her word. Running at this time wasn't the answer, for more than one reason. She trusted God to provide the answer in His perfect way and in His perfect time. If she was to run, He'd make it perfectly clear. If Roger was to change, she'd welcome the change the moment it happened. She only hoped the Father's time would come soon.

No matter when it came, it never would be too soon for her.


The earthy, musky scent of the dark rickety barn that stood a handful of yards behind the general store embraced Faith as nothing else did these days. Her kerosene lamp gave off a golden glow in a halo around her, casting shadows in every nook and corner of the immaculate barn. Gentle snuffles and shifting hooves on hay let her know her presence was noted and mighty welcome. She smiled.

"Maisie, my girl." Faith picked up a small tin pail of alfalfa chunks, and approached the odd, wide stall where Roger housed their animals. While he could have built three proper stalls, one for each creature, he certainly hadn't been willing to go through the bother. A cross between a horse's whicker and a donkey's bray burst from the animal's lips. "Hush! You don't want Roger to hear. I'll have to leave, and you won't get any treats if I do. You want these goodies, right? Tonight I brought you carrots. They're awful sweet."

The mule propped her chin on the stall door, rattling it under the weight of her head, her lips baring chunky ivory teeth. With a lightness that never failed to impress Faith, Maisie nipped up the alfalfa in the middle of her palm, gave it only the briefest chew, then gulped it down. Another whickery bray followed.

Insistent stomping broke out a few feet down the length of the stall. "Wait your turn, my friend," Faith responded.

At the spot where Roger had placed the next feed bin in the stall, Daisy was already waiting for her share of goodies. She greeted Faith with a warm, damp nuzzle on the neck. "Be careful there, my dear one. Don't you go getting any spit on Roger's old coat." She snugged the wool garment closer, and ran her hand over the lapels to check for moisture. "You'd think he'd have given up on this old thing, what with all the mending I've done to it. But he's just as tetchy about anything happening to it as if it were his newest one."

The old coat was the warmest garment available to Faith. She used it any time she came out to see the mules at night, when Roger was sleeping off another bender. Her knitted wool shawl wasn't adequate for the winter weather here halfway up the mountain. Still, she loved it, since she'd raised and shorn the sheep that had provided the wool, she'd spun the yarn and knit the wrap. It was the last one she'd made before the Indian raid.

The stomping at the third bin let her know someone was impatient. "I told you many a time. It's ladies first."

A snort told her what the male mule thought of that.

Faith rubbed Daisy's head and received another loving nuzzle in response. "You're a sweetheart, too, missy."

Maisie gave her distinctive whickery bray.

Faith sent the mule a sideways glance. "Ah, you're jealous, are you? Never to worry. I love all three of you, and you all know it. But you, my Maisie? You've got yourself a special corner of my heart all to yourself."

The sweet, gentle animal had shown Faith an uncommon affection from the moment she arrived at the Nolan property. Many a night, she'd spent hours weeping into the thick coat over Maisie's warm neck, despairing of ever finding any more joy in her days than what she found with these animals. They always welcomed her, responding to her tender care like flowers did to rain. Roger wasn't rough-handed with only Faith.

More stomping. This time, the stall door rattled in unison with the irritated, impatient clomps.

Faith chuckled. "Well, mister. I suppose it is your turn, now, isn't it?" She slipped the pail's wire handle over her arm, then sidled over to the last mule. He was waiting for her. "I fed you already today, didn't I? You can't be as hungry as you make it seem. Besides, all I have for you tonight is alfalfa and carrots."

It didn't matter. He would eat anything and everything

she offered him, and always asked for more. He had been growing rather plump around the middle, a fact that Faith had noted and was taking pains to correct. "You can't spend your days sleeping and eating, you know. Why, the girls work more than you do. And you're supposed to be the bravest and strongest one, the leader of our little pack. But, no. You leave that job to Miss Maisie, don't you?"

Oh, yes. Stronger, he was. But he was also prone to complain whenever asked to do his duty. Each time Faith loaded the three animals to take the supplies up to the logging camp, the girls went fairly well. At least, Maisie always did. Daisy followed placidly along behind Maisie.

But this fella...?

"You know, big boy?" She scratched his head. He rubbed the velvety area between his forelock and muzzle up against the underside of her chin in gratitude. The big, old foot-dragger was a sweet boy, too. "Roger did at least one thing right. He gave you the perfect name, now didn't he? I've never known a more slothful critter than you, Lazy!"

Holding out the last carrot to the greedy animal, Faith sighed. Who'd have thought she'd end up all alone but for three mules as friends? "Isn't that a sorry state? But, at least you are here. I'd have gone mad, pure raving mad indeed, if I hadn't had you."

She thanked the Lord for providing the easy, undemanding, unquestioning, and never belittling companions. True, she knew practically everyone in Bountiful, the nearest town to her parents' ranch and also to the foothills at the base of Mr. Bartlett's mountain, where the small Nolan spread sat. But she never could abide the pitying looks they all gave her these days. It would seem Roger had earned himself a reputation for his willingness to argue and his speed with his fists. While she knew she'd hidden the bruises well the rare time she went to town, she feared everyone there knew what was what.

"Well, friends"—she returned the pail of alfalfa to the hook where Roger always wanted it kept—"I'd best be on my way back in. A body never knows when he'll snore himself awake, he's so loud. Reminds me of a train rumbling on nearby rails—very, very near."

Always mindful of the danger of fire, she took care when she picked up the kerosene lantern, as she headed to the privy. Pines surrounded the structure, and while during the day their emerald presence reminded her of a protective embrace, at night they seemed to loom with a touch of menace, a stark warning that an inexperienced soul could get lost in their midst, never to be seen again.

She shuddered, and swiftly took care of her needs. When done, she gripped the lapels of the much-repaired coat with one hand and the lantern with the other, and headed back to the house.

Everything within her rebelled. Every instinct reared up. Every bit of her being recoiled at the thought of returning to Roger's side.

If only she'd known.

If only she'd had a better choice. Perhaps if she'd chosen the young ranch hand . . .

"Why, Lord?" she asked for the latest of countless times. "Your Word says you'll never leave me nor forsake me. Have you forgotten me? Do you hear my prayers? Must I endure this for the rest of my life?"

# Chapter 2

"This last order...well, I have to say I'm troubled," Nathan told Matt Murphy, a fellow war veteran and his employee of longest standing. "The reality is that we still have to have supplies. Woody says we're running low on some of the foodstuff staples we need to see us through to spring. It's a concern. Especially since winter's just around the corner. But I hate to have to count on someone as unreliable as Roger Nolan."

"Then don't." The wiry redhead crossed his arms and gave Nathan a challenging stare. "It's not as if I haven't pressed you to do what I reckon you'll likely have to do in the end."

Nathan ran a hand through his hair. "I struck a deal with the brothers, Matt. It rubs me wrong to go back on my word."

"Looks to me, boss, like they break their word to you over and over again without the least bit of shame. Been wondering, how'd you get yourself in this pickle, anyway? I thought you said your pa owned this whole mountain. But when I came out to join you, there they were, right happy as hogs, squatted on that piece of land."

"I thought my father had the deed to the whole thing, too, but they were here before I even had the chance to go scout out a good spot for the logging camp. Seems they'd come out west a short time before the end of the war..."

The men exchanged pained looks.

Nathan cleared his throat. "Yes, well, they produced a deed when I asked them what right they had to the land, so I couldn't run them off. Looked like some sort of home-steading agreement."

Rusty eyebrows drew close as Matt narrowed his eyes. "You sure that deed's all legal-like? Wouldn't put it past those Nolans to try and pull a swindle over on you."

"Looked all legal to me. Besides, they've settled down there, close enough to the edge of my land that it doesn't make much sense to argue. There's enough land in these parts for the Nolans and me."

Matt shook his head. "Looks to me like you're too good-hearted for your own good."

Nathan shrugged. "I have this recollection of my mother saying over and over when I was little that I needed to treat others like I wanted folks to treat me." He stood, began to pace. "But this isn't about me. It's about them. They seemed interested in setting themselves up as businessmen when we started out, and they offered to supply me and my men. They already had those three sturdy little mules, plus the cash to buy the supplies so they could add the back storeroom to their place. They insisted they wanted to handle large orders for the camp."

"A body would reckon they'd be obliged to you, seeing as you didn't chase them off the mountain—your mountain.

I'm thinking you surely could have. After all, it's your regular orders for supplies that's let them open their general store."

Nathan chuckled. "Yes, since I provide the bulk of their business, I should be able to expect superior service. And at first, that was the case. Lately things have not gone as well."

"Indeed they haven't." Matt slapped the tabletop, making the two empty enamelware coffee cups rattle. "How many of these paid shipments have mysteriously disappeared between Bountiful and the Nolan Brothers' General Store?"

"This one's the third. The two other times, Roger came through with our order just as we were about to run out of food. He's yet to offer a single word of apology for his unreliable service."

"Hope you're not still waiting for that apology."

Nathan shrugged. "The first time, I didn't make much of this kind of thing. The second time, it irked me, so I had a talk with Roger. But that doesn't seem to have done much good, now does it?"

Matt stood. "Nothing, I'd say. I reckon you're going to wind up opening your own store sooner or later, so if it was me, I'd open it sooner."

Nathan shook his head. "I don't have the animals to get the supplies up here, nor do I have the cash to buy them."

"Seems to me you do have one thing you can do. You can finish that flume, and fast as you can, so's we can sell enough lumber so you can open yourself a store."

"I do admit, I wouldn't mind if I never had to deal with either of the Nolans again. I haven't seen it myself, but I hear Theo's temper has landed him on the wrong side of Marshal Blair's jail more than once."

Matt rolled his eyes and shook his head. "Theo is little more than a ne'er-do-well. He spends the better part of the day sitting out front of Folsom's River Run Hotel with his pal Hector Swope, the two of them, more often than not, drunk no matter what hour of the day."

Nathan weighed the wisdom of discussing something else he'd heard last time he'd gone into Bountiful. He figured Matt was a discreet and sensible man. "I'm not one for gossip, but I've heard talk about Roger. I hear he's made connections with some of the soldiers who came to fight the Bannock War down south of here by the Malheur Reservation awhile back."

"I've heard the same. Rumor has it, the Nolans charge a pretty penny to supply them with spirits."

Nathan grimaced. "I've heard the same. I can't imagine Captain Roberts approves. He seems too sensible a man to have his men drinking while on duty. But I hear the Nolans will sell the stuff to anyone willing to pay for it."

Matt placed his coffee cup in the washbasin, then headed for the cabin door. It was late, and he likely wanted to call it a night. The other men had already gone ahead, and had hours of sleep on the poor fellow. "Doesn't surprise me none."

Nathan followed his friend to the front door of the logging camp's main cabin. "Can't say it does me, either. But it is alarming. Liquored men's minds are mighty changeable. One never knows how they'll react."

"Sounds to me, boss, like the perfect mix for trouble of some kind."

"We've had enough of that around these parts. Nothing good's going come of all this, I'm afraid."

"Reckon you're right, boss. I only hope it happens far from here."

Nathan figured it'd be better to pray the Lord kept any such disaster far from his budding business rather than hope it happened that way. He couldn't afford to expand as he needed, much less could he afford to start all over again, no matter what the cause.

Later, hours after he should have been asleep, Nathan continued to mull over the state of affairs with the Nolan brothers. He'd known from the start most men in his position opened up a company store of their own. That way, they could control what came in and what went out, and, he suspected, sooner or later he'd have to do just that. But, as he'd told Matt, his funds were much too tight at the moment, and he had a partly built flume to finish.

Now that a spur line was coming to Bountiful, he wanted a direct means to get his lumber to the railroad. He couldn't see his way to where he could finish the flume and open a store at the same time.

On the other hand, he couldn't very well run an efficient operation if the camp lacked the most basic supplies because of a pair of scoundrels at best and dishonest crooks at worst. That would simply endanger his men.

On top of all that, he now felt a great deal of distaste whenever he had to deal with the Nolan brothers. Nothing upright or decent about either one of them.

And yet, in the middle of that mess, one found Mrs. Nolan running the store a good deal of the time, working far harder than either Roger or Theo ever had. She was much younger than her husband, and he knew she'd married him after her parents had been killed by a band of rogue Indians. Nathan understood her desperate need back then, but why had she chosen Roger from among the men in the area? Surely at least one other bachelor had offered for her. He himself would have helped her out and given her his name if he'd known what had happened. But he'd been minding his business up the mountain.

Maybe what Eli Whitman said was true. Maybe he was turning into one of those wild mountain men, like the ones that had settled up in the untamed Rocky Mountains years before, trapping fur animals for a living.

It wasn't that he had any great liking for a hermit's life. It was more a matter that he'd come back to Oregon with too much in his head. Even all this time after the war, he couldn't get away from all of what he'd seen.

Death.

Everywhere.

A ravaged land.

His mother's family, dead or destitute, devastated.

They hadn't been the only ones. After the fighting was over, Nathan had known he had to return to Oregon. He couldn't bear to see what had become of the South. He couldn't bear to hear one more horrible tale.

Indeed, war was truly Hell on earth. He couldn't imagine a worse fate for those who rejected the heavenly Father's gift of His Son.

A sudden thought burst in his head. He wondered if life with Roger was for Mrs. Nolan a war of some kind. On occasion, he'd seen spurts of panic in her eyes, flashes that she'd quickly masked, wrapping herself in her calm, cool dignity, and displaying a regal bearing so much at odds with the man she'd wed.

Those forest-green eyes of hers always wore a sadness that tore at Nathan's heart. In spite of all he'd witnessed and experienced during the war, he'd never found himself truly desperate. He'd always known his father had provided for him, and funds to start a new life were waiting for him in the Bank of Bountiful. What must it have been like for that young woman to find herself without any alternative? How could she have reached a point where Roger was all she could see as an answer?

Nathan didn't know. But one thing he did know. Faith Nolan was twice the person either of the brothers would ever be.

And, with his suspicions growing at full steam, he decided to keep an eye on the goings-on at the general store.

A week after the fiasco with Mr. Bartlett's missing supplies Faith had gone outside to gather a basketful of dried wash, when a strange commotion made her drop one of Roger's clean shirts. She swooped down to scoop it up before it soiled again, crammed it into her basket, and hurried toward the barn. Before she got there, however, she identified the source of the noise.

Plodding toward her were the three little mules, Maisie in the lead. "How on earth did the three of you get out of the pen?" She hurried toward them, but came to an abrupt halt when she saw the tear in the flimsy fence around the pen at one end of the barn. She'd asked Roger at least three times to repair the weather-beaten boards tacked haphazardly to posts made of the stripped trunks of slender pines. She knew the two brothers had enclosed the area when they'd first home-steaded their land, but they hadn't made any repairs since.

At least they'd done a better job with the snug, sturdy cabin that served as business and home for the three of them. She and Roger made use of the sleeping loft upstairs and the kitchen and tiny sitting area that took up the right side of the building. Theo's quarters were in a shedlike structure at-tached to the left side, the general store side. Not that he seemed to spend much time there.

To Faith's intense relief.

Something about the way her brother-in-law looked at her made Faith's skin crawl. He'd never done anything untoward, nor had he said anything inappropriate, but the look in his eyes always made her feel...dirty—dirtier.

Hard to imagine, since marriage to Roger had done that from the first night.

Maisie trotted up to her side, nuzzling the thick wheat-colored braid in which Faith kept her hair for sensible com-fort. The mule's trademark whickery bray nearly deafened her.

"You are a troublemaker, aren't you, Maisie, my girl? Now I'm going to have to keep the three of you locked in the barn all day until Roger takes the time to fix the fence. Not that he's likely to, I'm afraid."

As she spoke, Daisy nudged her shoulder, trying to get as close to both Maisie and Faith as she could. She scratched the two animals, surrounded by their affection. Even the grim re-ality of life with Roger didn't dim the pleasure she got from her animals. That got her to thinking. Where was the third mule? He had been there a moment ago. She couldn't see him in the clearing, but she heard the heavy plodding she associated with the ornery male. "Lazy!" she called. "What are you doing? Where are you going?"

The plodding continued. But it didn't come closer. Instead, it moved farther away from where she stood with the two girls. She craned her neck, searching the tall pines that surrounded the Nolan spread, but couldn't see Lazy. She glanced from Maisie to Daisy, and hesitated. Did she take the time to lock them up in the barn and risk Lazy wandering too far into the woods? It was past four already, and sundown came fast this time of year. Weak sunlight did little to illuminate the space between the trees much farther than five to ten feet in. The thought of searching for the mule in the dark and cold was more than she could abide.

She shuddered, pulled Roger's old coat tighter around her, and set off after the rapidly escaping mule. "Lazy! Stop your nonsense right now." She glanced over her shoulder to find the girls following after her. "You're supposed to mind, you two. I've enough with Lazy to cope with."

But of course, Maisie didn't slow a bit. Daisy, as always, followed right behind her dearest friend. And so, Faith took part in the most unusual parade she could imagine.

Which embarrassed her no end when she realized she was no longer alone in the clearing. "Oh, goodness! I didn't see you there, Mr. Bartlett." She looked to either side of the lumberman on the horse, but saw no sign of her runaway mule. "Um...was there something you needed from the store?" She blushed, thinking of the man's missing supplies. "Or...did you come for your order?"

The logging camp owner doffed his hat and shook his head. "No, ma'am. I figure it's not here yet, or surely Roger would have sent word up the mountain, right?"

Warm brown eyes the color of fresh-brewed coffee pinned her to the spot with an intense stare.

She shook her head. "No, sir. The shipment won't be into Bountiful for another week, maybe ten days. I'll be sure and have either Roger or Theo take it all up to you. No reason to make you come down yet a third time for what you bought and paid for, and expected days ago."

"Roger? Theo?" A knowing grin tipped up the corners of his mouth. "Are you sure one of them will be bringing the supplies up the mountain?"

Faith's cheeks heated. "Well, I reckon it will end up being me who brings your things. If you don't mind, that is. Because if you do, why, then I'll make sure one of them does it." No matter what kind of excuse those two came up with, and she knew they could come up with plenty.

She squared her shoulders. "Yessir, Mr. Bartlett. I'll make sure you get your supplies as soon as they get here."

"I'm sure I'll be seeing you up at the camp with your three mules—speaking of them, I only see two. Did something happen to the third one?"

Her cheeks blushed hotter still. "They got out of their pen, and Maisie and Daisy came after me. But Lazy plain took off. Who knows where he's gotten to by now."

Mr. Bartlett grinned again. "Maisie, Daisy, and Lazy? Hm...interesting names."

"You can ask Roger about that. He'd named them before we...married up. He did do well naming them, though.

Especially that scoundrel, Lazy." She started off in the direction where she'd last heard the male's hooves tapping away. "If you will excuse me now, sir. I'll be after finding my missing mule."

Faith heard Roger's bellow before she saw him stomping down the trail behind her. "What have you done with my animals down there, woman? Don't you know they're what keeps food on our table? Why, if you weren't a woman I'd—"

"I certainly do hope you're not threatening a woman, Nolan," Mr. Bartlett said, his voice calm, measured, but full of warning.

Roger stopped short and jutted out his chin, covered in stubble. "What's it to you, Bartlett? She's my wife. And don't you go getting no ideas about her. I don't cotton to no indecent—"

"Roger!" Faith cried, horrified.

"I'm sure you didn't mean that comment as it came out, right, Nolan? Your wife has done nothing but greet me as any good storekeeper would greet a customer. I *am* your customer, or have you forgotten that already?"

Roger had the decency to flush a dark red. "Well, no, I ain't forgot nothing. Just making sure everyone knows what's what."

"About that mule," Mr. Bartlett said, changing the subject, to Faith's relief. "Your wife was trying to find it when I came through on my way back up the mountain from Bountiful. It would seem there's a problem with the fencing around your animals' pen."

Roger frowned. "A problem? What kinda problem?"

Mr. Bartlett gestured for Faith to speak.

She grimaced and turned her gaze down to the ground. "I...ah...told you the fence was coming loose in a couple of spots. Two or three times, I...ah...told you."

Out of the corners of her eyes, Faith saw Roger shrug. "I been busy." He puffed out his burly chest. "Earning a living, you know. I'll get to it soon's I get me a minute or two."

"Seems to me," the logger said, "you might be a mite late already. Your mules broke it down and were running loose when I rode up. Your missus has the two females, but the male's taken off. Let's not waste any more time finding him. It's getting dark."

"Of course," Faith said, her voice sounding more courageous than she felt. "I'll put the girls in the barn, and go look for Lazy."

"No, ma'am," Mr. Bartlett said. "The forest's no place for a lady, especially not at night. Roger and I will find the mule. You go take care of these two, then go on inside."

"But—"

"Now, don't you fret, Mrs. Nolan. We'll find the runaway. You go ahead. I give you my word."

A sideways glance told her Roger wasn't pleased, but he was also not about to take on the man who paid him the bulk of his earnings, the man on whose property the Nolan brothers had squatted. Illegally, at that. She'd heard the two brothers mocking the gentlemanly logger one night after they'd consumed enough whiskey to float a tugboat upriver.

She turned toward the barn, and heard the familiar pattering of two sets of hooves behind her.

"Come on, now, Nolan," Mr. Bartlett said. "Let's find that mule of yours."

As she bolted the stall door closed after the girls went inside, Faith didn't need to wonder what would happen when Roger returned.

Faith gave the potatoes and chunks of sausage sizzling in the skillet another stir and tried not to fret over the missing Lazy. As unwilling to work as he was, he was also that ready for mischief. Not that the girls fell far behind. She suspected Maisie was the guilty party in the matter of the torn-down fence. Nothing made the leader of the pack happier than to follow Faith as she did her chores.

Unfortunately, Lazy wasn't so inclined. He loved to wander.

A quick glance at her pocket watch told her it was taking the men longer to find the runaway than she'd hoped. On the other hand, their search put off the time when Roger would return to the cabin.

"...but she sure does make up some fine vittles," Theo said as he stamped his boots this side of the kitchen door.

Faith's heart pounded. She knew well what cruelty Roger was capable of meting out, but Theo remained a mystery, one she didn't want to try to solve.

Without so much as a greeting for her, Theo went on. "And it smells like she done made us some already. Two strangers followed him inside. Hector Swope, Theo's fellow sluggard, brought up the rear.

Panic struck; Faith saw no escape.

"Evenin', Missus Nolan," Theo said, his voice a taunt, his

eyes leering. "Me and my friends, why, we're in need of feeding." He checked the table. "I'm seeing here where you only have three plates set out, but now I've brought company home with me, we'll be needing us four. Get another one, and dish up fast. We're hungry."

Faith caught her bottom lip between her teeth. What should she do? Although she always made a bit more than she expected the three of them to eat, in case the two brothers were especially hungry, she didn't have enough in the skillet to feed five men. She knew Roger would be famished when he returned, as was the case every single night. He wouldn't be happy to find his supper eaten by his younger brother and the three visitors. On the other hand, she doubted she could hold off these fellows until Roger returned.

So she picked up the heavy iron skillet with a hand wrapped in a towel, hurrying to dish up. She'd have to peel more potatoes and open another jar of the sausage she'd put up last August. She prayed the second batch cooked up quick. At least the Excelsior cookstove had plenty of fuel, and was hot as could be. It might not be so bad, if Roger took a while longer to return.

But no matter what time her husband found that rascal Lazy, she would be alone with the four scoundrels until he came home again. A quick glance toward them left her no doubt as to their thoughts. She'd seen that same unholy light burning in Roger's eyes many a time in the years since she'd married him.

She turned away, quaking inside. At the stove, she thudded the skillet down, the clatter surprising even her. "S—sorry," she said, her voice weak to her own ears.

Another glance, this one at Theo, made her shudder. His small, dark eyes were narrowed more than usual, and he stared at her, intensity in that dreadful gaze. "What's wrong with you, woman? Can't a body and his friends eat in peace around this place? Don't you go forgetting I own this place as much as Roger does."

His three friends laughed as though he'd told a funny tale. Faith saw nothing of humor in his rude words, much less in the implied threat behind them.

Knowing Theo would likely take advantage of any sign of weakness, as his brother always did, she squared her shoulders, and met Theo's insolent stare. "Nothing. The pan slipped from my hand, is all. Go on. Go on and eat, please."

As the men lost interest in her response and resumed their meal, she breathed a touch easier. She peeled and sliced two small potatoes, then mixed them with sausage and onions in the still warm pan. While it all cooked, she turned to her washbasin, filled it with hot and cold water, and shaved slivers of yellow soap into the pan. Once swishing them with her fingers had dissolved them, she washed and dried the lone coffee mug she'd used earlier when she'd come in after the escapade with the mules. Until the men had eaten she wouldn't have anything further to keep her busy. She whispered a prayer as she twisted the dish towel in her hands.

"Father, don't leave me now. Hold me in the palm of your hand and protect me from all harm. If it be your will, please end this torment in the best way possible..."

The cabin door banged open again. Faith looked over her shoulder to see Roger and Mr. Bartlett enter the room. Oh, dear. Would she have yet another man to feed with more food barely started?

Before she had a chance to ask, Mr. Bartlett noticed Theo and his companions. "Sam, Lee! What are you two doing here? Did you come after me? Is something wrong back at the camp?"

The two loggers pushed away from the table, their cheeks ruddy, their eyes darting from corner to corner, their hands swiping their lips clean of grease.

"Aw . . . well, see . . . it was like this, Mr. Bartlett—"

"Well, no, boss. We was making our way back with—"

Both stopped at the same time and glowered at each other.

Roger tore his stare from the half-empty plates and turned it toward the pan of fresh-sliced potatoes and chunks of sausage on the stove, to Faith's rapidly blanching face, and roared. "Where's my supper? Ain't I toldja time and time and time again I need food when I git finished with my work? I come home after slaving to provide for ya, and this is all what I get? Today! Especially today. Today I had to chase after them silly mules you've taken such a shine to. You're s'posed to be watching them, ain't ya?"

Faith shook her head, made every effort to maintain a calm appearance, shrugged. "Theo came with his friends, and . . . why, I . . . um, reckoned you'd want me to show guests here at your house the proper hospitality."

"Hospitality?" His face turned redder with each syllable. "With my supper? Why, I'm going to show you what hospitality—"

"Mr. Nolan," Mr. Bartlett said from where he still stood at the threshold to the room. "I wouldn't fault your wife for feeding hungry visitors. It shows you're a wise man, wedding someone like her. She's quite a compliment to your good taste."

At first, Faith wondered if the man had lost his mind. Then she saw Roger relax, puff out his chest, rub his belly, and smirk.

Her husband leered at her. "She's right easy to look at, too."

Theo let out another of his snorts of laughter.

The lumbermen next to him chuckled until their employer silenced them with a stern glare. "I do believe," Mr. Bartlett said, "that we've overstayed our welcome." In a respectful gesture, he nodded to Faith. "'Evening, ma'am." He donned his hat, and with a friendly smile, tapped two fingers on the brim as he faced Roger again. "Please let me know when our order arrives, Nolan. I'll make arrangements to have some of my men pick it up. Don't want to impose on you."

Roger shrugged without much interest. "Like I said, I'll let you know."

Theo let out another laugh. "Your order...sure, Roger'll let you know."

The logging camp owner looked ready to say more, but he instead gestured for his employees to follow him. Roger trailed along behind them to close the door as soon as they stepped outside. He turned to Faith, a mean light in his eyes.

"So, *Missus Nolan*...are you having a hard time recollecting who you wedded?"

*As if she could ever forget.* "No, Roger. Of course not."

When she turned back toward the sizzling food, he went

on. "Well, you make right sure you keep on recollecting, hear?"

She didn't turn, but made a production of stirring the food. "Of course, I will."

"Hmph! And now, what's that about my supper? How's about you showing me some of that there hospitality you show so quick-like to Bartlett's men? Where's my food?"

She jabbed a thick slice of potato with her knife. Relief filled her when the metal pierced right through with ease. "It's coming right now. As soon as I set out a clean plate for you. Do you want to take time and wash up, or are you ready to sit?"

The sound of the chair legs scraping across the wood floor was Faith's only answer. She set a blue-and-white enameled tin plate in front of Roger, and handed him a clean fork. A moment later, she returned from the stove with the skillet full of savory food. He barely waited for her to finish dishing up the generous mound before he fell to it.

Back at the stove, Faith slid the pan to the back, where her portion would remain warm but not overcook, in case she felt the slightest bit hungry later on. "Here's a glass of water and the pitcher of milk. I'm going to feed Lazy, since I fed the girls after I put them back in their stalls. I won't be long."

Roger grunted.

On her way out, she saw Theo pull out a bottle of whiskey from the box.

It looked like it was setting up to be another long night.

# Chapter 3

Days went by and Nathan heard nothing about his order. One night, after supper had been eaten, the long oak tables cleared off, and the thick, white pottery dishes cleaned, dried, and put away, he sat with Matt and Woody, his ornery but decent and hardworking camp cook, all three nursing by-now cold cups of coffee.

"No, Matt," he said, "I haven't found a solution yet, not since the last time you pestered me about it a couple of days ago. No matter which way I look at my circumstances, I can't come up with any source of extra dollars. I exhausted all the money I could get my hands on to finish the work on the flume."

"What about that there bank of your pa's?" Woody asked. "Thought it was part yours now."

"I'm only a minor and always silent partner—by my choice, I'll have you know. I don't call the shots there, and I can't use it as my personal money well where I can go dip a bucket whenever the fancy strikes."

Matt leaned his head back, a thoughtful look on his face. "I know how you feel, since you've told me plenty of times, but are you willing to consider a loan yet? Especially since a store of your own would solve so many of your supply problems."

"Ya mean all of 'em, Matty-boy, don'tcha?" Woody's faded blue eyes sparkled with mischief. Matt hated the childish nickname.

"I've told you not to call me that, Old Man." An impish light burned in his own gray ones. "What's wrong? Getting forgetful under all that gray hair—oh, that's right. Most of it's fallen out by now."

"The Good Lord's just making it easier for a body to comb with less and less every day now." The cook broke into cackles of laughter.

"Enough, you two." The jabs and jests were all in good fun, since the two men sincerely liked and respected each other, but they did like to egg each other on, and could go on like that for hours on end. "We're not discussing the state of Woody's head right now."

Matt let the chair drop down onto all four legs.

Nathan arched a brow.

"Sorry. I forget how you don't like that." At least Matt had the grace to look remorseful. He also looked as single-minded as ever. "Back to the store and the money. It would seem to me that a loan for this kind of reason shouldn't rub you quite so wrong. Would you consider borrowing?"

Nathan sighed. "I've all but reached that level of irritation. Sadly, my friend, the Bank of Bountiful has little liquidity at the moment. Don't forget how rough these last couple of years have been on Hope County. The droughts and the grasshopper plagues killed the crops and dried up the land, even the creeks. Many of the farmers and ranchers had to mortgage their properties. Eli—have you met Eli Whitman?"

"Can't say I have," Matt answered.

"Yup." Woody crossed his arms over his portly middle. "Good man, Eli Whitman is. His pa raised 'im good. Good man, too, his pa was."

"Eli's my partner," Nathan continued, "the bank president. I met with him a number of times to take out the funds for the flume. He's struggling, too, since he used the bank's liquidity to help the men hang on to their land. They won't have the means to repay those loans until they bring in some decent harvests or until their sheep can be sheared for the wool or are plump enough to take to slaughter. And you know cattle's also got to be well-fed to sell well. No one's herd out here's in any condition for that."

"So there won't be no help there."

"I see no way to make a camp store a reality, not right now. No matter how much I want to be free from the unreliable actions of the Nolan brothers."

Matt leaned forward on the table, the fingers of his hands laced together. "I can see how it galls you to have to depend on someone like Roger Nolan."

"I can hardly stomach it any longer. But, I only have one option left. I'll have to work even harder than I already do, sell more lumber, ship it out to more markets, so the logging operation can earn the funds to support a general store."

"Hoo-hoo-hoo!" crowed Woody. "When this boy makes up his mind to do something, look out! Heaven will be the only help the fool what gets in his way is gonna have, Matty-boy."

Matt chuckled, letting the use of the name slide on by. "The man knows you, Nate. That is you in a few choice words."

Woody took out his battered silver pocket watch. "Hmph! Dunno 'bout you youngsters, but a man's gotta get his sleep, if he's gonna get up in time to make biscuits and coffee in time for others to eat."

Nathan stood. "Now, don't you go making things sound worse than they are. Matter of fact, how are things in the larder? I know you at least have beans left from supper, so breakfast will be a sight more than just a pile of bread and your muddy brew."

"Muddy brew!" Woody stroked his grizzled beard. "Hmph! Let's see what you say when you get up a day and can't go opening them eyes on your own. S'pose my muddy brew will be right fine then, now won't it?"

"You have a point, Woody. If nothing else, your coffee could wake up a bear in the dead of winter. But that doesn't tell me much. Don't sidestep my question. We need to feed the men. How're we doing on food?"

Woody shrugged. "Not so good. I have a while's worth of beans left, but they're not so toothsome if I cook 'em up with only water and lard. I'm running real low on dried beef, the bacon's nearly gone, and canned foods...well, you can look in the pantry. Don't have us too many of those, either."

A knot formed in Nathan's gut. "Why didn't you lay it out like this to me before?"

"Didn't wanna burden you no more'n I had to, boss. I reckoned the Nolans would get us set back up soon enough. Can't figger why they're taking so long. It's just food. How hard's it to bring up sacks of beans, flour, salt, sugar, dried beef, some jars of molasses, buckets of lard? I fetched us a passel of hams from when I helped Perry Larrabie with them hogs of his. He promised hams, an' I took 'im up on them."

Nathan's tight middle seemed to drop. "So we have hams. What else?"

"Bushels a apples an' eggs an' canned chicken an' garden stuff I put up in September. But that won't fill men's bellies long enough."

"No it won't." Before Nathan could come up with something else to say, Woody went right on.

"Other things you ordered?" He snorted. "The tools and stuff, why…that all showed up like a deacon with a collection plate of a Sunday morning. But I can't be dishing up tasty saws and seasoned axes to hungry loggers."

"That you can't." Thoughts whipping in his head, he forced a smile on his face. "Don't you go worrying, Woody. I'll figure something out. Even if I have to head out to Pendleton, buy me a pack of mules, and haul the food up here myself."

Matt, who'd been silent uncharacteristically long, rose, the heels of his boots scraping the floor. "See? You're already heading in the direction of a company store. I know me a thing or two about mules. I'll help you pick out some sturdy ones."

The knot in his gut loosened, but only to set his middle swimming sickly as he thought back on the balance in his bank account. "I wasn't serious—"

"That's a problem," Matt said, no-nonsense this time. "You have to get serious about this mess with the supplies and the Nolan brothers. You've good men here, Nate. They're counting on you—we all are." He turned toward the door. "Sleep on it. Then get moving to do the right thing."

Since there was nothing more to say, they parted ways, Nathan and Woody heading for their separate rooms in the main cabin, one on either end of the large dining hall, and Matt to the bunkhouse, where the other lumberjacks had gone earlier in the evening. But even though the conversation had ended, Nathan's thoughts returned again and again to the matter of the store and the fix he was in because of the no-account Nolan brothers. As troublesome as his situation was thanks to them, he couldn't imagine how Mrs. Nolan tolerated living at the store, married to someone like Roger. But no matter how dire her situation looked, he had to respect the decisions she'd made. He respected her.

Roger was not much more than a brute, and Mrs. Nolan looked as delicate as a forest fern, but she must be made of stronger stuff, since she was managing to endure. Strong, graceful, and capable. She struck Nathan as quite the image of ladylike loveliness.

She was tall and slender, and he liked to watch how her thick, wheat-blond braid swung with purpose across her back as she went about her work at the store. Her forest-green eyes took in everything, and revealed a quick mind. He'd noticed how her delicate jawline could take on a determined firmness, and her skin looked as soft as his late mother's velvet cloak. Her pretty, feminine features, the gently curved cheeks and straight nose, went well with her willowy frame.

Every time he stopped at the general store, Nathan couldn't escape the thought that, because of her circum-

stances, like a willow, surely she must have the inner strength
to bend and sway as the winds of life buffeted her.

Yes, indeed. He admired and respected Mrs. Nolan. Even
if he doubted he ever would understand her.

A week later, Roger hitched the mules to the store's generous
flatbed wagon and hauled a new order to the store from the
nearby small town of Bountiful. He and Theo stacked cases
and crates of supplies in the storeroom corner they had as-
signed to the logging camp's orders. Remembering the camp
owner's kindness toward her, Faith gathered up her courage
and approached Roger.

"Will you or Theo be going up the mountain to let Mr.
Bartlett know his supplies are here?"

Roger shrugged. "Tomorrow, maybe. Or the next day.
Tonight, I've a friend or two coming in to...um...play
cards. I'll get 'round to Mr. Bartlett soon enough. Don't you
go pestering me with it."

Distaste and dismay warred in Faith's heart. Dismay because Mr. Bartlett would have to wait longer for items he and
his men needed up at the camp before the weather turned.
He'd come down to the store twice now. She doubted he
took the trek for his health. Mr. Bartlett had bought and
paid for the food, and they were probably close to running
out. The upper heights of the mountain were surely covered
with snow by now, and soon the snow line would reach Mr.
Bartlett's property. No one at the logging camp had pack
mules. Horses weren't built to haul large loads like the one in
the storeroom up a mountain trail. Her three mules, on the
other hand, were.

She felt enormous distaste, because whenever Roger and Theo had "friends" in, the visit—drinking bouts, more like it—went on into the wee hours of the night. As dreadful as it seemed to her, it appeared that was all the Nolan brothers cared about. She felt even more unsafe, if possible, at those times.

On warm nights, she would slip out to the barn and sleep on a blanket spread over a bed of fresh hay in a quiet corner, but with the temperature dipping as low as it had of late, that wouldn't be a good option. She reckoned she'd have to stay in the sleeping loft above the sitting room and pray for safety.

As for supplies, she would wait for the right moment to do the only thing her conscience allowed her to do. When she found her opportunity, she would load the mules and deliver Mr. Bartlett's order before Roger managed to make it mysteriously vanish again.

Before Roger noticed what she was up to.

She'd much rather suffer the consequences after she'd done the right thing.

Yes, she would have to watch for the right moment, for the chance when she could slip past Roger's much too watchful eye.

When the sun rose the next morning, well after the visitors had left but the brothers continued drinking and playing cards, Faith came down the stairs one step at a time, as quiet as could be. She knew what she would find on the first floor of the cabin. It had happened too many times already.

In the kitchen, it became impossible to escape the thunderous rumble of snoring. Both brothers remained sound asleep. It was the perfect time to carry out her plan.

With a hammer and a chisel, Faith pried open the crates and boxes in the storeroom. She separated the supplies into manageable bundles, then tied the bundles on the mules as she'd often helped Roger do. Once she'd loaded the three animals to the maximum they could safely carry up the mountain trail to Mr. Bartlett's logging camp, she slipped inside the house again to check on the sleeping men and grab her wool wrap. To protect herself against the chill wind, she draped the warm shawl over her head and tucked it carefully around her ears, neck, and shoulders. Finally, she crossed the ends over her chest, fixing it in place with a long, polished wooden pin that had belonged to her mother. She hurried back to the stall.

"Come along now, Maisie, my dear. Quietly, now, if you can. There's a good girl."

As she was about to guide the pack leader out of the stall, she heard the unmistakable sound of Theo, still half asleep, stumbling into the stable. It sounded as though her brother-in-law was headed out, as he regularly did. Who knew where he might be headed. Not that it mattered. She only cared that he didn't bumble his way into the farthest reaches of the barn, near the mules' area, and find her and the loaded animals.

She scooted to the back of the stall, making sure the mule's body hid her as much as possible. She hoped Theo wouldn't look too closely in her direction. His boots plodded back and forth in an erratic rhythm until he seemed to trip over his own feet. A vile curse burst from his mouth, but since Theo often used such language, Faith wasn't surprised. Bothered and offended still after all this time? Yes. Surprised? No. Nothing much about the Nolans surprised her any longer.

Her heart pounded so hard that Faith wondered if Theo could hear. If not her heart, then surely he could catch the ragged sound of her rough breaths. Eyes closed, she drew in air, then held...held...held it, eased it out, bit by tiny bit.

As she strained to remain undetected, he muttered more curses each time he knocked another item off the hooks on the walls. The tremendous ruckus he raised made the animals restless. All three shuffled in the hay, the sound a soft susurration in the open building. Maisie let out a low whickery bray.

"Shhhh!" he hissed. "'S only me, ya dumb beasts. I'm not wanting nothing with the three of you, especially not your noise. Don'tcha know my head's fit to burst like a dropped egg?" He crossed to the stall where he usually kept his horse, and banged open the door. His horse whinnied.

"Aw, c'mon. Not you, too. Don't give me no what-for right now. I'm of no mind to put up with yer foolishness. Lesss go! I gotta get me down into Bountiful, and I can't be letting you make me late."

Man and horse made for the barn door.

Faith daren't let herself ease up on her cautious, soundless breathing—not yet. One never knew when Theo might notice he wasn't alone in the barn. If he found her, he'd immediately alert his older brother, and then, not only would Faith pay a price for her desire to do the right thing, but Roger might keep the supplies longer out of spite. Once winter arrived for the duration, no more shipments could be taken up the mountain. It would be too dangerous, not only for people, but also for the mules. The moist soil of the forest froze when the weather turned winter-cold, and ice wreaked havoc on any unsuspecting traveler, be it human or animal.

Maisie shuffled her feet again. Faith ran a hand down her flank. Although she knew a soothing word would calm Maisie, she also knew Theo would surely hear that. They would all have to be patient for a while longer.

After what sounded like multiple clumsy attempts to saddle and mount his horse, Theo and the animal clomped out of the barn. The initial blast of cold air from the opened door struck Faith in the face, then as fast as it had come, it stopped with the final slam of the door.

Only at that moment did she allow herself a deep breath. It took minutes longer for her heart rate to slow down to a more bearable beat. "Oh, Maisie," she crooned under her breath. "I think we're safe now, but Theo's still close enough that he might see us if we leave. I need you to stay still a bit longer. It'll be soon, now..."

She strained to hear anything outside, from either a possibly returning Theo or a rousing Roger.

As the minutes eked past, the silence of the woods remained undisturbed. Faith's middle eased back to normal, and her shoulders released the tension they'd assumed the moment she'd first heard Theo. Only then did she slip out of the mules' stall. She closed the door behind her and hurried to the window to check for the brothers out in the clearing. When she saw no one, she crossed back to Maisie's stall to guide the lead into the middle of the barn. Then she let the other two join her, first Daisy, then Lazy.

With one hand, she adjusted the wrap more tightly around

her face. With the other, she opened the heavy door. Moments later, she led her small parade through the clearing and onto the mountain path.

She hoped Roger slept long and deep. It would take a while for her to reach the camp. Upon her return, she'd have to face the consequences of her actions. But it had to be done. The hardworking men up at the camp had to eat. How Roger could disregard that fact Faith would never understand. Especially since Mr. Bartlett and his lumbermen had come to the Nolans' aid a number of times in the past when stray Indians had roamed the area and an attack appeared imminent. Most had been moved by the military to a reservation in Idaho, but some had eluded the soldiers' efforts. Desperate and angry at the white men in the area they considered theirs, they were known to attack without mercy.

Faith knew Roger had drawn the threat upon them. He had on occasion traded alcohol for the Indians' horses. Who bought the horses from him, she never knew, but he'd made a tidy sum in those transactions. Those times when he hadn't wanted to trade, or hadn't had what the Indians wanted, they left the general store none too happy with the Nolan brothers. It was in those times, when Roger refused to supply the irate Indians with that to which he had accustomed them, that the loggers had ridden to meet the Indians and cut off their hostilities at the pass.

Roger never should have forgotten those kindnesses. He never should have returned evil for good.

Partway up the mountain, chilled to the bone, Faith heard the distinct sound of something—or someone—moving between the trees and underbrush. Her heart skipped a beat. Two....

Dread filled her.

Should she have come at all?

Had she put herself foolishly in danger by wanting to do good?

She patted the lead mule's neck to urge her along. "Move, Maisie. We must get there soon."

As she always did, the animal responded by picking up her pace. Daisy followed. Lazy...well, Lazy insisted on continuing as he'd begun. He always lagged behind, even when it was crucial that he follow Faith's orders. Like now.

But, no. The ornery critter dawdled as her fear continued to build.

She heard it again, the sound of an approaching...what? Animal would be best. They were usually more frightened by a person than the person was of them. It might not be anything more than a deer or some such thing. But a stranger in the woods? One thing Faith had learned: You could never trust a person by simply seeing them or even listening to them. You had to get to know someone, truly know them, before you could trust. She didn't trust anyone anymore.

"Whoa!" a man cried.

Faith spun around.

A stranger indeed, the disreputable-looking fellow hastily doffed his stained, tattered hat and bobbed his head, the matted dark hair never moving with the gesture of greeting. "Well, hello there, miss. Strange sight for a body to see, a lady walking in the woods."

Heart pounding, Faith stood tall, determined to give at

least the appearance of confidence and assurance. She hoped this filthy person was one in need rather than one with wicked intent.

"I've a shipment of supplies to deliver to the logging camp. We're on our way there. And, you, sir? Who might you be?"

"I'm David Worley, at your service, ma'am." He made a small bow, and in spite of her common sense, Faith found herself being charmed. He went on. "Ain't that something? It happens that I'm on my way right there, right now, myself. If it wouldn't be a bother to ya, I'd much 'preciate the honor of escortin' you there. A lady ain't safe out here like this, you know."

Only after she'd heard his voice clearly and taken a better look at him did she realize he was quite young, perhaps not much older than her own twenty-two years. How did a man let himself get like . . . *that*?

As seconds lengthened into minutes, Faith watched Mr. Worley's expression change. Deep disappointment replaced the eager good spirits. In the mottled light of the forest, she thought she saw a shadow of pain, perhaps shame, cross his face. Guilt struck her.

"Your company would be my pleasure, Mr. Worley." She prayed that would remain true. "Having a fellow traveler will help make the time go by much better. Why don't you tell me about yourself?"

"Me? Oh, I'm not interesting, ma'am. How 'bout you tell me your name?"

She did, then smiled. "Now tell me where you're from."

As they followed the trail, Faith leading Maisie and the

other two in their usual positions behind her, Mr. Worley on the other side of the animals, they carried on an easy, mostly one-sided conversation. Faith found it easy to draw him out, since her new acquaintance clearly liked to talk.

"I'm from Pendleton, Miss Faith, and that's where one Mr. Nathan Bartlett and I met up. He come out on business, he did, and he knew someone I knew, too, so that's how we met one day. We got us to talking, and he told me 'bout how he had lumbering work and needed men to do it. I told him I was his man."

"So you followed Mr. Bartlett out here."

"Indeed, Miss Faith. Man's gotta jump when he hears of good, steady work, you know? But it took me a while to make it out to this mountain of Mr. Bartlett's, seeing as I had to work my way here, not having much money to count on when I started my trip, see." He looked around them at the dense forest, awe on his face. "It's right big, ain't it, now?"

She chuckled, but didn't say anything. There wasn't much to say. Mr. Bartlett's mountain was impressive.

"Yessir, ma'am. I been in woods before, but not like this. It sure is big, and full of trees, like Mr. Bartlett said. A feller can see how he would want to sell off some of 'em for lumber. And now I'm here, why, I'm ready to work. Been a logger for a span of years past, and I ain't married up yet. How about you?"

The light of interest in Mr. Worley's eyes made Faith blush right up to her hair. "I'm married. To Mr. Roger Nolan, the owner of the general store at the bottom of this trail. That's why I'm taking their supplies up to Mr. Bartlett's camp. They ordered them and my husband . . . well, it was best for me to bring them straight away."

The conversation never flagged, mostly on account of Mr. Worley liking to chatter. Faith appreciated his company, since he distracted her from her thoughts. Anything that took her mind off what lay before her upon her return to the general store was fine by her.

Right around midmorning, Nathan thought he heard people on the trail to the camp. Since he hadn't been expecting anyone, he hurried toward the mouth of the path, curiosity and alarm mingling. A man never knew what might come his way on this untamed mountain. To his amazement, he found a shivering Mrs. Nolan with her three mules, loaded to the utmost, hurrying toward him. The logger he'd met the last time he'd gone to Pendleton walked alongside the lead mule.

"What's happened to Roger?" he asked. "How about Theo? Why are you the one who's had to bring up this order? It's turned mighty cold these last few days. I never would have sent a lady to do a man's job, Mrs. Nolan." He turned toward his would-be employee. "And how come you're with the lady, Worley? Although, I'm glad you're finally here, seeing as how I can use an extra hand, we've so much work. I had hoped to see you sooner."

Mr. Worley took off his ragged hat to greet his new employer and give him a long-winded account of the various delays he'd faced. When done, he turned back to Maisie and went to work on the knots around one of the bundles, as Mr. Bartlett had asked him to do.

Nathan then walked over to Faith's side. "You haven't said what happened to the brothers, ma'am."

She blinked and, almost as if she'd been a slow-thawing

mountain stream in springtime, responded after a minute or maybe more, as though she'd needed to register his words. She surprised him with how long it took her to respond, since he didn't think he'd said anything too complicated to grasp.

"So—sorry, Mr. Bartlett. Roger is...well, indisposed, and Theo's gone. He was no longer around by the time I left."

Her response struck Nathan as more vague than necessary, and he wondered if she'd lied. Why? He couldn't imagine. Before he could probe, however, she went on.

"I was the only one left who could bring your supplies. I—I hope you don't object too much, sir."

Anger boiled in Nathan's gut, but he squelched it. It wouldn't do to take out his disgust with the lazy, good-for-nothing brothers on this decent, hardworking woman. "No, no. Of course, I don't object. But, really, now. They never should have sent you out on a day like today. It's mighty chilly out in these woods, ma'am."

She shivered, clearly in agreement. "I couldn't let your supplies stay in our storeroom for any length of time, especially when you and your men need them. It would have been wrong, seeing as how you didn't get the order when you expected from the start."

He arched a brow. "As it was wrong for them to send you out to do their work, no?"

"Oh, but they didn't send me out."

When she blushed but didn't continue, Nathan didn't prod. It became obvious by what she didn't say that the brothers had no idea she'd come to make the delivery. She'd taken it upon herself to do right by him and his men. He could only wonder what might have led to that situation, but he could easily imagine various scenarios that might come to pass when she returned home, none of them pleasant for her.

He set his jaw in a hard line. He'd have a talk with Roger as soon as he could get down there to be sure she suffered no consequences for her actions.

"In that case," he told her as he led the way to the main cabin on the compound, "why don't you take a minute to rest while we unload? I'm sure you want to be back home before the sun begins to set."

She shook her head and turned back toward the mules. Nathan couldn't see her face, and he found himself irritated by her minor evasion. He'd wanted to see her response to his mention of her return to the Nolan household.

She only murmured, "I appreciate your understanding."

He kept walking. At the door to the large main log cabin at the center of the semicircle of buildings that made up his camp, Nathan scraped his boots against the metal bar his cook had attached to a slab of lumber. Rough as bark himself, Woody still liked to keep the floors as clean as possible.

Nathan opened the door and called out. "Sam! Davey... Woody? We need you to give us a hand unloading supplies. Mrs. Nolan has most kindly brought them to us, and we need help to get her back on her way to the general store."

The two loggers he'd called came out and between them, Worley, and Nathan untying bundle after bundle, they relieved the pack animals of their loads in no time.

As they worked, Nathan couldn't help but admire the healthy condition of the mules. The day he helped Roger find the wandering male, he'd learned Mrs. Nolan was the one who saw to the animals' care. From all he could see, she did an excellent job of it, as she also did an excellent job of running the general store.

Seeing how she did so much, he had to wonder...what *did* Roger and Theo do?

She really was an asset. He couldn't understand why Roger didn't appreciate her. He wouldn't mind hiring her to run his general store, not that he thought Roger ever would stand for that.

He heard a familiar limping gait from inside the cabin. Woody stuck his nearly bald head out the door. "Ya pulled me away from my baking," he muttered, scratching his grizzled beard. "Better be for a good reason, boss."

Faith gasped.

Nathan cast a look over his shoulder.

Worry drew a pair of fine lines between her delicate, arched brows. She caught her bottom lip between her teeth. Her green eyes sped from Woody to him and back to the cantankerous cook. She took what appeared to be a protective step toward the older man.

Nathan clenched his jaw. He'd always had his suspicions about her situation at home, but she'd covered it well. Now, reading only too well the expression on her face, Nathan knew he had to make light of the moment, even though intense thoughts as to Roger's fate sped through his mind. As if there was any way to take Woody's harmless complaints other than with a dose of good humor. He laughed.

"Is that all the thanks I get?" he asked the camp cook. "All I've heard from you for days now is how we've been on the brink of disaster, seeing as we didn't have much more than sacks of flour and beans left. Hope you'll be happy to hear

Mrs. Nolan has been kind enough to bring the supplies I ordered. Come on out here. Give us a hand, why don't you?"

As Woody limped toward the mules, another stream of muttered protests pouring from his lips, Mrs. Nolan continued to study the two of them, not moving one whit from where her feet seemed planted in the hardscrabble soil of the clearing. Moments later, Nathan watched as she appeared to will herself to relax.

He relaxed as well. Woody was harmless, all talk and vinegar, but as big-hearted as any man could be. He himself was rightly fond of the old codger. If the tough old-timer even had a whiff of what Nathan feared was happening to the lovely young woman who stood before them, he doubted the Nolan men would withstand Woody's fury.

After experiencing the atrocities of war, Nathan wanted nothing to do with any kind of fighting. Even so, he was having a hard enough time himself resisting the urge to rush down the trail and confront the pair. But that would doubtless lead to some kind of physical altercation. Even if he ignored that, if they survived, Mrs. Nolan would ultimately pay the price for their injuries.

He'd seen too much precious blood spilled, too many lives lost.

He'd told God he would never condone so much as a flying fist. He wasn't about to change his promise to his heavenly Father now. He'd have to find another way to protect the gentle woman who'd risked her safety in more ways than one to do what she believed was only right. For his benefit, at that.

Her courage was something he never would forget.

# Chapter 4

All the way back down the trail, Faith alternated between praying and wondering how long ago Roger had awoken. The one thing she knew with certainty was his reaction once he'd finally roused himself, and discovered her gone and the camp order missing.

Regardless, she'd spent long enough without doing a thing about righting some of Roger's wrongs. No more. She couldn't stomach any more years—even a day—of cowardice. While she'd been little more than a girl with no practical knowledge when her parents had died, she'd lived a lifetime in the last three years. A dreadful one, at that. In that time, she'd learned that she ultimately answered to Almighty God instead of to Roger Nolan, no matter what her husband thought or said.

The closer she drew to the general store, the more unsettled she became. Her shoulders grew rock-hard, her stomach churned with each step, and her head pounded. She knew what she was about to face, and she dreaded every second of it.

But when she walked into the clearing, she spotted three horses tied to the hitching rail Roger had installed for the store's customers. She let out the breath she'd been holding as she hurried to the barn. The three mules followed her, one right behind the other.

She quickly brushed them down, made sure the water in the trough wasn't crusted over with bits of hay and corn or a film of ice, since it had grown increasingly colder during her return trip, and double checked the stall door to make sure it had latched properly. Once, when Lazy had managed to open the stall, he'd made his way to the alfalfa pail and had himself a grand old time eating all that had been left in the bottom. There hadn't been much. Lazy hadn't agreed with Faith's relief at the small quantity. He'd banged the pail against every surface he could find, letting anyone within a broad and wide area know his opinion.

A prayer on her lips, she hurried to the general store. Once inside, she realized the business portion of the building was deserted. From the living quarters, however, she heard the men's voices. At that moment, they were laughing.

She gave thanks for the hilarity, since that meant Roger should be in a passable mood. At least right then.

Before she'd left that morning, she'd set a crock full of soaked beans on the back corner of the stove, letting them cook slowly with molasses, chunks of bacon, and a good handful of onions. As she approached the doorway, the scent of the cooking food met her senses.

Head held high, she hurried into the room, all the while she unwrapped the shawl from around her head. "Will your guests be staying for supper, Roger? I'm thankful I started the beans before I left. They need a long cooking time, and by now they're most likely done."

As she hooked the wrap on a peg on the wall, she heard movement behind her. She turned, and saw the two officers rise to their feet.

"'Evening, Missus Nolan," said, Captain Roberts.

At his side, the younger one nodded, his gaze firmly on Faith. "Nice to see you today, ma'am."

She cast a sideways look as she crossed to the stove. No one could have missed the barely sheathed anger on Roger's face. Because he had company with him, however, he turned toward the three other men at the table with him, and asked if they cared to eat.

"That'd be right nice," the captain said, seeming to speak for all of Roger's military guests. She blushed at the memory of the last time they'd met, the time when he'd spotted the bruise on her wrist. Embarrassment flooded her, but she couldn't let her discomfort show. She had a meal to serve.

"It won't take long," she said.

"See that you don't take long," her husband snarled. "It's far past suppertime."

She winced.

"Thank you kindly, Mrs. Nolan," Captain Roberts said as she checked on the beans. "I do appreciate it."

She cast another glance over her shoulder then spoke to the other guests, to make sure what was expected of her. "Will you be eating with us, too?"

The other man, a sharp-featured soldier with thinning, sandy hair, nodded absently.

"Very well." She stirred the beans with a long-handled wooden spoon. "I'll have fresh biscuits ready in no time."

As shamed as she felt, and as much as she dreaded the time

when she'd have to face Roger after what she'd done, she felt the need to do her best with the meal. If not for Roger, then for Captain Roberts's sake. The few times she'd met him, he'd treated her kindly, with a proper, businesslike demeanor. And while his pity rankled, she suspected it stemmed from a compassionate nature.

The least she could do was feed the men, since the guests' presence offered a cushion between her and Roger's displeasure. Even if it would only be a temporary barrier. She mixed up an extra measure of biscuit dough in gratitude.

She stepped to the cabinet on the far kitchen wall, and took out tin plates and cups. She placed them on the broad work shelf the brothers had built for her between the Excelsior and the back kitchen door, then returned to the stove for the bean crock. By the time the aroma of the biscuits let her know they were close to done, she had everything else ready for the meal.

"Gentlemen," she said in a low voice. "If you would excuse me, please? I'd like to serve supper for you."

With scarcely a nod her way, the men continued their discussion. They were talking about the few Indians still angry about the recent war between the Bannocks and the soldiers south of Hope County. By now, most had been removed to reservations, but a few had slipped through and stayed behind. The Army continued to help protect settlers in northeast Oregon in the hopes their fate wouldn't be the same as that of her family.

When the men finished their meal, she cleared the dishes and washed up, wondering all the time whether she should escape to the relative safety of the barn or if she should retire to the sleeping loft. As the captain brought out a pipe for himself and cigars for the others, including one for Roger, she came to an easy decision. She couldn't abide the smell.

"I'll be checking on the mules." Without waiting for a response, she ran to the barn and into the stall, easing in close to Maisie. She leaned on the animal, let the welcome heat seep into her, and sucked in large gulps of cold night air to catch her breath.

Sooner or later, she'd have to go back inside. For the moment, she'd enjoy the safety of the barn, its comforting, earthy smells of hay and animal, and the relative safety it offered. Roger rarely went there.

Faith stayed with the mules until she heard the military men head outside. While she couldn't make out the words, she did hear a curt exchange between one of the men and Roger. She reckoned they had figured out her husband shorted their order by a good amount. Just as he'd done to Mr. Bartlett. She wondered who'd offered Roger a minor ransom for the goods this time.

Eventually, she heard them all ride away. So as to not enrage Roger any more than he already would be, she wrapped the shawl more securely around her neck and returned to the house straightaway.

By this time, Theo had come back and was in the process of eating a pile of bacon and beans and the last of the biscuits. He paused long enough to give her a rude stare, which made her draw herself up to her full height. With far more calm than she felt, she stepped past the brothers and to the ladder to the loft.

"Don't s'pose you got any more of this bacon, do ya?"

Theo paused only long enough to voice the words, then shoveled more food into his mouth.

"I served all I cooked, Theo. Sorry. Your brother had company, as I'm sure you noticed when you arrived, and I reckon they were hungrier than I'd thought."

Since he didn't say anything more, she hurried up to the loft, crawled into bed, and pulled the heavy quilt over her head. In the middle of her prayer of thanksgiving, seeing as God had given her a reprieve brief though it might be, she dozed off. Hours later, she opened her eyes to find the house still pitch dark. The silence of the night enveloped her.

Faith slipped out of bed, walked to the railing across the loft, and looked down into the sitting room. There, she found a too-familiar scene. Roger had fallen asleep in his large, overstuffed brown leather chair, while Theo lay on the old velvet sofa, legs crossed at the ankle, his decrepit, dingy-gray slouch hat over his face. Roger let out another of his stentorian snores.

As she studied the man she'd married with an abundance of good intentions, she felt a wave of disgust and bitter disappointment so powerful it near to smothered her. A germ of a harsh emotion stunned her in the speed with which it flared into a searing red lump of hate lodged in her heart, as it had begun to do from time to time in recent months.

Faith could honestly say she'd never known hatred until her wedding night. These days, however, it ebbed and flowed, and tonight it flowed like molten metal. The arrogance and prideful attitude of the Nolan brothers astounded her. After all the deplorable treatment they'd heaped on her, they believed her so incapable that they slept unguarded in a room adjacent to a kitchen where she kept a pair of sharp-bladed knives.

She caught the glitter of their edges in the flicker of the flames in the hearth.

She supposed many would consider whatever action she took with those knives justified, the harvest of what the men had sown. She took a step. Caught her breath. It was the first time that foreign notion had crossed her thoughts.

Could she use one of those knives to rid herself of her tormentor? As quiet as she'd tried to be, Faith realized she'd failed when the brothers began to stir. Then Theo stood, belched, scratched his head, and shambled to the door. "Gotta go. Shouldn't'a stayed so long."

Roger shrugged. "So now you've slept on it some, brother, have you changed your mind? Toldja you were wrong all along. T'ain't right, Theo. I always know what we ought and oughtn't do better'n you."

On his way to the door, Theo shot Roger a belligerent glare. "Don't hafta do what you want all the time, not on account of you being older."

A smug look on his jowly face, Roger scratched his rotund middle. "But you do hafta do what I want when it comes to my money."

Theo shoved an arm into the sleeve of his threadbare coat. "It's my money, too."

"Then get yer sorry self outta here," Roger growled. "Get moving, and go earn us some more, seein' as you're always being so quick to claim what comes in as yours. You said you were heading back to Bountiful tonight, and then tomorrow going on to—"

"Well, well, well!" Theo's small brown eyes narrowed to where they were mere slits in his plump face. "Lookee here, brother. Looks like yer missus is a-missing you, sleeping all alone up in that cold loft. Must get lonely of a night. Ain't that right?"

Faith shuddered. Now that the brothers had seen her, there would be no feigning sleep. It appeared the time to face the consequences had arrived.

"Would either of you care for...for fresh coffee?" It was all she could think of at the moment. Coffee, of course, might do some good, if it served to help them fully sober up, maybe even work some of its civilizing gifts on the two louts.

"Nah." Roger stared at his brother. "Theo here was jist leaving, weren't you, now, Theo?"

Theo shrugged. "Why, sure. Sure, Roger. Too bad I won't be having none of that coffee. You do make one fine pot, Faith."

She couldn't remember ever giving her brother-in-law leave to call her by her given name, but he'd taken the liberty anyway. She nodded acknowledgment and descended the stairs.

After Theo slammed the door shut, she turned to her husband. "Can I get you anything to eat?"

"Nothing," he said in a biting voice. "And you'd best sit until he's had time to go down a ways. You and me...we have us some talking to do."

*A real man didn't do any kind of talking with his fists...*

The thought flew through Faith's mind before she could catch it and turn it over to the Lord. It lodged in her heart like a lead ball, and she feared it might prove impossible to dislodge. One more truth she'd learned the hard way. One more reason to count herself a fool. She sank into the sofa, thankful, at least, for its proximity to the warm stone hearth. She felt iced to the depths of her being.

It took no effort to follow Theo's movements outdoors. He fancied himself quite the singer and filled the quiet night with the foul words of another one of his carousing ditties. She blushed, as she always did.

For a while, she wondered if Roger had fallen asleep again. He sat in his chair, immobile, only his chest rising and falling with his breath. She daren't try to climb back up to the loft, or even escape her fate, since she doubted she'd get far. More than likely, he was biding his time, waiting until Theo was far enough away. He never let his temper fully loose on her when anyone else was around.

A short spell later, or so it seemed to Faith, he opened his eyes again and stood. "Didja think I wouldn't know?"

Faith stood as well, hoping the movement would disguise the shudder that ran through her. She'd never heard Roger speak in that slow, deadly low voice. And she didn't need to pretend she didn't know of what he spoke. "No. I reckoned you would notice quite fast."

He took a step toward her. "Then why'dja go and do something like that?"

As she watched, he opened and closed his fists, his face growing redder by the moment. After she'd sent a prayer to heaven for help, she took a deep breath. "This was the second time the camp's order had come in. Mr. Bartlett paid for it up front, Roger. It wasn't right to keep him and his men waiting, especially for their food. It's getting cold, and any day now the path will be too dangerous and slippery—icy, even—to take the mules up far enough. Those men work hard. They need that food. I did what my conscience demanded I do."

He came another step closer, so close that Faith could smell the sour odor of the spirits he'd consumed hours earlier. "So who's more important? Your husband or your conscience?"

This time, he didn't stop coming. She had to take care how she answered that question, now that he stood but steps away. But no matter how she answered, she feared the outcome would be the same. Roger's face had twisted into the familiar enraged contours, and his nostrils flared with each sharp gust of breath he drew in.

The hands never stopped fisting.

"Both." She held her chin high, kept her eyes on his, made her voice as firm as she could. "Both are equally important, but . . . at times one outweighs the other, as it is with anything in life. I had to consider the men's lives—"

"NO!" He dropped hands like hams on her shoulders and gave her a shake. "No! Your husband is the only thing what matters, 'specially when it's something 'bout *his* store."

He shook her again, calling her by a vile name.

She winced, but let her body grow limp, since she'd learned the buffeting shakes would leave her in less pain that way. Sometimes, a fair amount of shaking and yelling would satisfy him. She prayed that would be the case again.

But he continued his assault, and instead of purposely emptying her head of any thought, as she usually did, this time, something inside her snapped.

*Enough!*

Faith would never know if she cried out or if she only thought the word, but she did know she fixed her eyes on his, brought her hands up to shoulder height, and clasped his thick wrists. With reserves of strength she'd never known she had, she yanked sideways, and pushed his hands away from her body. The shock that registered on his face allowed her to spin away.

She didn't get far.

He grabbed her braid. "Git back here!"

Immobilized by the pain in her scalp, she glanced everywhere, hoping to find something, anything to help. Holding her breath, she realized she stood only a step or two away from the hearth where Roger kept the fireplace tools. One of them, a heavy iron poker, leaned against the stone face. Faith summoned that foreign strength again, rotating her body away from her husband, gritting her teeth against the pain of her aching head, swerving back toward the hearth. By the grace of her merciful Lord her outstretched fingers made contact with the poker, and she clung fast.

"Let me go!" Her plea rang out raw and rough, unrecognizable even to her. At the same time she voiced her demand, she swung her arm up and around.

Roger caught the poker on its downward sweep. "Never! Let me have that you . . . you—"

But Faith didn't give up quite so easily this time. She clung to the metal with all her will. Roger did as well. They fought for the weapon, pulling, twisting, tugging, and wrenching it back and forth.

Her unexpected rebellion against his domination only enraged him more. On her part, he had pushed Faith well past her limit. She couldn't surrender to this life for another moment. She fought on.

Roger soon had enough of Faith's efforts to protect herself. With the hand holding the poker, he yanked her toward him, breathing hard...grunting, then with the other he reached out and gave her a breath-stealing shove. She flew backward...stumbled...lost her footing.

The metal piece slid across her palm, out of her grasp.

She fell...into utter dark.

# *Chapter 5*

When Faith opened her eyes, it was still night. She blinked, and although she lay motionless, a piercing stab in the back of her head cut through her disorientation, serving to rouse her fully. The deep silence pressed down on her like the heavy weight of an anvil. In seconds it became a smothering force all around her. Her head pounded; she felt a great deal of pain, right in the back where it rested against what she thought must be the stone hearth. She reached a hand to rub at the ache, but found the throbbing spot unexplainably damp.

She brought her fingers forward to see if she could identify the moisture, and by the light of the still-glowing embers in the fireplace, she saw the dark stain on them. The rusty odor of blood struck her right away.

In the relative dark of the room, she looked around to orient herself, moving her head as little as possible. She lay on the floor by the fireplace, right where she last remembered... oh! The memory of the fight blazed into her mind, the expression on Roger's face vile and vicious. Faith couldn't quell the wave of shudders that wracked her.

Drawing on her last ounce of strength, she pushed up on her elbows, slowly rising in spite of the overwhelming pain in her head. She blinked in an attempt to focus her eyes, especially on the large, dark form stretched out like a mountain range at about the halfway point across the large room. When her vision cleared, she almost wished it hadn't.

Roger lay sprawled facedown, out cold, as far as she could tell.

Cautiously, she worked her way up onto her knees, never looking away from her husband's prone figure. A sick sensation swirled in her middle, and dizziness threatened to topple her back down again. But something about the sight of Roger on the floor like that felt dreadfully wrong. She had to see why he was there, what had happened while she'd been unconscious.

The thought of having lost consciousness made her feel faint once more. But she couldn't. She bore a responsibility toward her husband; she had to see what was wrong with him, even if he hadn't earned one bit of her concern. She fought her body, and by sheer willpower remained steady.

When she tried to stand, the room whirled around her. It appeared she wasn't ready to walk yet. Very well, then, she would have to crawl, and like a child make progress from creeping to crawling to walking and more. Her conscience wouldn't let her do otherwise. No matter what stray and sinful thought she might have entertained during the wee hours of the morning.

By the time she'd almost reached Roger's side, she began to tremble, wishing somewhere in the most lily-livered corner of her being that she hadn't started the effort in the first place. Evil filled the place, as surely as the dreadful smell that assaulted her senses. That coppery tang was one you never forgot.

Blood.

And not only her own.

At the same time she drew a deep breath, Faith pushed herself up to her feet. She immediately wished she hadn't. *Oh, Father in heaven...*

She would never forget the shadowy sight that met her gaze. The poker she'd tried to use in her own defense had somehow found its mark. At that moment, it protruded at a hideous angle from the back of Roger's head. A pool of blood had gathered on the floor beneath the wound.

Faith stumbled backward, hand over her mouth to cover the scream that fought to escape her lips. "Dear Lord...what happened here?"

How could she not know how something like this had happened?

The last thing she remembered was Roger shoving her, then falling against the hearth. The blow to her head had shot a bolt of pain through her, and darkness had consumed all her senses. How had that poker found its way from Roger's hand, where she'd last seen it, to his head? Two things she knew without any question. She could not have done it while unconscious, and he hadn't put it there himself. But then, who had struck her husband?

Not just struck him. That much blood...

Who had killed Roger?

As she stood, frozen in place, her grip on sanity suddenly weak, she became aware of a panicked shriek outside oddly blunted by a strange crackling sound. At almost the same time, she noticed another acrid odor, faint but growing stronger, and more familiar than that of blood.

Smoke!

And it didn't come from the fireplace.

Faith spun on her heel. Dizziness struck. She extended her arms in search of balance, and as she did, she noticed the reddish glow outside the kitchen window. *Oh, sweet heaven...Almighty Father. How could that be?*

As her husband lay murdered at her feet in their sitting room, something was burning out back behind the cabin. Close. Too close.

She had to get out of the house or risk dying herself. In jerky, uneven motions, she turned to look for the old coat. She'd worn it out to the barn. She'd come back inside... where had she put it—there! She'd hung it on one of the hooks by the back door.

She ran to get it, and the closer she got, the redder the glow outside appeared. With an economy of motion, she pulled the garment on and around herself, then wrapped the warm woolen shawl over her head and across her chest. As a final precaution, she snagged Theo's old cap, a musty-smelling dun-colored thing. She crammed it down over the thickness of the shawl to hold the heavy knit closer to her head and ears. In a moment of what she vaguely recognized as hysteria, she reckoned she'd never looked odder than at that present time.

The smell of raging flames outside grew more pungent by the second. She had to get out of the cabin. Since the flames were at the rear of the structure, Faith ran to the door from the living quarters to the store. But before she reached it, she pulled up to a halt. Smoke, thick and gray, seeped in through the gap under the door. Crackling...the hiss of consuming flames sent her back a step. Escape by that route would be impossible.

"Father God...please don't leave me now."

She would have to get out from the back, even though that was where she'd first noticed the blaze. On that side, she had only two possible means of escape. She would either have to go out by the door or she would have to climb onto the counter where she kept her dishpan, throw open the window, and climb out, coat, shawl, hat, and all. It was too cold outside to consider leaving any of that behind, even if it would make her exit much easier.

From where she stood about ten feet away, she could see the flames now dancing outside the glass of the window. She couldn't go that route.

With another prayer on her lips, she pulled open the door. Heat and smoke slapped her. Her eyes watered, and she could barely see. A solid wall of fire roared to her left outside the kitchen window, the flames she'd watched from inside. To her right, the short pile of firewood Roger kept by the kitchen door had caught fire as well. Smaller flames licked at the two wooden steps below the door.

If she was to make it out safely, she would have to do it right then. And she'd have to go over or through those smaller—but just as dangerous—flames close to her feet that came closer every second she delayed.

Eyes shut tight, arms wrapped around her chest, she ran out, into the heat, into the thick smoke. She ran, ran, *ran*.

When she couldn't bear the not knowing any longer, she stopped and opened her eyes. To her amazement, she'd made it past the steps and into the small area between the house and the barn.

Faith cast a quick glance over her shoulder. She watched the flames eat away at the threshold to the kitchen. Beyond the fire, in the middle of the sitting room, she could still make out the faint bumpy contours of Roger's body. Guilt filled her.

She hadn't spared a thought to getting his corpse away from the raging inferno. Shame and remorse writhed in her heart. She should have taken him outside.

But...could she have?

Roger was—had been—a heavyset man, taller than her by a couple of inches. Logic told her she couldn't have carried him. Still, logic wasn't taking the lead right then.

Could she have dragged him? In spite of her bulky clothes and the flames at the door?

She glanced down...and saw the hem of her skirt scorched and still burning a hungry path upward. She dropped to her knees, slapped the fabric against the hard-packed dirt, paying little attention to the state of her hands.

Moments later, her skirt was once again safe. *She* was safe.

Or so she thought.

A rattle sounded out from somewhere to her right, from the vicinity of the barn.

The barn!

The mules...

A pang of anguish and fear squeezed her, and she raced to the ramshackle structure, another prayer in her heart. She glanced over her shoulder, and saw sparks catching at the scraps of dead grass beyond the back steps. Could she outrun the encroaching flames and get the mules to safety?

Panting, she dragged open the slightly ajar barn door and rushed to the pen. To her horror, that door was wide open, swinging on its flimsy hinges, the latch hanging uselessly by only one nail. "Maisie . . . ?"

A quick look around the dark confines of the barn revealed nothing unusual, no movement, no mules. Her heart quaked as she realized the mules had panicked and broken out of the poor pen to escape out the open barn door. Relief filled her.

Almost on its heels, a knot blocked her throat and a tear rolled down her cheek. While she was relieved by their safety, the thought of them being lost to her tore her heart in two. Where would they have gone? Would they be warm enough wherever they went? Would they find food, water, shelter?

The snapping and spitting flames sounded closer than before.

She had to get out—get away. With a last look at the empty stall, she slipped back outside, and was horrified by how close the flames had come. The heat struck her from that side, sent her stumbling in the opposite direction.

Catching her footing, she stood frozen, dazed and distressed, heart heavy, thoughts in chaos, terrified. She swept the clearing with her gaze. While she saw nothing unusual but for the burning building, her heart didn't pause or slow a single beat of its ferocious pounding. Thoughts of escape found footing in her mind.

Followed by questions that began to urge her forward. Roger was dead. She hadn't killed him. Was the killer still around? Was he watching her? Was he about to pounce?

Her husband's killer wouldn't hesitate to kill her, too.

She had to get away.

Fast.

She took one cautious step, and peered around again. Nothing, no sign of any animal, no human, nothing to fear.

Except the flames.

Another step. Nothing happened once again. She walked farther into the center of the clearing, out in the open, in full sight of any creature that might care to do her harm.

A second later, she stopped, clasped her head. What was she doing? Where was she going? Should she try to find her way, in the dark, to the town of Bountiful?

Reason told her she'd never make it there on foot. Even by horse or by wagon, it took hours. That only left her one choice. She had to wend her way up the forest trail for the second time that day, only this time, in the dark. She stood a better chance to make it to the logging camp than to seek safety anywhere else. Surely Mr. Bartlett would remember her efforts on his behalf when she showed up. Surely he would offer her shelter in her moment of greatest distress.

As she stood, gazing for a last time at the place she'd called home for three years, a gust of wind carried a sharp, familiar smell past her nostrils. Kerosene! Horror overwhelmed her. The only way for kerosene to give off its pungent odor in the outdoors was if someone put it there.

Faith crushed a fist to her mouth, stifled a cry. While she

might escape the fire, she couldn't escape the truth. Someone had set the cabin, the general store, on fire. After they'd killed Roger.

They *had* tried to kill her.

She prayed that someone was by now long gone. Even if she didn't know for sure, she wasn't about to stand there and wait to find out.

She ran to the mouth of the path, praying the forest canopy didn't prove too thick to let in the scant glow the sliver of moon cast down. Without light, she didn't know how she would find her way along the twisty trail. In spots, the cleared path grew narrow and hard to find.

Firm determination in place, Faith started her trip to the logging camp, heart pounding, the will to live pushing her on. "Go, go, go!"

With each step, her thoughts sorted themselves out more. Bits of memory flashed through. Echoes of fear...a wild flight...embers of devastating fire...

She couldn't believe how eerily this night paralleled that afternoon years earlier. She'd come back from town, the flatbed wagon filled with Mama and Papa's order from the mercantile. Nothing could have prepared her for the sight of the farmhouse ruins, still burning here and there, a haunting silence over the devastation, broken only by the occasional crack of smoldering wood. The stench of smoke swirled around her. Nothing remained. The house and the barn had become piles of ashes. Few boards still stood.

Bitter tears scalding her face, she'd flown back to town.

And here she was, fleeing another place where she'd lived, fearing for her life, horror-filled by yet more loss of life.

Had Indians struck again?

She sped up, keeping her gaze on the ground to avoid tripping on the uneven surface of the trail.

The times Indian men had come to do business with Roger, the thought of what their kind had done to her parents had sent her seeking refuge in the storeroom. She had to wonder what her husband could have done to enrage any of the stragglers from the reservation to such a pitch as to lead them to this atrocity.

A shudder racked her, and she nearly lost her footing. She gritted her teeth, focused on her goal.

She'd never thought it wise for Roger to sell to the Indians. This might prove her right. *If* the culprit was an Indian.

Behind her, a crash resounded, reverberating against the trees.

She moved faster still.

Her breath came in pants of steam. The wind pierced through her outer garments, chilling her. The odd sounds of the forest had always frightened her, but tonight they terrified her.

She kept going.

Then she heard what sounded like horse's hooves.

Close.

To her rear.

No! She was nowhere near the camp. She had to get there. *Keep moving!*

A glance over her shoulder revealed nothing in the dark. Wrapping her determination more closely, she began to run, more afraid of what might be coming her way than a twisted ankle. In an effort to calm down, she told herself she must have only heard sounds from the raging fire. Or a small forest animal, fleeing the flames.

But when she heard them once more, closer to her this third time, she could no longer deny the truth. Someone was after her.

It had to be Roger's killer. He must have waited after starting the blaze, watched the destruction from near enough to witness her escape. Was he on the way to finish the job? Or maybe he didn't know she was here, was only riding along the path. She couldn't risk him catching up to her regardless.

Panic—panic—*panic!*

If he was following her she couldn't outrun her pursuer if he was on horseback, but she was fairly certain she could lose him among the trees. She doubted a tall, somewhat delicate horse could pick its way through the dense forest undergrowth.

For a moment, she hesitated. Could she maneuver the pitfalls within the forest herself in the dark? She had to. It was the only way out of danger. She had to get away, find a place to hide until he passed. She darted off the path into the damp and dank embrace of the trees. Despite the hush within the thickness of the foliage, she still could hear the distant crackle of flames and the sound of hooves growing louder on the path. But instead of continuing whoever approached on the trail seemed to veer off it as well. In her direction.

The only thing that fit inside her head was her desperate need to escape. That, together with the ever-louder sounds of her pursuers. Too many hooves for only one horse.

Faith's chest burned with the sharp, shallow breaths of icy air she'd been taking since she'd left the house. She couldn't keep up the furious pace. She slowed. The hoofbeats drew closer with each passing moment.

Then she fell, tripped over a rock or a root, a dead branch, she didn't see which.

Now the riders sounded almost upon her.

Eyes shut tight, she shivered and prayed...

Until a warm, wet nose rubbed her neck. "Maisie!"

Relief rendered her weak. She laughed a nervous titter, utterly unlike her. Tears of joy ran down her cheeks.

Daisy nuzzled her left cheek.

Faith reached up to pat her. "How did you get here? Both of you!"

And then, to make it all the more absurd, Lazy butted her head from the right side. "Oh, goodness gracious. All three of you. You poor things. You must have been so scared—"

The shriek she'd heard while she'd gathered her senses after coming to must have been from one of the mules.

"All of you are clever critters, aren't you?" For once, she was elated Roger hadn't bothered to make things right. The damaged lock on the door to the stall must not have given them much trouble. After that, it was simply a matter of doing what they always did. Maisie led, and the other two followed her out.

None of the mules was talking.

"Thank goodness you're all safe. And now here you are. With me."

She nearly wept, she so appreciated their company out in the dark. Her confidence grew by the minute. "Amazing what a few staunch companions can do for a body, wouldn't you say?"

Maisie let out her gentle bray.

The others responded, and it seemed to Faith as though they'd echoed the lead mule's sentiment.

"Well, then. We'd better be on our way. It's a long walk up the mountain, and all of us are tired from the first time we made the trip today. We need to get there, and soon. Before the fire spreads much farther."

And before Roger's killer found her.

Determination firmly in place once again, Faith resumed her flight to the logging camp and the relative safety it would provide.

Under her breath, she prayed Mr. Bartlett would help her.

She had no one else to turn to.

# Chapter 6

After what felt like hours of wandering in the dense woods, Faith collapsed on a fallen log. She had to admit the truth.

She was lost.

Hopelessly and completely lost.

With three mules who trusted her enough to follow wherever she led.

Tears of frustration burned in her eyes, spilled down her cheeks. "What am I going to do now?" she asked her faithful companions.

None, not even Maisie, answered. They did, however, surround her, their warm bodies giving off the steamy heat they'd worked up.

Faith's limbs felt as heavy as the mossy, rotting piece of tree trunk where she sat. Her muscles quivered from the unaccustomed exertion. Her back ached in unfamiliar places. Her toes had grown numb from the cold, and her fingers were icy and stiff. Her cheeks stung from the bite of the cold night wind, whose eerie whistle kept her on edge.

She'd never felt so weak. Exhaustion drained her of all her strength. And still, she had no idea where she was or how she was going to get them out of the woods, much less to the camp. How was she going to get them all to safety?

The weariness led to a yawn. The thought of sleep filled her with a sense of longing, of something that might solve the unsolvable, and if not solve it, then at least to put it out of her conscious mind for a peaceful while. She rubbed Maisie's head. "What a fanciful and crazy notion, don't you think?"

Maisie snuffled, drawing closer to Faith. Then, in a gesture heartwarming in its understanding, the mule lay down at her side. While she knew her animals slept lying down at times, usually they rested, dozing, while on their feet. They rarely ever allowed themselves the luxury of fully resting, choosing instead to remain ready to flee at the first sign of danger, a trait inherited from their equine parents. The donkey half did the same.

"You're tired, too, aren't you?"

Lazy answered by following Maisie's lead, choosing to bed down as close to Faith's back as he could get.

The toll of the long day and horrifying night felt too great to bear. Her eyelids felt heavy, sleep the only thing she could envision right then.

Of course, there was the matter of finding her way out of the forest. She'd have to wait until daylight, or she'd most likely wind up even more lost than she was. Then, too, the mules were counting on her. They trusted her, knew she'd provide all their needs, and in her current state she would do none of them any good. Sleep was the best option.

"But here?" She looked around, taking in the trees in all directions where she looked, the forest floor, dense with fallen pine needles, the one log where she sat. The heavy silence held no hint of approaching danger.

She noticed how the mules' bodies had formed a small space where her body would fit just right, cradled within their warmth, sheltered in the protection their bulk offered. Daisy remained on her feet, as Faith suspected she would do until one of the other two animals awoke and relieved her of her sentry duties. She'd seen the three do it before.

Her head found a cushion close to Maisie's neck, and she only drew a breath or two before slumber overtook her.

Peace...

"You'd better come see this, boss," Purcell told Nathan as soon as he'd opened his bedroom door. "Don't know where it's at, but it looks like a pretty big cloud of smoke."

"Smoke?" He pulled on his boots. In the forest, any hint of fire presented too great a danger to ignore. A blaze found too much fuel wherever one looked. "Show me."

The two men ran outside, and in spite of the night's darkness, Nathan saw the billow that had alarmed Purcell. It rose from the lower reaches of the forest, and swelled as it rose. A faint orange glow reflected off the gray smoke, clearly visible against the dark winter sky.

He spun and headed back to the cabin. "Get the others. Tell them to dress well, but to be ready. Fighting fire in the woods is an ugly matter."

Less than ten minutes later, Nathan pulled on his heavy coat, a knitted cap, and thick winter gloves. The other five men did the same, and between them, they carried the camp's three buckets and assorted empty food supply tin pails. In silence, they set off down the path, carefully guiding their horses on the rugged trail, unsure where the actual source of the flames might lie, in doubt about where they'd get the water they would need to douse the blaze.

After they'd gone a substantial way down, a sick suspicion gripped Nathan. Could the general store have caught fire? The trail led directly to the store, and the smoke seemed to come from that direction. If so, were the Nolans safe? Had the slovenly brothers grown careless and allowed a blaze to break out? And what about Mrs. Nolan? Was she in danger?

He remembered her courage. How could he not? She'd braved not only the woods, but also Roger Nolan's anger to help him and his men.

"Let's go straight to the store," he said. "We can get a better idea of what's happening once we get there. It's in a large clearing, and without the trees overhead, the location of the fire might be easier to identify."

Matt matched his steps to Nathan's. "Let's not rush in there. I'm thinking that smoke's rising from somewhere awful close to that store."

Nathan cast him a glance. Matt didn't look his way, looking instead up toward the smoke-filled sky. "That's what I'm afraid of."

A grim nod was his only response. He picked up his pace. The others followed suit.

The closer they drew to the Nolan's property, the greater their certainty grew. The blaze was indeed at the store. When they finally reached the clearing in the woods, they dismounted and looped their reins over branches of trees a safe distance from the fire. The moment drew out, sickening in the reality before them. They were too late to save the building. The barn, however, still stood, although flames were creeping closer, even as they watched.

"There's a good well," Nathan called out, pointing in the direction of the water source. "Let's start there, and see if we can't save the barn."

A knot formed in Nathan's gut each time he looked at the ruins of the general store. Had the Nolans perished in the blaze? He had to find out. He couldn't continue to worry and speculate.

"You fellows work on the flames. I—I need to check over there."

From his men's expressions, he didn't need to say more. They understood his mission.

As he approached the smoldering pieces of wall that remained standing, the mounds of charred furnishings, the skeleton of the store, bile rose in his throat. Would he also find the remains of the three who'd lived there?

His endeavor proved gruesome indeed. He didn't need to go far to spot what remained of one human body, partly covered by burning debris. If he had to guess, he'd say it was Roger, since he'd been the largest member of the household. Taking all precautions possible, he nudged aside chunks of what had become charcoal with a metal rod he'd found a few feet away from the house. It might once have suspended Mrs. Nolan's wash line.

He found no trace of the other residents of the place.

"Barn's empty, boss," Woody called out. "No animals here."

Where were Mrs. Nolan and Theo Nolan?

If the blaze had been an accident, wouldn't it have made sense for her to head for the logging camp for help? Why hadn't they met them on the trail? Surely they wouldn't have tried to get all the way to Bountiful.

Nathan wouldn't have answers to his questions until he and his men doused the flames. He dropped the metal piece and picked up a tin pail, then headed for the well. With a load of water in hand, he joined his men and helped them bring the fire under control.

Not much later, they all stood still, faces streaked with sweat and soot, surveying the wreckage in the clearing. While the blaze was out, thin curls of smoke rose here and there, where embers had been doused as recently as minutes before. The oppressive silence bore an ominous weight, and Nathan couldn't shake the vague sense of foreboding that enveloped him.

The sound of a rapidly approaching horse came from the opposite section of the path from where he and his men had come. Into the smoke-colored approaching dawn, Theo Nolan galloped, anger drawn on his round face.

"What'd you do to my property?" he asked as he drew the horse to a stop before Nathan. He dismounted, and the belligerence in his voice spread to his face. "Didn't ya have enough with the rest of the whole mountain? You that greedy, Bartlett?"

"Take a breath." Nathan kept his words even, his expression bland. "My man Purcell saw the smoke from up at our camp. We came down to see if we could help."

"Help yourself to what ain't yours, is more like it."

"Hang on, there," Woody said. "No one's helped themselves to nothing, here. We came down, used your well water to fill our buckets, and we been puttin' out your fire ever since. Where were you all this time?"

Theo cleared his throat with a loud *harrumph*. "I was supposed to be off to Bountiful. But when I got me to the end of the trail and before I headed that way I turned around for a moment. That there big cloud of smoke was what I seen. Turned myself right back around again and got back here soon's as I could. You're what I found."

"Sounds pretty close to what we did," Nathan said to the enraged man. "I must say, I'm sorry about your brother. It looks as though the fire caught him while sleeping, and he didn't get out."

A series of emotions sped across Theo's features, and he worked his jaw in an attempt to control them. "Roger?" he asked. "You sure 'bout that?"

Nathan shrugged. "As close as I can get. There's what's left of the poor soul who died, spread out on the floor. It's a man, and it's not you. Was anyone else here?"

Theo shook his head. "Only Roger and Faith—Faith! Where is she? Where'd she go after she lit my poor brother on fire?"

The sick sensation that had hovered in the pit of Nathan's stomach lurched to full force. "Whoa there, Theo. No one's seen Faith or the mules. Maybe she opened their stalls and took them with her to safety."

*He hoped.*

Theo narrowed his eyes. "You saying the mules is gone, too? With that woman?" He spat on the ground. "She stole 'em. After she kilt my brother with fire. Burned down all's we got. Gotta find her. Ain't right, what she done to my brother. And me."

Woody held out his hand. "Now wait up a blazin' hot minute, there, why don'tcha, Theo? We don't know what happened here." He shook his grizzled head. "Don't you go sayin' nothin' too crazy, nothing what's gonna come back and kick ya in the behind, if you know what I mean."

"I'm only saying what I see, clear as day." Theo was known for his obstinacy.

"And all you see," Nathan said, seeking more patience within him, "is a burned building. Look"—he pointed toward the fence around the animals' pen—"how the board is still broken, right where the mules got out not so long ago. I was here that day, helped Roger round them up. But it seems no one's fixed it since then."

Theo scoffed. "Them mules were in the barn when I fetched Charlie, here, and left not so long ago. Even you gotta know they couldn't'a got out on their own. They're mules, right?"

It did sound far-fetched, even to Nathan, who was trying to see all sides of the situation. Still, without knowing everything about the night's events, he had to try to keep matters on sensible footing.

"Why would Mrs. Nolan steal her own mules?"

Theo's small brown eyes flashed with outrage. "They ain't her mules, Bartlett. They're mine. Mine and Roger's, that is. We paid for 'em. All's she did was clean up after them, and give them food. Nothing more."

"But she was Roger's wife. Surely, as husband and wife, they saw the animals as hers, too."

Theo jutted out his chin. "Weren't hers. Mine and my brother's. That's it. Now you're saying he's gone?"

"Go take a look."

Color drained from Theo's padded cheeks. "I . . . s'pose."

He dragged his feet as he walked closer to the ruined store. Nathan watched him cast a quick look at the body and then, with a sharp inhalation, the white-faced Theo turned away and came back to Nathan's side.

His throat worked with the large gulp he took. "S'him, all right." He gave his fat- and flesh-padded jaw an unexpected squared-off firmness. "Someone's gotta go fetch Marshal Blair. Cain't do it myself, on account of that man plumb hates me. But he's gotta come out here straight away and arrest that Faith woman. She kilt my brother, destroyed our property, and stole what's left. She ain't better'n no common rustler. Way I see it, she's pert near a horse thief, what with mules being half horse, as they are."

A sinking feeling struck Nathan. His worst fears had been voiced. And by someone whose word would carry weight in the eyes of the law.

Was Theo right? Had Faith harmed her husband? Had she stolen the mules?

Or was she, as Nathan hoped, a frightened woman who'd run from a fire, leading her animals to safety?

Only the Lord knew.

He looked around the clearing, praying for the right way to handle the moment, hoping to diffuse the tension without letting matters get any further out of hand. But it seemed the forest he loved so much, the woods that normally gave him a sense of shelter, of comfort, of peace, today reminded him of an oncoming Union battalion. The shadows loomed in ominous silence, seemingly encroaching upon them, threatening to swallow everything and everyone in their path.

He'd never thought himself particularly fanciful, and he realized he was letting his fears and worry get far ahead of him, but the sense of foreboding wouldn't let him shake it off. The moment lengthened as thoughts coursed through his mind. What should he do? What was the truth of the matter? Was there any way to help Mrs. Nolan? Or was Theo right?

What should Nathan do in this sorry situation?

Nothing came to him, no answer to any of his questions. Still silent, he strode to the barn, and found the large door ajar. He slipped inside, only to see the oddest stall he'd ever seen. It was wide enough for at least three, and the door swung lopsided from flimsy hinges. The meager latch hung down, one of the nails that once held it in place gone. While he couldn't be sure, it would seem that the mules had panicked at the scents and sounds of the fire and had busted out of their quarters. More than likely, they'd run off, seeking safety.

Had Mrs. Nolan gone to find them? Was there any way she was trying to make off with them, as Theo had said? Was she safe in the forest? Or had something befallen her as well? Could someone—whoever set the fire—have taken her and the mules? There were a lot of hoofprints around, but it was a general store.

Had been a general store.

Frustrated, he went back outside. He realized that no matter how much he wanted to resolve the matter there was only one thing to do. "We didn't see her on our way down, and if you didn't see her coming up the other side of the trail, then we're not sure where she might be. Goodness knows it's a big mountain full of trees out here. She could be anywhere, lost probably. We need to find her."

"Poor thing could be hurt," Woody offered.

"Bah!" Theo said. "You're right 'bout one thing, Bartlett. We gotta find her. And someone has to fetch Marshal Blair straight away. He'll know what to do with the likes of her. Does it all the time, I reckon."

If anyone knew the truth of Theo's assertion, it was certainly him. Over the span of years Nathan had known the brothers, the younger of the two had found himself only too often on the diligent marshal's wrong side.

A sense of doom dropped down on the men. Matt offered to go to Bountiful and return with the marshal, since it didn't seem as though Theo had any intention of backing down from his demand. The rest of the men were resolved to find Mrs. Nolan.

Nathan separated the small group into sets of two. He and Woody headed up the trail, while the other pairs spread out into the woods around the store. Anything could happen to a lost traveler in the dense foliage. He prayed someone would soon find her.

He prayed they found her alive.

Faith awoke when Maisie leaped up from where she'd lain, offering her a perfectly adequate pillow for her throbbing head and a source of warmth for her chilled body. The throbbing wasn't likely to improve any time soon, since her head crashed down onto the ground at the mule's sudden move. As to the cold? Well, winter was only just beginning.

The three animals set up a loud braying as Maisie took off at a fair clip. Daisy followed in close pursuit, and Lazy, as always, trailed behind the girls at a far less vigorous pace.

"Hey!" Faith cried, rubbing the spot where she'd banged her temple. Now she hurt not only at the back of her head, where she'd hit the hearth the night before, but also to the right and almost at the hairline next to her eye. Perhaps she should have set off toward Bountiful as soon as she'd found the runaway mules after all.

What could have spooked Maisie? Where had those three critters gone now?

"Maisie? Where are you? Daisy...Lazy! Come back." She looked about at the trees that loomed all around. Her plan of hiding in the darkness of the forest from pursuers during the night didn't look to be all that wise when examined in the pale gray of the woodland's dawn.

As she tried to think things through, somewhere close behind her a shot rang out. No, not a shot. The snap of a dead branch cracking under the weight of an approaching person.

Faith jumped up and away from her erstwhile bed as fast as her mules had done moments earlier. Heart pounding, she hastened after her animals, praying she wouldn't trip on any of the dense forest debris underfoot. Even if it wasn't someone coming after her, it could be someone out hunting who would mistake the mules—or her—for game. She didn't want to alert whoever it was to her whereabouts until she knew their identity. But she couldn't move quickly enough and remain quiet, and she could hear the rustling of someone moving rapidly closer.

"Lookit here! Toldja she'd a-taken off with our—er...*my* property, dinnent I? She was even talking at 'em—but... where are they? Where's them mules, Faith?"

As Theo and one of the loggers crashed through the undergrowth right up to her side, his loathsome voice pinned Faith to the spot. Her feet seemed to have become tree roots, her boots uncommonly leaden in weight. Her heart skipped a beat, pounded a flurry of speedy thumps then skipped again, at no time giving her the impression it intended to return to its normal pace. The damp chill of the woods snaked in past the meager protection of her borrowed coat, as the icy fingers of the dawn's wind crept under the shawl she'd earlier wrapped around her head but by now had loosened and drooped down around her shoulders.

She shuddered, shot looks all around, but found no clear path toward escape. It wouldn't have helped if she'd found one. Theo pushed his bulk into her line of sight any time she turned even the slightest bit, working his well-padded jaw, waving his arms in wild gyrations, sending condemnation her way from his small, dark eyes.

Bile burned her throat.

Her stomach heaved.

She gagged.

"Don't jist stand there," her brother-in-law yelled at her. "Go get them, Faith. Ain't it bad enough I caught ya trying to make off with 'em? Now you're gonna jist stand there and watch 'em run? You were a lousy excuse for a wife for my brother, and now you're even a lousy excuse for a horse thief—"

"Mules," she said before she could stop herself. "They're mules, Theo. And I didn't steal them. I ran from the fire, hoping to make it to the logging camp and get help before the buildings burned away. They followed me, but I got us all lost in the dark. It's thanks to them I didn't die frozen during the night."

"More's the pity," the angry man spat out, his voice cracking a time or two. "Why'dja go and kill Roger? Dinnent he give ya a home and food and clothes and all after your kin left ya with nothing at all? He was good enough to keep ya, but you were too good to keep to your vows?"

"I didn't kill him." She forced her voice to stay as steady as she could manage. "We had a . . . disagreement. I . . . ah . . . fell and hit my head against the hearth. See?" She turned around and pointed to where her hair was still stiff from the blood she'd shed. "The fall knocked me out. When I came to, I saw Roger lying on the floor. I saw blood, too, his blood—a lot of it. And smoke. The cabin was in flames. Without a doubt, your brother died sometime while I was unconscious. I couldn't save him. It was too late. Please remember, Roger was a big man, much bigger than I am. I would have died, long before I managed to get his body outside. That's why I left him in the cabin. I . . . well, I had to run, to get help."

Theo spat a glob of chewing tobacco juice at a tree trunk.

Her stomach lurched again.

"Don't believe none of what ya say," Theo muttered.

Before she could speak in her defense, another man ran up to her brother-in-law's side.

"I see . . . you found . . . her." Nathan Bartlett's words came out choppy, his breath labored. He'd clearly been running for a spell. He turned from Theo to Faith. "Let's head back. My men are looking for you and the mules. We need to let them know we've found you. Are you hurt? How'd you get here? What happened back at the general store?"

As they hurried along the path, Faith struggled to keep up with the tall man. Before long, she'd begun to draw hard, fast breaths. With each question the lumberman fired at her, Faith's breathing became further impaired. By the time he paused, she could only gasp small gulps of air that didn't reach the depths of her need.

Her head still throbbed from when she'd fallen against the hearth. The skin on her face stung from the cold wind, and possibly from her rush through the flames at the door. She hadn't thought to take an inventory of her aches and pains at any time. She'd slept cradled against a dead tree trunk, between two mules, and now she needed to think clearly. The lumberman expected her to make sense.

She felt dizzy from the multitude of images spinning through her head.

"I—" She had to stop, rub her temple, try to slow her racing heartbeat, ease her choppy breathing.

"I'm so sorry." Mr. Bartlett stepped up to her. "I'm forgetting myself. We need to get you to the camp soon. I'm sure you're near frozen, and you have scrapes and red spots on your cheek and jaw. Woody can see to those."

Welcome relief swept through her, and she resumed walking. She wanted nothing more than to find the warmth and shelter he offered. "I'm sorry. I hate to put you out, but I'm afraid I've nowhere else to go—"

"Don't fret about that, Mrs. Nolan," he said, taking her elbow and leading her toward a group of horses tied to trees at the mouth of the trail up ahead. "It's only neighborly. What any decent, church-going man would do."

A tentative smile curved her lips, but before she could say anything in response, he paused and turned back to the gathering men. "I'm going ahead with Mrs. Nolan. She's hurt and needs to warm up and rest. You can catch up to us when you've made sure you've left no burning embers anywhere."

"Good thinkin', boss," Woody, the older logger, said. "I'll ride on up with you two. Make sure there's something hearty to stick to her innards, and some hot coffee to get her blood a-runnin' again. Or tea. Reckon she looks like a lady what drinks herself some fine tea."

"I doubt she'll want your muddy brew," Mr. Bartlett said, glancing sideways at her, gauging the success of his mild attempt at lightness.

She appreciated his effort, but all she could muster was another weak try at a smile. She certainly didn't want any "muddy brew" coffee, much less food, since she didn't think she could swallow a bite, but a cup of tea did sound like a good possibility right then. "Thank you," she said softly as she wondered how she was going to make it all the way up the trail again.

"Are you ready?" Mr. Bartlett asked.

She glanced around her and shuddered. "Yes. Yes, I am."

Strong arms wrapped around her before she realized what

was coming. She flew up through the air in their secure clasp, a feeling of safety and shelter embracing her, foreign and a touch alarming to her. "What—"

"Don't fret," the logger said in his calm, resonant voice. "Horace here might be a tall one, but he's gentle and smooth as any horse I've ever known."

Mr. Bartlett set her on a dark chestnut horse, who stood quietly waiting. With an abundance of care, he settled her on the saddle, not one built for a lady, but still, at the moment, perfect to her. Her initial reluctance to put the lumberman to any trouble began to fade, since she doubted she could make it to the camp on her own steam.

"Ready?" he asked.

"Yes."

He took the reins in hand and began to lead her mount up the trail. "Wait!" she called. "Where's your horse—oh, no! You can't give up your horse. It wouldn't be right for me to ride, while you have to walk."

"Well," he said, his voice again striking her as purposefully light, "it's all sorted out already. You're on Horace, and I'm walking next to the two of you. I'd hardly let a lady walk while I ride. And, well, begging your pardon, but you looked ready to fall. After all you've been through, I'm not surprised. But you're safe now. You can ride easy, and let the horse do the work."

Again that word, that sensation she hadn't felt since her parents' deaths. Until Mr. Bartlett appeared, offering protection...safety. It felt good and strangely right.

To her amazement, the logger continued to walk apace with the horse—Horace. Mr. Bartlett kept a hand near the animal's rump, and on the rare occasion when the fine animal stumbled on the debris strewn over the trail, that hand flew to steady her.

A woman could get used to such kind treatment, especially one who'd never known a man so kind and protective. Aside from her late papa.

With that sense of protection firm in her mind, she let darkness enfold her, the only sounds breaking the forest's hush those of the horse's hooves leading her to the shelter of the logging camp.

After what seemed like only seconds, but couldn't have been, she opened her eyes and realized they were no longer out in the woods, but at the edge of the clearing at the camp.

"Let's go inside," Mr. Bartlett said, a hand extended to help her dismount.

She blinked. Pain in her head and dizziness threatened to drown her. Her surroundings swam around her.

"How could I have lost track...maybe even dozed? And on a horse, at that."

"You've been through a lot, Mrs. Nolan." With another measuring look, the camp owner reached and grasped her by the waist. A moment later, she stood unsteadily on the ground.

"Ooooh!"

"Careful there," he said, his steadying hand at her back. "I'd say you may have a bit of a concussion, from the look of the wound on your head. It could make you mighty lightheaded, and I wouldn't want you to fall. You've already been hurt enough."

The double meaning of his words brought a wash of

shame over Faith, but at the same time, the warmth and compassion in his expression and in the sentiment he expressed couldn't be discounted. Sincerity radiated from the man.

"Thank you," she whispered. She had to navigate the wide clearing and make it to the main cabin across the way—

"Here we go!" Strong arms again swooped her up, but this time, he held her close, as his legs made short work of the walk. With a booted foot, he pushed open the door, which evidently Woody had left ajar.

Moments later, he set her down carefully on an upholstered piece of furniture in the shadowed room.

When Faith's eyes grew accustomed to the dimmer indoor light and she managed to focus, she noted she'd been placed on a large leather sofa. A moment later, she was covered with a heavy woolen point blanket, its distinctive green, yellow, red, and indigo stripes against the white background bright in the light that seeped in through a nearby window. She also caught sight of well-chinked log walls; saw the small glassed windows at various spots in those walls; made out the large, black iron stove toward the back of the room; rejoiced in the vast stone fireplace where a warm fire crackled and spat; became aware of the brawny tables and chairs scattered about; even glimpsed a few braided rugs sprinkled under various pieces of furniture. The place looked like a haven for rugged men should.

"Lady..." Theo muttered as he stomped in. "She ain't no lady. Ladies don't go 'round killing off their husbands, and then running off with their brother-in-law'ses inheritances."

Faith pulled herself into a full sitting position. She grasped the tight woven edge of the blanket, almost as though the item might offer her strength. But it couldn't. She was on her own. And with the Lord.

She tipped up her chin. "I didn't kill Roger." Then, before Theo could argue again, she squared her shoulders and continued. "You know I didn't run off with anything. I already told you what happened. I fell during a . . . a disagreement between Roger and me after you had left the cabin. I bumped my head and fainted. When I woke up again, I saw Roger dead on the floor, and the cabin going up in flames. I had to run outside to keep from dying in the fire myself."

Theo rolled his eyes. "You weren't nowhere—"

"And," she said, cutting off his argument, "while I was trying to get here—to safety and to ask for help—the mules showed up. They began to follow me. You know they often do that. Since I'd gotten turned around off the trail and was lost by then, I couldn't lead them back to the barn. I decided to rest until sunrise so we wouldn't get even more lost than we already were." When he opened his mouth to respond, she held up a hand. "Please, wait. I'd like to know what you would have had me do. Would you rather I had turned them back then locked them in the barn? Risked them dying if the fire spread? I didn't steal anything."

"Did so steal 'em. Saw you with my own eyes. All what you jist said is nothing more'n a story you cooked up once you got caught with 'em. It's awful lucky one of Bartlett here's men heard them mules running in the woods where you had them go. Otherwise, why . . . I can't begin to figger out how much these three fine, sturdy animals are worth. How could I have replaced 'em, now the store's all gone? And I'm needing them to haul things out here from Bountiful, at least to the barn, if I'm going to earn my decent living. But you? Well, we all know you're jist plain worthless."

Although Faith knew she shouldn't take the sharp, hate-filled words to heart, it still hurt to hear them spoken out loud. Even if the one speaking them was only Theo.

Before she could compose herself enough to come up with a passable response, Mr. Bartlett stepped up to her brother-in-law. With a large, work-roughened hand, he took Theo by the arm and led him to the door.

"I think we all need to catch up on lost sleep before we do much more talking," the lumberman said. "It's always better to think a thing through before one says something one will later regret."

Much like the mules, Theo dug in his heels. "I ain't said nothing I'm ever gonna regret. And I'm not starting to, nei-ther. I always speak my mind. I'm not about to stop doing that, no matter what story she cooks up."

Mr. Bartlett nodded. "That's fine, Theo. Let's get some sleep so that you can continue to speak your mind some more once you're rested."

From the chair at the head of one of two long tables in the large room, the older lumberjack Mr. Bartlett called Woody made a sound much like a snort. Faith narrowed her eyes, but the man's heavy, wiry gray beard concealed much of his expression. He continued to ply his wicked, sharp knife over a chunk of wood, as he whittled away the excess from what-ever he was busy making.

Theo also turned to the old codger, stared at him with his small eyes. But he must have seen as little as Faith herself had because he shrugged and let himself be led right up to the door. "This ain't over, you know, Bartlett. The marshal ain't here yet, and jist on account of your man finding my mules, it don't mean she's not a thief. She was about to steal them, and she would've, too, if we hadn't'a caught her. And them."

"Then you have your mules back?"

"Yeah, I got 'em," he grumbled.

"Good. In view of all that's happened tonight, then we must be thankful you suffered no further loss."

Faith couldn't tell if Mr. Bartlett was using his mild words and tone to rebuke Theo for his lack of response to his bereavement or if he merely wanted him out of the building.

"Like I said," the lumberman added, "we all need sleep. I can offer you a bed in our bunkhouse. It won't be fancy, but it's clean and the boys don't snore. Much."

Beds!

Oh, dear. What had she done? She'd never even given propriety the least thought. She couldn't stay here. It was a place for men. She'd have to figure out somewhere else to live, and soon. But where? She had no money for a room at Folsom's River Run Hotel, and while she did have a passing acquaintance with most in town, she could count few as close friends. Her head throbbed viciously the more she thought about it.

It seemed her problems were just beginning.

# Chapter 7

After an extended, uncomfortable silence, Woody scraped his chair back away from the table. It shrieked against the floorboards. He approached Faith with his odd, bowlegged limping walk.

"Here, boss," he said, walking up to Theo. "You can see to Missus Nolan's situation while I go ahead and take Theo on down with me to the bunkhouse. Wouldn't want *him* getting hisself lost out there, now would we? 'Sides, it'll do the both of us a passel of good to snore some ourselves."

The two loggers nodded to each other, their communication obvious but unclear to anyone but them. Mr. Bartlett opened the door, let Woody stomp out, and then gave Theo a gentle push outside. He closed the door with a gentle but firm *click* from the iron latch as it fell into place on its own.

Did these men let the door lock them out of their own house?

As Faith allowed herself a curious appraisal of her surroundings, she noticed three doors at the rear of the room. Two were on either side, almost against the back wall. She suspected they might lead to additional rooms. The third was located near the stove with a window to its right that showed the tall trees outside. That door sported a latch much like the one at the front of the cabin.

"It locks all by itself, too." Mr. Bartlett's eyes twinkled with humor. "We don't want bears getting in here, you know. If one of the men forgets to close the door, a bear can give it a swat and come inside."

Faith couldn't stop the shudder. "That's dreadful! Roger never told me we were in danger from anything like bears. I knew they were about, but I never thought they'd try to get inside. The only animals I've seen near the general store are the squirrels and deer. Oh, and he and Theo did talk about spotting foxes every once in a while."

"Indeed." The corners of the logger's lips twitched. "Don't want to mess with foxes, either, Missus Nolan. They're serious animals."

Foxes? From what she'd seen they were small creatures, but of course, he'd know more than she would. To think she'd been living in complete ignorance of all she might have faced out here on the mountain.

Or . . . was that a smile trying to break free?

He wouldn't make fun of her, now would he? Surely not.

She stood carefully, pushing herself upright with her hand against the sofa. "Very well, sir. Then I'm sure you'll understand why I must get back to Bountiful. The Good Lord didn't fashion ladies to be subjected to such savage creatures."

Mr. Bartlett crossed his arms across his broad chest. "Can't say you have much chance of making it back to Bountiful if you leave now. You got lost in the first place, didn't you?

Would you want to come up against one of those bears or foxes alone out there in the trees? I imagine there's a mountain lion or two about as well. And it's a long, long walk to Bountiful."

Faith felt the blood drain from her face. Her stomach lurched once again, and then sank all the way down to what felt like her toes. The man was right. It didn't matter if he looked a mite like the mountain himself, tall, rugged, strong. His plaid black and white shirt and denim trousers with the knees worn to almost white gave evidence to hard work and the powerful muscles that permitted that hard work. Perhaps not totally dangerous. Just not wholly tame.

His wavy golden-streaked hair did make Faith think of the animals from other lands in the books her mother had read to her when she was still a little girl. A lion came to mind every time she saw the man. And the way he'd handled Theo . . . well, it took someone with little fear and great courage to confront the often angry younger Nolan brother. He had a reputation, gained by his actions and hot-tempered nature.

Clearly Mr. Bartlett had bested Theo.

Oh, how Faith wished she could do the same. She appreciated his effort and would have to find the words to thank him—yet again—for the way he'd intervened on her behalf.

" . . . are you quite all right, ma'am?" he asked, concern drawing lines across his brow. "Can you hear me?"

When she nodded, he went on. "I imagine that bump you took to the head could've done something grave to you. You do need to do like Woody said a bit ago and get yourself some rest. You don't look very well, you know. What I mean is . . ."

The blush and the way he ruffled his hair gave him a youthful look, endearing in an odd way.

"I do understand. I must look a fright by now. Don't worry one bit."

She took a step toward the back door, since a glance in that direction revealed that latch didn't seem to have dropped into place when last it closed. "I appreciate all you've done for me, and your concern for my welfare. But I really must be on my way—"

"And here I thought we'd gone through this and agreed you didn't want to meet bears or foxes today."

She clenched her fists at her side. "Of course, I don't. No sane woman would. But I must get back to civilization, to where there are other women—proper *ladies*—and where I can . . . can . . ."

"Yes, ma'am. From what I can tell, it's time for you to get some sleep." He came to Faith's side and grasped her elbow again. "I'm sleeping in the bunkhouse tonight, and Woody has his own room to the back here, right by the kitchen. You'll use my room. It is quite comfortable, even if I do say so myself, with a wool blanket plus the quilt my mother made years ago. You can rest well and in peace there."

Before she knew it, they stood before the door on the right-hand wall of the large main room. As she'd thought, it led to another room built onto the structure. Mr. Bartlett opened the door, and when she caught a glimpse of the plain but neat appointments inside, she nearly swooned from the longing for rest.

The bed lured her inside.

"Oh, but I'm sure this isn't fair to you," she argued against her own wishes and best interest. What was right was always right. "This is your room. I'm sure I've imposed enough already. I could never presume—"

"Don't you like the room, ma'am?" he asked, that expression of genial humor on his face and in his voice again. "Please answer me that. At no point would I think you've presumed. I did invite you to take my room, after all."

How could she answer the man? She would never—could never—lie again, not now that Roger's demands no longer hung over her head, like an anvil about to fall. "Of course, I like the room. It's lovely, and like you said, has a lovely quilt on the bed"—made of what seemed to be bits and pieces of men's suits—"But—"

"Buts don't come into this, ma'am. I insist. Go ahead. We can talk about anything you want later on, but do yourself some good—and me, too. Woody has taken quite a shine to you, and he won't be happy if I don't take proper care of you. Especially since you're a guest to the camp. Please accept my offer and get some of that sleep you need so much."

Seeing the urgency in his face, Faith realized the search for her had exhausted him, too. He needed sleep, but his manners made it impossible for him not to ensure her comfort while she remained under his care.

She patted the large hand on her arm. "I think I will do as you say, after all. I'm sure you have something more important to do than argue with me."

"Why, yes, ma'am." The eyes sparkled with leashed mischief again. "I do indeed. I have some sleep to get, too."

When she stepped fully into the bedroom, Mr. Bartlett

closed the door behind her. His boots strode across the main section of the cabin, and seconds later, she heard the front door open and close again, the latch clattering into place. Only then did Faith allow herself the luxury of examining her new surroundings.

A simple wood-framed rope bed held a plump mattress, over which Mr. Bartlett had spread the quilt, whose shades of grays, blues, tans, and browns made for an attractive patchwork. The point blanket the logger had mentioned lay folded over the foot of the mattress, and Faith remembered the comfort the one that had covered her on the sofa a short while earlier had offered. She could almost feel the warmth it would give once she curled up under it. Puffy pillows—two of them—sat at the head, their clean, white covers a pleasant contrast to the richer colors of the quilt.

Two large windows, on opposite walls, let in plenty of daylight, but the muslin curtains pulled to a side of each would offer her welcome shade. Faith went straight to them, let loose the cream-colored fabric from its ties, and as they fell into place, soft, soothing shadows dropped across the bed, to the side of the pine dresser and the spindles of the rocking chair in a corner.

Even in the dimmer light, the small table at the side of the chair gleamed with care and a welcome lack of dust. Underfoot, a colorful braided rag rug cushioned her steps.

She struggled with the urgency brought by a pang of something she couldn't quite identify as she admired Mr. Bartlett's bedroom. Although she'd tried to keep the cabin as nice as possible, to her dismay the Nolan brothers hadn't been so inclined. No sooner had she neatened the sleeping loft than Roger would drop something on the floor, sprawl on the smoothed bed, leave dirty bootprints and the dirty boots themselves strewn about, or carry a stack of boxes up from the store for what he called "safekeeping." Theo had done the same downstairs.

She often wondered what on earth could be important enough for Roger to bring to the loft where they slept. Surely it would have been safe enough if he'd left it in its place on a shelf or stacked in a corner of the general store. She'd never understood, because she'd never dared to sneak a furtive peek, and Roger had never said.

At any rate, she'd always known tidiness didn't last long.

In contrast, this room . . . why, it was lovely. In a manly sort of way.

The bed, so neat and fluffy and comfortable-looking, drew her further into the room, right up to its side. She leaned down and untied the laces of her boots. When she'd lined them up in the corner nearest to the bed, she went on to undo her brown flannel skirt, slip out of it, and place it over the arm of the rocking chair. Her muslin blouse followed.

Once she stood in only her chemise, soft cotton petticoat, and black stockings, Faith pulled back the quilt and slipped into the bed. To her amazement and delight, the mattress was a deep, full featherbed. The softness welcomed her as she sank in.

The pillows, also filled with soft feathers, bore a pleasant scent, fresh and slightly piney, outdoorsy. She couldn't help but wonder if it came from some soap or grooming lotion Mr. Bartlett used. It was his bed, after all. She liked it very well.

Feeling safe and cradled, Faith barely managed a "Thank you, Father" before she fell asleep.

"You know I've never been one for wasting precious daylight work hours by sleeping," Nathan muttered to Woody. He'd met up with the older man when he'd gone to check on Theo in the bunkhouse. As the older man went to speak, he held up a hand to stop him. "That's why I'm still awake. I know, I know. I should at least try and get some sleep. The night was a tough one, I'll agree."

One of Woody's bushy gray eyebrows rose. "Seems to me you hardly need a body to have yourself a conversation, seeing as how you think you know what I'm thinking so well." When Nathan sputtered, Woody chuckled. "Had ya going, didn't I? It sure was an irregular night, all right. But was there something else you woulda done?"

The two men stood outside the door to the bunkhouse, the brisk breeze snaking down their coats' necks and up their sleeves. Nathan cast a glance toward the mouth of the trail. "Of course not, but it was draining. And now we're losing a day's work, since I can't push my men to work without sleep. That's how loggers lose limbs. Even their lives."

With a one-sided shrug, Woody leaned against the wall to the left of the door, his posture almost too easy to fool Nathan. Moments later he got around to speaking again.

"Don'tcha find it some interesting how them mules follow her 'round the mountain? Seems they think they're hers. But Theo Nolan, he sees them as his inheritance. Man's gotta wonder what's what."

Back to the subject of their guest. Not surprising. "I suppose if one looks at it from the legal side, then Theo will inherit whatever Roger owned. That means the mules are his, no matter how much they love the Widow Nolan."

Woody's beard jutted out with the stubborn cast of his jaw. "Uh-huh, but can you believe him when he says he wants them animals to keep up with the business? Don't recollect you ever talking about meeting with him or doing any kinda business with him when you went to the general store. It was always Roger or his missus you talked about. He's always been too busy walking in and out of Marshal Blair's jail cells, that one."

It was Nathan's turn to shrug. "Theo's going to have to find a way to earn money. Might as well continue what he and his brother started."

"Hmph! Don't know if that one's ever done an honest day's work in his lazy life. Don't know if he's about to start now, either."

Nathan chose to avoid that kind of speculation. "I have noticed how well the mules respond to Mrs. Nolan." He paused, wondered if he should voice his suspicions. "I've been afraid the brothers have roughed up the animals. What if the reason they like Mrs. Nolan so well is because she's the one who's shown them the only kindness they know?"

"Oh, fer heaven's sake, Nate. Of course, Roger and Theo's been too rough with them. Forget about worrying about them three mules. I was just getting roundabout to it. This has not much to do with them, and you know it. It's that little girl what worries me. Did ya see all that blood dried up on the back of her head? Blond hair don't hide much, you know."

"Yes," he said, in a voice weary and worried. "I saw the blood. You heard her. All I could get from her when we found her was that she'd hurt herself during a disagreement with her husband."

Woody jammed his fists on his hips. "You wanta tell me what kinda disagreement knocks a lady out like she said, and leaves her bleeding on the floor like the deer a body's hunted for the coming winter's eats?"

He winced. "Only a . . . fight of some sort can do that kind of damage."

"And now that there Theo is dead set on seeing her blamed for stealing when she ain't done nothing but suffer and try to do right by a man who's done nothing to earn it."

Nathan nodded. "Seems to me, if a man mistreats his wife, the woman he vowed to cherish and protect, then what's to stop him from dealing out even worse punishment to his pack animals?"

"There's nothing would stop 'im. And that explains why them mules are so fond of Missus Nolan. To say she stole 'em is just plain nonsense."

As serious as the situation was, Nathan couldn't stop a smile. "They sure are fond of her. They even broke out of their pen—twice, more than likely—to be close to her. I can vouch for it. The first time I helped Roger round them up. That male's the most ornery critter I've ever met."

"He's a mule, ain't he?"

He chuckled. "He is, at that. But if Theo was part owner of the store, and the mules are part of the business, it seems he owns them whether they like it or not. The law will take his side."

"You doing like 'im, and calling her a horse thief, now?" The bearded chin jutted out again. "I can see that dirty Theo Nolan doing that, but I'm wanting to think a mite better from you."

It took Nathan a great deal of determination to control the shudder that threatened to shake him. "Be careful using terms like that so easily. I'm not calling her a horse thief. Theo is the one trying to. But if it does come to that, then this ugly mess could turn out uglier still in the end. Around these parts, horse thieves are thought pretty much the lowest of the low. Some think even hanging's too good for them."

"Who you telling, Nate?" Woody shook his head, disgust on his features. "I been out here since pretty near before you were born. I know a man needs his horse to survive out here. A body steals something as big as a feller's horse, why he might as well leave him to die." He ran his fingers through the low ruff of hair on his nearly bald head. "But it'll take a whole lotta talking to prove to me she's stole as much as a pin from them Nolan brothers, never mind three ornery mules."

Mrs. Nolan's fate wore heavy on his mind. "Do you think a woman would be treated as harshly as a man accused of such a crime?"

"I'd like to think folks out here would have themselves a load more sense than to do something so thick-headed. But..." He shook his head. "Sometimes, a body can't find no accounting for some's foolishness."

Chills wracked Nathan. The notion didn't even bear considering; it was too hideous for words. The image of the slender widow burned in his mind again. She'd already borne more than he cared to imagine at the hands of the crude brothers. Would she be forced to face even more? This time, would the last living Nolan brother demand her life in trade for the ownership of three mules?

"Do you think Theo's accusations come from grief?" he asked. "The fellow did lose his brother."

"Dunno. Do ya think that fool man thinks his sister-in-law's responsible for Roger's death?"

"I don't know how anyone could think that, under the circumstances. But regardless what he thinks, it seems he's determined that she pay for his brother's life with hers."

A painfully short time after her eyelids closed, raised male voices not too far away roused Faith from a deep and peaceful sleep. She faced a momentary disorientation, since she didn't recognize her surroundings at first. But only too soon she remembered. As the images sped through her thoughts, she wished she hadn't woken up. Who would want to find herself confronted by the consequences of all that had happened?

At least she didn't have to go out there, where the men were. Certainly, not yet. The latest spurt of belligerent discussion on the opposite side of the door sounded as though it came from Theo Nolan. She had no desire to see him so soon again—if ever. But if she stayed in Mr. Bartlett's bed much longer, anyone could come looking for her. She didn't want that.

As she considered her limited options, the conversation outside became a full-blown argument. She had no idea what the disagreement was about, but it didn't take a particularly clever person to suspect it might have something to do with her and the events at the general store. For the first time in her life Faith chose cowardice over courage and burrowed deeper into the comfort of the bed.

From the relative safety of her warm cocoon, she strained to make out the words. But no matter how hard she tried, she couldn't clearly hear what was being said. Curious, probably too curious for her own good, and frightened about her immediate future, she pushed aside the covers and tiptoed to the door.

By that time, however, the men had lowered their voices, and she still couldn't catch the gist of the conversation, but there did seem to be a new and authoritative voice added to the mix. That could only mean one thing.

Marshal Blair had arrived.

Faith's heart began a steady, increasingly hard pounding in her chest. Her temples started to throb again, and the rhythmic beat quickly rendered her lightheaded. Fear was a dreadful emotion, one that she wanted to eliminate, but she found it impossible to do. Theo had a mean streak as deep and wide as Roger's had been, and he wanted to punish her. She was sure his vindictiveness stemmed from more than the supposed theft of the mules.

Theo blamed her for not saving Roger's life. He wanted someone to blame.

"...I tell ya!" Her brother-in-law's voice was unmistakable. The volume had risen with each word, and she was only too familiar with his ill will. Theo was out for blood.

Her blood.

The time had come to put an end to her distasteful cowardice and confront her accuser. With that fact firm in her mind, Faith dressed, and then laced her boots back up. She stepped up to the washstand to splash cool water on her face. She dried off with the length of towel hanging over the washstand's dowel rod at the right of the basin, undid her braid, and ran her fingers through her hair until she reached the blood-encrusted strands. Distaste made her stomach churn. Determined to get on with things, she dampened the hair until it softened again, and then she used the towel to daub off the mess. Once it felt as though she'd cleaned off the worst of it, she wove her hair into the usual plait. When ready, Faith squared her shoulders. Chin up, she strode to the door, and then on into the midst of the gathered men. Her approach put an immediate end to their discussion.

All eyes focused on her.

Fear again fluttered in her middle, but one more time, she called on the disgust she now felt toward the weakness she'd demonstrated for three years to help her force it aside. "Hello, gentlemen. I'm glad to see all of you gathered in one place. I do believe the time has come to put an end to the foolishness that led to your meeting here today."

"Foolishness!" Theo shoved his chair away from the table. One of the legs caught a rough edge on the puncheon floor, and the chair fell with a clatter.

He ignored it. "You can't tell me it's fine to go killing my brother, and then jist call it silliness. See?" He turned to the sturdy gentleman with keen silver eyes. "I toldja she was evil. She kilt Roger, burnt the store, stole my mules, and now goes and says it's all silliness. She's gotta pay for all she's done. We hang murderers and horse thieves in these here parts. You're always so full of your job, Marshal Blair, so, here. Do it. See to it she hangs for her crimes."

He was accusing her of murder now? Nausea swirled in her throat. Still, Faith couldn't let Theo see any sign of weakness in her. She squared her shoulders. "I can't imagine anyone believes I harmed my husband, much less that I'd try and steal the mules."

Theo stood and approached her. "Is Roger dead?"

What was he up to now? "Yes."

"And you was in the cabin, right?"

Again, she answered. "Yes."

"Really, now," Mr. Bartlett said, "is this—"

Theo glared the logger silent as he took another step toward Faith. "Was anyone else in the cabin with you and Roger?"

She'd reached the end of her patience. "This is silly. You know I was the only person with Roger after you left the cabin."

He spun, faced the other men, arms opened wide. "See? She done said it herself. If Roger died, it's on account of her. He didn't do himself in, and no one else was there what coulda done it. Arrest her, Marshal Blair!"

Faith gasped.

Woody clomped to her side.

Mr. Bartlett crossed his arms and squared his jaw to rock-like firmness as he watched Theo.

The marshal, a man who all in Bountiful considered wise and willing to suffer no fools, narrowed his eyes. "I'll admit it's a strange situation here, but I don't know that I have enough details to do such a thing. What exactly did happen, Mrs. Nolan?"

In the calmest voice she could muster, Faith went over

everything she could remember about the day before. She told about her trip up to the logging camp with the supplies, she told of her return, she mentioned Theo's presence, and she told of the time she spent out in the barn with the mules.

She even mentioned her argument with Roger.

That caught the lawman's attention. "What were you quarreling about, ma'am? It's important."

Her cheeks heated, and she daren't look at Woody or Mr. Bartlett or the red-haired logger she'd heard called Matt. "Well, sir, it's not quite so simple. You see, Mr. Nolan—my husband, *late* husband—ran the general store. And...well, I'd made a decision to do something that affected the store and he didn't approve."

"Did you know he wouldn't approve when you decided to do that...thing?"

Faith's cheeks felt on fire. "Yes, sir."

"See?" Theo said again. "She was up to no good all along."

Her brother-in-law's comment irked her mightily. "If anyone was up to no good, why, it was Roger. And maybe you, as well."

A gasp.

A sputter.

Feet shifted.

A chair creaked.

But no one spoke.

She went on. "Roger had done some things *I* couldn't approve. Things that were wrong, that went against all that is good and honest and righteous. I couldn't go along with him and still face myself, much less God, every morning. I had to right his latest wrong. My husband didn't much like that."

Mr. Bartlett made an odd sound deep in his throat. "Did he . . . did Roger strike you?"

Shame made her shrink in place. How could she tell a man so confident, so strong, that she'd been too weak to stand up to Roger? How could she face him, knowing she'd stayed with a brute because she'd had nowhere else to go? How could she tell him she and Roger had argued over the supplies he himself had ordered and paid for?

How could she tell anyone how cruelly Roger had dealt with her, how his hand had connected more often than not?

She couldn't.

"No, sir. Roger didn't strike me." *Not that last time.* "I was near the hearth, and had the fireplace poker in my hand. He reached for it, and—ah . . . well, I stumbled and fell. I don't know what happened after that, seeing as I lost consciousness after I struck my head. By the time I came to, Roger was on the floor, and a whole lot of blood had pooled all around him. I have no idea how that happened. I was unconscious."

"Now, ain't that convenient?" Theo said, his sarcasm jabbing at Faith.

"No," she countered, her gaze firmly on the marshal, "it's truly most inconvenient. I can't give an accounting of those minutes, more than likely close to a half hour, where somehow Roger died."

"Yes, ma'am," Marshal Blair said. "You're right about that. It would indeed be most helpful if you could tell us what happened. Are you sure you didn't strike your husband with the poker?"

"Not while I was conscious, I didn't. But since I was out for a bit, I can't say exactly what I did. Still and all, I don't think it's likely I got up, took the poker from him and cracked his head with it, then went back and lay down where I fell against the hearth. All with no recollection—"

"Aha!" Theo exclaimed. "She jist said she don't know what she did. Can't have it both ways, Faith. You hafta know you didn't kill Roger or you can't know you *dinnent* kill him."

"Well, there goes the farm," Woody added, not quite helpfully.

The marshal looked around the room, clearly taking note of the various responses. Then he turned back to Faith. "What's this about stolen horses?"

She took a deep breath, shook her head. "There are no horses involved, sir. And there is no theft involved, either."

"Sure is, Marshal Blair." Theo's smarmy grin vanished right off his face. "There's the thievery of val-u-ble livestock taken place here."

The marshal's gaze never left her face. "In your own words, if you please, ma'am. Tell me what all this is about stolen horses—or livestock, whichever it rightly might could be."

She quickly told the lawman about the mules, the broken fencing, and how dear they were to her. She also told him how they'd tracked her down during her escape from the burning building.

She noticed how his luxurious mustache twitched when she named the mules, evidently stifling a chuckle. Purcell, Mr. Bartlett's newest lumberjack, didn't fare as well. He barked out a laugh. His employer's swift glare made him throttle any further outbreak of humor.

But when she described Lazy's antics in detail, especially his tendency toward dawdling, and how he'd lagged behind Maisie and Daisy in the woods, Marshal Blair let out a laugh. Even Mr. Bartlett and Woody joined in.

She smiled. "They're quite clever at times. One has to spend time with them and give them a chance. They're lovely companions."

"I must say," the marshal said when he'd stopped laughing. "It does look as though you've bested the Brothers Grimm. They had the Pied Piper of Hamelin, and we have us the Pied Piper of mules."

"Huh?" Theo said. "Ain't seen her with no pies for them mules, even if she does bake a nice pie every oncet in a long while of Sunday suppers. Her apple pies're right good." He narrowed his eyes. "I just know I seen her stealing the— er . . . *my* mules in the woods. See, I owned half of all's what is Nolan property. That means them mules is mine, all mine, seeing as how Roger's dead now. She was stealing them, and I want her arrested."

Again, Marshal Blair tried to keep from laughing but failed. "What makes you say Mrs. Nolan was stealing the animals? I only heard about runaway mules."

"Why, she was hiding 'em, I tell you. I found her chasin' 'em off when we was about to see 'em. I reckon she was going to wait with the mules in them woods there until light, thinking no one would find them, woods being so thick and dark. Then she'd run off and I'd never see none of them ever again."

How could any reasonable soul take his accusations seriously?

The marshal ran a hand over his full mustache, then crossed his arms. "See here, now, Theo. I don't know how I can do something like arrest a lady, you know. It's right irregular. Especially since I don't see where she stole anything—"

"You telling me," Theo said, his voice menacing, his face contorted with ugly rage, his steps deliberate and threatening as he approached the lawman, "that you're gonna listen to her? She's no better'n the girls at that fancy Lillybelle's Palace down to Pendleton. She done wed Roger for all he had, and she's now taking off with the most val-u-ble things he has left, now he's dead and burnt."

"Now, Theo—"

"Don't you go now-Theoin' me," he cut in. "Tell me now, Mister Marshal Blair. You gonna take my word on her crimes, or are you gonna take the word of nothing more'n a preacher-cleaned-a-wedding floozy? You gonna take the word of nothing more'n a—er, a . . . *woman* on this here matter of my brother's death?"

# Chapter 8

How anyone could come to the conclusion that Faith Nolan had stolen anything simply because she and the mules had run from a raging blaze, Nathan didn't know. He did know, however, that she didn't belong in Bountiful's small jail. Faith was too delicate, too lovely for such rough quarters. He glanced over to where she now sat on the sofa. They'd been arguing over the matter for hours and she looked pale and should be resting, but he didn't know how she could under the circumstances.

"Is your mind made up?" he asked Marshal Blair. He couldn't take one more round with the stubborn Theo either. "You're going to listen to him and arrest Faith—er...Mrs. Nolan?"

The lawman raised his hands up near his face in a gesture of frustrated surrender. "Do you hear the"—he cleared his throat loudly—"injured party backing away from any of his claims?"

Nathan pinned Theo in place with a pointed stare. "I'm afraid he refuses to see reason."

"Ain't so," Theo objected, aggrieved. "I see every single

last reason why the marshal here has to take her in and lock her up. My brother's dead, ain't he? And she said herself there weren't no one but her there and she don't know that she didn't kill him. That makes her guilty, don't it?"

Nathan turned back to the marshal. "If you do feel the need to take her back to Bountiful while you sort this out, I must insist on at least some allowances, seeing as Faith—er...Mrs. Nolan is...well, a lady, and not some common criminal."

"She *is* a crook, all right," Theo muttered. "Common or uncommon don't make no difference to me."

Nathan clenched his fists, but didn't let himself be drawn in another time. "Don't you agree?" he asked Marshal Blair as if Theo hadn't spoken.

Wariness narrowed the marshal's eyes and furrowed his brow. "What kind of allowances were you thinking, there?"

"You can't seriously consider taking a lady like her to the jail. It's no place for her, no offense meant to you and your deputy."

"Right, right. I agree," the marshal said. "What do you suggest?"

"That you find someone who'll take her in, perhaps a family to help her at this time."

Blair rubbed his chin. "Know anyone who'd take kindly to housing an accused killer?"

Nathan sucked in air. "I'd have to think on that a bit."

"You see my problem, then."

"I never said it would be easy." He shook his head, a wry smile on his lips. "I don't suppose anyone ever told you your job would be, either."

"You're right there, too. No one did. But it doesn't solve our problem, now, does it?"

Nathan thought over the residents of the small but growing town of Bountiful. He didn't imagine Faith had remained especially close to anyone in town after her marriage. She'd once mentioned she rarely made it even to Sunday services. It would seem Roger had kept his wife practically a prisoner in that cabin.

"We all know that Reverend Alton's a decent man, right?" he said at last.

Murmured "Sures" and "Yeses" flew around the room.

"We can also say no one doubts he's an honest, upright man of God, right?"

"'Course he is, Nate," Woody blurted out. "What are you saying? Are you wanting to ask the preacher-man to turn himself into the lady's jailer or some such nonsense?"

"Not exactly, but he and his wife might take in Mrs. Nolan, if only for a spell while this all gets sorted out. Surely Mrs. Alton could use the help, especially with winter setting in." Everyone knew Mrs. Alton was afflicted with a bad case of rheumatism.

"Hey!" Theo yelled. "Visiting the preacher ain't no punishment—"

"Well, now," Marshal Blair drawled, a slight smile tipping up the ends of his mustache. "Don't rightly know if we should be thinking along the lines of any kind of punishment yet. Nothing's been proven against the lady. She deserves to have herself a jury decide the matter, as the law of the land requires."

Theo frowned. "What land you talking about, Marshal?"

"This great land of ours, Theo. The United States of America."

Nathan's shoulders eased a fraction. He allowed himself a glance at the newly minted widow, and saw an echo of his own relief bloom across her pretty features. The pinched look she'd been wearing for long hours now smoothed into the more familiar beauty of her calm, even features, her forest-green eyes, and her lovely, gentle smile.

"Well, then," he said. "Seeing as we're all agreed, now"—he turned toward the massive cook-stove, where Woody had been stirring something that smelled good and savory—"why don't you dish up some of what you've been making there, Woody? I'm sure everyone's tired after all the excitement, and at least for myself, I wouldn't mind an early bedtime."

"Meaning we should head out for Bountiful early, as well," the marshal said.

"Well, good mornin', Martha!" Woody muttered. "It's about time someone showed some sense hereabouts." He clomped to a cabinet next to the iron stove, shaking his shaggy head. "Seems like all of them's gone pure mad, Lord. Whoever's heard of jailing a lady?"

Theo pulled out a chair and sat for the first time in a long while. "He don't know what he's saying. If she didn't kill my brother, who did? She done kilt him, set the house alight to hide what she done, and then tried to steal my mules on top."

His words gave Nathan pause. Even though he was certain Faith had no more killed Roger Nolan than she'd tried to steal the three mules, Theo's certainty sent a pang of unease straight to his gut. What if—

But, no. He couldn't be such a fool as to let a well-known drunk's disgraceful claims muddy his mind. He cast a glance at Faith, noted the direct way she met his gaze. She didn't strike him as a person intent on hiding some dreadful truth.

No, he couldn't stomach even the suggestion that Faith might have had a hand in her husband's death.

All through that night, images of Roger's lifeless body and of the raging fire showed her no mercy at all. They returned to haunt her time and time again, no matter how hard she'd tried to banish them, how hard she'd prayed for the Father's peace to fill the remaining hours of her night. She heard the crackle of the flames, smelled the stench of burning wood, felt the intensifying heat.

Would she suffer from these visions the rest of her life? However long that might prove to be?

True, she hadn't loved Roger, but she'd never wanted to see him harmed, and the sight of his dead body had hit her hard. Horror and grief and sadness filled her once again, tears burned her eyes. The loss of what might have been ached in her heart, and the tears fell.

Roger *was* dead. What a lost life he'd led.

If she, who had been hurt so badly by her husband, had never wanted him dead, then who could have done such a hideous thing? The Army men had left; she'd heard them herself. And Roger hadn't begun the argument until he was certain Theo had made it a fair bit down the trail to town. Roger always made sure no one, not even his brother, was near enough to witness their confrontations.

At no point could she have done something so vicious as

to strike Roger's head with an iron poker. The notion purely turned her stomach. To hurt someone...to end a life...

How could Theo think that kind of evil lay in her heart? He'd only ever taken notice of her when he'd wanted food or more coffee, so why had he become so dogged about her supposed guilt? If nothing else, he did know she had never done him or Roger any harm, and goodness, she'd had ample opportunities. She could have poisoned them any number of times, if that had been her intent. Could grief at the loss of his brother blind him to such a degree? Faith didn't think she'd acted that foolishly when Mama and Papa died.

As the light before dawn woke her, she shook off her grief and melancholy with strong determination. She washed with the water, soap, and a piece of toweling provided on the washstand, then dressed. Now that she was ready for the day, she couldn't wait to start down the mountain and then over the road to Bountiful. Anything was better than being the only woman in the camp's world of men.

Well, to be fair, neither Woody nor Mr. Bartlett seemed too quick to condemn her. And the marshal struck her as trying to keep a level head in the midst of the situation. Still and all, a lone woman in a crowd of men always stuck out. And Faith didn't much care for the way that kind of visibility made her feel.

More than one of Mr. Bartlett's loggers looked at her in ways that made her uneasy. She'd been unable to escape that kind of scrutiny when Woody had served the evening meal the night before. The men had inspired the wildest urge in her to run. After all, she no longer benefited from the protection her married state had provided.

After she wove her hair into two skeins and coiled them into a coronet at the top of her head, she slipped out of Mr. Bartlett's room. A few feet away, Woody stood before the stove, a large wooden spoon in one hand and a folded red-and-white towel in the other. A wave of heat and delightful aromas swelled toward her from the hot stove.

"Good morning," she said.

"'Morning, ma'am. Did you get yourself some rest last night or were you too worked up to do more than wrassle your covers?"

She gave him a small smile. "Sleep didn't come until late and not too easy."

"Are ya ready to face the folks out to Bountiful?"

"You don't think they're likely to listen to Theo, do you?"

The old logger gave the fragrant contents of the large skillet another stir with his spoon before he turned to face her. "Wish I could tell you what you want to hear, Missus Nolan—"

"Please." She held up a hand, stopping him. "Now that Roger's gone, please don't call me that. I'd be honored if you'd call me Faith."

His wiry gray mustache gave a wiggle, and she thought it signified a smile. "I can sure do that, ma'am—er...Miss Faith. I do understand. I most certainly can. Do that, I mean. For you."

It hadn't been a smile, not when his words had come out in such a tight, choppy way. It seemed he'd been trying to restrain his anger, anger perhaps toward Roger for what he had done to her.

He knew.

It appeared Woody knew how badly Roger had hurt her.

Shame sent fingers of heat into Faith's cheeks. She didn't think she could bear the pity.

"I would like to go see the mules." She turned, then stopped partway to the door, but didn't face him. "I wouldn't want to head out and have Theo think again I was trying to make off with them. I don't see anyone else up yet who could vouch for me."

"Oh, fer goodness' sake!" He shook his head. "Some fools are so blind they can't see the tips of their toes but for their noses. You go right on ahead, Miss Faith. I know you won't be running nowhere. Not if you never did run from Nolan hisself during all them years. You are the sort who do what you say you will, aren't you? Even when it ain't so easy a thing to do."

She turned and drew a trembling breath. "Mama and Papa put a lot of stock in saying what you meant, and then expected you to follow through with the word you'd given. This moment...well, I can't think of a single reason why I'd want to put myself into a worse position than the one I find myself in. A fugitive straight off is guilty of a crime. My only crime is that I married Roger Nolan."

"Amen to that, ma'am."

His enthusiasm made her smile ruefully. "I won't be long."

"I'll be waking up the men in...oh, how 'bout half an hour or so? They'll be hungry, so I figger I better be dishing right up oncet I do. I'm not seeing my way clear to you leaving us without a meal in yer belly, either, so don't go telling me none of that 'I'm not hungry' nonsense."

Faith laughed outright then. "How can you know me so well? We only met yesterday."

"When a body's knocked around God's Earth long's I have, something's gotta have rubbed off on him along the way. You get to learn to read folks real good when you have to count on 'em. If you can't know who's right and who's wrong, why, then you sure ain't gonna be living long, are you? Not out here on this land, you're not."

She started walking toward the cabin door again. "And you think you know which I am—the right or wrong kind?"

"It ain't nothing like me thinking I know what you're like, Miss Faith. I *know* you're the right kind. You didn't hurt that Roger Nolan any more'n I did."

At the door, she turned a bit, arched a brow. "And what about the mules?"

He stared for a second...two. "That there's a mite harder to read, ain't it? But if I was the betting sort of fella—and I'll have you know that I'm not, never have been, neither—I'd have to say you haven't taken half of what the Nolans owe you for all the grief they've piled on ya these long years. *Hmph!* Even three mules don't add up near to that. 'Sides, them mules love you just as much as you fancy them. And you didn't take them nowhere, did you, now? I figger Nathan had it right. I recollect the day he came home so late at night saying he spent all that time helping Roger round 'em up. Did Roger ever fix that fence what Nathan said was broke?"

She shook her head.

"There you have it then, Miss Faith. They ran away, sure as sure is."

Tears welled in her eyes. "Thank you, Woody. I appreciate your trust. I know how dear trust can be, and how hard it is to come by. I won't betray it."

"I know you won't." His voice quivered with emotion, but as fast as she took notice of it, he cleared his throat. "Now go on out there to your critters. I was them, I'd sure be missing you right about now."

The strangest urge to hurry over and hug the crusty gentleman filled her, but she knew she'd embarrass him if she did any such emotional thing. Instead, she hurried out the door and across the clearing. The rosy tones of dawn and the crisp, evergreen-scented breeze made the day feel fresh and new and full of promise.

She hoped it didn't bring her any more trouble. After all, how much could a body bear before she broke under the weight of it all?

*The Good Lord only gives you as much as He's sure to help you to bear*, Mama used to say. Some days it proved mighty hard to believe.

As she let herself inside the lean-to shed at the back of the largest building in the camp clearing, a trio of greetings rang out. The mules' welcome warmed her heart. Faith practically ran to Maisie, threw her arms around the sweet girl's neck, and finally let the floodwaters fall.

She wept in huge, harsh sobs. She cried for her situation, for the nightmare her marriage had been, for the loss of loving parents who'd wanted nothing but the best in life for their only daughter, and died working to give it to her. She wept for her lost illusions, for her dreams of a loving husband and dear little ones at her knee, for her uncertain future, for all those times when Roger had hurt her but she hadn't let herself cry.

Maisie's bristly coat absorbed the moisture, leaving no

trace behind. When her misery was spent, she went to the other two, and spent a moment with each. She wondered if they were the reason she hadn't curled up into a lump of hurt months and months ago, and... well, she didn't know what followed that notion, what she would have done. She merely knew the three sweet animals had saved her from madness.

"Leaving you at the mercy of the likes of Theo turns my gut into knots," she whispered as Lazy nuzzled her cheek. "But right this minute, I don't even know how I'm going to get past this madness of his, much less protect you three. When things are sorted out again, I'll find a way to get you back. I can work, and I will buy you three from Theo. I won't stop until you're all mine again."

As long as her brother-in-law didn't destroy them—and her—before then.


Shortly after breakfast, they set out on the trail. Mr. Bartlett and Woody insisted Faith needed a mount or a buggy, pointing out she couldn't very well walk all the way to Bountiful. Since no one had a buggy, they walked down to the place that had once been her home, where the general store's serviceable wagon would have to do the job. She could have ridden one of the horses, but Mr. Bartlett had insisted the lead mule was the right one for Faith to use. She'd been relieved, since Maisie was such a bright, gentle creature, and her companionship gave her comfort.

The two loggers had also insisted the other two mules should stay at the camp with Woody and Matt in charge of their care.

"That's purely foolish," Theo argued. "It don't take two

men to watch two mules. I tell you, we need to take 'em with us. I'm gonna be needing them soon enough."

"Then you can come fetch them soon enough, cain't you?" Woody had argued, his voice a low growl. "See to setting Mrs. Nolan up in a proper home in town first off, and then you can come back to the mules. I'll take good care of them for her, seeing as how she loves them so much and they love her right back."

Theo's jaw jutted out. "Won't matter how much she loves them mules after she's in jail, will it?"

"Trial first," Woody countered, eyes narrowed. "Right and proper, and with a judge and a jury and all, you hear? Once *they* declare she's the one what killed your brother and started up that fire, if they're all struck stupid and mad and can't see what's in front of their own eyes, then you can go ahead and jaw all you want about jail."

Once they'd reached the general store and hitched Maisie to the wagon, Faith fell back to let Maisie set her own slower pace. The whole length of the trip, Faith dreaded their arrival in Bountiful, and she prayed silently for the Father to go before her, to prepare the hearts of the reverend and his wife, and those of the rest of the good folks in the town. She accepted the truth. She needed a place to go, now even more than she had three years ago. She'd been offered a number of different options, but pride and stubbornness had led her to refuse them all in favor of marriage to Roger.

Now, the thought of winding up in the jail if the Altons refused, surrounded by brawlers, drunkards, bank robbers, or worse—true killers—chilled her. She shuddered every time she thought of the iron bars over the windows of the small, squat building at the far eastern end of Bountiful's Main Street.

"Don't fret," Mr. Bartlett said in a soft voice.

Faith swiveled her head. She hadn't noticed him drop back to her side. Maisie continued her easy, rolling pace.

"This has all been so odd—oh, no. No, no. Odd is such a poor word, but I'm afraid I don't know a better one—strange, maybe, or perhaps peculiar would do better. You must believe me, though. I've never hurt another soul. I could never do such a dreadful, sinful thing as...as..." She couldn't even say it. "You should have seen Roger on the floor, blood all around him..."

"Hush. Don't think about that now. Let's pray the Altons are willing to take you in. I could almost assure you, even without talking to them, that'll be the case. I've never known anyone kinder."

Faith glanced sideways, met the logger's gaze in the faint light of dusk. "I wish I could believe that as easily as you. I—they offered to take me in back when my parents were killed, but I said no. I didn't want to impose. Then Roger offered marriage, and I accepted *his* proposal. I'm afraid they might feel slighted or worse, offended."

"Doubt it. Besides, that's all in the past now. Look to the future. You need to put all this Nolan nonsense where it belongs, in your past."

She gave a humorless chuckle. "Wish it were nothing more than nonsense. But I'm the one who married Roger, who fed both of the brothers, who worked day after day in the general store and the cabin and...and...well, everything. None of that was nonsense, Mr. Bartlett."

"Please, ma'am. Call me Nathan. I'm not used to being called by my last name."

"Then you must call me Faith." She sighed. "I would like to never be called Mrs. Nolan again, but I suppose that's not possible."

"That will change once you marry again."

"Never!" She grimaced. "I'll never do that to myself again."

"I'm so sorry. But, Faith, you're a young and love—er...well, yes. You're a young woman still. I'm sure you want a family of your own?"

Tears stung her eyes, and a pang struck her deep in her heart. "It was my fondest wish, once. I'm afraid after these years of marriage, I'm not sure children are worth all the rest that comes with it."

"The Good Book says children are a gift from God. He's a good, merciful Father, you know. I doubt He ever left you alone all that time, nor will He fail you again."

It took a great deal of effort to get a breath down past the lump in her throat. "For a while after Roger and I married, I was furious at God. I couldn't understand how He could have let that happen to me." She met Nathan's gaze full on. "My parents had been murdered. Savages had taken their lives. How could God leave me at the mercy of another sav—"

Oh, dear. Had she really said that? She'd never told anyone, not outright. Would he be as disgusted by her weakness as she was? Would he back off and take his support away?

She didn't know if she could bear that. As alone as she'd

always felt, his acts of kindness over the past few days had become shining treasures to her. A sideways glance revealed no disgust on his face.

As long as she'd gone this far . . .

She squared her shoulders. "I did ask God how He could have left me at the mercy of Roger. But I never got a full answer, and with time my anger burned out. After a while, I remembered Jesus' words to His disciples. He said He wouldn't leave them alone, that He would send a Comforter to them. I came to know that Comforter mighty well. He was always there, giving me the strength to go on."

A tear rolled out of each eye. She didn't bother to wipe them away. She had no idea how she could talk so freely to this man, practically a stranger, but she felt his genuine interest in a lonely spot in her heart. As hard as it had become for her to trust, something told her she could trust him with these sad things, with her life.

She prayed the Lord wouldn't let it come to that.

After a brief spell of quiet, while behind them the red sun continued to creep closer to the darkening, purple horizon, Nathan spoke again. "We're almost there. I suppose you're afraid, and it's struck me I never even considered your feelings or opinion when I insisted on this solution."

"What other choice did I have?" Faith shifted in her seat. Her body ached with the unaccustomed effort of driving the general store's wagon for such a long time.

He shook his head, then shrugged. "I don't know. Theo is one stubborn—"

"Mule." She smiled. "That is one trait the brothers share with the animals. It's endearing in the real mules, but it became most infuriating in those two, almost as soon as I moved into the cabin."

The logger laughed.

Faith felt surrounded by the goodwill and understanding in that spurt of good humor. She stole a glance at Mr. Bartlett and noticed again, in a different way, a more *real* way, what a truly fine-looking man he was. She'd always been aware of his great height. She'd always been tall herself, which had always set her apart from other girls as far back as when she'd been in school, and even from the ladies the few times she'd gone to church since she'd married. Now, though, she noticed the line of his jaw, the angle of his cheekbone, the arch of his brow line. When he turned to face her, she blinked.

Goodness! Those features melded together to form a most attractive face. And his smile warmed a spot in her heart that had grown icy-cold since the day she wed Roger Nolan. Since the night he first brutalized her.

When she realized she'd been staring, a rapid rush of heat filled her cheeks. She turned to face east and gulped in a sharp breath. The first buildings of the town were now close. She would soon face the folks who'd pitied her once before. That possibility—probability, perhaps—didn't sit well with her. Would they condemn her now? Would they believe Theo over her?

What about the Altons? Would they take her in?

Would they take pity on her again?

# Chapter 9

As the sky turned a deep, deep navy blue on its way to a nighttime black, their small group rode right up to the church. The modest but adequate parsonage sat beside it, a bit farther back from the road than the white, steeple-topped building with lights burning bright in the windows. As they approached the hitching rail on the western side of the church, the front door opened and two women stepped out onto the stoop, clearly limned against the lamplight within. Their animated chatter rang out over the otherwise vacant street.

Faith's stomach clenched.

*Please, Lord.*

She slipped out of the wagon, aided by Nathan's hand at her elbow. Although he let her go as soon as her feet touched the ground, he stayed by her side when she paused to pat Maisie's warm, exertion-dampened neck. When she couldn't reasonably postpone the inevitable any further, he walked with her to the front of the pastor's house. They joined the marshal and, of course, Theo, who'd turned the corner of the building moments before she and Nathan did.

Some small, hidden part of her had conjured up the pleasant fantasy that her brother-in-law might somehow have changed his mind during the ride to town. But, no. He hadn't.

"Still cain't see why you hafta put her up in some swanky house," he groused. "There's a perfectly good jail here in Bountiful."

"You would know, wouldn't you?" Nathan asked.

Faith gaped. She couldn't believe he'd actually said that. She wished she had that kind of courage, that daring. She couldn't see herself ever saying something like that. Even though it was true. Many times Theo had failed to come home for the weekend, as he was expected. When he did show up, he would complain about the time he'd spent in one of Marshal Blair's cells.

Her admiration for the lumberman grew even more.

A few steps away from the front stoop, Faith recognized the lady in the dark green wool cape with the pastor's wife. It was Olivia Moore—well, Whitman, now. She'd married the owner of the Bank of Bountiful a number of months ago. Faith had always liked Olivia, not that she'd known her well. Their two families had lived outside of town on their farms, and aside from meeting first at school, and then occasionally at church over the years, their paths rarely had crossed.

"My goodness!" Mrs. Alton cried. "What do we have here? Jeremiah! Please come to the door. There's a passel of folks come by right this minute, just as dear Olivia was on her way out."

The plump lady bustled down the front steps, while Olivia stayed at the top of the stoop. "Mrs. Nolan?" the pastor's wife continued. "You're part of this peculiar party, too? Oh, dear, dear me. What's happened? Are you unwell?"

Faith met Mrs. Alton's gaze. "I'm as well as can be expected, under the circumstances."

"Under the circumstances?" Reverend Alton said in his resonant voice, as he came from the depths of the house. "What is going on, gentlemen? And you, too, Mrs. Nolan. Is there a problem—"

Theo snorted. "She done kilt—"

"Well, Reverend," the marshal said in a voice that drowned out Theo's. "There's been a fire up to the Nolan Brothers' General store. 'Fraid the place is gone, and somehow Roger's wound up dead. Couldn't get a good sense as to how he'd met his Maker, seeing as how everything was more ashes and embers than much else."

"Oh, heavens!" Mrs. Alton wrung her hands as she hurried to Faith's side. "What's wrong with me? Please, please do come in." She slipped a comforting arm around Faith's waist, and *tsk-tsked* as she helped her up the front steps and inside. "Here I am, babbling away like some spring-fed brook after a May shower, while you stand out here in this cold. Are you warm enough? Can I get you a cup of coffee? Or perhaps tea?"

Faith couldn't eke out a response. She stood frozen in place, and not because of the weather outside. All she could take in was the impression of a lovely room with green curtains, a number of polished tables beside various upholstered pieces, bright kerosene lamps, a soft rug underfoot, and a crackling fire in the hearth. Bric-a-brac had been sprinkled over every flat surface, and a couple of books lay on a side table, an open leather-covered Bible on top.

This reminded her of what she'd dreamed of someday having. Instead, she'd wound up in Roger's rough cabin, where only the most functional items found a home.

"Here." Mrs. Alton indicated the tan velvet wing chair next to the fireplace. "This armchair is the nicest, plumpest one we have here in the parsonage, and it's in the warmest spot, too. Please, sit, dear child. Let me fetch you that cup of something. Will you have coffee or tea?"

Arms crossed, the reverend watched his wife, a tender smile on his face. Once she'd sputtered silent, he stepped toward the lawman. "How can I help you, Marshal? Do you want to arrange for Roger's burial? Will there be a service? How many days ago did it happen?"

Faith dropped into the chair, dizzy, queasy, her knees as firm as calf's-foot jelly.

"Coffee or tea?" the reverend's wife asked again.

"Coffee," Faith answered in a shaky voice. A tremor shook her. "P—please."

As Mrs. Alton hurried toward the parlor door, Faith felt a soft hand on her arm. "I'm so, so sorry," Olivia Whitman said. "I can't imagine what you're feeling, but you have my sympathy. Is there anything my husband or I can do to help?"

The unexpected kindness brought tears to Faith's eyes once again. "I can't think of a single thing."

"If you do, please don't hesitate to ask. I'll be praying for you."

Faith nodded. "Thank you. I appreciate your offer more than you can know."

"...then it's settled," Nathan said, relief evident in his

voice. "Thank you, Reverend. Your help in this matter is a godsend."

At Faith's side, Olivia turned to look at the logger. "Hello, Nate. I hadn't noticed you."

The tall lumberman smiled. "You're doing something far more important than greeting me. Besides, you and Eli see me often enough these days. I have yet to turn down an invitation to the Whitman dining table since the two of you wed."

Faith glanced at the banker's wife to see her cheeks tint a pretty rose shade. "I'll tell Cooky you said that. She's begun to enjoy her work more since she's heard nice things from the children. Besides, she has a soft spot for you."

Now Nathan was the one who blushed. "I wouldn't know." He ran a hand through his golden-streaked brown hair, while with the other he tapped his hat against his thigh. "How are the children?"

Olivia's face came alive when she smiled. "As challenging as ever. Well, perhaps not so much now as when they were running wild. But they do keep me busy all day."

Mrs. Alton returned with a steaming cup in her hand. "All they needed was a loving mama, and you're that plus plenty more, my dear." She placed the coffee on the table to Faith's right. "Drink up, Faith. You look near to frozen, and half scared to bits. There's nothing to frighten you here, where I'm going to insist you stay, now that you don't have a home. I have a perfectly good, empty bedroom upstairs. No need at all for you to fret about where you'll go. I'd be right pleased for you to stay with us as long as you want."

The offer left her nearly breathless. Mrs. Alton was echoing what she'd heard Nathan agree to with the reverend. But the lady hadn't been in the room to overhear any of what she knew he must have told her husband. She'd offered Faith a room without a qualm.

Faith didn't think it fair to keep her hostess in the dark. "I must tell you why we're here before I accept. It's only right for you to know everything."

"Everything, dear? What do you mean?"

Faith glanced at Nathan, who smiled and nodded encouragement. "We don't know quite how Roger died. We...he and I, that is, were having a disagreement, and I fell."

Mrs. Alton gasped. "Are you hurt?"

"Not really." She went on to describe the events that had led to their arrival at the parsonage.

A time or two, Olivia gasped and Mrs. Alton wiped away a tear.

To Faith's amazement, after she'd told them about Theo's insistence on having her charged with the fire and Roger's death, even after she said she'd likely be tried, neither woman looked disgusted. If anything, they'd come closer to her, and now stood tall as a pair of pillars at either side of her chair.

"Now that you know all the details, you don't have to let me stay. I know it's quite an imposition under the circumstances. I can go with the marshal."

At Faith's left, Olivia dropped down to her knees, her cloak pooling on the gold, cream, and black rug underfoot. "Tell me one thing, and not because I need to know, but because you need to say it. Did you do it? Did you harm your husband? Did you set the general store on fire?"

"Of course not." Faith glanced at Theo, who began to

stammer. "At least, not that I know. As I said, I fell and lost consciousness. I can't be sure what happened during that time. I can assure you, though, that Roger was alive and well when I fell, and the general store as fine as always. There was no fire."

"Well, my dear girl," Mrs. Alton said. "That's all I need to know. It's perfectly clear that anything at all could have happened. Your husband could have gone into the store side of the building, knocked over a lamp, tried to carry you out, and fallen himself. Only the dear Lord knows, and I'm not Him." She turned to the cluster of men. "There's nothing decent or proper about a woman in a jail. Go on—all of you. This child needs to be in bed. I suppose you can sort out all the details among yourselves in the morning, if indeed you must. Go. *Go!* And good night."

A smile curved Faith's lips. The tension in her body began to melt away. She hoped to someday become a woman with the self-assurance Mrs. Alton displayed. She showed no uncertainty when chasing a passel of men out of her house, and they left, on her word alone.

The reverend, if the indulgent smile on his face was anything to go by, had no objection to her directness.

Olivia turned to Faith. "I see Mrs. Alton is taking charge of the situation, and that means you're in excellent hands. I must return home now, since I'm certain my dear husband will be ready for me to take over our children's nighttime routine." A faint line appeared on her brow. "If it won't be a bother to you, I'd love to stop by and visit with you tomorrow morning, after I walk my youngsters to school."

"Bother?" She shook her head. "Not at all. A visit will

likely be a good distraction. I don't care to think over and over again about..."

"I can understand." Olivia reached for Faith's hand and gave it a little squeeze. "But please don't forget that God has a way of working things out. Even the most unlikely, dreadful things are as nothing for Him. Just don't give up hope."

Faith found it impossible to respond, so she nodded and blinked away the tears that threatened.

Moments later, the front door closed behind Olivia and the men, including Nathan Bartlett, who had insisted on seeing Olivia home. It turned out that Mr. Whitman and Nathan were partners in the bank, and friends, as well. Just as he'd shown Faith a great deal of kindness and compassion, he offered his friend's wife his protection as she returned home in the dark. Her respect for him grew.

Theo, on the other hand, lobbed a final glare at Faith as the marshal walked him out.

"Well, then," Mrs. Alton said when silence reigned in the parlor. "I roasted up a nice leg of mutton on Sunday. Could I offer you a plate? Perhaps a sandwich?"

Faith shook her head. "I don't think I'd be able to eat."

Mrs. Alton *tsk-tsked*. "It must have been dreadful to hear Theo Nolan, of all people, say such horrid things about you. Especially since they're none of them true."

"But you don't know they aren't."

"Pshaw!" The reverend's wife gave a carefree wave. "I'm sure something happened, but I doubt you had anything to do with it. Not if you didn't do anything to those two brutes all those years you were out on that mountain."

Faith stood, shaking still. She shouldn't be surprised the

Nolan brothers weren't well liked, but she didn't expect the reverend's wife to be so blunt. Or to have such clear understanding of all that had gone on, all she'd thought hidden, all her shame. "I don't know how you can say so with such conviction. Especially since I can't be certain I didn't have anything to do with the fire or even..." She shrugged. "The rest."

"See?" Mrs. Alton smiled. "You can't even bring yourself to say it. Come on. Let's be done with this silly conversation and get you to your new room. You need rest. I'm sure you'll see things more clearly once you've slept."

Faith followed the plump lady toward the stairs, crossing paths in the hall with Reverend Alton as they walked out of the parlor. "Thank you ever so much, sir. I doubt I could have abided the jail cell."

He chuckled. "Thank Mrs. Alton, dear child. I stand aside and watch her. She is a formidable force when she gets moving."

"Oh, I do. I'm most grateful. To the both of you."

"Reverend Alton," his wife said from the top of the stairs, a twinkle in her cocoa-colored eyes. "I do believe you have a Wednesday night sermon to write. I'll take care of our guest."

As if in a daze, Faith followed Mrs. Alton up the stairs, down the corridor, and into a room on the right. "I filled the pitcher with hot water when I went to fetch that coffee for you—I wasn't about to let you leave this house, child. I set a couple of things on the bed for you, too. If there's anything else I can do for you, please let me know. I want you to feel at home."

*Home.* She hadn't been home since that long-ago day she'd come into Bountiful to pick up a wagon-full of supplies her father had ordered at the mercantile in town. How she wished she could believe the sweet woman.

As if she'd heard Faith's sad thought, Mrs. Alton patted her arm. "All is well now. The worst is finally over."

Faith's heart stuttered with a skipped beat. Hope, it seemed, hadn't died. But although she wanted to believe her hostess was right, the last three years loomed too real.

The day after Faith arrived at the Altons' home, Olivia Whitman did indeed come to visit. She chattered in a lively way, discussing everything in general and nothing in particular. Faith wondered if, after Olivia left, she would be able to relate any bits or pieces of what the banker's wife had told her. She did, however, feel a deep appreciation for Olivia's simple offer of friendship, something Faith had long lacked, ever since her move to her husband's home had isolated her. They laughed over tales of the Whitman children's antics, and sympathized over the loss of Addie Tucker's grandmother, a sweet lady Faith remembered from back when she'd been a regular part of the congregation. Then Olivia stunned Faith.

"You do know," she said, "that my dear Mr. Whitman and I wed for a multitude of reasons, none of which was abiding affection for each other."

Faith's eyes widened. "No, I had no idea. Ever since I moved to the mountain, I've known little about the goings-on around town. I didn't come in much, since I was so busy at the store, and neither Roger nor Theo was particularly sociable. I doubt either one paid much attention to what happened in Bountiful, unless it affected them. I never knew you'd married until this last Christmas, when I persuaded Roger to bring me to church for the service."

"Well, it's a long story, but what I learned is God works miracles every day. You never know what day He's going to work yours. All I can tell you is that if you close yourself to His gifts, you might miss something as marvelous as the tenderness my husband offered me a few months after our marriage began."

Faith caught her bottom lip between her teeth. "And yet, during all my time on the mountain, He didn't see fit to work that miracle for me. Believe me, I prayed for one, begged Him to work His will in my dilemma. I was sure He hadn't planned a marriage like that for my life. But, nothing. He never answered my prayer. I—I don't know that He even heard."

"Of course, He did." Olivia reached out, laid a hand on her arm. "It seems clear to me that the Father has another man in mind for you. That's why you can't set your mind against men. Not all of them are like—well, like Mr. Nolan."

Immediately, the image of the handsome logging camp owner overtook Faith's thoughts. Olivia was right. Nathan Bartlett was nothing like Roger. He'd already proven himself a gentle, caring, respectful, and even hardworking and industrious man. She also couldn't discount how safe she felt in his company, or how attractive she found him.

Heat flooded her cheeks. She couldn't think of the man in such a way. He'd never done anything to invite such thoughts.

On the other hand, her conversation with Olivia revealed

an unpleasant reality, one she'd begun to grasp since the moment Woody made it clear he knew all about Roger. It seemed everyone in town knew all there was to know about her dead husband's worst traits. She cringed at the thought of reading pity on all those faces.

Before shame could consume her, Olivia surprised her with an invitation. "Please join us on Sunday after church," she said. "The Ladies' Bible Society is holding a box lunch auction to refill our empty coffers. Six weeks ago we shipped a crate full of Bibles to missionaries headed to China. Can you imagine? China! What an enormous mission field that is."

Faith sighed, fear finding fertile ground. "I hold no illusions, Olivia. I doubt anyone will want to buy a box lunch I prepare."

"Please, stop that kind of talk. No one will know it's yours until well after it's sold. Then whoever buys it will eat lunch with you, and they'll see what a lovely woman you are. That's the best way to counter that horrid Theo's tales."

Faith shrugged. "I can see the good sense in your plan, but I'm not sure I can bring myself about to take part in the auction. Besides, I'm a new widow and in full mourning."

"You can still mourn Roger while you help the Bible Society."

"I don't know..."

The banker's wife discounted Faith's objection with a shake of the head. "There is something we haven't talked about yet. You're in quite a bit of a fix right now. From what you've told me, all your belongings went up in smoke with the general store. Do you have as much as a change of clothes? Anything at all?"

Faith thought about Maisie, Daisy, and Lazy.

But, no. Even though her heart saw them as hers, she didn't have even them.

She shook her head. "Aside from this"—she waved at her dusty, smoke scented, and wilted flannel dress—"that I was wearing when it all happened, and the calico dress and cotton petticoat Mrs. Alton found among the items her daughter left behind, I have nothing. Oh, there is the wagon...but I'm sure Theo will say it belongs to him."

"Well, then, we must do something to change that. A sooty dress and a summer-weight calico aren't enough for the winter. We might even get snow soon, it's so cold this year." She tapped her chin with a finger as she thought things over. "I have an idea, and I think it's a lovely one." She turned toward the rear of the house, where their hostess had discreetly disappeared after greeting Olivia. "Mrs. Alton! Could you please join us for a moment? I've a question for you— and a favor to ask, as well."

Moments later, the reverend's wife bustled into the parlor, wiping her damp hands on a blue-and-white ticking towel. "Have you girls—forgive me, *ladies*—had a nice visit?"

Olivia smiled. "Splendid!" Then she gestured toward Faith. "But we do have a problem. She has nothing, absolutely nothing. It all went in the blaze. What do you think if we gather the women from the Bible Society and hold a dressmaking bee? It wouldn't be too different from a quilting bee, I would think."

Mrs. Alton clasped her hands together, brought them up to her gray wool-upholstered, carrier-pigeon chest. "What a lovely idea! Of course, we must do something for dear Faith. She can't possibly go on without a stitch to wear."

Faith stood, shaking her head. "Oh, please don't put any-one to so much trouble. I can certainly stitch up a dress or a skirt and blouse myself. I have little else to do while I wait to see what the marshal will do next."

Olivia stood as well, a determined tilt to her head. "Excel-lent! You can sew alongside the rest of us. That's the whole point of a bee. Everyone is busy. And that's how we take care of things in Bountiful. When one has troubles to bear, others come alongside to take a bit of the burden off those weighed-down shoulders."

Faith was stunned. "But I'm not from Bountiful, not really. I grew up at my parents' place outside of town, and most recently, I've lived on the mountain."

"You went to school with us here in Bountiful," Olivia argued, her features set in a firm expression she'd surely per-fected disciplining her children.

"It was a long time ago—"

"You're here now," Mrs. Alton said in a voice that left no doubt where she stood on the matter. "And as the president of the society, why, I do declare, dressing you should be our next project. We can start with a meeting day after tomorrow. At that time, we can talk about the box lunch auction, too."

No matter what excuse Faith put forward, the two strong-willed women dispatched it with remarkable ease. By the time Olivia donned her cloak to return home, Faith had agreed to go along with the plan. They assured her no one in Bountiful would be foolish enough to believe a word Theo said.

She wondered. She really wondered.

And still, hours later, she couldn't believe her future would unfold in such a tidy fashion. Surely not the future of a widow accused of murder and arson.

"Are you ready, dear?" Mrs. Alton asked two days later. "I'm excited for you to meet the rest of the ladies. They're all so sorry these terrible things have happened to you, and they want to help in any way they can. You'll see. They're very welcoming. Not that there are all that many of us here, yet."

Faith focused on the less worrisome part of Mrs. Alton's comment. At least if there weren't many ladies in town, there would be fewer people to scorn her.

Faith knew, better than most, that the West was still a man's world. Too many women who tried to make the move out to the territories breathed their last on the way across the plains. The railroads had made things much better, but it was still a costly journey, and many couldn't afford train fare for a whole family. They chose to fill wagons with their belongings, join up in a train, and make the crossing that way.

Those women who survived the journey often died in childbirth, since there were so few doctors caring for so many, and over such sprawled-out areas. Then there were the ladies that refused to follow their men. They knew what to expect . . . or they thought they knew what awaited them.

Faith's family had come by wagon, but she didn't remember much. She'd been very young. But after growing up out on the farm, losing Mama and Papa to an Indian raiding party, and then the years spent living with Roger in the back of the general store on the mountain, Bountiful looked quite nice and civilized to her.

With a perceptive glance toward Faith, Mrs. Alton stepped outside and, reluctantly, Faith had to follow. The cold wind slapped her face, setting her back with its power. "Goodness! I'd forgotten it could get like this. I suppose I grew used to the trees blocking out the wind on the mountain."

"Sure," her hostess said as she closed the door. "There's nothing here to break that wind—no trees to speak of, no hills near enough to matter, and too few buildings to shield Main Street."

They started down the street, heading toward Metcalf's Mercantile, where the owner had let the Bible Society set up a large quilting frame in his store's back room.

"I'm surprised a gentleman storeowner would let a group of ladies use his establishment to come together and quilt."

"Oh, Zebediah Metcalf is one shrewd businessman," Mrs. Alton said, her smile full of humor. "Where do you think we buy our dress goods? Our thread?" She nodded, an astute expression on her soft, plump face. "Mm-hm. He knows he'll make a tidy sum from our purchases."

"And this will be the best place for a Bible Society meeting? Not the church building?"

Mrs. Alton hooked her arm through Faith's. "We often sew for the missionaries who distribute the Good Book. Since that's still our society's main focus, we haven't seen the need to change the name. But we've tackled another project or two before, as well as the quilts. Because of the quilts, we set up a suitable meeting space in the store, since Reverend Alton would not find it amusing if we had us our great, big quilting frame in the middle of his sanctuary. By now we have a good supply of scissors, pins, and tapelines there. It's the most convenient location, with it being right in the middle of town."

Faith tried to escape the keen scrutiny of the reverend's wife by gazing straight ahead toward their destination. But she must not have succeeded in shielding the worry on her face.

"Don't you fret now," her hostess said, her voice a gentle scold. "The ladies all said they'd like to help get you back on your feet again. They know how difficult things can be for a woman out here. Besides, the walk will be excellent exercise for us. I've eaten a few too many slices of pie over these past few weeks, and you're looking a mite peaked, if I do say so. It'll do us both good to get out of the house."

Faith touched her cheek with her free hand. "Peaked? I reckon I may be a bit..."

"Pshaw! Healthy is healthy. And, as I told you, this outing will do you a world of—OH!"

Mrs. Alton stumbled toward the ground, the force of her momentum flinging Faith off balance. As she fought to right herself and pull her older companion upright, something struck her in the middle of the back.

A gust of air exploded from her lips.

Pain stole her breath.

Her hands flew out as she tried to brace herself. It didn't help. She hit the road surface.

Sparks danced in her head.

As darkness took over, she heard Mrs. Alton's cries. The sounds of her friend's pain and the pounding of hooves were the last Faith consciously registered.

# Chapter 10

An eternity of black stretched out past Faith. As she identified the existence of the expanse, she realized a blacksmith had taken residence in her head and begun to clang away at the inside of her forehead.

*Clang! Clang! Clang!*

The pain left her unable to move even as little as it took to draw breath. Something dry and gritty filled her nose with each attempt.

She moaned.

A red haze filled her throbbing head.

When she tried to shift, a wave of nausea stunned her. The simple attempt let her know she was lying face down on a hard surface covered with something puffy, gritty—

The road.

Since it would seem she could only think right then, Faith tried to sort out the impressions she had, to pair them with what vague memory floated into her mind. The last thing she remembered was the blow to her back, right after Mrs. Alton had tripped.

Oh, no! Had that dear lady been hurt when she tripped in

the road? As for herself, what had struck her in the middle of her back? Pain radiated from the point of impact to all other parts of her being.

She moaned again, but the sound came out muffled at best. She had to stand, couldn't remain sprawled out on the dusty surface of Main Street. She had to make sure Mrs. Alton wasn't hurt.

Calling on all her strength, Faith placed her head cheek down, and then rolled her opposite shoulder back toward that side. Another moan ripped from her dirt-clogged throat. Even so, her lower body followed her head and chest.

On her back, she lay still, as surge after surge of pain wracked her body and her head, weak gasps past her gritty throat the only things between her and asphyxiation. As if from a great distance, she heard the murmur of what she assumed were voices. But whose voices?

She strained against her reluctant eyelids again, but her head swam at the effort. Dizziness took hold, and the black curtain behind her eyelids glowed a pulsing red again. Clearly, she was in no condition to move, not even to look around. The only way to conquer the pain in her head and stave off the queasiness was to remain as still as possible.

Moments later, she caught the murmur of voices again, this time closer, maybe. Perhaps louder.

" . . . She movin' a'tall?" a man said.

"I can see she's breathing," a woman answered.

As she strove to corral her thoughts if not her actions, she entertained a fleeting thought. Perhaps she was on the verge of dying and the pain would end any moment now. Were the voices she'd heard those of angels greeting her in Paradise? She'd always understood from years of reading Scripture there wouldn't be any pain in heaven.

"What're ya thinking happened to her, Thelma? She don't stink of spirits none," the man said.

Outrage gave Faith a rush of determination. Who was this . . . this angel?

Through lids still parted a fraction, she counted a number of faces . . . two . . . three? They seemed to float at a short distance above her.

"Would you stop all that staring at her, Elmer Myers? Help us get her somewhere more comfortable. Or is looking at a pretty lady all you're good for? I woulda thought you'd gotten past that, you being so long in the tooth. Does she have to suffer your silliness, too, after nearly getting trampled to death?"

"What about Mrs. Miriam?" the man—Elmer—shot right back.

"Miriam's fine." The woman's voice had grown peevish. "Doc Chambers is with her, and I'm sure someone's fetching the reverend."

Hurried footsteps approached. "How's her breathing?" the newcomer asked.

"Ah . . . Doc Chambers," the woman said, relief in her words. "It's awful good to see you. Don't it beat all? This poor girl's been hit by a crazed horse. I saw it myself. Right out our front window. See, Elmer? I told you I was right about putting that expensive glass in the shop. I saw all what happened out here today."

Doc Chambers. Faith knew the name. He was Bountiful's physician.

She hadn't died after all.

And the strange voices weren't angels, either. They were folks from town, even though she knew she'd never met an Elmer Myers.

"Did that horse hit Miriam Alton as well, Mrs. Myers?" The doctor's voice betrayed his concern.

"Aw...call me Thelma, please. We're fixing to be neighbors, now that Elmer and I are settled into our tidy little butcher shop."

"I'll call you Thelma, then. Did you see the horse strike Miriam or did it spare her?"

"I don't know. Didn't see any such thing. I looked out the window when I heard a cry. I can tell you Miriam tripped and stumbled and tried to right herself. But this girl? Poor thing, she fell on her face." Thelma paused. "It did all happen so fast...I reckon it could have happened that way, that both of them got hit by that great wild beast."

"Then again, maybe not," the doctor said. "Look at her. Miriam's faring better'n Mrs. Nolan."

Something cool touched Faith's forehead...her neck... her wrist.

"Can I help?" another man said.

Faith recognized that voice—Nathan Bartlett. She was most certainly alive. And rousing, though all she could remember was heading down Main Street with Mrs. Alton toward Metcalf's Mercantile.

She knew she shouldn't have tried to go to the society's meeting.

Mustering her determination again, Faith managed to crack one eye open, wider still. As muted as the light of early dusk was, it nonetheless made her wince, which in turn intensified the urge to gag. She fought the pain and the nausea, as she kept her eye open a broader slice. Above her, she could now make out the features of a handful of concerned faces.

"D'ya see that, Doc?" Elmer asked. "That's one right pretty green eye she's got there, ain't it? Since I can see it, it must mean she's waking up again."

"Oh, for goodness' sake, Elmer!" Mrs. Meyers said. "Why don't you get back to the store? I'm sure you can find a haunch of meat to cut for one of our customers, or a...a...kidney to cut up for some suet. There must be something you need to do."

"Anything to get away from your vinegar—er...honeyed words, dear."

Faith couldn't stop the smile. And while the pain in her head continued unabated, the queasy feeling didn't strike as strong. She pried open her other eye.

"Wha—what happened?" she whispered. The words grated in her throat, sounded rough even to her.

Nathan knelt down beside her. "A horse got loose. He must have hit you and Mrs. Alton. You fell, and now have a bump on your forehead. But neither you nor Mrs. Alton is seriously hurt, right Doc?"

"Well, Miriam's got herself a twisted ankle and a pair of scraped hands, and it would seem Mrs. Nolan here has herself one nasty concussion. She needs to be watched, but unless something unexpected comes up, I'd say she'll be right as red hot pepper and twice as sassy, if I recollect her late mama right, in a couple days or so."

"Then I'll see to getting her back to the Altons' home."

Nathan glanced up the street. "It looks like the marshal and the reverend are already helping Mrs. Alton there."

With impressive ease and smooth motion, Nathan gathered Faith in his arms. He murmured, "I'm sorry. I don't mean to jostle you. You can't stay in the street."

Fireworks exploded before her slightly open eyes. The out-of-control blacksmith resumed his clanging inside her head, which felt as though it was about to burst into pieces. She reached up and clasped it, one hand on either side. But that left her supported only by Nathan's arms, a somewhat precarious and wholly mortifying position in which to find herself. On the other hand, it was one that was becoming almost a habit.

"Oooh!" The off-balance sensation won out. In a reflexive gesture, she reached out and gripped the broad shoulders mere inches from her rapidly closing eyes.

"You're safe." His arms secured her more closely against his chest. "And we'll be at the Alton home in a moment."

*Safe...*

Not if a mere walk down the street could nearly get her killed.

Certainly not when someone could come into her home, kill her husband, and try to burn her, as well.

How could she ever be "safe?"

What had made the horse bolt?

That question buzzed without mercy in Nathan's head. And what fool left a horse that poorly hitched on Main Street?

What if instead of tripping two grown women the horse

had trampled a child? The thought didn't bear entertaining. He'd have to make sure Marshal Blair got answers to his questions.

The way things had played out was bad enough. Mrs. Alton's injuries were minor, but Faith had been laid out cold in the middle of the road. She could have been killed. A hoof to any adult's head would be as devastating as to a child's.

After he helped Faith onto the sofa in the parsonage's parlor, he went straight to the jail. The squat building looked the part. It was an unadorned box, a row of windows across each side, each covered with iron bars. Wholly unpleasant, and nowhere anyone of sound mind would want to stay.

He grimaced at the thought of Faith caged in that place.

Inside, the door to the marshal's office was open. Since the situation was too serious to waste time on niceties that led nowhere, Nathan went straight to Adam Blair's desk, and dispensed with any useless greeting.

"What have you learned about the horse? Whose is it? Who is the fool too careless to make sure he'd secured his horse? There must be something you can do to keep it from happening again."

Marshal Blair raised an eyebrow. "I'll grant you that accident was frightening, and it's too bad Mrs. Nolan was hurt so bad, but I don't see what a body can do to keep a horse from running off."

Nathan felt his grip on his patience slip. He crossed his arms to keep himself from making fists. "You know we have more than enough hitching posts and rails and who knows what else for a man to tie down his horse anywhere up and down Main Street. You know it was all the fault of the horse's careless owner."

"Did anyone see the horse? Does anyone know whose it is?" the marshal asked. "I mean, d'you know if the new butcher and his wife saw anything that would help? I know Thelma made sure I knew she'd seen it strike Mrs. Nolan."

Nathan shrugged. "I would ask them every question you can think of. From what I can tell, the missus is mighty keen on the goings-on outside their shop. She might be the kind that sells a pound of gossip with a Sunday roast."

"Oh, we already know her pretty well in town. She's a busy-body, all right, but she means well. And she is awful new to town. I figger she's lonely, and trying to learn as much as she can about the place where she's come to live. Keeping an eye on what happens on Main Street would give her something to chat about with the other women around these parts."

"I suppose you have a point." Nathan's anger had begun to burn away under the influence of the marshal's calm manner. Now, it seemed to fizzle out completely. "Do you know where the two women were going? I think I heard something about quilting."

"Not exactly. The Ladies' Bible Society was about to have themselves a dressmaking bee. Looks like they want to help Mrs. Nolan."

"That's neighborly. Fai—er...Mrs. Nolan lost all she owned in the fire. She has nothing but the clothes she's wearing."

The marshal smiled. "Even if they're busybodies like Thelma Myers, the women from the Bible Society are good folks, too."

In spite of the anxiety he'd felt since the moment he'd heard Faith had been hurt, Nathan smiled. "I agree."

The men fell silent. After a handful of minutes had gone by, the marshal spoke. "Are you staying in town again?"

Nathan shrugged. "It's too late to head back out to the camp today."

"At the hotel?"

"No. Eli and Olivia insist I stay with them. Have to admit, as decent as Folsom keeps his hotel, Olivia does run a fine home. Their extra room is clean and comfortable, and Cooky does make tasty meals. I'm not likely to pass up either luxury."

The lawman laughed. "Can't say as I blame you. I'd do the same if it were me."

Nathan headed toward the door, hat in hand. "You will speak with Mrs. Myers, right?"

"Sure. I'll see what else she has to say. Who knows? She might have seen the horse's owner walk away from the animal. That would help us identify him, and then he and I would have us one fine chat."

"On the matter that he can't endanger the citizens of your fine town again."

"Something very much like that."

Nathan had to be satisfied with that. "I'd best let you get back to what you were doing."

"I was fixing to head home. But first, I reckon I'll stop by the dining room at the hotel. Can't quite make myself eat my own cooking every day. Cookery isn't my strongest suit."

"You're saying you're better with a gun than a skillet in your hand?"

The lawman arched a brow. "I'd rather keep it in its holster."

"Fair enough." Nathan clapped his hat on his head. "I'll stop by here before I leave town, see what you've found out."

Adam Blair nodded, but Nathan could tell he'd turned his attention back to the papers on his desk. He walked out, closing the jailhouse door behind him. A final glance over his shoulder made him shake his head. To think Theo Nolan wanted to lock Faith up in that place.

Not that he meant the marshal any disrespect, but it was no place for a lady.

And Faith Nolan was a lady. No matter what Theo had to say.

Nathan doubted he'd ever forget how it had felt to shelter her in his arms. She'd trusted him. He hoped he always proved himself worthy of her trust.

It took three days for Faith to no longer feel the discomfort of the concussion or the sharp pains from the blows she received on her back and her forehead. Olivia had visited every day, and she'd taken it upon herself to arrange a new time for the dressmaking bee.

The members of the Bible Society were expected to arrive at the church by mid Saturday morning, where they would proceed to measure in the entry foyer, cut down the center aisle, and pin while comfortably seated on each individual seamstress's preferred pew. All were to come together on the first two pews to apply their needles to Faith's three new dresses-to-be to sew the patterns' pieces together.

The nervousness she'd experienced the first time they'd

tried to have the gathering returned. How would these women respond to her? She'd been involved in scandal after scandal over the last couple of weeks.

Faith was ready to end her time as Bountiful's entertainment.

When they arrived, the women surprised her. Either they hadn't heard Theo's accusations, which she didn't think was the case since he'd made no secret of them, or Mrs. Alton and Olivia were held in great regard, and their sponsorship counted an equally great deal. Whatever the reason, they welcomed her, and in no time, everyone was busy with their part of the dressmaking venture.

Olivia introduced Faith to a striking redhead, whom she identified as her dearest friend. Addie Tucker, the wife of the town's livery owner, sat next to her, and asked every question imaginable.

After a bit, Olivia marched up to their side and waggled a finger at her friend. "For goodness' sake, Addie Tucker, if your needle moved as fast as your tongue, you already would be done with Faith's first dress."

Addie laughed. "I'm just making the best of my time. Now that I've a little one running into trouble at all times, I've learned to not waste a single moment. And I'm quite impressed with how Faith managed to run that general store on the mountain."

"Well," Faith said, "it's at the foot of the mountain. Our customers wouldn't care to have to climb too high to do their shopping."

"Who are—were—the customers?"

"There are sheep farms along the rest of the foothills, and

those farmers come to us for supplies. Also, the handful of soldiers at the post a few miles south of us come in when their military shipments are delayed. Back when I first married Roger, we even had a handful of Indians come by a few times for blankets and some other items. Now that most of them have been moved to reservation lands in Idaho, I haven't seen any for a while. Our main customer is Nath—Mr. Bartlett and his logging camp."

While Faith had tried to catch her slip of the tongue, the looks Addie and Olivia exchanged told her she hadn't succeeded. The two friends displayed admirable discretion when they didn't say a word.

Mrs. Hadley, Addie's mother, walked into the sanctuary doorway and clapped her hands. "Ladies, Olivia's outstanding cook has sent us an assortment of delicacies for refreshment. I'm sure we can all stop our work for a bit, and enjoy our luncheon."

Eight women around a laden library-type table made for a great deal of chatter. Laughter abounded, and the excellent food satisfied their appetites. But a short while later, even the happy hubbub couldn't mask the stomping up the front steps.

Mrs. Alton, still somewhat unsteady on her twisted ankle, wobbled toward the door. "May I help—"

"I come after that woman what kilt my brother," Theo said. "It's been days and days, and that there marshal ain't done one blamed thing about her. She owes me plenty for burning down my store, too."

Faith's breath caught in her throat. The floor beneath her feet seemed to tilt, and she felt as though the dizziness from the day of the accident had returned. All from hearing that hateful voice.

She shot glances 'round all corners of the sanctuary, the urge to run and hide more powerful than she would have expected. Where could she go? And was running the solution?

No. It wasn't.

She'd decided to choose courage over cowardice. She had done nothing to run from. Faith squared her shoulders, held her head high, and walked into the foyer entry of the church as though she were in her Sunday best. Anna Alton Carlisle's calico dress would, of course, have to do, and the ugly bruise on her forehead didn't help her confidence one bit.

Stripped of all external trappings, Faith relied on God.

She waved toward Mrs. Alton. "Why have you come to bother these folks, Theo? You know the marshal said he would take care of looking into the matter of Roger's death—"

"Don't you go forgetting the fire." His jaw pushed out. He thumbed his worn hat off his forehead. "It's cost me plenty, losing all. I ain't even got a place to sleep. Can't sleep in the barn."

It couldn't have cost him anything, since she was certain he hadn't tried to replace the cabin much less the stock at the store yet. And that barn had been good enough for her plenty of nights. But experience had taught her not to bait her brother-in-law. "Yes, the fire as well. Have you been to the jail to speak with him?"

"Been down there already, and he weren't there." Theo narrowed his small, dark eyes, fixing her with one of the mean, hate-filled stares she had come to know too well. "I hear you had yourself an accident. And even Bartlett's gone back to his camp by now. I reckon it's time to have us that there trial without wasting any more time so's they can hang ya for your sins right away."

The chorus of gasps reminded Faith of the women on the front pews. As much as she'd enjoyed the morning, she doubted any of those lovely ladies would ever spare her the time of day again.

"I didn't kill Roger, and I didn't burn down the cabin." She decided to try to use logic, even though she'd never known Theo to indulge in the habit. "Why would I want to kill my husband? Why would I want to burn down our business and home? I have nowhere to go now, and no means to provide for myself. I'd never be so foolish."

Theo jutted out his chin. "All's I know is you was trying to steal them mules. I figger you must'a wanted to sell them off. They're worth something plenty. You'd have enough to...oh, I dunno. Do whatever you womenfolk do with cash."

"Really, now, Mr. Nolan," Olivia said as she strode up to Faith's side. "That sounded like a most offensive comment. I do hope I misheard you. You can't be berating a brand-new widow, can you? I'm sure you wouldn't be so quick to insult Mrs. Nolan."

"I figger by offing my brother she at least insulted me, if not lots more'n that. He were my brother, ma'am. M-my *brother*." He slapped his worn hat against his leg. "She's nothing but a killer and a thief."

"Has it occurred to you, Mr. Nolan," Addie offered from

Faith's other side, "that you could be mistaken? That you might be accusing her wrongly?"

"I know what I know—"

"Mr. Nolan," Marshal Blair said, clapping a large hand onto Theo's shoulder. "I would hope you haven't made yourself a nuisance with the ladies."

Theo shook off the lawman's clasp. "I thought you said you'd be setting up to try this killer, but it's been days since we come to town, and you ain't done nothin'."

The marshal leaned against the doorframe. "Well, now, Mr. Nolan. I reckon you know we need a judge to have us a proper trial, don't you?"

Faith's brother-in-law frowned. "I suppose."

"See here. I've taken it upon myself to send to Portland for one. It could take the fellow some time to travel here to Bountiful."

"But—"

"There's no other way to do this," the marshal said. "You'll have to wait him out. He'll get here soon enough. That is, if you're still wanting that trial."

"'Course, I want her tried. My brother's still dead, ain't he? And she's out here, having herself a ... a ..." He glanced around the sanctuary, his gaze pausing at the table. "Is that a ladies' tea? After she kilt Roger? How long you gonna make me wait to take care of her"—feminine gasps erupted in a furious flurry—"er ... to do some kinda justice? She kilt Roger, so she needs to hang."

Mrs. Alton stepped up to Theo's side. "You'll have to wait at least as long as it takes the good Lord to get the man here, I'll have you know. God's time isn't necessarily our time, but it's always the perfect time. Now, I'll thank you to take your leave. The ladies and I are mighty busy with Bible Society business. Unless you'd like to join us in our work?"

Horror widened Theo's eyes. "No, no. I suppose I hafta wait, seeing as I cain't go fetch that judge myself." He spun around and stalked off, muttering under his breath.

Faith suspected he'd go find his pal Hector Swope, and the two of them would cook up a fresh serving of their usual trouble. Regardless, she felt a great deal of relief. As long as he didn't come to look for mischief anywhere in her vicinity, she'd rest much easier.

Marshal Blair turned to her when Theo had gone a ways down Main Street. "I bought us some time, ma'am. Now it'll be a matter of me finding who did kill Roger."

"You believe me?" she asked.

The lawman studied her intently. "Can't say I see a reason why you woulda killed him. And the store?" He shook his head. "It would make no sense for you to light the place on fire."

She let out a heartfelt sigh. "Thank you."

"Enough of this," Mrs. Alton said. "I have a lovely luncheon set out on the table. Please do join us."

He laughed. "You'll have to forgive me, Mrs. Alton, ma'am, but I don't think I'm suited to a sewing party, even if the meal's wonderful, which I'm sure it is."

Her hostess's eyes twinkled. "I hear you take all your meals at the hotel these days, Marshal Blair. I'm sure I can fix that small problem soon enough. It's all a matter of finding you a fine wife. It's about time you settled down."

Although the marshal tried to disguise it, alarm hit him hard. "As I said, Mrs. Alton, I'll be leaving you ladies to your needlework. I have plenty of work waiting on me down at the jail."

Olivia and Addie chuckled as he hurried down the front steps. "He does need a wife," Olivia said. "And I've decided I'm going to find him one."

"You don't have enough to do with a husband and two children?" Addie asked her friend, a russet eyebrow raised, mischief in her voice.

Olivia gave her friend what struck Faith as a secretive smile. "Hm...I can always do a mite more." She turned toward the table. "Now then, how about if we return to our meal? And the dressmaking bee."

Faith closed her eyes briefly. Who knew how the rest of the women would receive her, now that they could no longer ignore all the dreadful accusations Theo had flung her way.

But when she reached the table, they all swarmed around her.

"What a horrid man—"

"How did you survive all that time with those brothers?"

"And he says you did what to the—"

"The gall!"

To Faith's amazement, not a one seemed to have believed a word Theo had said. They were all outraged on her behalf. Little by little, as the early afternoon unfolded, she began to let go the tension that had been her constant companion for so long.

But still, she wondered how long that time the marshal had bought would last.

# Chapter 11

"You recollect me of a bear with a sore tooth," Woody complained. "Cain't you find a spot to sit still for a spell? What's on your mind?"

Nathan felt a wave of heat spread from the back of his neck up to his hairline. He'd thought he'd hidden his worry from his men. Clearly, Woody had a talent for observation greater than he'd thought.

"Nothing much." He stole a glance at his cook and friend. "I'm just thinking. I have to figure out how I'm going to get supplies out here, now that the general store's gone."

Woody scratched his chin through his grizzled beard. "You got a point there. What are you thinking?"

"I suppose I'll have to put in that road we talked about and open my own store. In the meantime, I may make Theo an offer for those three mules. I don't think he really wants them, no matter what he says."

"Bah!" Woody shook his head. "There's something else there. Don't reckon that lazy Theo's gonna feed them animals or muck the barn out. Can't think why he'd be so stubborn about them. Even for the store. All's I can reckon is he's wanting the place to set someone up to run the business, and he figgers he'll take in buckets of gold without busting a sweat."

"I doubt anyone's going to make the place pay besides Faith. She was the one who handled the orders, who ran the store, who stocked the shelves, and she even had to deliver the last load. He'll never work half as hard as she did."

"And about them mules . . . well, he ain't come for 'em, you know."

"I know." He resumed his pacing.

Woody seemed satisfied.

For the moment.

More pacing.

A handful of minutes later, the old logger shoved his chair back and limped to the stove. "Here," he said shortly. "Have yourself some of this coffee. Y'ain't gonna sleep none tonight, so you may as well fret wide awake."

"Well, that tar you brew sure will keep me from sleeping all night."

"Watch what you call tar, son. It's what wakes you up—"

"I know, I know. It's what wakes me up in the morning. Tell you what. How about you go to sleep? I can fret over my finances all by myself. *Without* need of your foul coffee."

Woody nodded. "I'm going. A body cain't be keeping up with you young bucks without a blink of sleep. Ain't been too many times lately I been able to get even that much." He headed off to his room. At the door, he paused. "Ain't a whole lot going on up here, son. Why'n't you stay in town and keep an eye on her? Y'ain't gonna rest until you do."

Nathan didn't respond. There wasn't much to say. As

usual, with his homespun way of seeing the world, Woody had identified the problem without Nathan spelling it out.

He knew Theo had stayed in town after he'd returned to the camp. The younger Nolan brother wouldn't drop the matter of the trial. He was too cussed a . . . well, mule.

Olivia and Eli had tried to persuade him to stay with them until Adam Blair heard back from the judge he'd contacted. But Nathan wasn't one to shirk his responsibility at the logging camp. And Mrs. Faith Nolan wasn't his responsibility.

Even though it sure felt that way.

He'd never forgive himself if something happened to her while he continued to cut down trees without a care in the world.


The box lunch auction had been postponed after the accident that injured both Mrs. Alton and Faith. In spite of the warm friendship the Bible Society ladies had extended her, she hadn't wanted to attend such a public town event. But she hadn't been able to come up with an excuse her hostess would accept. Or Olivia.

"You must get your mind off your troubles," her new friend had insisted one afternoon as they put the finishing touches on two of Faith's new dresses. "It's not right to stay inside and do nothing but fret yourself into a sickbed. And since you do need to eat, all you have to do is make two or three servings, then pack it all in a box, and tie it up with a pretty ribbon bow. Who knows? One of the local fellows might buy it and sweep you off your feet."

"Olivia! I couldn't possibly. You know I'm still in mourning. For at least a year."

She scoffed. "Never you mind that, Faith. You've lived out here most of your life. Those things don't matter so much in the West. You need a husband, that much I can see. And all these lonely fellows...well, we have few unmarried ladies in Hope County. I'd say that's the perfect recipe for a wedding."

Memories of her marriage struck fear in Faith's heart. "Not at all for me. I've learned those kinds of basic needs aren't what make for a good marriage at all. Don't forget. I already walked down that path. Waiting for the Lord, that's what works. But honestly, I don't think He's going to have me wait for a future husband. Not after I made such a mess of things the first time around."

"That's your fear talking."

"What's wrong with learning from your mistakes?"

Olivia hadn't been able to counter that nugget of wisdom. By the same measure, she hadn't been able to extract a promise from Faith about the upcoming auction. After a bit, she'd stopped pushing. Faith's relief had been almost palpable. She hadn't wanted to make more statements only to have Olivia take them apart, word by pointed word.

But she wasn't about to go.

Which determination got her absolutely nowhere, since on the Sunday chosen for the rescheduled event, Faith found herself walking to the church across the wide yard between the two buildings, Mrs. Alton on her one side, Olivia on the other. All three carrying the lunches they had prepared.

"You do know you're a mite persistent, right?" she asked, resignation in her voice.

Olivia's smile could have lit up the entire sanctuary. "My very dear Mr. Whitman tells me so all the time."

Faith shook her head. "Poor man never had a chance when you moved into his house."

Olivia pulled up to a stop, strong feelings clear in her serious expression. "Please tell me you're not saying I set my cap for the man, Faith Nolan. Because I'll have you know I did no such thing. It all happened as I told you—"

"I surrender!" she said, laughing. "A woman can't even make a silly comment without you pestering her into a stern discussion."

Olivia shrugged. "A woman can't give up when she knows she's right. Especially after town wags leveled that exact accusation at me back when it all took place."

When they reached the church, they set the lunches on a table outside with the others. As the women took their seats in church, Olivia with her family, and Faith with Mrs. Alton, Olivia's words continued to wend their way through her efforts to focus on Reverend Alton's sermon. Was God trying to tell her something through her friend's words? Was she giving up too easily?

Had she given up in the face of Roger's mistreatment too quickly? Had she tolerated the intolerable? Then again, what could she have done differently?

Before Faith knew it, the service was over. She had no idea what the reverend had taught, or even what hymns the congregation had sung. Guilt struck, and she confessed her failing to her heavenly Father, asking forgiveness for her distraction.

Instead of a steady stream of departing churchgoers, all the congregants in the church bustled around the sanctuary, helping to move the pews out of the way. A number of long, sturdy tables were brought in from various neighbor homes and set up in the large room, then covered with snowy-white tablecloths. A mountain of cleverly decorated box lunches was stacked in front of the altar, and as soon as the flurry of setting up was done, butterflies swarmed in Faith's middle.

Her nerves made swallowing difficult.

Even though it could prove mighty embarrassing, she decided she hoped no one would buy the box tied with ribbons of green-and-white gingham left over from a dress Olivia had helped her daughter fashion over the past summer. Faith didn't think she could abide making light chatter with someone who'd later boast he'd broken bread with a vile killer.

Even though she'd killed nobody.

As Faith fretted in silence, a rustle of whispers erupted in the church when the door opened again and in walked five men in military attire. She recognized Captain Roberts and Sergeant Graves right away. Olivia had mentioned that an invitation had gone out to the nearest post. It would seem the soldiers were interested in home-cooked luncheons and female companionship. This, even though they'd missed the Sunday service. Faith thought a couple of the military men with the captain and sergeant looked familiar, and reckoned they might have shopped at the general store or visited Roger once or twice before, joining the officers on their buying trips—trips that often turned into . . . more. Her husband hadn't been particular about drinking companions.

Amid the hubbub of greetings that surrounded the arrival of the soldiers, the gathered congregants settled out into two groups, the men on one side of the sanctuary, and the women on the other. Reverend Alton led the auctioneer, Bountiful's carpenter, Mr. Tom Bowen, to the front, and in minutes, the event got started.

"What have we here?" Mr. Bowen asked in his booming voice. "It's a right pretty lunch, and I can say it smells awful good. I might could be talked into skipping lunch with my family for this fried chicken—"

"Thomas Bowen!" a plump lady in a nice blue dress trimmed in gray lace exclaimed. "Stop your nonsense right this minute, or you might find yourself without a dinner from now on."

"Aw...Irma," he said, pretending to be chastised, but his eyes revealed his mischief. "I'm sure you don't mean that, darling. You know I'm partial to your cooking. It's just that..." He shrugged. "We have us some right good cooks here in Bountiful, it seems."

Somewhat mollified, Irma gave a loud "Hmph!" and retreated to her chair.

The men on the right side of the sanctuary laughed.

The women echoed Irma's exclamations of disgust.

"Let's see now...where was I?" Tom made a great show of forgetfulness. "Ah, yes! I'm seeing who the lucky fella will be what'll buy this lovely lunch. Who'll offer me five cents to start the bidding? And remember, the money's for a good cause. Our ladies want to continue to supply missionaries with copies of the Good Book, so's they can reach unchurched folks in China."

Chatter broke out as some of the men gathered to stand in a small crowd in front of Tom. Eventually, Sergeant Graves began the bidding. Tom's voice carried throughout the large room, his antics amusing the attendees, as he teased ever-increasing amounts for the brightly decorated lunches. He displayed quite a talent as an auctioneer, as he interspersed his sing-song patter with laughter and additional commentary. For the most part, husbands bought their wives' concoctions. Those purchases elicited scant attention. It was when only the last few lunches were left at Tom's side that everyone's keen interest was piqued.

Those remaining boxes were the ones known by most to have been packed by the few unwed ladies in the area. Only five boxes had yet to be sold. One of them was Faith's green-and-white bow-bedecked offering. A queasy sensation sloshed around her middle. She gave the front doors a longing glance. She would much rather be just about anywhere but here.

For the first time since the auction had started, Tom Bowen fell silent. While he'd held on to his audience's attention with his humor up until then, his sudden silence was even more effective. The overall hubbub in the church slowly died out.

"Well, now," the carpenter said when a fly might have been heard bat its wings. "I see we've arrived at the best part of the auction. It's the single ladies' turn to charm us men—er...the *unmarried* men among us with their cooking charms."

Male laughter rang out again.

Faith looked toward the door another time. As crowded as the room had grown, she thought she still might manage to sneak out and no one would be any the wiser. That is, they wouldn't be until someone bought her lunch and she was nowhere to meet the buyer. She sighed.

Still, the urge to get away ran deep. She started to rise from her seat, but the auctioneer's resumed prattle brought her up short.

"I see here a nice-looking box," he said. "It does smell an awful lot like someone's packed roast lamb. Any of you men like lamb? Because I can tell you all that I sure do. And I'm so hungry my belly's growling's almost drowning all your noise out."

Good-natured catcalls rang out.

Mr. Bowen's eyes twinkled. "Irma, my darling, I think I'm going to pass on your good chicken sandwiches today, after all. I may just make myself a feast with lamb."

Boos and hisses sped through the crowd of women.

"Can't do that to Irma."

"You're already married."

The bachelors all tried to outdo each other in their varied comments.

"I'm ready to eat with a pretty—"

"Hurry up, Tom. I'm hungry!"

Faith dared a glance at the carpenter and gasped. The box in his hands was hers.

She blushed, and the urge to run had her up and moving toward the door again.

"Isn't it exciting, my dear?" Mrs. Alton said, appearing at her side. "He's about to raffle yours. Is there anyone you'd like to eat your meal with?"

Faith shivered. An idea occurred to her. "Yes, indeed. I'd love to eat with the reverend today."

Mrs. Alton laughed. "Nah, nah, nah! That won't work. He's already bought mine, and his waistline doesn't need two meals, I can assure you. Besides, we wouldn't like my dear husband to leave a poor, single fella to go hungry."

"But I'm a new widow," she argued, panic nipping at her heels. "You know I'm in mourning, Mrs. Alton. It won't do for me to take part in such frivolous nonsense so soon after Roger's death—"

"Pshaw!" Mrs. Alton hooked her arm through Faith's and led her back toward the altar again. "I'd buy that answer if I had any illusions about your marriage. I know you didn't wish that man ill—if you had, he wouldn't have lasted as long as he did after the two of you married. But I know you suffered at his hand, and his passing is as much a relief as it is a dilemma for you. Now that I've come to know you a mite better, I want nothing more than to see you wed to a good, kind man who'll know how to treasure you as you deserve."

Tears stung Faith's eyes. "I still can't believe you're able to trust me like this. Especially since Theo continues to accuse me."

Mrs. Alton made a face. "You can't expect me to put much stock in the words of a shiftless bum, can you? Theo Nolan spends most of his days in a rocking chair out on the front porch of the River Run Hotel. He'll say anything, depending on which way the winds blow his hat off his head."

"...So do I have fifty cents for this lovely lamb lunch?" Mr. Bowen asked.

"Fifty-five!" a gentleman cried from the far side of the room.

"My goodness!" Mrs. Alton exclaimed, craning her neck to see who'd spoken. "That is an excellent starting sum for your lunch. I wonder who that is doing the bidding."

Faith's cheeks heated. "I wouldn't know."

Her companion twisted around in her chair, bobbing her head, still intent on catching a glimpse of the bidder. "Ah...but wouldn't you *want* to know?"

Oh, goodness gracious. "To be honest, I'd much rather let him enjoy it on his own while I return to the lovely room at the parsonage."

"Sixty-five!"

"We have us a sixty-five," Mr. Bowen echoed. "And now, how about seventy?"

The bidding continued. When her curiosity got the better of her, Mrs. Alton practically dragged Faith up to the front, reminding her of a proud hen who leads her chicks to a choice spot where worms abound. Faith was mortified.

The bids continued to mount.

By the time it was all done, the lunch went for the princely sum of two dollars and ninety-nine cents. The average box lunch had sold for ninety-five cents.

Faith doubted there were many men hankering for lamb that day, but instead many more burning with nosiness. She wished the ground would open up beneath her and swallow her whole. No such thing happened.

"Come on up here to collect your prize, Mr. Parham," the auctioneer said. "And will the lovely lady who prepared this meal come and join us, please?"

As Faith fought the urge to shrink, a gentleman hurried toward the altar, and Mrs. Alton pushed her toward him.

Panic mounted.

She stepped back.

The reverend's wife prodded her forward.

"No, no!" Faith held her ground. "How am I going to eat with that man? I have no idea who he is. I've never even seen him before."

"Don't worry, dear." Mrs. Alton spoke in a tone both encouraging and excited at the same time.

It did nothing to help Faith.

The reverend's wife continued. "He's a nice gentleman. Eli Whitman hired him about a year ago. He's the bank secretary, and as I'm sure you can see, he's a nice-looking fellow. I hear he's also sober, churchgoing, and clearly holds an excellent job. A lady couldn't do a whole lot better, if you ask me, and could certainly do far worse. Such good prospects don't come around often enough."

Without waiting for Faith's response, Mrs. Alton raised her hand high in the air and waved at Mr. Bowen. "Yoo-hoo, Tom! Mr. Parham has bought himself Faith Nolan's lunch, lucky fellow. She and I cooked the leg of lamb together, and I know all about the other delicacies she packed with the meat and fresh-baked bread. I can tell you they'll have themselves a fine feast."

A chorus of chuckles burst forth, all of them feminine. Mr. Bowen gave Faith a questioning look, his scrutiny intense. A few of the other men turned their heads in her direction, faces full of curiosity. Mr. Parham's expression echoed theirs, even if a bit more discreetly.

She had nowhere to go. Faith forced a step in the direction of the occasional auctioneer... then another. Moments later, she stood before Mr. Bowen at Mr. Parham's side. She watched as money exchanged hands, and then as Mrs.

Hadley, Addie Tucker's mother, came in her capacity as treasurer of the Bible Society to collect the loot.

Cash in hand, she smiled at Faith and hurried off. Mr. Bowen resumed his auctioneering. Faith and Mr. Parham stood awkwardly at the front of the church, the box of food in the bank secretary's hands.

"Pleased to make your acquaintance, ma'am," he said in a pleasant voice, his expression polite. "Would you care to find a place to sit before the others hurry to crowd the tables? I'm sure Tom Bowen doesn't have many more lunches to raffle off."

Tongue-tied, Faith nodded, then followed her luncheon companion to the table farthest from the crush of nosy event-goers. Mr. Parham set down the box. She took a seat in the nearest chair. He gave her a nod.

"If you'll excuse me for a minute," he said, "I'm parched. Would you care for coffee or will water do?"

"Coffee is always good."

"Good to see we agree." With another nod, he crossed to where Addie held court with a large coffeepot in hand.

Faith bit her bottom lip as she rummaged in the box for the white napkins she'd packed. *Oh, Lord. I can't remember a more uncomfortable moment in my whole life. Please don't leave me. Give me the words to speak to this nice man, give me the strength to endure as long as the meal lasts. Even if you do know I'd much rather be at the parsonage reading your Word.*

"Mrs. Whitman makes a fine pot of coffee," Faith's meal partner said moments later at her elbow, startling her, two large coffee cups in his hands. "And I understand it's fresh. She said she'd just brewed this latest pot."

Faith nodded as she set out the dish with the slices of roast lamb on one of the napkins. She continued to focus on serving the meal, aware in a vague way of Mr. Parham's trivial chatter. The gentleman seemed nice enough indeed, and she realized how dreadfully rude she was being, but she couldn't help herself. She felt as though she were a bystander, someone other than herself, a witness to the scene instead of the one living it. No matter how hard she tried, she couldn't bring herself back into the moment at hand.

Fortunately for her, the bank's secretary continued to keep up a lighthearted conversation, and she managed to keep up her part by merely murmuring agreement where appropriate. While Mr. Parham ate with great gusto, Faith managed to chew and down a couple of bites of the lamb, some crumbs of bread, a small piece of one slice from the juicy apple, and a single bite of good yellow cheese. She couldn't dredge up even the semblance of an appetite when she knew she was under such great scrutiny.

Oh, sure. The residents of Bountiful by now had begun to enjoy their box lunches throughout the rearranged church sanctuary, but at no point did Faith feel herself free of their curious stares. Certainly, Mr. Parham didn't let his attention stray from her, either, even though he didn't pursue any intense sort of questioning.

And then...

One moment, the bank secretary was discussing some intricate financial transaction he'd saved from collapse due to his meticulous attention to detail, and the next he moaned, clutched his abdomen, and fell off his chair, retching, twitching, and convulsing. The man's face turned an alarming shade of purple-red.

A cry of horror burst from Faith's lips before she could stifle it.

Olivia flew to her side a second later.

Mrs. Alton rushed to her other flank.

The buzz of gossip broke out.

Addie Tucker bustled right up, stared at the man on the floor, and called for Doc Chambers. Then, in a voice not to be ignored, warned the rest of those gathered in the church. "Don't any of you others come and crowd us here. Curiosity won't help Mr. Parham. Doc Chambers is the only one who will. The rest of you can pray. Starting right now."

The physician, napkin still tucked into the collar of his blue-and-white striped shirt, ran to Mr. Parham's side, his black leather satchel in hand. He opened the case, tore off the napkin, then turned his attention to his patient.

With a cautionary glower for anyone who might entertain the notion of coming nearer, Addie stepped closer to Faith. When she seemed certain no one would get in the doctor's way, she reached out a hand. The warm touch, as unexpected as it was welcome, helped to ease Faith out of the semifrozen state in which she'd found herself for quite a spell. Tears threatened, but she fought them back, horrified to think the reluctantly dispersing crowd might witness her moment of weakness.

As though she'd awoken from a horrid nightmare, Faith blinked. Around her, bodies hurried from each corner of the room toward the twin doors to the sanctuary, heads still turned, gazes glued to the men at her feet, others staring at ... well, at her.

An arm wrapped around her waist. "Come with me, my dear." Mrs. Alton's gentle voice coaxed her along. "There's not much we can do to help, and we don't want to get in Doc's way, as Addie was so wise to say."

"Oh, but I couldn't leave without knowing—"

"We don't have to leave," Addie said. The pretty redhead, still at Faith's side, smiled. "Let's do something worthwhile. Let's pray."

The four women, Mrs. Alton, Olivia, Addie, and Faith, crossed the room and sat in chairs hastily abandoned by the other event-goers. Faith joined in the prayers offered by her friends, but at no time was she able to fully remove her attention from the motionless man on the floor and the grim-faced doctor hovering over him. To one side of the two men stood Reverend Alton, Mr. Whitman, Mr. Tucker, and ... oh, my!

Nathan had come to the box lunch auction. Faith hadn't noticed him in the crush of folks inside the church.

" ... amen."

Faith caught her breath. Once again she'd let her attention wander when she should have been praying, turning to God for comfort and guidance at this turbulent time. *Oh, Lord, forgive me.*

"What happened?" Olivia asked, concern in her features.

Faith shrugged. "I'm not sure. I must admit I wasn't paying much attention to Mr. Parham. He did most of the talking, and almost all the eating. I'm afraid I was quite rude to him. But, you see, I haven't been particularly hungry since ... well, since the day Roger died."

Mrs. Alton stood, *tsk-tsking* softly. "I can see where that would be the case. I wonder if Mr. Parham's prone to fits. Has your Eli mentioned anything, Olivia?"

"Never. And even though I don't spend much time in the bank, I've never known him to twitch or any such thing."

"I wonder if he's come down with some dysentery," Addie said. "I hope it's not something we have to deal with here in town. The children . . . well, it can be awfully dangerous to little ones."

"Not only to little ones," Mrs. Alton countered. "Dysentery can take anyone's life. It just depends on how sick a body gets. And it looks to me as though Mr. Parham is quite sick."

Doc Chambers glanced their way, a deep groove carved across his brow. "I'm afraid you're right. But it's not dysentery. At least not if it's what my examination's making me suspect. Something's gone mighty wrong here, and I need someone to go fetch Marshal Blair for me."

Gasps burst from the four women.

The men traded glances, shrugged shoulders, looked at the doctor once again.

"I'll go after the marshal," Josh Tucker said, heading toward the door. "What do you want me to tell him?"

The physician stood, his expression ever more troubled. Dread pooled in Faith's stomach, twisting and turning and sickening her when his gaze met hers. "I've been practicing medicine a long, long time," he said in a somber voice. "Ain't never seen this in all those years, even though I've read some on such cases when I trained back in Boston, and even a time or two in newspapers since then."

Her shoulders tightened, and Faith felt as though she had

to brace for a physical blow, almost the same sensation she'd often experienced during her marriage to Roger. Her pulse pounded through her body, beat loudly in her ears, made drawing breath a great challenge.

"What is it, Doc?" Olivia asked. "Do we have an epidemic in town? Do we have to guard the children?"

He paced back and forth in front of the prone body, the silence growing unbearable. Finally, he paused, shook his head.

"I don't reckon we have us an epidemic here, Livvy, but it wouldn't hurt to watch out for the children some—and watch for ourselves, while we're at it, too. Something's plumb wrong when a young man is poisoned in church on a Sunday morning."

# Chapter 12

"Poisoned!" Faith cried, dizziness making her falter. "How could that be? That food was fresh. Food poisoning only happens when food is spoiled."

Her words seemed to break through the dam of silence in the sanctuary. After her, all spoke at once, the questions tossed out in such a way as to eliminate any chance to understand. The men's deeper voices drowned out the women's higher ones, and Faith once again felt that odd sensation of separation from the moment she was living.

The doctor's gaze grew, if anything, more piercing at her words. "Why don't we wait until the marshal gets here before we take a stab at all this? I don't want us to have to go over what's happened more than once, not without him being here."

An icy chill ran through Faith when the doctor looked at her. He couldn't possibly think she . . . could he? In the face of Theo's accusations, Mr. Parham's apparent poisoning while in her company eating food she had prepared hardly helped her appear innocent. But she didn't know the doctor well enough to read his expression.

Perhaps that trial would happen sooner rather than later. She'd hoped it wouldn't happen at all.

Not another word was uttered in the wake of the doctor's comment, and the minutes seemed to stretch into hours... maybe days' worth of time. Faith wanted answers, she wanted them right then, and she wanted the marshal in the sanctuary so that she could extract those answers. Her life depended on those answers.

And still they had to wait.

She bit her bottom lip, shifted her weight from foot to foot, and laced and unlaced the fingers of one hand from those of the other. She glanced at her new friends, and to her dismay, saw her own concern etched on their faces, especially on Mrs. Alton's kind, motherly face. As she studied the older woman, Mrs. Alton turned her way, and their gazes met.

Instinct prodded Faith closer to the lady who'd taken her in.

Mrs. Alton met her partway, her arm wrapping again around Faith's waist. "'Fear thou not,'" the reverend's wife whispered, "'for I am with thee.'"

Faith had always believed that particular one of God's promises. That is, she had, but after all that had happened to her in the last three years, how could she still believe God was with her? How could she still believe He held her in the palm of His hand? How could she still trust that she mattered more to Him than that one sparrow fallen from its nest?

And yet... although she felt abandoned, she wasn't alone. Hadn't God provided her with Mrs. Alton, Olivia, and Addie, as well as Nathan Bartlett and Woody, in her time of need?

Was that how the Lord was showing her how much He really cared?

The sound of the church door opening cut into her thoughts. Marshal Blair walked in, followed by Mr. Tucker. As the door swung to close, it crashed open again, banging against the wall with a crack that ricocheted through the room as though it had been a gunshot.

Theo Nolan stormed in, rage on his round face. "Dinnent I tell you she was dangerous? Dinnent I tell ya, ya should've locked her up? I toldya she needed to hang for killin' my brother, but none of ya listened to me, didya?"

Faith's stomach heaved. Perhaps God wasn't on her side after all. Surely, if He was, He wouldn't have let her brother-in-law show up right then.

"Easy, Theo," Marshal Blair said, his voice even, his expression calm. "We don't know what we have us here, do we? All's I know is that Josh came after me, saying Lewis had taken sick at the church. How's that got a thing to do with your brother?"

"Lewis ain't got nothing to do with Roger," Theo said, "but she sure does. She's kilt both of them, sure as sure. Now what're ya gonna do about her?"

"For pity's sake, Theo Nolan," Doc Chalmers groused. "Who's said anything 'bout this feller pushing up daisies? Lewis ain't dead. He's feeling mighty puny, I'll give you that, but I'm praying he's past the worst of it. With a coupla weeks of rest and good nursing, I'm thinking he'll be right as frog's fur."

Faith glanced at Mr. Parham, who, as far as she could tell, hadn't moved since he'd last convulsed on the floor. "But—"

Mrs. Alton's arm tightened around her waist. "Shh..."

She clamped down on her tongue before another sound could escape. The reverend's wife was right. The less Faith said, the better off she would be. No one seemed ready to pin Mr. Parham's misfortune on her other than Theo, and so far, no one seemed too ready to give his wild statements much credit.

"What exactly did happen, Mrs. Nolan?" Nathan said.

His return to the use of the more formal title didn't escape Faith's notice. Neither did his serious expression. The slight sense of relief she'd begun to experience vanished. How could Nathan be the one who looked at her with suspicion? He knew her a bit better than the others did. How could he suddenly doubt her?

On the other hand, the man on the floor did pose an obstacle to belief in her.

She shook off her emotional response. Mr. Bartlett was no one to her, she reminded herself. He was only a former customer who'd shown her kindness during those times when they'd done business, and then after Roger's death. She had to steel herself against trusting anyone, especially a man. Even one as appealing as Mr. Nathan Bartlett. Perhaps God had led him to ask the question to open Faith's eyes to reality.

She squared her shoulders and related to the marshal every detail she could remember. When she was done, the silence in the sanctuary felt thick and suffocating. Marshal Blair rubbed his chin with a long, blunt finger, his gaze straying toward Mr. Parham a time or two.

As Faith felt certain she would go mad with the growing anxiety inside her, the patient let out a groan. That galvanized Doc Chambers into action. He dropped down onto one knee and closed his satchel. "It's time to get this fella to a proper bed—his bed. I hear he's taken a room in Widow O'Dell's house. Is that right, Eli?"

"You know what goes on in this town better than I do," the bank president said. "But as far as I've heard, yes, Lewis does rent Mrs. O'Dell's extra room."

The men planned the transfer of the patient as though it were a military maneuver. Josh Tucker ran out in search of a board from one of the buildings under construction a short way down Main Street. The others propped Mr. Parham into a seated position, supporting him on both sides to keep his unsteady body from flopping back onto the floor. Faith's nerves felt stretched to the breaking point, but there wasn't much she could do.

Before long, Mr. Tucker was back with his board. The gentlemen wrapped the long slab of wood with one of the tablecloths, and then laid the support on another cloth. Finally, with great patience and care, they helped the bank secretary down onto the makeshift litter.

The men headed out with the patient, and the women stayed behind to clean up the debris from the church's by now mostly forgotten social event. They parted ways when they'd eliminated all evidence of the ill-fated meal. Regrettably, the memories wouldn't fade that easily for Faith.

Neither would the memory of the odd look Nathan sent her way as he'd left the church. She couldn't be sure what had been behind it, but she did know one thing. He harbored questions about her. He didn't trust what she'd said.

She feared he might be succumbing to Theo's wild accusations.

And the inexplicable happenings around her.

He might have begun to suspect her, to think she might be guilty.

To think she might have killed Roger Nolan after all.

Nathan hadn't wanted to believe a single one of Theo's accusations. He hadn't thought a woman as gentle, hardworking, and appealing as Faith Nolan could be capable of such a heinous crime. Had he been foolish in his desire to believe her?

It would seem so.

Why on earth else would Lewis Parham collapse during that box lunch auction? Was there something truly sick and evil about Faith Nolan? And if so, then what? While one could almost understand a woman who had suffered as much as she had turning on her attacker, one couldn't grasp why she might ever do anything to harm a stranger.

Why would she wish to poison the bank secretary?

He had seen what some people were capable of during his years at war, even those who in other circumstances would appear to be the soul of innocence. But the war was past, and there was no acceptable reason for the kind of viciousness it would take to harm either Roger or Lewis. He couldn't abide the evil in the soul of one who might be guilty of such actions.

He couldn't excuse the one who'd done it.

But . . . had Faith turned on Roger? Had she actually killed her husband? Had she then set the building on fire to hide her crime?

It made no sense for her to destroy her source of income, her home.

What about Lewis Parham? What could she possibly have against the man? Or was it a matter of the bank secretary knowing something about her? About Roger *and* her?

If so, what did the man know?

Hours after they'd taken the ailing secretary to his room at Widow O'Dell's place, Nathan had been unable to relax. He'd paced the Whitmans' parlor for long minutes, but felt too much like a caged mountain cat, so he'd stepped out onto Main Street to continue his attempt to exercise away his nervous energy. In the cold night air, he strode up to one end of town, where the train station was being built for the railroad spur line. The stacks of wood on the road and the skeleton of the building took on eerie shapes in the shadows cast by the moonlight. In the dark, one could imagine another's evil intent.

Aware of how fanciful and silly his thoughts had become, Nathan turned and headed back in the direction he'd come . . . and kept going to the far edge of town, his thoughts no clearer for the additional walk. There, he stopped in front of the newest emporium in town. It was a sure sign of the town's growth that Bountiful could now boast of a nearly finished saloon, not a place he ever expected to patronize.

"Need an ear?" Eli said from behind.

Nathan spun. "You're lucky I no longer carry a weapon."

Eli shrugged. "The war's over. And I know how you feel about weapons and fighting and killing, and all. Didn't have a worry about it in my mind."

"I'm that predictable?"

The bank president laughed. "I wouldn't call you predictable, my friend, but rather a man I know fairly well."

He nodded slowly. "Fair enough." He slipped his hands into his pockets. "Anything you needed?"

"No. Just realized you'd left the house, and I thought you might appreciate a friendly ear. I watched you today at the church. What happened there hit you hard, didn't it?"

Instead of answering, he asked a question of his own. "Have you spoken with Doc Chambers since we left Parham in his room?"

"He stopped by a short while after you left to march up and down the street. I'm surprised you missed him."

Once again, Nathan chose to ignore his friend's comment on his actions. "What did Doc have to say?"

"That Lewis doesn't know how he could have swallowed the rat poison."

"Rat poison?"

"Exactly."

"Easy enough to find the stuff just about anywhere."

"Sure. Metcalf's Mercantile has boxes and boxes of the stuff on the shelf, and has sold even more of it since they opened their doors for business years ago."

"As I suspect the Nolan Brothers' General Store must have done as well."

Eli shot him a questioning look. "Surely you've bought your own box or two. I'm certain you've had rodents out at the camp." When Nathan didn't respond, he went on. "Don't tell me you've begun to believe Theo's foolishness."

Nathan shrugged. "I don't want to believe a word he's said."

"But...?"

"But I can't set aside reality. Her husband's dead, and now the man who shared a meal with her has turned up poisoned. What would have happened if Doc Chambers hadn't been there? What if instead of vomiting, Lewis had continued to convulse, his stomach full of the poison? I'm sure you know the answer to that."

"I know he could have died. That doesn't mean Faith is guilty of anything."

"Lewis was eating the meal she prepared."

"So was she, and she's not had a fit of any sort yet. Or do you think she was in the frame of mind to kill herself? She couldn't have known who would buy her box lunch."

He ran a hand through his hair, looked up and down the street, glanced at his friend again, but couldn't bear to hold that earnest stare. He focused on the packed dirt road surface. "I don't know what to think. I only know what I saw."

"And not just today, right?" Eli waited, but Nathan only shrugged. His friend continued when Nathan didn't speak. "You can't get past the war in some ways, can you?"

"You wouldn't be able to either if you'd seen what I saw."

"I'm not challenging you, but rather stating a fact, one I think is clouding the way you see the world around you. And it may be leading you to come to wrong conclusions."

"Are you saying that you can be certain Faith had nothing to do with Roger Nolan's death? Even after the man subjected her to unspeakable cruelty for three years?"

Eli took a moment to weigh Nathan's words. "Yes, I think I am saying that. I don't think Faith Nolan is capable of hurting anyone."

A spark of something light began to flicker in Nathan, but he didn't let it burn. "So the poison Lewis swallowed . . . appeared inside the fellow. All on its own."

"I didn't say that." Eli waited for Nathan to meet his gaze. "Has it occurred to you that it might have been meant for her? And not placed there by her own hand?"

Nathan felt as though instead of words Eli had thrown a punch at his gut. It took him a handful of minutes to sort through the possibilities. "I suppose that could be the case, but it strikes me as far-fetched. Why would anyone try to poison her? Why her?"

"I couldn't begin to tell you. It's a different possibility I felt you hadn't considered. Had you?"

"No, I hadn't, but the fact that I'm considering it now doesn't mean I think it's likely. I need a reason for her to be poisoned."

"You also need a reason for her to poison a stranger."

Nathan couldn't argue that point. But he also couldn't deny the events of the afternoon. And he refused to be taken in by a pretty lady in a bad set of circumstances. He had to make sure he knew what had happened. "Someone put poison in that food."

"How were they going to know what portion Lewis would eat and what portion Faith would serve herself?"

"You're making my point, Eli. She's the one who would have known what to serve herself."

"But even if she had something against Parham, which seems unlikely, she couldn't possibly have known he would win the auction."

Nathan stared at his friend for a long moment.

"I think it's time to head home and to bed," Eli said at last. "Things usually look clearer in the light of day, *after* a good night's sleep."

While Nathan didn't see how this would look much better simply because he'd slept, he didn't feel like arguing any further with his friend. And he suspected the puzzle was one he wasn't going to be able to solve on his own. No one would be able to solve it by virtue of willing it. From where he stood, it seemed only One could see clearly through the many possibilities.

Only God was in the position to know a person's heart.

Only God could know the guilty party's reason.

Only God knew why.

Only He knew who.

Olivia's, Addie's, and Mrs. Alton's encouragement and support made but a small dent in Faith's anxiety.

"I saw the looks those men gave me," she said when the four of them stood inside the Altons' entry foyer. "I understand you want to comfort me, but no matter what all of you say, I doubt your husbands will soon become anywhere near as sympathetic as you are."

"No, my dear," Mrs. Alton said. "You have it all wrong. My husband is a most understanding man. That ability to put himself in other folks' shoes is what has made him such an excellent shepherd all these long years."

"I'm sure that's the case in normal circumstances," Faith countered. "Let me remind you that this is anything but a normal circumstance. Theo is sure I murdered Roger—you heard him yourself. I know that the way things happened makes it look worse for me than it otherwise would. Seeing as I can't prove I did nothing of the sort, your husband isn't going to be particularly sympathetic toward someone who looks as much like a killer as I do."

"Give the men a chance," Olivia urged. "They can't possibly be such fools as to listen to someone like Theo or ignore what's before their noses. What did you pack in that box lunch, Faith? Did you put anything in there that could have harmed someone?"

"Of course not! I only packed wholesome food. Besides, I also ate some of the lamb, the bread, even the cheese and the apple. True, it only added up to a handful of small bites, but I did have some of that food."

"The reverend and I ate the same things, as well. You and I packed the box lunches together, if you'll remember."

"See?" Olivia said, triumph in her voice. "You shared the same things others might think were tainted. What madwoman would risk her own life that way? Or Reverend Alton's? Or Mrs. Alton's, either?"

Faith donned a crooked, wry smile. "You said it yourself. A madwoman, that's who."

"Are you mad, then?"

"No, but is there any reason to believe they don't think I'm that unstable?"

"They're not stupid," the bank president's wife said. "And they're going to see that truth soon enough."

Faith shook her head. "Soon enough? I would hope so, but I'm not nearly as sure as you seem to be. Besides, I doubt it'll make a difference, seeing how things stand. We are waiting for a judge from Portland, remember?"

"That may be the best thing in the end," Addie said. "A judge will make sure all sides are presented and considered fairly."

Faith remained unconvinced, but she was too exhausted to continue the discussion. "I suppose I have no choice but to wait for them to act."

"Act?" Olivia's eyes narrowed. "What are you afraid they might do?"

Faith opted for a touch of humor—dark, true, but humor nonetheless. "Run me out of town on the newly laid rails is one possibility that comes to mind."

"Bah!" Addie joined Olivia, presenting a united front. "They're no ogres, and you'll soon see that. They're good men."

"I have no doubt they are," Faith said. "That's why I don't think they can put themselves in my shoes. They've heard over and over again from Theo how I've done the unthinkable. With that thought in their minds, I doubt they can see me for who I am. They certainly won't understand my horror at the thought of hurting another being, and that's human as well as animal. They don't know what I saw or felt when I returned home from town the day Mama and Papa were killed. They don't know me well enough."

When her three companions objected, Faith held up a hand. "You hardly know me either. Good sense alone says you should be at least a bit suspicious of a practical stranger. You know I haven't spent hardly any time in town since I wed Roger. And I'm a different woman from the girl who went to school here years ago. That's why I don't blame them. I don't understand how the three of you have decided to trust me after all that time I spent away from the life of the town."

Her words seemed to bring the three wives some soothing. It also had them declaring their complete trust in her, in spite of what had happened at the box lunch auction, in spite of everything else. And it allowed the four women to part on good terms. But it did nothing to ease the fury of Faith's troubling thoughts.

After all, what was she going to do next? Theo had no intention of letting the matter of Roger's untimely death fall by the wayside. He intended to extract his pound of flesh from her. He'd never liked her; why would he show her the slightest mercy now?

Mercy?

Oh, goodness. How silly of her. How could a man who had no understanding of God's gracious gift offer it to her in turn?

He couldn't.

And that was why she feared the future she faced would be bleak indeed.

The next afternoon, Faith made her way across the churchyard, a brimming pail full of hot water and slivered yellow soap in one hand, three thick cotton rags in the other. She'd persuaded Mrs. Alton to let her repay them for their hospitality by letting her clean the sanctuary. When her hostess had argued, saying it was her pleasure to have her company in the parsonage, Faith had insisted she needed something to do, if for no other reason than to keep from going wildly crazed thinking and fretting her hours away.

At that, understanding had dawned on Mrs. Alton, and she'd agreed.

When she reached the doors to the sanctuary, Faith set down the pail and used the heavy key the reverend's wife had given her. Once inside, she made her way down toward the altar, where she left her supplies to go search for the broom Mrs. Alton told her they stored in her husband's office.

Faith found the broom straight away, but she also found much to draw her attention away from her planned clean-up. Reverend Alton kept a tall pair of well stocked book-shelves behind his desk. They drew her like magnets did iron filings.

It had been a while since she'd indulged her love of read-ing. Roger hadn't put much stock in books, seeing as how he and Theo were barely literate, so Faith hadn't had much choice during her years of marriage. She'd never been al-lowed to order books in any of the many shipments she'd received while she ran the general store. The long drought had left her so thirsty for the written word she couldn't have kept herself from reaching out and running a respectful fin-ger up and down the spines of any number of the tomes ranging the shelves even if an angry rattler had sat atop them.

She pulled out a thick volume at random, and brought the book up close, wrapping her arms around it, hugging it to her heart. She drew in a deep breath, pleased by the famil-iar scent of paper, ink, and leather binding. It brought Mama and Papa to mind.

Tears in her eyes, she turned the book to see the title on the spine, but before she could read it, she heard a sound out in the main room of the church. Strange. She'd thought she'd closed the door behind her, and she hadn't expected company as she worked.

"Hello?" she called.

No one answered.

The silence, instead of reassuring her, made her uneasy. She set down the volume of Greek history on Reverend Alton's neat desk and, prayer on her lips, stepped back out into the large expanse of the sanctuary.

"Who's there?" she asked.

Once again, her question received no response. This time, her heart rate kicked up, and her nerves made her muscles tight. Her hands seized down and her shoulders stiffened. Determined not to let something as silly as a creaky floorboard get the better of her, she tipped up her chin and marched out toward the front doors.

Before she reached the entrance to the church, however, she found the source of the sounds. Inside the wide wooden doors sat a large basket covered with a piece of brown flannel. As she approached, the tiny golden head of a young pup, one barely old enough to have opened its eyes, shoved the fabric aside.

The pup and the basket couldn't have been there even ten minutes.

"Where did you come from?" she asked, unable to ignore the poor thing even though all her instincts urged her to run. "Who left you here?"

The young animal let out a sharp bark, the same squeaky sound she'd heard while in the reverend's office, and her heart melted. She dropped down to a crouch, making soft, soothing sounds, hoping to reassure the little fellow. Faith ran a finger over the puppy's head, and was thrilled when her caress was rewarded with a lick of the warm, raspy tongue.

Had someone known the Altons would make sure the puppy would find itself a good home? Faith had no doubt the reverend and his wife would never let the defenseless creature suffer, and she knew their congregation knew it as well. How she wished she were in a position to be the one to raise the young dog into a strong, loyal friend and companion. She certainly needed that kind of presence in her life.

But she had no means to do as her heart urged her to do. She sighed.

"You sweet thing," she said. "How could anyone abandon you here? I could never do that. Did they have no way to provide for you? They must have cared enough to bring you—"

Blinding pain struck her temple, cutting off her words. As darkness took over, Faith had only one thought.

*This was no accident.*

# Chapter 13

The by-now familiar pounding inside her head told Faith she was still alive. A third blow to her head. Surely this couldn't be good. Neither could it be passed off as a coincidence any longer. Someone had tried to—

Well, someone had tried to...*harm* her, and not only this time. In her heart of hearts she knew the episode with the runaway horse on Main Street had been meant to hurt her.

Maybe even...oh, goodness. Did she have to consider *that*? Had someone really tried to...to kill her?

Again?

Could it be?

Who was behind these attempts? Was it the same person who'd killed Roger? And why had they killed her husband? Why would they want to kill her? Who hated her that much? While she knew most folks in Bountiful, she didn't know any of them especially well. Surely not well enough to make someone want to kill her. Who wanted her out of their way so much as to risk being caught, attacking as they'd done in plain daylight?

The troubling thoughts whirled in Faith's throbbing head,

no answer coming to her as she considered all that had happened in her immediate past. A chilly gust of air raked icy fingers over her sprawled body, and she shuddered.

She blinked, and through the pain in her head took stock of her surroundings. She remembered coming to the entry foyer of the church, and from what she could see, she hadn't left...or been moved. Since that was the case, there shouldn't have been such a cold wind coming in. With a great deal of caution and all her strength she fought the queasiness and rose onto her elbows. Her surroundings turned hazy for a moment, and she blinked four or five more times to clear her vision.

The double doors she'd carefully closed when she'd arrived, and that had still been closed even after someone had dropped off the puppy—

The dog! Where was he?

Faith struggled to a sitting position. "Hey, little one. I'm still here. I didn't leave you..."

But when she forced her eyes to truly focus, she realized the basket was gone. A deeper sense of disorientation struck her, and she turned to look back toward the altar. She found no sign of the basket. Or the pup. Had she imagined it? Did she have the order of events correct in her fuzzy mind? Could she have dreamt the dog in the basket *after* she'd been struck?

"What on earth...?"

Someone *had* struck her. Of that, she remained certain. She hadn't fallen, hadn't hit herself against anything. She was certain she'd found a dog a few feet inside the door. She hadn't imagined it, hadn't dreamed it. Also, the walls on either side of the entrance area were at least four or five feet away to her left and her right. There was nothing in the church foyer she could have hit, even if she'd slipped and fallen.

Someone had indeed hit her.

Calling on all her strength, she rose to her knees, and then to her feet. Another wave of dizziness threatened to fell her again, but she fought to cling to her senses. Only when she felt able to stand without danger of falling did she slowly step toward the open doors. Even being so weak, she knew she had to close them. Whoever had hit her could return and finish the job she feared they'd started out to do.

She didn't think their goal had been to merely stun her. They'd likely left the pup in the church to distract her. Did they think she might identify them later? No. They didn't want her to call for help ... or fight back or run. The more she thought about it, and it being the third attempt on her life, she was now sure the goal had been—and still remained—to kill her. But then, why was she still alive?

Although she was prepared to go home to her heavenly Father whenever He called her to His side, she didn't want her departure from life to come about because of some criminal bent on doing away with her. At present, Faith didn't feel her time had come to see her Savior face to face.

After she locked the doors behind her with the key that had still been in her skirt pocket, she turned toward the front of the church and slowly approached. A few feet away from the altar, right where she'd left them, she found her cleaning supplies. The bucket of now-cold water sat in the same spot, and the pile of rags hadn't moved either. She made her way to Reverend Alton's office again, and found that door open, just as she'd left it when she'd gone to see what had made the sound in the sanctuary. She gasped.

"Goodness!"

The previously neat desk was no longer clear on top. A slurry of papers flooded the polished oak top, and poured off the right side and onto the floor. Faith stepped inside the room to approach the desk. But before she got there, she realized all the drawers had been pulled open. A couple had papers sticking out, clear proof, if any more was needed, that someone had ransacked the place.

While she stood, shocked by what had happened, Faith sensed she was no longer alone. She spun around. Reverend Alton stood in the doorway, a thunderous expression on his normally calm and pleasant face.

"What is the meaning of this?" he asked in a clipped, stern voice.

The blood draining from her face, Faith found she couldn't get words out past her tightened throat. "I—I . . ."

"Why would you do such a thing?" He ran a hand through his thinning gray hair. "My wife said you'd come to clean the sanctuary. There was nothing about rifling through my papers in that proposition."

Fear knotted her stomach, but righteous indignation gave her the strength to go on. "I . . . didn't do this. I did come to clean. Mrs. Alton said I'd find the broom here, and that's all I did—well, I did take a book on Greek history from one of your bookshelves, but that's it. I put it down on your desk when I heard the puppy crying out in the sanctuary. Oh!" She pointed. "See? There it is."

He blinked, clearly bewildered by her response. "A puppy? In the sanctuary? Oh, what am I talking about? You're saying you took the time out to read when you were supposed to clean? I don't understand."

Of course, he didn't. She'd lived through the events she'd enumerated, and she failed to understand. Still, she somehow had to make him see she hadn't done a single thing wrong.

"I can see where it's confusing," she said. "I'm confused, myself."

"Then please try to help me understand."

"Gladly, sir." Slowly, and with due attention to detail, Faith proceeded to describe her afternoon to Reverend Alton. He didn't interrupt, but even when she'd finished, she could tell she hadn't made any progress.

The silence lengthened. Then, without warning, the reverend let out an exclamation. "Oh, no!"

He hurried to the far side of the desk, pulled the deep bottom drawer all the way out, and then shook his head. "I'd hoped..."

Against her better judgment, Faith took a step forward. "What? What is it?"

When he looked up at her, his features were set in what seemed a deliberately mild and neutral expression, but the piercing look he sent her wasn't. It was clear he'd hardened his mind-set toward her. "The box where I always keep the offering is gone. It was especially full today, what with the money the ladies made on the auction. On Mondays, I make a deposit late in the afternoon, and of course, I hadn't done so yet."

What he didn't say, but made clear to Faith without a

word, was that he believed she'd done something with the box. She couldn't let him keep that wrong notion, however, so she tried to explain.

"I don't know who took it," she said. "Maybe it was whoever hit me in the head. If you care to check, I have a knot where they struck, and a throbbing headache."

"You were hit in the head. Again."

It wasn't a question. Faith could almost touch the skepticism in his voice, and she knew she couldn't blame him. Even she could scarcely believe it had happened. Yet again, as he'd said.

How could she expect anyone to believe *any* of it?

She sighed. "I suppose you must feel the same disbelief I do, sir. Probably more. As I tell you the details, they sound improbable, even to me, but I promise you, Reverend Alton. It all happened as I've told you. I don't have a better explanation because it's the only one. That is what happened. I can also assure you I *don't* have the box."

The reverend arched a brow. "Really, now, Mrs. Nolan. Does the box matter one bit?"

She knew what he meant. "I don't have the missing money, either."

"I see."

His expression remained neutral, but his voice again reflected what she could only term his disbelief. Before she could further defend herself, not that she thought a defense had even a remote chance to help, he continued.

"I must send for the marshal. The church has been robbed. It's a matter for him to investigate. We'll have to accept whatever he finds."

Faith took his words as a somewhat ominous warning. As if her life had had anything but ominous overtones lately.

But that didn't matter. The marshal did indeed need to be fetched. "Of course," she said. "I would also like to know who has been after me. After today's episode, I am convinced someone means for me to follow Roger into death."

Reverend Alton's gaze cut to her. His lips tightened, his eyes narrowed, but he didn't speak. In the silence, Faith's heartbeat clanged louder. She hated the vacuum of sound, but what could she do? What could she say?

She had to wait.

"I'm glad you agree, Mrs. Nolan. Allow me a moment. I'll stick my head out the door to see who might be passing by so I can send them to fetch Marshal Blair. Go ahead. Since you say you were hit, it likely makes sense for you to take a seat while I go."

"Thank you, but"—she couldn't, just couldn't, tell him she was afraid to stay alone, even in his office—"I'd rather follow you."

Again, his eyes narrowed as he studied her face. Then he nodded. "Suit yourself."

Faith hoped the marshal came quickly. Her nerves couldn't bear much more.

Nathan couldn't believe his ears. Not only had Faith Nolan been at the side of Lewis Parham when the poor fellow had been poisoned, but now it appeared she'd been at the church at the precise time when the full offering box had vanished. How would she try to explain this latest incident?

"You coming with me, then, Nathan?" Adam Blair asked him after the carpenter Reverend Alton had sent to fetch the lawman left the jail.

"Of course. All that has happened in the last few days seems to have been put into motion by Faith's—*Mrs. Nolan's* decision to bring my order up to my camp."

The lawman leaned back in the chair behind his desk and studied Nathan. The close scrutiny of those keen eyes made him feel as though Adam could read his every thought about Faith, even the ones that weren't especially negative. Nathan's cheeks warmed as the seconds ticked by.

When he feared he would lose his mind waiting, the marshal spoke again. "You really think it's about you?"

"Well, yes—er . . . no. Not exactly."

Adam crossed his arms, a hint of amusement on his mustachioed face. "Care to explain that to me?"

Nathan's cheeks burned hotter. "I think there's likely something in what she did that led to her husband being killed. Don't ask, seeing as I can't imagine what it might be. And I'm afraid that's the reason the cabin was burned down, the reason she was attacked at that same time."

"I can rightly see your reasoning behind that notion, but what does any of that have to do with the offering box at the church?"

He shrugged. "I don't know what one thing has to do with the other, but . . . well, it will sound crazy, but my gut tells me none of this is random. It can't be. How many coincidences can happen in a matter of days?"

"I agree. But why do you think it's someone who's done all this *to* Mrs. Nolan rather than Mrs. Nolan having done it all herself? I can't quite see my way clear to your kind of reckoning anymore."

Nathan ran a hand through his hair. "I've asked myself the same question more times than I can count, but I come back to the same thing each time. Why? Why would a reasonable lady act against her interests, killing her husband who provided for her, and burning down her home? She's homeless now, remember? She no longer has the mules she loves so much, she's under suspicion for any number of crimes, and now she goes and steals money from the church? That seems...well, if not mighty stupid, then at least foolish. Faith—*Mrs. Nolan* doesn't strike me as a stupid or foolish woman. But, I suppose I have to agree with you in a fashion. If not her, then who?"

The marshal shook his head, his grin broadening. "You sure you're not after proving her innocent 'cuz you're after marrying up with her? She's an awful pretty thing, ain't she?"

Again, Nathan feared his feelings were emblazoned across his face, but he steeled himself against the embarrassment. "No such thing, Adam. I'm grateful the lady helped me and my men a handful of times, especially that last shipment of food when we were dangerously low, and I do feel sorry for her. She suffered a great deal at Roger's hand. But none of that means I'm set on marrying. Not her or any other woman. Not right now. I have a flume I'm in the middle of building. Now that the general store is no more, I'm of a mind to open up my own company store for my camp and my men, seeing as how I'm going to have to do something to get supplies up the mountain. At the least that's going to mean I have to carve out a road from that forest. On top of all that, I have to cut enough lumber to sell to the mills west of here so I can pay my men. None of that leaves me room for courting or wedding a woman. From all I hear, sweethearts and wives take up a whole lot of a fellow's time."

The lawman smiled. "That there's an awful lot of words to tell me no. Have to wonder if you're arguing more against yourself than you're arguing against me."

To keep from saying anything further, Nathan turned to face the door. "Coming?"

Adam Blair laughed out loud. "Oh, I would think it's right fair to say I have no notion of missing any of this. Whatever 'this' might turn out to be."

Nathan faced his friend. "And that's supposed to mean . . . ?"

"That you're arguing too much, my friend, and you're much too interested in the lovely widow lady's fate."

"Does that mean you don't think she's guilty of all she stands accused of?"

Adam donned his hat and cinched his gun holster a notch tighter. "You'd'a asked me yesterday, I'd'a said, that's right. Now? Can't say as I know yet what I rightly think." The lawman shot him a sideways glance. "But if I had to take a guess, I'd have to follow my gut. It's telling me she's as innocent as you or me."

Nathan felt more conflicted than ever, relieved by Adam's words, but still faced with damning evidence against Faith. "Really, now. I have to wonder what leads you to that opinion. We've seen a lot against her."

"Experience." Adam walked outside and locked the jail behind him. "And instinct. Just like you." The marshal led the way down Main Street, the keys to the jail clinking against his gun. "Always known you to have solid, trustworthy in-stincts, and a good head about you. Doubt you'd ever be so sweet on a woman if she even had a chance of being prone to violence of any sort. And no matter what you tell me, Nathan, you're sweet on Faith. No shame in that, my friend. No shame at all."

Shocked, Nathan followed Adam to the church, not a word breaching his clamped-shut lips.

There was no truth to Adam's assertion. He wasn't sweet on Faith Nolan. He couldn't be.

Impossible.


*Oh, Lord . . . how did I ever reach this point?*

Although, mercifully, the marshal hadn't used handcuffs on her, nor had he pulled his gun, Faith knew all eyes in Bountiful were focused on her from behind doors and win-dow curtains as she was led to the town jail. She couldn't imagine a more shameful or mortifying experience.

Even if Marshal Blair had insisted she was not under arrest nor was he in the process of locking her up. True, it might not be his immediate intent, but Faith was certain by the time all was said and done she would find herself behind bars inside the ugly box of a building. After all, this time, even Reverend Alton believed she was guilty of theft.

And from the church, no less.

How wicked did a person have to be to do such a thing?

She didn't think she knew anyone that evil, not even Roger. Theo? No, not really. Not even the Nolan brothers could be that bad. But one had to know a body fairly well to know how sinful they might be.

How could she get these people to know her well enough to understand she wasn't capable of stealing from anyone, much less a church? She didn't know. She supposed it had to take time, time spent getting acquainted, time seeing how one acted in all kinds of situations.

Time she simply didn't have.

"Stop fretting," Mrs. Alton whispered at Faith's side. The older woman had bustled out of the parsonage when Marshal Blair had led Faith out of the church. "I promise you, it all will turn out fine. The Good Book promises us. Remember, my dear, that all things will work together to the good of those who love the Lord, to those who are called according to His purpose. And while that doesn't mean our lives will be a delightful walk through a garden of roses, it does mean that God is using all the horrid things that happen to our ultimate good, to help us become more Christlike."

Faith sighed, grateful for the lady's staunch belief in her innocence. "I know what Scripture says, but sometimes I feel I'd like to get a look, even from a distance, of that garden of roses you mention."

Mrs. Alton waggled a finger at her. "Ah, ah, ah—"

"But I also know how I feel. By that verse's measure, sometimes I reckon I must be coming close to Christlike by now." When Mrs. Alton's eyes widened, Faith gave her a wry smile. "I know, I know. It sounds almost blasphemous, but you don't know how dreadful it's all been."

At that, her stalwart friend relaxed. Tears glittered in her eyes. "I suppose," she said, "that if one were to look at your situation that way, it's easier to understand why you feel that way."

"I'm exhausted."

"That I don't doubt."

There didn't seem to be more to say, so the women continued in companionable silence.

But when they reached the jail, there was nothing companionable about the atmosphere there. Along the way, they'd walked past the River Run Hotel. As usual, Theo had been ensconced in one of the rockers, his pal Hector Swope at his side in the other. No sooner had her brother-in-law laid eyes on her in the company of the marshal than he had joined their small party. Like before, he'd advocated for her immediate imprisonment.

"Been tellin' all of ya . . ." he said. Over and over and over again until they reached the jail.

Inside Marshal Blair's office, all eyes turned on her. Faith steeled herself against the scrutiny. She refused to speak, to give the appearance of any need to defend herself. If they were going to accuse her, well, it would be their choice. She wouldn't give them the opening to start. She squared her shoulders and stiffened her spine.

"Let's see here, Missus Nolan," the marshal said. "It seems trouble's following you mighty close, doesn't it? I know you've already given me an idea of what happened today, but I suggest we hear the whole story all over again. You might could recollect something you forgot earlier."

Faith drew a long breath. She went over the events of the day with the same patience and detail as she had done twice before already. At the end of her retelling, the men remained silent, staring at her.

Every one of them, that is, except Theo Nolan. "See?" he

crowed. "I done nothing but tell ya she's the one what kilt Roger. Then she tried to kill that other feller yesterday. I tell ya, she's always been big on sprinkling rat poison here, there, and everywhere. Always sayin' foodstuff in the store drew in rats like not much else. Never seen such a one fer sweepin' an' washin' and fussin' 'bout dirt and stuff all the time. That's one more reason she's the one." He shook his head.

The marshal leaned forward, listening intently.

Reverend Alton's jaw jutted, and his eyes displayed disapproval.

His wife drew closer to Faith.

Faith shook inside, but fought to not let it show.

Mr. Bartlett raised a brow, glanced from Marshal Blair to Theo to Faith and back to her brother-in-law, his expression quizzical and intent.

No one spoke. No one but Theo, of course. "Now," he continued, "she's gone and stole the church's money. Ya cain't deny she's a bad one, Marshal. Ya gotta lock her up before she does worse."

The lawman seemed reluctant to speak, so the silence drew out. When Faith was about to defend herself, Reverend Alton shuffled his feet and spoke out.

"I must admit, folks, I didn't want to believe ill of Mrs. Nolan. Not when she first came to us, you understand." He gave her an apologetic nod, then glanced at Theo, before turning back to Marshal Blair. "But when odd things start to happen all of a sudden, and the only element that always remains the same is one person, why...a conscientious man can't continue to deny what he sees."

"Why, Jeremiah Alton!" His wife's usually sweet, gentle

face donned a thunderous expression. "I'd best not be hearing you cast a stone in this dear child's direction."

"I can't simply indulge you this time, dear." His jaw, in turn, set in a firm line. "I don't know what's happened, but enough has that I have to doubt Mrs. Nolan's innocence on all these many counts. I suggest it's best for the marshal to handle this matter from here on in."

She shook her head. "But—"

A serious husbandly look silenced Faith's defender.

Her knees weakened and a shudder ripped through her. An overwhelming wave of fear swirled up and around her.

*Fear thou not, for I am with thee...*

As the Scripture verse bubbled into her memory, Faith began to pray silently. To wait upon the Lord. And to wait for the men to make up their minds.

The first one to speak came close to breaking what last little speck of heart she had left. Nathan stepped up to the marshal's desk.

"I have to agree." His voice rang out with regret even Faith could hear. "I've leaned more toward trusting Faith— Mrs. Nolan—from the start, but too much has happened by now. I can't let this last go without insisting on the law stepping in. Either she is guilty of these crimes, or she is a victim of them. Either way, it seems it is safest for all, Mrs. Nolan included, if she remains in the jail. A judge is on his way, and it's best to let him see this through to the end."

Mr. Whitman, who'd hurried into the jail mere moments earlier, clapped a hand on his partner's shoulder. "I know how fond Olivia's grown of Mrs. Nolan, Nathan, and I don't know how I'm going to tell her what's happened. But I can't say I'm comfortable leaving her free after a robbery at the church, since she was the only one there when the box went missing. Then, too, she's been hurt again. She must be kept safe from any more attacks . . . incidents—accidents perhaps— no matter what." He shook his head. "Don't know what's in Bountiful's best interests. Or hers. All I know is these things that have happened do call for a complete investigation. For everyone's sake."

Tears burned her eyes. She felt as though a fist were squeezing her chest, breathing had become such a challenge.

"Dunno why ya've not listened to me," Theo said. "I've been right all along. Who knows what else she's likely to do, if ya go on letting her loose."

"Ridiculous!" Mrs. Alton exclaimed. "Jeremiah Alton, I suggest you get yourself off to Folsom's River Run Hotel tonight. You'll be needing a place to rest your head. I'm so angry, I'd much rather not argue with you right down to the wee hours of dawn."

With that, the lady marched out of the office, her abundant maroon sateen skirts swishing with her every step. She slammed the door for punctuation.

Faith felt weak, shaky, and without anywhere to sit she began to sink to the floor.

As she went down, Nathan caught her. Her gaze, previously blurred with tears, cleared as she stared into his eyes. He didn't flinch, and stared right back, his gaze questioning but no longer warm, kind. The moment stretched in awkward, charged silence.

Through the flannel of her gray dress, Faith felt the warmth of Nathan's arm around her back, his strength as he supported her, his growing righteous rage as he stared at a woman he feared capable of such heinous crimes.

That thought gave her the strength to right herself. She was innocent.

Faith took a step away from the logger and closer to her jailer. "I'm ready to face whatever I must, Marshal Blair. I know what I've done, and what I haven't, and I'm determined to prove myself incapable of any of these dreadful charges. I am also ready to trust my Lord to see me through. How soon will that judge of yours arrive? I cannot wait to put an end to this madness."

# Chapter 14

Two horrid days later, Faith wondered what could possibly have possessed her to accept being locked behind bars so easily. Especially since she hadn't done anything to warrant imprisonment.

Nevertheless, rough brick walls chinked together with lumpy mortar surrounded her. Against the far wall, the marshal had set a narrow cot with a thin mattress that gave off a musty scent. It offered scant comfort, seeing as it was stuffed with either straw or hay or corn husks. The ticking itself was dingy, and she cringed any time she had to let it touch her skin. The boards on the wooden floor hadn't been put in too well, and wide gaps had grown on either side of each wobbly one. Iron bars covered the single window, and precious little light ever stole in, even during the daytime hours.

The worst indignity, however, was the chipped and discolored enamel chamber pot the jail provided to each cell, sitting right out in the open. Faith cringed whenever her body demanded she surrender her self-respect and put the disgusting thing to use.

She'd asked for a Bible, but had been denied due to the jail's utter lack of reading material.

"You're the only prisoner who's ever asked, ma'am," Marshal Blair had told her, a touch embarrassed by his need to turn her down.

As soon as Mrs. Alton came to visit, however, a tasty meal in hand, Faith repeated her request.

"What do you mean, he didn't find you a Bible?" the reverend's wife asked, aghast. "That was a most reasonable request, Faith, my dear. How could Adam do such a thing? Him a Christian fellow, and all."

Faith experienced a momentary pang of sympathy for the marshal, who was about to feel the exquisitely polite wrath of the righteous lady. "He mentioned I was the first prisoner to ask for anything to read, and in particular for the Good Book."

She shook her head, her lips pursed and her brows drawn close together. "Well! I do declare."

"Don't be too hard on him, Mrs. Alton," Faith said, her sympathy growing. "I'm sure he was doing his job."

"Hmph!" She clapped her hands together. "And none too well, I'll say. We'll see about providing all the prisoners with a copy of the Father's Word from now on. That'll be the Bible Society's newest missionary outreach, and here in our own backyard."

True to form, the reverend's wife marched out of the jail after she gave Marshal Blair an earful, and less than a half hour later, she returned with a lovely leather-bound copy of the Good Book in hand, one Faith suspected had come directly from the reverend's office. She didn't want to think how the man would feel about the woman he believed had stolen from him and his congregation winding up with his book. Perhaps he'd see it as ministering to a sinner who needed God.

"You do know you could go into my room for my own Bible," Faith said.

"This was much quicker than rummaging through your things."

Nothing she said had dissuaded Mrs. Alton, and after the lady left, Faith spent hours reading, soaking her bruised heart in the Father's love.

The slow-moving time in jail had also provided her with a great number of hours to think. While she knew, without any doubt, that she hadn't done a thing to put Mr. Parham's life at risk, nor had she taken a penny of the church's money, much less the collection box full of the Bible Society's funds, she had begun to question her memories of the night when Roger had died.

Then, when Olivia came to visit, the two women went through Faith's memories over and over again.

"Tell me one more time what you know—know for absolutely sure—happened the night your husband died," Olivia requested.

As her anxiety sharpened again, Faith paced the narrow cell. "It all began when I went against Roger's wishes that morning, and took Nathan's supplies to the camp."

Each time the two friends shredded the meat off the bones of an event, Olivia would give the details a different turn under the light of scrutiny. And, as had happened each time they'd talked about the relevant parts of the last few weeks,

Olivia again gave careful consideration to Faith's words, and soon enough came up with yet one more new question.

"I don't believe you've told me exactly why you felt you yourself had to take the order up the mountain," Olivia said. "I would think it's more a job for a man than for his wife. Besides, you know as well as I do that there were two perfectly able-bodied Nolan brothers who could have—and should have—done the job themselves."

Faith shrugged. "Roger wasn't especially meticulous about carrying out his duty to his customers. This was at least the second or maybe third time that Nathan's order disappeared after Roger and Theo brought it to the store from Bountiful but before Nathan came after his supplies."

"Disappeared?"

"I don't know what else to call it." Faith's frustration with Roger had yet to dissipate, in spite of his untimely demise and the time gone by. "One moment everything was stacked neatly in the back storage room, and the next it was gone. I never saw where it went. I never even knew if someone picked it up while I was...oh, busy with the laundry or baking or seeing to the animals in the barn."

"Do you think Roger might have taken it on his own? Did he ask Theo to deliver it? Or perhaps, as you said, someone did come for it and you simply didn't realize it."

Faith took the time to consider the possibilities. "Now I think about it, I don't think so. I always took care of the mules, so I knew each time he took them anywhere, and during the three years of my marriage, Theo never had anything to do with them. Goodness, the whole town knows Theo spends almost all his time down here in Bountiful, far too busy loitering to do any work around the general store."

"Very well, then. I suppose we can rest assured he didn't take those orders anywhere." She thought for a moment. Then her expression grew alarmed. "Don't tell me Roger charged Nathan more than once for those missing shipments."

"Oh, no. Roger wasn't stupid enough to try anything like that. He just didn't have any scruples about the timely delivery of a complete order."

When Faith sat back down on the nasty cot, Olivia stood and paced a bit herself. "So you're saying the supplies Nathan ordered disappeared more than once. What happened the next time you realized they were gone?"

"I didn't know any more than that I'd helped store the supplies in the back room, but then, when I had to fetch something from the back, his order was no longer there."

"What did you do?"

"Nothing. Roger had been listening. He came into the store, and took over. Sent me to see to supper."

"But you'd been running the store when Nathan arrived."

"That's right. I was there when he arrived, serving a customer. One of his new hired men had come to lay in what he needed for the winter up at the camp." She shrugged. "Roger gave Nathan a silly answer, but as soon as he left, Roger did put in a new order to replace what had disappeared."

"I see..."

Faith let out a burst of breath. "If that's the case, my friend...why, I must say, you see far more than I do."

Olivia grimaced. "I'm sorry. I used that phrase more as a

simple comment. I have to agree. I don't see too clearly, either."

Faith's frustration gained yet another head of steam. "Yes, Olivia, I understand very, very little of what's happened so far. All I can tell you is that I made up my mind to get the camp's replacement supplies up to the men the moment they arrived, no matter how or why they disappeared."

Her friend's expression turned thoughtful again. A few moments later, she asked another of her incisive questions. "Do you suppose Roger sold them?"

"Of course, it's possible. Nathan paid when he ordered, so Roger had the cash to get the supplies. He hated giving credit but didn't mind receiving it from suppliers. Cash was always tight. Someone else might have offered to pay more to get the same supplies without waiting on an order, seeing as how it takes a while to get shipments into Bountiful and then to the store. But I don't know who that might have been."

"That's an interesting possibility. Have you mentioned it to Adam?"

"I haven't thought much about the fate of the order. I should say something, I suppose."

"Indeed." Olivia propped her elbows on her knees as she leaned forward, closer to Faith, her chin on her laced hands. "One might wager that's the explanation to that odd disappearance—I just am not the wagering kind."

Faith chuckled. "I'm not either, but you're likely right. At that moment, though, it didn't occur to me. I didn't want to give Roger any opportunity to . . . 'disappear' Nathan's order again."

A smiling Olivia sat up and clapped. "Good for you!"

Faith waved the cheer away. "Oh, I don't know about that. It's just what I did."

Leaning against the odious bars, she rubbed her forehead, working hard to remember even the slightest of details, since anything had the potential to help clear the cloud of mystery that surrounded those days. "As I said, once the replacement supplies arrived, Roger and I stacked them in the back, as always. Then I watched and waited—not for long, mind you—until he was again...well, indisposed—"

Olivia scoffed. "Oh, piffle! Call it what it is. The man was drunk, Faith. Repulsively full of spirits, is what your husband was."

Faith couldn't stop the chuckle. "Very well. I waited until Roger was snoring away late into the morning after he'd had too much to drink. I loaded the mules, and the four of us hurried up the mountain."

"You went back down after Nate's men unpacked the mules?"

"That's right. That's exactly what I did."

"What did Roger do when you returned to the cabin?"

"Nothing right away. He was...um...busy with some men who'd come to see him."

"Busy?" Olivia narrowed her eyes.

Faith shrugged.

"You said men? What men? Who were they? Were they customers placing orders? Or...well, I don't know. What were they doing with Roger?"

Faith laughed without much humor. "They were drinking. Again. Nothing more than that, certainly not from what I could see. It seems that's all Roger and Theo ever did with any regularity."

"Goodness. That man did like his liquor, didn't he?" Olivia shook her head in what seemed to Faith like growing horror. "You're telling me he overslept because he'd had too much to drink, and then, by the time you returned from making a delivery he was too drunk to make, he was drinking again? I can't quite take in such a thing."

"Do try to imagine it, please, because it happened too many times."

"Did he say anything when he realized you'd returned?"

"Oh, yes." She shuddered. "He said we'd 'discuss' what I'd done later, after his guests were gone."

Olivia grimaced. "I'm sure you knew what he meant."

Faith saw no need to respond.

"How long did they stay? What did you do while they were there?"

"The same thing I did whenever things became too dreadful in the house. I went to the barn, and spent the time with my mules."

Olivia stood. "Oh, you poor dear!" She hurried to Faith's side. "You didn't spend the whole, cold night out there, now, did you? How perfectly dreadful."

"If I had spent the night with the animals, it wouldn't have been the first time, nor would it have been the worst thing to happen. The worst usually came later, when Roger let loose his temper."

Olivia covered her lips to try and muffle her gasp. It didn't work.

Then she reached out and embraced her friend.

"Don't, please. Don't let it upset you." Faith stepped back and squeezed her friend's hand. "It was dreadful, yes, but well before I took the first step up the mountain, I knew what would come once I returned."

"Even knowing, you went ahead with your plans?"

"I did what I had to do, what I knew the Lord expected from me."

Olivia nodded, kindness and understanding in her expression. Then, to Faith's surprise, her expression changed, this time to disgust.

"Bah!" she said, turning to pace a few steps in the other direction. "I'll never understand men. How those silly creatures can think you would hurt, much less kill, that fool Roger . . . well, it's not something I can fathom."

"Don't be too harsh with them. Even I can't be sure what happened."

Olivia crossed her arms. "You were unconscious. How could you do anything, lying down?"

"I can't be sure about what went on. Clearly, someone struck Roger in the head. They . . . they killed him. Then they set the store on fire. But I have no idea who might have arrived while I lay unconscious. How could I know? All I know for certain is that he was killed. I didn't witness the killing. And then, the cabin was in flames when I opened my eyes. Of that I'm sure. But I don't know who did it . . . and I want to know. Believe me, I *need* to know." Again, she rubbed her forehead, which by now throbbed mightily. "I might not remember because of the blow to my head, you know."

"Who do you *think* could have done it?"

Faith sighed. "I reckon just about anyone. Roger was no

one's favorite." She glanced down. The pain she suffered when she saw the truth of the man she'd married returned. "He never became mine."

"Pffft!" Olivia waved. "What about the church money?"

When Faith couldn't answer on account of her tight throat, Olivia shook her head. "Oh, never you mind. I reckon that's the same situation as with what happened in the cabin, since you were hit. That knot on your head and the blood in your hair...I hear it was plenty hard to miss." She gave a disdainful sniff. "How absurd to think you could be as honorable and decent as to deliver Nate's supplies when you knew—*knew*, mind you—that Roger would... would pummel you for it later, and yet steal the princely sum of twenty-four dollars and seventy-three cents from the church."

Faith couldn't help but laugh at Olivia's indignation. "Put that way, it does sound silly, doesn't it?"

"Silly?" Her friend stomped her black-booted foot, then resumed her pacing. "It's far worse than silly, Faith. It's purely ludicrous for these men to even waste a thought on such a stupid notion."

Aware that she was arguing against herself, Faith had to be honest. "You must accept reality. I can't explain much to anyone's satisfaction."

Olivia halted her agitated march. "What do you mean?"

"We can't get away from the truth. I was the only person in the cabin with Roger, and there's nothing I can say about how he died and how the cabin caught fire. Same thing with the cash box at the church."

"Crazy. Plumb crazy, Faith Nolan." Olivia shook her head.

"Are you trying to tell me you lost consciousness, and while you were unconscious you up and killed that brute—forgive me, I know he was your husband, but he was a brute—and then took kerosene and a match to your home? You could do this while you were still unconscious?"

"We-ell..."

"Well, nothing. That's pure absurdity, Faith Nolan."

"The way you describe it does sound ridiculous, but I can't be absolutely certain I didn't do those...those dreadful things before I hit my head. I might not be able to remember on account of the injury. That I do know happened, because I bled enough out the back of my head to outrage Woody up at the camp."

Olivia tilted her head and studied Faith. "Why don't you tell me a mite more about that quarrel, as you like to call it? Tell me each last, bitty thing you can recollect about the fire-place poker."

Faith told Olivia how Roger had made them wait in the sitting room in that awkward silence. She described how they'd waited until he was certain Theo had gone far enough down the mountain trail to not hear what was about to happen back at the cabin. She told her friend how Roger had scolded her, how he'd raged at her, and she told her friend how she'd eventually stood, fed up with Roger and his unreasonable anger, and begun to resist.

"I do recollect reaching for the fireplace iron as clearly as if I'd done it a minute ago," she said. "And I remember Roger grabbing the other end. We each tugged, back and forth a few times. And then I tripped."

"Tripped, huh?" Olivia's expression turned speculative.

"Did you *really* trip? All on your own? Or did Roger push you?"

"No matter how hard I try, I can't bring back a single clear memory of that particular moment." She shook her head. "He might have. I do know I fell. I also remember the horrid sensation of the world dropping away from me, and the darkness that swallowed me immediately after that."

"Did you have the poker in your hand when you came back to?"

Faith thought and thought, but eventually had to shake her head again. "I have no recollection of the poker after I fell, so I don't think I did."

Olivia tried again. "Do you think he might have taken it or do you think you dropped it in the fall?"

She shrugged. "I don't know . . . I can't remember."

"It's madness to suggest you might have done anything wrong, much less criminal."

"Well, then," Faith said, challenge in her voice. "If you're so certain it wasn't me, then pray tell, who?"

They considered a list of names.

"There's always Theo," Olivia said. "You've said they always argued."

"True, but he still cared for his brother. You can see it even now. He's grieving, if in his own odd way."

Olivia thought for a bit. "How about those Army fellows? You said the captain and others, too, were there that night. One of them, maybe?"

"I must ask you the biggest question, then. Why? Why would any of them kill my husband? They all got along, and he entertained them. They wouldn't have wanted to put an end to those times."

"How about the other customers? You said sheep farmers shopped there, too." She raised her eyebrows and jabbed a finger in the air toward her friend. "Aha! The Indians. Didn't you say they shopped there from time to time? That laggards still stopped by? Did any of them especially like Roger?"

Faith shrugged. "I wouldn't say any of them especially *liked* Roger, but I also can't say any of them loathed him enough to kill him."

"Oh, for goodness' sake," Olivia burst out. "I don't know who killed that man, but you certainly didn't do it while laid out cold on that floor, bleeding out the back of your head, and all."

After Olivia's pronouncement, Faith couldn't persuade her friend to even entertain the possibility of her guilt. On the one hand, Olivia's staunch defense was gratifying. On the other, she hoped the men wouldn't think the two of them had come up with a story to excuse criminal acts simply because they'd become friends. They parted shortly after that, with Olivia's final words hanging between them.

"Your name . . . let it be as a reminder to you." Her friend's eyes twinkled. "Have faith in our Father. You're always in His loving care. Have faith."

"I've been here long enough," Nathan told Eli and Olivia as Cooky cleared the supper table that night. Eli had dismissed the children, who'd argued, making clear they should be allowed to stay up with "Uncle" Nate. "I must be getting back to the camp. I am the one responsible there."

Eli arched a brow. "You're telling me you're prepared to leave town before the judge gets here? Before the trial? Before we learn Mrs. Nolan's fate?"

A sick sensation swam in Nathan's middle, especially uncomfortable after, if unrelated to, supper. "I don't want to, but I have a duty to my men."

"Have you learned anything that makes you think Woody's had trouble up there?"

"No, Eli, I haven't." Sometimes Nathan wished his friend weren't quite so direct. "It's more a matter where I can't see my way clear to surrendering my responsibilities onto his shoulders."

"Vastly capable shoulders, at that."

Nathan smiled. "You're persistent, you know. Yes, he's quite capable. That's why I hired him in the first place."

"I don't know," Olivia said after sitting quietly for far longer than Nathan remembered her doing in a long while. Her speculative expression made him uneasy. "It would seem you also bear responsibility toward Faith."

"What?" He shook his head, hoping to clear it. "What responsibility could I have toward a virtual stranger?"

Satisfaction filled her broad smile. "Her troubles, these latest ones, began after she took your order to the camp."

The guilt he'd carried since that fact had dawned on him a week earlier returned. He fought it with all he had. "Do you mean to say that decision of hers makes me responsible for her louse of a husband and his sorry way of running his store?"

"No, Nathan." Her voice practically dripped excessive patience. "The responsibility comes when you consider how that brute she married treated her to his anger *because* she went to the camp to do what was right in the Lord's eyes."

He sucked in air as though Olivia had leveled a blow to his midsection instead of hurling words his way. She'd given voice to the thoughts he'd tried to avoid since the morning of the fire.

Unwilling to continue with that conversation, he tried to divert her attention. "Maybe, but I'm still not a man who can simply sit and do absolutely nothing. I'll go right crazy."

Eli chuckled. "You could always come to the bank with me, *partner*. You do remember your position there, don't you?"

"I remember. *Silent* partner's what I agreed to, what I've always been."

"But when you have nothing better to do with your time, it wouldn't hurt you to come take a look at the bank's current situation. We're coming out of the problems caused by the drought and the grasshoppers quite nicely. Slowly, yes, very slowly, but at a steady pace."

He stood and paced. "I'm not sure, Eli. What do I know of banking?"

"Enough that you've said you need more funds than just for the flume, but not enough to know what that means to the bank," Eli countered. "That flume's taking a good part of the bank's liquidity, since we're still holding a number of the farmers' and ranchers' mortgages. Now you've said you'll be needing money for the road, as well. You should spend time looking over the books. I promise not to let it become too painful a chore."

"Excellent idea." Olivia pushed back her chair. "That'll keep you busy here in town until the judge arrives."

Nathan raised his arms in surrender. "Fine, but I'm heading down to the River Run Hotel. Can't be abusing your hospitality any longer."

Olivia frowned. "Have we done anything to give your that silly notion? We truly enjoy having you stay here with us. And the children especially love their Uncle Nate."

He smiled, remembering his latest chess game with Luke, and Randy's recent inquisition as to the merits of blue hair ribbons versus rose. "I'll admit I love them, too."

She stood, a satisfied smile on her lovely face, and headed for the door to the hall. "Then it's settled. I'll let Faith know your decision. I'm sure she'll appreciate your support."

Before he could stop himself, he blurted out, "I don't know that I can offer her my support. I can't stand behind a person who's done what she stands accused of doing. Never, Olivia. Do you understand?"

Standing in the doorway, Olivia faced him. "But she's innocent—"

"You *think* she's innocent." His gut roiled at the thought of Faith actually killing Roger, of her trying to kill Parham. And then, stealing the church's offering...

He wanted to prove her innocence, he had all along, but as the days went by and the events piled up, his determination on her behalf took on tints of doubt. Evidence against Faith continued to mount. He'd always been a practical man, prided himself on his common sense. He couldn't discount what a whole town had seen.

Still, he couldn't deny Faith Nolan's vulnerability, not to

mention her delicate beauty, tugged on his emotions. And there lay his problem. What part were his conflicted emotions playing in his internal turmoil? How much were his feelings affecting his reason?

Were his gentle feelings for Faith pushing him to seek to prove her innocent while he discounted the growing evidence of her possible guilt?

"For everyone's sake," he said, striving to keep his fear for Faith, his growing anxiety and desire to do right by her and the town of Bountiful, from coloring his words, "I hope you're right. I hope she's as innocent as you say. All this violence, the killing..." He shuddered. "I can't stomach any more of it. Never."

Olivia excused herself, saying she needed to inspect the children's schoolwork for the next day. Eli and Nathan moved into the parlor, where Cooky brought them a fresh pot of coffee and delightful apple-spice pastries. They settled in, at first discussing bank matters in general terms. Then the discussion turned toward Faith once again.

"You know," Eli said, "the outcome of the trial isn't certain, and that troubles me. No matter how evenhanded the judge might be."

Nathan hated to hear his concerns voiced. It made them seem more substantial, more threatening. "I've thought about that. But I do believe the trial is needed."

"I didn't say otherwise."

Nathan set down his coffee cup and met his friend's gaze. "I'll grant you that I'd much rather we prove Faith innocent, but we haven't found anything to prove—prove, mind you, not speculate—that someone other than her was at the general store that night. No one has found anything that might point blame away from Faith and onto anyone else."

Eli tapped the bowl of his pipe into the small tray on the table at his side, then used a sharp, wicked-looking tool to scrape the inside. "It occurred to me, as well."

"I'm afraid too much of the town's sentiment will be set against her. The men I've spoken with haven't shown much compassion for her, and they are the leaders of the community."

Eli began to defend his fellow citizens, but Nathan held out a hand to halt his objection. "I understand the reason for their concern."

"I can't argue with them, either." Eli sat back. "I hope you realize that, even if she is found innocent, as I believe she is, their suspicion could make life here tough for her."

Nathan frowned. "Are you saying you don't believe we will prove her innocence?"

"No, no. I haven't given up, but innocence isn't always all that's needed to bring about acceptance. Her days might turn into an ongoing nightmare, no matter what. Olivia was the one who pointed that out. She faced a certain amount of the town's condemnation before we married. She knows what might await Faith."

"Let's hope they don't repeat that history."

"I agree." Eli stood, crossed to the hearth, stirred the glowing embers, and, while gazing into the red coals, continued. "I'm merely trying to think ahead. I wouldn't be the kind of man I strive to be, the kind of Christian I hope I am, if I didn't look at all sides of Faith's situation. You know me. You know I tend to plan for the worst while I pray for the best."

"Are you saying you have a plan? What is that plan?"

Eli laid an elbow on the mantel, turned toward Nathan again, but failed to meet his gaze. "It involves you."

An uneasy feeling lodged in his gut. "Me?"

"Indeed." The banker shot him a glance then shifted his gaze back to the window fire. "I fear the worst, to be honest. Too many of the men in town are suspicious of a woman they see as shrewd, greedy, and a possible killer. The jury will be picked from that crowd. They could always find her guilty of murder because fear clouds their better judgment. I don't blame those who don't know her for not wanting her around their families."

Although something inside him again went against logic, Nathan had to agree with Eli—to a point. "You know my experiences in the war. They marked me for life. I admit I've struggled with that, myself. Killing is a sin, one I can't stomach. But..." He shook his head and shrugged, unable to continue.

"I don't think you have anything to fear in that regard, Nate—"

"But?" he cut in, impatient as his unease grew.

"But I'm increasingly certain Faith is innocent. I've dealt with any number of clients at the bank and with members of my late first wife's family, and have become fairly able at sniffing out dishonest folks. Faith doesn't fit the mold, and she's too straightforward. Besides, Olivia assures me of Faith's decency, and I tend to believe my wife's intuition. I can tell you to rest at ease in that regard. It's just that I can't reassure the whole town."

Unexpected relief seeped through him. He stood and made for the door. "Well, then. You've echoed my deepest feelings. We're agreed Faith's innocent, and we're committed to prove her so. I need some cool air—"

"We need to double our efforts to uncover the culprit," Eli continued as though Nathan hadn't budged from his chair. "That means we need to learn more, ask more questions, speak to those who might know something about that night. Or the poisoning at church."

"Don't forget the cash box and the runaway horse."

"Indeed. We can come up with a plan. We need the facts before the judge arrives. Besides, it would give you something to do, instead of saying you're just wasting time."

"I completely agree." Nathan smiled, feeling encouraged. "I do feel better when I take action. I'm not one to just sit and wait for things to happen. It's a relief to know we're agreed, that we've settled—"

"No so fast, Nate. That's not all we need to discuss."

His eyebrows shot up. "Another problem?"

"I'd rather you don't see it as a problem. It's more a matter of setting up the best outcome for any verdict at trial. It'll be especially important if we can't persuade the jury of her innocence, a jury we both feel could be poisoned against her."

He gave his friend a tight smile. "I'm not a complicated fellow, Eli. What are you trying to tell me while still not saying it straight out?"

"What should be most important for us is to protect

Faith. I can't see them finding a lady like her capable of even attempted murder. It's the other charges that worry me." Eli gave Nathan a speculative look. "I know of a way to ensure her safety and her future, and you're the only one who can carry it out." He took a deep breath. "You can offer her marriage, and then assume her debts as your own. That will prevent the horse-thief hanging sentence. Once you clear the debts—once you make restitution for Theo's losses and the church's cash box, she's out of danger. And your good name will go a long way to make people around here feel easier about her."

Only two words penetrated. Both were critically important.

Hanging... marrying...

Nathan faced the need to weigh the horror of hanging a woman against the challenge of marrying that same woman. And paying off her substantial debts while still facing his need to invest in the logging camp.

He fought to force words past his tight throat. "Marriage is a serious matter."

"So is death by means of a rope."

He shuddered. "You didn't have to be so blunt. You know I have no funds to cover the loss of the general store. And, since I know how she feels about them, Faith would want to buy the mules outright. Neither of us trusts Theo with the animals' well-being. The animals are about all I might be able to cover. Unless things have eased even more at the bank and you can offer me some kind of mortgage."

Eli shook his head. "We'll go over the books as we discussed, but you know what these years have been like. We have few liquid assets. Still, whatever we have I could offer against some of your land as collateral."

"I suppose we could reach an agreement, and Theo is the sort to take whatever he can get without having to put out too much effort." Had he lost his mind? Could he possibly give this mad notion even the slightest consideration? Nathan couldn't believe the words that poured from his mouth without any seeming thought behind them. "I just don't know if we can come up with enough to suit Theo."

Indeed. He *had* lost his mind. Thinking of restitution for Theo Nolan...

"That's Theo, all right." Eli barked out a humorless laugh. "But don't forget how he doesn't think of much besides his next drink. I suspect we might satisfy him with less than the whole amount up front. You could then agree to pay the rest in quarterly sums, or something of the like."

So far, he'd responded to Eli's suggestion with mild comments, and yet, Nathan's thoughts were anything but mild. A dose of panic spurred them, and he didn't know if he could see his way clear to offer Faith marriage.

Eli waited.

Finally, Nathan tugged his coat tight and made toward the door. "I need to take a walk, clear my head to think this through. And I'll have to pray about it, Eli. It's not something a man can agree to without seeking the Lord's will. Marriage is a sacred covenant, as you well know. I'll have an answer for you, but I don't know when. I can't rush an answer to prayer."

"I don't think we have the luxury of time. And yes, I do know how sacred a marriage vow is. Remember, though, sometimes the Lord answers our prayers in unusual and un-expected ways. I'd promised never to remarry after Victoria's death. Then . . . well, God brought Olivia into my life."

Nathan couldn't stop a crooked grin at the memory. "On the heels of misbehaving boys and a runaway pig."

Eli laughed. "Unusual and unexpected. But a true bless-ing, as I'm sure you'll agree. Who's to say the Father's not brought Faith into your life for the same purpose? Who's to say He's not after blessing you as He blessed me?"

Nathan's stomach churned as his thoughts spun. "I'll take that into consideration, Eli. But I'm sure you, of all men, can understand when I tell you I won't come to any decision lightly. It's the rest of my life."

"It's her *life*."

The truth hit him hard in the churning gut. He nodded and stepped toward the hall. "Let me think. And you do your part. Come up with a list of those you think we need to see. Maybe even some of the questions you and I have. Let's see what we can learn, before . . ."

He didn't finish the thought. He didn't have to. Both men knew the rest. Both understood his reluctance.

As Nathan paced the length of Main Street in the night-time chill, he couldn't deny that reluctance. He'd never been one to jump into anything without a great deal of thought, planning, prayer, and consideration of all possible angles.

The judge was on his way. The town wanted a speedy trial—a quick verdict. Faith needed protection. He needed guidance. Answers. From God and all those involved.

Urgency nagged at him. "What should I do, Lord? I need time to think, to look at all the problems that might arise. Eli wants an answer. Faith *needs* an answer. But...I don't know if I can do it. I'm not one to rush into things that truly matter, surely nothing that matters this much."

*You've never had a life depending on your decision.*

Although God didn't yell at him, Nathan felt the response as though he'd heard it loud and clear through the cold, dark night. It brought him unexpected comfort. True, he didn't know what he was going to do, but the assurance of God's presence encouraged him. He'd have the answer in the Lord's perfect time.

As had happened other times in his life, Nathan acknowledged he could trust in God, in his Father's guidance and his Father's wisdom. He'd need both this time more than he ever had before.

Marriage.

To Faith Nolan.

Was he about to marry her even though he knew it wasn't the right time?

And what about the question, so loud in its unvoiced state? Neither he nor Eli had dared mention the most devastating possibility. What if the jury did return a verdict of guilty to the worst charge? What if they found Faith guilty of murder?

Would they hang a woman for that?

He couldn't let that thought take root in his head. It was too ludicrous, too ridiculous. Too improbable. Too horrifying.

*Father, don't withhold your answer. Please don't delay.*

# Chapter 15

Hours and hours on his knees later, Nathan watched the light of dawn slip in between the blue curtain panels over the window in the Whitmans' guest room. The Bible in his hands had been his companion in the longest, most torturous night of his life.

Did he truly believe in Faith's innocence?

Yes.

Did he trust the Almighty to work things out for Faith? For him?

Yes.

In the end, it all came down to one single truth. What did his heavenly Father want him to do? What did a righteous, just God expect of a man who claimed to honor Him? What was God calling him to do?

In the last hour, he'd begun to feel a weight on his heart. Could he let a mob of foolish, blinded men ruin a woman's life? Could he stand by as a more than likely innocent woman's life was stolen years before a Holy God would want it to end?

Could he stand by and let evil triumph when he could stop it?

When he stripped all the details out of his thoughts, he was left with only one question to answer. What if he were in Faith's shoes? What if during the war he'd been caught, held on trumped-up charges by the enemy, sentenced to a firing squad? What if he knew someone could save him from that fate? What if that person didn't act?

Before God, and with the thought of unjust but certain fate clear in his mind, he let the decision come on its own. He set the Bible back down on the nightstand by the bed, walked to the window, and opened the curtains to let in the morning light. Bathed in the rosy glow of the new day, Nathan admitted he'd known all along what he would do. He'd tried to deny it, had let fear and reluctance take the lead in his thoughts, but all along a part of him had held a kernel of longing.

There was something about Faith Nolan that drew him like a magnet drew a shard of iron.

Respect, admiration, and the normal recognition of the appeal a pretty woman held for him had melded into a true attraction. He could no longer deny it, not after all these hours face to face with his God.

But could he make Faith Nolan his bride?

Faith didn't sleep. She'd spent the night hours storming the Father's throne with prayer. She didn't want to spend another minute in this jail, didn't want to die. She loved God, wanted to someday see Him face to face when her life was done, but she hadn't begun to live yet.

"Father God...if there's a solution, a way for me to avoid this gruesome end, please show me what it is. Fill everyone involved with wisdom, convict the heart of whoever plotted against me, bring to light the evil that's been done. As dreadful as the jail cell has been, the noose would be far, far worse. Please spare me such a fate—if it's in your holy will."

As the sun began its trip up the eastern horizon, she found herself oddly at peace. When the marshal led Mr. Folsom to her cell with a dish of eggs, bacon, and flapjacks from the hotel's kitchen, she was able to offer the men a smile.

"Good morning," she said. "And Mr. Folsom, thank you for your kindness. I do appreciate the good food you're providing me while I'm behind bars."

The hotel owner, who'd worn a frightening scowl, blushed and set his jaw. He wouldn't meet her gaze as he handed her the covered plate and utensils. "You're welcome, I'm sure."

The moment she took hold of the tray, he scurried out faster than necessary. Faith chuckled. The Good Book did say a kind word turned away wrath. She was glad she'd spoken kindly.

After she'd eaten and washed up, Marshal Blair approached her cell again. Faith expected him to gather her breakfast things, which he did, but he didn't turn to leave right away. Instead, he studied her for a moment.

"You've an early visitor," he said. "May I bring him back?"

"A visitor?"

The lawman nodded. "Nathan Bartlett's here to see you."

She was torn at the news. On the one hand, she couldn't deny how kind the logger had always been to her. On the other, she knew he harbored doubts. Somewhere in the depths of her heart, she'd longed for him to stand behind her, to champion her innocence. But he'd not taken that strong a stance.

Still, she couldn't refuse. He'd come to see her. His actions spoke volumes.

"You can let him in," she said.

As the lawman went after her visitor, Faith prayed for the Lord's hand to rest on the meeting, for Him to give her the right attitude toward Nathan, and for the Holy Spirit to measure her words. In spite of her better judgment, anticipation made her heart beat faster.

Nathan walked in wearing his brown coat open down the front to reveal a navy, black, and white plaid flannel shirt and his usual jeans. His gold-shot hair was ruffled by the wind and his cheeks ruddied by the cold. He looked, if possible, more attractive than he ever had. If only....

"How are you?" he asked in a subdued voice.

She blinked, setting her fanciful thoughts aside. "It may surprise you to know that I'm quite well. I've rarely felt the Father's presence as strongly as I did last night."

He nodded, his expression thoughtful. "It might surprise you to know that I understand. It's on account of a night of prayer that I'm here today."

She arched a brow. "Prayer brought you here?"

"Prayer, and the conviction that I'm doing the Father's will." He took a breath so deep his shoulders lifted the open coat enough for her to take note. "It all became clear during the night. I now know what I'm called to do."

"And that is?"

"I know this isn't what you'd want, but I know the Father's led me to you. Please marry me, Faith."

She gasped. "Wha—what did you say?"

His features still cast in serious lines, Nathan nodded. "I can't bear the thought of a jury sentencing you to hang. Not without anything solid to prove you've done any of what Theo says you did, and, well . . . I'd like you to be my wife."

Confusion filled Faith's thoughts. "I'm trying to make sense of your explanation, but I'm afraid I don't understand. Are you saying that marrying you has something to do with whether they hang me or not?"

He blushed. "Something like that, only I didn't say it all quite so well. I'm not a fellow for a lot of fancy talk. I have nothing but respect for you, and I can't abide the thought of all that's happened to you. If I were to legally take up your debts and make good on them, you'd be freed from here, and you wouldn't face a hanging."

"Take up my debts? What do you mean?"

"If I marry you, I can become responsible for paying up for you, since Theo's main complaint is the loss of the store— well, it's also Roger's death, but it's unthinkable that anyone would convict a lady like you of murder, much less sentence you to hang. Especially since there's nothing to tie you to Roger's killing. Besides, Theo himself was there that night, and the soldiers, too. Who's to say if they all left as they insist they did?"

She took the time to think through what he was trying to say. What struck her most was how embarrassed he appeared, how vulnerable, and yes, kind. As always, Nathan Bartlett spoke with a depth of kindness that touched her soul, came through in all his words.

She'd not allowed herself to ponder what life might have

been like had she married someone like Nathan rather than Roger; she'd dismissed the thoughts as pure foolishness. Now, he was offering her the chance to learn.

But sadly, she couldn't accept. "I appreciate your kind offer, but I can't marry you. I understand what you've said, and I don't want to face that mob again, but this"—she waved vaguely—"this isn't right."

"But—"

"I already married once because of my situation, Nathan. You know how that turned out." She stopped the sob that threatened to escape. "I can't see wedding again to save myself from trouble ahead. If I'm to marry, it'll have to be for the right reason. I'll need affection, a man who's interested in me rather than doing a duty, as honorable as that is. I want the love that'll see two people through years and years of joy and sadness, of abundance and lack, of comfort and work."

He ran his hand through his hair, ruffling it even more. "I do care, Faith. I care what happens to you in the future. And, sure. I don't know you well enough to say I'm truly…well, *fond* of you, but I'm sure we can get there in time."

She was tempted. Oh, yes, she was. But in the end, that hunger in her heart won out. "Perhaps. But I can't take that risk again. I know too well how things can turn out if love doesn't bind two lives. Thank you, Nathan, but no. I won't marry you. I'll have to trust the Father in this."

"I understand if I can't change your mind." Regret mingled with relief on his face. "But I stand by my word. If you decide to take a chance on me, why…send me word, and I'll fetch Reverend Alton straight away. My offer of marriage will still stand."

A knot formed in her throat, and Faith recognized what she was turning down. She didn't know another man as honorable as Nathan, and while the thought of marriage to the logger held unspeakable appeal, she was determined to stand her ground.

"I can't saddle you with my troubles," she murmured in little more than a whisper, unable to muster a strong, clear voice. "It wouldn't be right, no matter what you say. I do appreciate your kindness and decency, and will always be grateful for all you've done on my behalf."

"Your mind is made up." It wasn't a question.

She nodded.

"Very well. But you won't be able to send me away so easily yet. I'll be here, in case you need me, and if you should change your mind, until this is all resolved."

*One way or another . . .*

He didn't say the words, but they seemed to hang in the air between them. All Faith could do was nod once. She then turned her back on Nathan. She couldn't bear to see him walk away.

The sound of his departing footsteps after the clang of the cell door rang in the hollow jail.

Only then did Faith let the tears fall. They didn't stop for a long time.

A week after Faith was jailed the marshal surprised her by pausing outside the bars to her cell halfway through the morning. "Missus Nolan, ma'am, I've received a telegram telling me the judge will be here in a week's time. I reckon we'll be ready for the trial when he gets here."

What could she say? "I'll be ready—I'm ready right now."

He nodded, and with a kind look, went back to his office.

When Faith stopped shaking after he'd left, she pulled out the Bible Mrs. Alton had brought her, and began to read. Every so often, she paused to wipe tears from her cheeks. During the time she spent in her Father's Word, she sought answers to her questions and comfort, neither of which she found. After enough time, however, she did reach a measure of inner peace.

She was ready to accept whatever God might have in store for her life, even if it turned out to be a short one. Still, could she bear for the time she had left to be filled with the awareness that God had let injustice steal her days on earth?

A wash of regret for what she would miss flowed over her. She'd yet to know the mystery of falling in love, or the wonder of maternal feelings that came along with the birth of a child. A sharp pang pierced her heart. It hurt too much to even consider those losses.

If Theo had his way that was exactly what was in store for her.

How she wished she might not miss any of the magnificent things she'd dreamed about for years. She was still young enough that it could all happen. If she closed her eyes and gave her imagination free rein, she could picture herself pledging her life to another man, to one who would treasure her, to one rich with decency and dignity and honor, to one like . . . like Nathan.

And now he had offered.

She covered her face with her chilled hands at the pure embarrassment her foolish thought brought along with it. Up until a short while ago, none of their encounters had given her the slightest hint that anything like a courtship, a romance, or—

Heavens! Even after his proposal, any one of those things was out of the question.

Still, if she were to describe the kind of man she'd have wanted for a husband, why, it would be someone very much like Nathan Bartlett.

How wonderful it might have been if she could have let herself dream of a life with him, of the family they might possibly have had together. How splendid it would have been to watch those little ones blossom into the excellent, godly men and women the Lord surely would have planned for them to become.

How wonderful it might have been if she could have let herself accept his offer of marriage.

A sob escaped her tight throat.

Oh, my! Grandchildren . . . what an incomparable joy that could have been.

But not without love.

A trembling sigh slipped out. Those impossible imaginings were what hurt the worst. Death didn't trouble her. Not really. It was only a step she would take to enter eternity and see the face of her Savior. If it came in a week, well then, it was simply coming that much sooner than she'd planned. Or wished.

Oh, yes, she would miss a long earthly life, but not the one she'd known the last three years.

The thought of all the loss, of missing the joys her Father

had planned for her . . . that brought her deep, abiding pain. Tears washed her cheeks.

"Father?" She clasped the Bible close to her heart. "Are you here? I want to feel your presence in my days, especially if they're my last ones. I want to feel you near me while I make my way through this dreadful trial. I need you, Father, at my side. Fill me with the comfort of your Holy Spirit . . . and the truth of your mercy and goodness and love."

While she dreaded what she feared was about to come, she knew the One who sat on His eternal throne, and Mama and Papa were there at His side. That truth brought her the only spark of joy she could find in her dark situation.

Perhaps if she focused on that it would give her the strength she would need to get through the sad farewells she'd soon have to say. She had come to treasure the friendships she'd recently made. Mrs. Alton, Olivia, and Addie had shown her what she had missed growing up out on her parents' property. Yes, she'd known the girls from when she'd gone to school in Bountiful whenever weather had permitted, and she'd seen them as adults those times she'd been able to attend church in more recent times, but the kind of support and friendship they'd recently shown her was new. That encouragement continued unchanged, as did their daily visits. She appreciated them more than she could say.

"Missus Nolan?"

The lawman's voice startled Faith. She shuddered, and with the back of her hand, quickly swiped away the tears still on her cheeks. "Yes, Marshal Blair."

"You have visitors."

"Visitors?" Olivia had stopped by earlier, after she'd

walked her children to school. She hadn't expected anyone else, except for perhaps Mrs. Alton bearing the usual covered dish filled with a tasty supper. "I can't imagine who would be here. I suppose you can show them in. If you'll remember, I am your prisoner."

The marshal chuckled as he stepped aside. "Don't reckon I can keep them away."

To Faith's surprise, Nathan walked in, an older bespectacled stranger at his side.

"Hello, Faith," the logger said. "I've brought someone for you to meet. This is Mr. Peterson. Mr. Peterson, Mrs. Faith Nolan. If you'll accept him, he'll be your lawyer for the trial."

"Lawyer?" Confusion grew. "We don't have a lawyer in Bountiful, do we?" She shook her head. "That was silly. Of course, I can't have an attorney for the trial. I don't have any means to pay him. I'm so sorry you've wasted your time in coming to see me, Mr. Peterson."

"Don't worry about payment," Nathan said, his cheeks a ruddy red. "His services have been paid for. And he only came from Pendleton, not so great a journey. We fetched him to look out for you once the judge gets here."

Pride stung Faith. She sprang to her feet. "I'll have you know, I'm not one to accept charity, not even from friends. I suspect you've appealed to the ladies who've offered me their encouragement. I doubt their husbands would approve of your efforts."

A tight smile widened Nathan's lips. "Then you'll be surprised it's actually the husbands who insist you accept representation. They're the ones who've put up the funds to hire Mr. Peterson."

She gave him a doubtful glare. "I suppose you're about to tell me you're an innocent bystander in this effort?"

He blushed.

She had her answer.

He began to stammer. "Er...well, you see...I—"

"Save your breath, sir. I'll not be the object of anyone's pity."

"Don't be foolish." His jaw resembled a stony ledge. "We haven't offered pity. Can't you identify friendship and caring? Did Roger Nolan ruin you so much you can't see when they're being offered?"

It was Faith's turn to blush. "If you put it that way...I suppose you might have a point."

"If you'll both delay this argument until later," the lawyer said, a smile on his thin face, "we can get quite a bit done right now. Discussing the case, investigating the situation—situations, from what I understand—strikes me as a better way to spend our time than using words and pride as swords."

She sighed and gave the gentleman a quick nod.

"I suppose it's best for me to leave you alone to talk." Nathan turned to Mr. Peterson. "I'll be with Adam Blair. You can join me there once you're done. I can show you down to the River Run Hotel so that you can rest after your journey."

Once Nathan left, the silence seemed to deepen and draw out. Finally, when Faith feared she couldn't bear it for another moment, Mr. Peterson opened his briefcase and took out a small notebook and pencil.

His smile was warm and encouraging. "I'm sure you've

had to repeat your story more times than you care to count, Mrs. Nolan, but I'd appreciate if you would do so one more time. Please don't hurry. There's nowhere I need to be, and it's more important for you to recall everything possible—"

"If you please, Mr. Peterson." She smiled back. "You don't need to go on. You're right. I have been asked the same thing dozens of times, and have become a reluctant expert at telling even the least important of details."

The lawyer smiled, but didn't respond, his pencil poised over his notebook, a clear sign to Faith. She went over her story one more time, answering his questions as she went along. When she was done, she fell silent, clasped her hands in her lap, and sighed, exhausted, not so much by her speech, but by her situation.

Mr. Peterson paged through his notes a few times. "Well, Mrs. Nolan. That's quite a tale you tell." He met her gaze. "I must admit, I can't see a solid reason to believe you, but I also can't see a reason for you to do a single one of the things you've been accused of doing. Experience has taught me that criminals don't act without a cause."

His first statement set Faith's heart to a rapid, pounding beat. While his second statement eased her sudden fear, her general anxiety didn't lessen. "I can't understand how something like this can happen," she said. "Certainly not to someone like me. I've done nothing but tend to my home and the store for years. The only folks I saw during that time are the customers at the store, my husband, and my brother-in-law. I always made sure to keep to myself and to never offend anyone, not even Roger."

Mr. Peterson shook his head. "It's more than I can fathom. Tell me, Mrs. Nolan, is there anyone who might gain from your misfortune?"

She shook her head. "No one, not even Theo. When he first accused me, I doubted anyone would believe him, but..." She shrugged. "Here we are."

"What was Theo's part in the business?"

Faith chuckled. "That's a good question, sir. I never figured it out."

"What do you mean?"

"He didn't work in the store, and only once or twice helped Roger unpack the mules. He was gone much of the time. From what I've been told and noticed myself, now that I've spent some time in Bountiful, he's right fond of a rocker on the hotel's porch here in town."

"Hm...and yet he feels entitled to the store. And the mules, if I understand correctly."

"He says he put up money when they first opened the store."

Mr. Peterson tapped his notebook with his pencil, again going over his notes. "Are you sure he was not around when you and Roger argued?"

"He was quite drunk, sir, so he wasn't quiet. I heard him leave."

He nodded in a measured way. "Did you know the men who were with your husband when you returned from the camp?"

Faith shrugged. "I didn't *know* them. I'd met Captain Roberts and Sergeant Graves from the times they did business at the store, and I may have seen one or two of the others with the officers, but I rarely paid much attention to Roger's friends."

"It was safer that way, I would assume."

She jerked her head up and met his gaze. Instead of judgment, she found compassion there. Tears threatened, so she swallowed hard, blinked, and nodded.

He filled in the silence. "I take it by the time you and Roger argued they were gone as well."

She nodded again. Then, when she felt she could speak, she drew a deep breath. "The way I see things, someone wants me to pay for their sins. But who?" Tears welled, and this time, she couldn't stop them. One rolled down her cheek. "Who could do such a cowardly thing? Who despises me so much? And...well, why?"

Mr. Peterson removed his spectacles and cleaned them with a snowy handkerchief. Before donning them again, he pressed thumb and forefinger against the ridge between his eyes, which he closed, as though he could see the events pictured across his eyelids. "Theo Nolan insists you killed Roger and started the fire, but Marshal Blair can't find anything to prove the accusation. It all burned away."

"So here I sit, unable to help myself."

"Let's move on," Mr. Peterson suggested. "When it comes to the poisoned lunch, you're in a better position. Mrs. Alton worked with you to cook the food, and both of you packed the same things. No one but Mr. Parham was poisoned, even though you and the Altons ate the same food."

She breathed a mite more easily.

"To murky matters once again," he continued, his brows

knitting together, "even you can't deny you were the only one in the church when the collections box disappeared."

"I was."

"And you had a strange tale about a dog. It was there...and then it wasn't. The church door was closed, and then it wasn't. Reverend Alton insists it was locked when he came and found you in his office."

"Of course, it was. I locked it myself. *After* I came to."

Mr. Peterson shook his head. "Strange."

"I didn't take the collection box, Mr. Peterson."

He met her gaze square on.

She didn't flinch.

He gave a nod, then flipped to another page in his notebook, paused, read, and met her gaze again. "Here's something else. Theo is your brother-in-law. Tell me, Mrs. Nolan. How well do you know the fellow? How did the two of you get on? Did you ever have words?"

At the memory of Theo's beady eyes following her as she served and cleared supper, she shuddered. "I did all I could to stay far from him and on his good side. We rarely exchanged more than greetings or his requests for seconds at supper and coffee at all times."

"How about with your husband? Did Theo and Roger argue much?"

She chuckled. "All the time. At least once or twice on the hour. It meant nothing."

The lawyer's brows shot up over the upper edge of his silver spectacle frames. "Could they have quarreled more seriously while you were asleep? Could it have festered in Theo after he left, leading him to round back, and kill Roger?"

This time she laughed. "Only if that skunk changed his stripes. He would have had to decide he was prepared to put himself forward for the first time in his life. You see, Roger was Theo's only means of income. I ran the store, and Roger provided his brother with money. Theo never worked while I was there."

"A matter of the heart, then. Could Theo have been sweet on you and jealous of his brother?"

Her laughter multiplied. "Oh...oh, goodness me, Mr. Peterson. That is much too funny. No, sir. It could only have been a matter of the heart if the fellow had one for anything besides his next bender."

He arched a brow. "Well, then. How about enemies? Did your late husband have any?"

Faith shrugged. "Since his death, I've come to understand that most folks in these parts disliked Roger and Theo. But I'm not sure that dislike ever reached the point of hate or a wish to see either of them dead." A frightening image came to mind. "There were the Indians, though..."

"Indians? I thought they'd been removed to reservations after that last war to the south of here."

"Most of them were, but some escaped the Army's efforts to move them. There have been stray groups—more like two or three men—that have attacked farms and ranchers for the food and the livestock. It...it happened to my parents during the Bannock War."

"Your folks? Are they...?"

"They were killed, sir, and our farm burned to the ground. Before you ask, I wasn't home when they struck. I'd gone into Bountiful for supplies Papa had ordered from Mr. Metcalf at the Mercantile. When I returned, only the ruins, ashes and smoke, were left."

A pained look crossed his face. "I'm so sorry, ma'am. My condolences." The silence lengthened. Then the lawyer cleared his throat. "I would suspect that's when you accepted Mr. Nolan's proposal."

A wave of revulsion struck her. "Yes."

Mr. Peterson turned back to his notes. He riffled through the pages, tapping his pencil a couple of times. "These Indians. Did they ever argue with your husband?"

"If they did, I never knew about it. But they did come close to attacking the store one time."

Her words clearly piqued his interest. He pinned her with a sharp stare. "Tell me about that."

"There's not much to tell. They wanted more of the..." Oh, how foolish could she be? She shook off her distaste, and went on. "They wanted more liquor than they could pay for, liquor I reckon Roger promised, but when they came for it, he didn't give it to them."

"You do know, Mrs. Nolan, it's against federal law to sell liquor to Indians, right?"

She closed her eyes. Goodness! Roger had been breaking the law. She'd known his lack of respect for Marshal Blair, but evidently he'd flaunted his disdain in more than snide remarks. "I knew there was a problem with doing so, but I didn't know the details. Against the law? Are you sure?"

"I'm quite sure. True, it's not a law that many uphold, and authorities have more pressing matters to see to, but it is illegal."

"No wonder, then, that Roger made sure I was nowhere near the store whenever they came."

"A good thing, I'd say." The lawyer checked his notes. "You were saying about the one time Mr. Nolan didn't give the Indians the liquor they wanted..."

"Oh, yes. I never knew if they paid for it and he didn't have any or if he refused because they couldn't pay. In any case, they left, but came back that night, enraged and making quite the clatter, with screams and howls and—and well, it was blood-curdling."

Horror widened the lawyer's eyes, yet he still leaned forward, enthralled by her tale. "I can well imagine, but how did you escape?"

A faint smile curved her lips. "They never did strike. Evidently, Nathan Bartlett and his men realized what was about to happen. He cut them off at the pass."

The oddest light, almost relish, lit his face. "An old-fashioned battle, then. How many died?"

She chuckled. "None. That's what was so wonderful. From what Roger said, Nathan negotiated with them, without spirits, even, and somehow persuaded them to leave us alone. That was the last we ever saw of them—at least, the last *I* ever did."

Although the lawyer looked disappointed, he said, "A relief, I'm sure."

"I'll say. Blessed relief."

Mr. Peterson then took the time to scribble additional notes in his small book before looking at her again. "So we're back to no apparent explanation for any of this."

"It would seem so."

He closed his notebook with a gentle slap of the cover. "All right, then. It's my job to uncover that hidden reason."

"What do you mean, sir?"

The lawyer stood. "You strike me as an upstanding, believable woman, Mrs. Nolan. I don't think you've done any of these things, especially in light of the times you've been hurt. Once? I can see someone feigning an injury to distract the law. But all these times?"

She shrugged.

"No, ma'am. I don't think you're guilty. And so, it's up to me, Marshal Blair, and the rest of your friends to uncover what happened here. I'm fairly sure we'll have enough to show the judge the error in Theo Nolan's charge."

"Fairly sure..." Faith said. "That doesn't give me much to hang my hat on. I'd be far happier if you'd said you knew for absolutely certain you could prove my case."

It was the lawyer's turn to chuckle. "I never promise more than I know I can deliver."

"That's fair, Mr. Peterson. I can respect a cautious man."

"As I can respect an honest lady. An honest client, as well."

"All I can do now is pray the judge and jury will see me as your honest client."

Mr. Peterson ran his briefcase against the bars to alert Marshal Blair that their meeting was over. "I commend you for the prayers, and I'll join you, myself. We should all pray, Mrs. Nolan. It never hurts to bring our one true Advocate into any legal matter."

"I agree the Lord is righteous, sir, but it's His mercy I need most right now. That's where I'll hang my hopes."

"Let's hope I've learned my business some better than that." He put on the hat he'd left on the small table by the door, and rattled the bars again. "As promised, though, I will pray for His wisdom and justice. That's what it'll take for us to prevail."

# Chapter 16

Nathan refused the chair Adam Blair offered, getting straight to the point. "You know me fairly well by now, right?"

A smile twitched the marshal's heavy mustache. "Something 'bout your words tells me I'm not fixing to like your visit much today."

"I'm not here to discuss the weather." He dropped his hat on the empty chair and paced the short area in front of the lawman's desk. "It's about Mrs. Nolan—"

"How 'bout you drop that 'Mrs. Nolan' nonsense?" At Nathan's surprise, Adam chuckled. "We both know her name's Faith, and you're sweet on her. I reckon you oughta just up and marry her before letting any more time go by."

Nathan blinked. Could Adam have overhead his recent proposal?

Faith's refusal?

That would make matters embarrassing.

Then he took a closer look at his friend. "Hm...if you find marriage so attractive, and see Faith as such an excellent choice, I can't figure out why you haven't taken the lead and proposed yourself."

Adam bolted out of his chair, which clattered to the office floor. "I never...why, that's not...never said...I—I—I—"

"You sound something like a teakettle there, my friend." Nathan smirked. He crossed his arms and took time to enjoy Adam's discomfort. "I suspect you might be done telling me to wed the lady, don't you think?"

Adam's cheeks ruddied. "*Humph!* Let's see here, then. If you didn't come here on account of being sweet on Faith, then why did you come?"

As though a curtain had slid over a sunny window, Nathan's humor vanished. "Eli and I talked a few nights ago. We both agreed we don't have the whole picture of the Nolan situation. Something's missing, and the only way to find it is to—well, we have to ask questions. Have you spoken with the men out at the Army fort? And how much time have you spent with Theo? Aside from when he's wailed to you about Faith stealing his mules, which he's had no interest in since he got them back. They've been up at my camp, where my men have been caring for them all this time."

"I've spent time talking to him. Didn't get much. If he saw anything, it must'a been through buckets of booze."

Nathan gave a sharp nod. "Then how about the fort? Have you questioned the military men Faith mentioned? The ones who spent the night drinking with Roger?"

"I had me a chat with the captain. There wasn't much to what he had to say."

Nathan narrowed his eyes. "A chat? While Faith sits behind bars?"

Adam held out a cautioning hand. "Easy, there. The captain and I agreed he'd round up his men and bring 'em to see me."

"And when is this trip going to happen?"

"I reckon just about any time before that judge fixes to get here."

Nathan crossed his arms. "What's keeping you from heading out there instead? This morning?"

Adam checked the clock behind his desk. Nathan did the same. It showed a few minutes past nine.

The marshal then glanced out the window. Nathan did, too. The day was clear—no rain, and while it was cold, no snow had fallen as yet.

"Not much," Adam said at last. "I can head on out that way any time now."

Nathan tightened his jaw. "We, Adam, *we* can head on out any time now."

Adam tipped his head to a side, studied Nathan. "You're not about to let me change your mind about this, now are you?"

Nathan shrugged.

"Let's go then, my friend. Don't want to go making us too late coming back this evening. Sure would hate to make you miss one of Cooky's right fine meals."

Nathan waited for the marshal to step out from behind his desk. "If we get there at the right time, you may wrangle yourself one of those fine dinners, if you ask nicely."

Adam slapped him on the back. "Ask? Nah. Mrs. Whitman's always the one who's asked me to stay. So, what are we waiting for, then?"

The two men headed south, riding in companionable silence as their horses' pace ate up the miles. At no point, however, did Nathan lose his sense of urgency.

They found no trouble on their way to the fort. Once there, the drab appearance of the three unimpressive structures surprised Nathan. Built of logs from nearby mountain forests, they were little more than large cabins, the long walls broken only by small windows at shoulder height. Smoke puffed out of the three chimneys, and five horses stood in a large corral, ears pricked upright, tails switching as they watched the two new arrivals approach the largest building.

Nathan dismounted, tethering Horace to a hitching post at the right of the door. Adam did the same on the left.

They rapped loudly on the door, and waited as footsteps approached. "Who on earth—"

"Captain Roberts, sir," Adam drawled. "I decided we had us a fine day to give you the chance to make good on your offer to round up your fellers for me. You know, the ones who were up to the Nolan brothers' store that night of the fire. I'm needing to ask them some questions."

Nathan stepped forward. "You're needing to get some answers, I'd say."

Adam glanced over his shoulder, and while his expression remained serious, Nathan caught the twitch of the mustache that suggested a smile. "Those would be a mighty great help."

The captain stepped back. "Come in, please. It'll take me a spell to fetch them. They each have their jobs, you understand. That's why I meant to bring them in to you in town."

"Well, now," Adam said, his eyes narrowing a bit. "That's

mighty kind of you, but time's running, and I need to know what's what before the judge comes to town."

"I understand," Captain Roberts said. "I'll only be a minute or two. I'll fetch my wife. See that she offers you a bite to eat, iced water, coffee, something stronger—"

"Water," Adam said, cutting off the offer of spirits.

"Coffee," Nathan offered at the same time.

The captain snagged a navy uniform jacket from a peg on a wall and, shrugging into it, strode outside. Nathan took the time to study the room, curious about the fort. "Hm...not what I expected."

Adam gestured. "Not much more to look at inside here, either."

"Seems it does the job. They have a kitchen—it's over to the rear. The tables for meals are large enough." He gestured toward the right. "And that door likely leads to the captain's office."

"Sure, it works." Adam stood and walked to the nearest window, peered outside. "What d'you figure the other buildings are for?"

"I'm not that experienced when it comes to forts," Nathan said with a smile. "I fought in the war, but didn't spend any time on this kind of duty. I suppose one cabin's for the captain and his wife, and the other some kind of barracks for the rest of the men under his command. Plus, I think I saw what could be a barn a ways back before we got here."

Light footsteps crossed the narrow porch outside the front door. A brown-haired lady in a plain gray dress hurried inside. "Welcome, gentlemen! I'm Suzanna Roberts." She hung her cream wool shawl across the back of a chair. "That wind! I sure wish I were back in Ohio. I could do without the howling and kicking up dust." She scurried to the cook-stove without pausing to allow them a response. "Can I dish up a bowl of venison stew for you gentlemen? And I'll have a pot of coffee ready in no time."

Adam's mustache danced a jig. "Yes, ma'am."

In no time, they were seated at the table, stew, tender biscuits, and hot coffee before them. At no time did Mrs. Roberts stop her chatter, not a word of which mattered to Faith's future or afforded Adam or Nathan any clues.

As Nathan swallowed his last mouthful, the front door opened again. Three young soldiers stepped in, followed by Sergeant Graves and the captain. Mrs. Roberts excused herself, leaving the men to their business.

To Nathan's disappointment, none of the troopers had anything much to offer. They'd gone to the store to pick up an order, but had learned Roger hadn't had it after all. The captain returned from Bountiful with the sergeant to join his men at the Nolans' store and "visit" with Roger for a while.

Hours later, when they'd realized how fast time had passed, they'd said their farewells and left.

Disappointed with the results of the trip, Nathan stayed seated when Adam sent the soldiers back to their duties. When only Adam, the captain, and he remained in the room, Nathan turned to the officer. "Your story about the missing order is something I experienced as well. Had it happened before?"

The captain returned to his chair. "A time or two."

Adam leaned back against a wall, crossed his arms over his chest, moved his right ankle over the left. His eyes bounced back and forth between Nathan and the officer. Only a fool would have thought his stance lazy.

"What did you do then?" Nathan went on, seeing as Adam continued to keep his peace. "Didn't it affect the supplies you needed for the post?"

"Not much. I waited for Roger to let me know our things had arrived. You see, Mr. Bartlett, the Army supplies most of our needs. We've only had to make up the lack on occasion."

"The night of the fire, you did send your men to pick up an order, right? And you'd expected your things to be there."

"Of course. I'd seen Theo in town, and he'd said my order was in."

"But it wasn't?"

"Roger said there'd been a mistake. Our whis—er . . . our *supplies* were missing, and we'd have to wait for a new shipment."

Nathan met Adam's gaze. No wonder the man had counted Roger as a friend. It seemed he, too, indulged in the Nolan brothers' favorite pastime. Having nailed down that one detail, he turned to another topic.

"I hear you and your men are stationed here to make sure the Indians who've stayed behind don't make mischief," Nathan said.

Captain Roberts nodded.

"Do you deal with many?"

He smiled. "Not so often anymore. Most are now on the reservation in Idaho. The ones around these parts know we'll move them up north, but they don't give us much trouble anymore. We can deal with them."

Adam stepped forward. "Do you recollect if the night Roger died you and your men all came back here together?"

The captain started. "I—I . . . think so." He drew out the words, a thoughtful expression on his lean face. "I'd had a drink or two"—*or more*—"so I didn't pay as close attention as usual, but the men were tired. I'm sure they all made it back at around the same time."

"But you're not certain," the marshal pressed.

He gave a one-sided shrug. "I suppose I am certain. I went by the barracks before I headed to bed."

"You didn't see them ride back together."

His concentration deepened to a slight frown. "We all left at the same time. Don't see why they wouldn't have."

"And you?"

At that, the officer stood. "What are you suggesting, Marshal Blair?"

"Not suggesting, asking if you joined your men on that ride back. I reckon you wouldn't know if they did make the trip all of 'em together if you didn't ride down with them all."

Captain Roberts looked from Adam to Nathan and back. "I don't know what you're trying to get me to say. Of course, I came with them. Why wouldn't I have?"

"So you wouldn't have been at the cabin long enough to see who killed Roger Nolan?"

"I've answered more than once. Why are you asking these questions over and over again? I thought the man died in a fire."

Nathan had reached the end of his patience. "Someone struck Roger Nolan in the head before setting him and the store on fire. That blow's what killed him. Now his widow stands accused of murder. There's those of us in town that can't bear the thought of a woman being found guilty, much less sentenced to hang."

The captain's eyes bulged. "Murder! That lady from the general store? I'm sure no one in his right mind would find her guilty of killing that big husband of hers. And hanging?" He scoffed. "They're none of them fool enough in Bountiful to hang a woman—a *lady*. Who would ever do such a thing?"

"You're sure, now, you know nothing of the death or the fire that night?" Adam asked.

"Are you accusing me of killing Roger?"

"I don't recollect saying that."

A look of shame overtook the captain's lean face. "Look, Marshal. I'm not proud of the time I've wasted up at the general store or the times I've had too many drinks with Roger and my men, but I always found Mrs. Nolan a fine lady, one who had a heavy load to carry. I'm sorry she's had another burden with all this." He gestured vaguely. "I wouldn't go and do anything to harm her any further. If I knew anything that could help her..."

After that, the men exchanged a few niceties before Adam and Nathan said their good-byes. They mounted their horses, and headed back to town.

Neither spoke.

They had enough to fill their thoughts.

A week later, Nathan joined Adam, Eli, and Mr. Peterson to await the coach that was bringing Judge Michael Hess to Bountiful. Heightened anxiety filled him, and he found it hard to stand still. He shuffled, paced, shifted his weight from foot to foot. After about fifteen minutes in the clear, crisp, and cold morning air, a heavy hand landed on his shoulder, bringing him to a standstill.

"You've near run a rut in the middle of Main Street, what with that crazy marching you been doing," the marshal told him. "You're no longer in the Army, this ain't bringing Judge Hess here any quicker, and it ain't doing Missus Nolan any good. Take it easy, man."

Nathan blushed and raised the collar of his coffee-brown coat up for protection from the nippy wind. "I can't say as I feel anything but sympathy toward Faith."

Adam arched a brow, that half smile wiggling his fancy, full mustache. "You sure that's *all* you're feeling? Wouldn't be wrong if you have feelings for the lady, you know."

"That's not it at all." And yet, Nathan's conscience tweaked him. He pushed the pang aside. "She's had a rough time of it for years now. I saw the sadness in her eyes, a time or two, but there was nothing I could do. She always said she was fine."

"The lady's got starch and gumption," Adam said, the smile gone. "I understand what you're saying, but there ain't much a body can say when she's the only one around when the church collection box goes missing. I can't find a thing to say she didn't do it."

"But you haven't found the box, or the money, or anything that says she did, either, have you?"

"Other than her presence in the church," Mr. Peterson said, injecting himself into the conversation. "That's hard to overcome, Mr. Bartlett. Do believe me, please. I've spoken to just about all those who live in Bountiful, trying to find the one person who might have seen someone else go in and out of the church. Or the dog. But nothing so far. No one saw anything."

Acid churned his gut again. "I see. But…why? Why would a God-fearing lady do any of it?"

No one answered.

No one had to.

No one could.

In the distance, a whirl of dust announced the approach of the coach. The judge was nearly there.

As the coach came closer, Nathan caught an unexpected sound behind him. He glanced over his shoulder, and gaped at the sight of the women of Bountiful, led by Mrs. Alton, marching straight toward him and his companions. Each lady wore a right grim expression, and determination accompanied their steps.

Shocked into silence, Nathan nudged Adam, who still stood at his side. "This does not look like a friendly, welcome-to-town committee."

The lawman's eyes opened wide. "Not a welcoming party by any measure. They look more like a wagonload of trouble to me."

"What are you two whispering about?" Eli asked.

Nathan gestured with a thumb over his shoulder.

His friend turned. "Oh, no. There's my wife. We're in for trouble."

Eli grabbed Josh Tucker's shoulder, and swiveled his friend to face the female flock. The livery owner's face blanched.

Reverend Alton took a step toward his wife.

Mrs. Alton didn't slow her steady pace.

"What, pray tell, is all this about?" the man of God asked.

"This, my dear man," his wife responded, chin in the air, "is the town's conscience. We've met, discussed the situation, and come to a decision."

She looked to her right and to her left, to Olivia and to Addie. The younger women nodded. So did the others in the delegation.

The gray-haired ringleader nodded right back. "Since there are too many unreasonable men determined to believe the worst of our dear Faith, we're here to let this judge of yours know that things aren't merely as you men say they are."

Marshal Blair turned to the reverend's wife, a hopeful light in his gaze. "Have you found a witness to the theft at the church?"

"Well, no—"

"Has anyone confessed to tainting Mr. Parham's box lunch?" he asked.

Olivia sidled up to Mrs. Alton's side. "Not yet, but it's only a matter of time—"

"Most important," the marshal said, "has anyone uncovered a credible culprit in the murder of Mr. Nolan and the arson at the general store? At this point, the best way to guarantee her innocence is to present a real culprit to the court."

Silence descended. Only the hoofbeats of the team pulling the coach into town disturbed the uneasy hush.

Then, all at once, each woman began to object.

"There's no reason—"

"Not a one of you believes she did it—"

"Theo Nolan's guilty of slandering a good woman—"

"We'll have that list of names you want soon enough—"

"You might want to see about a room at the hotel again, Jeremiah Alton."

The men hurried to object.

The coach rolled up to a stop at the scene of the uproar.

Everyone fell silent again.

Nathan breathed a sigh of relief. He didn't want the judge to think of Faith's case as some silly notion from the foolish residents in a small town. A man had been murdered and a woman stood accused of the crime. She could hang for it. Even for the supposed theft of the mules, if Theo succeeded. Truth was, in these parts, mules were almost as valuable as horses, but only to a man who worked. No one could accuse Theo Nolan of hard work.

"Heaven help us," Mr. Folsom, the owner of the hotel, muttered as he joined the men. "Looks like Bountiful's womenfolk have decided to join that unnatural Susan Anthony woman. Think how impossible they can make life for us if they follow in her misguided footsteps. Let's hope this trial is over quick, and that Nolan woman is taken care of."

Nathan frowned. "I don't think it's a matter of 'taking care of' her, Mr. Folsom."

"Maybe not, Mr. Bartlett, but things in this town are mixed up enough as it is."

"Mixed up?" Eli asked.

"Sure," the hotel owner replied. "We're not a real proper town, you know. We're practically not here yet."

"That makes no sense," Eli responded. "The bank is here, as is the mercantile, the bakery, the milliner, the blacksmith— plenty more. And there are many, many farms and ranches spread out all over the county. Make yourself clear, Folsom. I don't understand."

"See? We're all standing here, eating dust, waiting for a coach to roll in. If we were a proper town, why, we'd have a railroad and station for folks to wait at for a real train. Thought you said we'd have a spur line in town a while back. Where's that railroad, Whitman? I only seen a short run of track so far. Not enough for nothing."

Eli shook his head. "Give it time. The railroad's coming to Bountiful, but it takes a great deal of work to lay track. What are you in such a hurry for?"

The hotel owner spat on the dirt road. "I'm trying to run a business in this sorry little town, but I can't even get the basics a hotel needs regular-like."

"Last I checked," Nathan offered, "Metcalf's Mercantile sells all those houseware needs."

"Not all I need," Folsom countered, "and not enough for all the rooms, the tables—you know, linens and dishes and . . . and—well, all a hotel needs to serve its customers."

"A little patience," Eli said. "Have a little patience, and the spur line will be done. You'll see."

"Patience! It's not as if I can even bargain with them Nolan brothers anymore, now Roger's dead and the store's gone. Even though they charged a pretty penny, I could get some of what I needed from them, now and again . . ."

The hotel owner shook his head and continued muttering. As disgusted as he said he was with the town, however, he didn't budge from the middle of the road, and "ate dust" like all the others as the coach drew to a stop.

"And now all this nonsense with Mrs. Nolan," Folsom

added. "A judge from Pendleton to deal with a troublemaker. Hope he doesn't take his time tying up this business." He gestured toward the furious women. "Look at all what she's managed to do while jailed up. She's dangerous, I tell you."

"Dangerous?" echoed a rotund gentleman in a black suit and brocade vest as he descended the coach. "Who might be dangerous in this lovely little town?"

The boom of his surprisingly loud voice cut through the commotion, capturing the attention of everyone, including the ladies.

As the group looked around, the sound of running footsteps came from around the corner. "It's about time ya got 'round to getting here," Theo called out to the judge. "There's still some as say she ain't done nothing, but I tell you, she's gone and kilt my brother Roger. She burnt down my store, too, stole my mules, and fed another fella her poisoned food."

"Theo," Nathan said, hoping to rein in the out-of-control situation. "You don't *know* any of that. There could be any number of explanations to all that's happened, and that's why the trial will be held, to hear *evidence* for and against."

Theo crossed his arms and jutted his jaw in belligerence. "Who's to say you weren't part of that there woman's plans all along? A course, ya wanna say she ain't guilty. But it all's happened." He turned and gave the gathered townsfolk a triumphant smirk. "She's pert near ruined me, near kilt that fella from the bank, and then she went and stole the church's collection monies, too. Plus, Roger's dead, burnt to a crisp. Ya still wanna say she ain't done a thing? Bah!"

The women let out a chorus of aggrieved cries.

The men countered with calls of alarm.

"Well!" exclaimed the judge. "What have I walked into?"

"Trouble, sir," a man Nathan didn't know suggested. "And from the looks of it, that there woman sitting in our jail is cooking up more. She's already gone and done this"—he gestured toward the angry ladies—"and she's likely provoking our women further still, to riot, even. It's time to get this trial done and over with afore she gets all our women... ahem...wearing trousers and running things."

Fear struck Nathan, unlike anything he'd had to face since the end of the war. He feared for Faith's safety. He feared for her life.

Before he could say a word, Theo scoffed. "Ya mean it's well past time Faith Nolan hangs!"

# Chapter 17

As if having to be dragged through the charade of a trial wasn't ghastly enough in and of itself...

Faith's final plateful of indignity was dished up when Bountiful realized no location in town was large enough to hold all the interested onlookers other than the just built and about to be opened Golden Door Saloon.

Never in her life had Faith thought she'd be forced to set foot in a place like that. Now her future—her life itself—would be decided in a saloon. At least the establishment hadn't begun its sordid trade as yet. She didn't know if she would have managed to tolerate the stench of spirits, so reminiscent of her worst moments at Roger's hand.

As she was washing up to go out and face that mob of men, the memory of the courageous women of the town, far fewer in number than their menfolk, made her smile. Even the lady from the butcher shop had joined the others in their support. She wondered if they'd attend the trial...in the saloon.

Disgust made her stomach roil.

"Are you ready, Mrs. Nolan?" Marshal Blair asked.

Faith jumped at his silent appearance outside her cell. She ran a hand over her neatly combed and pinned hair, waiting for her heartbeat to slow down to a more normal rate. "I can't imagine what more I could do to prepare myself, Marshal Blair."

His keys clanged in the hollow jail as he unlocked her cell. "I'm right sorry to have to do this, but the judge made it clear."

Marshal Blair held up a set of handcuffs. The thought of the walk through town filled Faith with horror. As he put them on, the chill of the cold metal sped straight to her heart. *Oh, Lord, don't abandon me now.*

The marshal took her elbow to help her out of the cell, and then to escort her all the way down Main Street to the saloon at the far end of town. To Faith's amazement, the street was eerily empty. On the one hand, she rejoiced she didn't have to face anyone while the marshal led her like that, shackled like any common criminal. On the other, she feared she knew where every last one of those respectable residents of Bountiful would be found.

When they reached the saloon, she found her suspicions confirmed. A number of men milled around the entrance. As soon as they saw her, they hurried inside. At her left, the marshal let out what sounded to her like a most irritated lungful of air.

She glanced at him.

"I'm so sorry, Mrs. Nolan." He shook his head. "I rightly do wish there was something else I could do."

"Don't take it to heart, sir. You didn't accuse me, and whoever did do the crimes is cunning enough to hide their tracks remarkably well. Most proper folks don't have anything to hide, so they usually don't have to learn to cover up things as well."

"You're as gracious as I feel you're honest, ma'am. And innocent, too. I pray the Good Lord helps us prove it today."

"Amen!"

He chuckled. But on the boardwalk in front of the saloon, outside the door, he stopped and released her arm. With the thumb and forefinger of his right hand, he smoothed his ample mustache. He struck her as unwilling to go inside, and, at the sound of the animated prattle within, so was she. When it became abundantly clear they could no longer delay the inevitable, the lawman hitched up his gun belt and sent her a questioning look.

She squared her shoulders. "I'm ready."

As they walked inside, everyone grew silent. Faith's entrance seemed to hold them all in thrall. The room itself felt as charged as the air before a thunderstorm's first flash of lightning. Her shoes tapped loudly against the fresh-milled boards of the floor. She kept her gaze lowered to those boards, unwilling to see any more condemnation, unwilling to reveal how close she was to tears.

A quick glance through her lashes revealed Judge Hess in a large, upholstered leather armchair at the farthest end of the room. Before him, someone had placed a table, and two plain wooden chairs were arranged a few feet away on either side. Marshal Blair led her to the one on the right.

Hand on a Bible, she was sworn in, and the proceedings began. She forced herself to keep her gaze fixed on Judge Hess. The judge started out by questioning Theo, who sat in the witness chair and told the same story he'd been telling from the outset. When he was finished with her brother-in-law, the judge motioned for Mr. Peterson to cross-examine the witness.

At first, Mr. Peterson took Theo back over the answers he'd given, apparently trying to see if he could rattle the man off his rigid view of events. But then, in a sudden turn, he changed his line of questioning.

"Tell me, Mr. Nolan," he said, "who were the gentlemen at the cabin the night your brother died?"

Theo blinked. "Huh?"

"How many men were at the cabin that night, and who were they?"

Faith leaned forward a mite, and saw Theo rub his forehead. He squinched his features in a sure sign of concentration—or at least a mighty effort to concentrate.

"Um...I think it were three of them, maybe one...two more," he finally said, shrugging. "It was a while back, you see. I cain't be expected to recollect what all went on other'n my brother dying and her being the only one there."

Mr. Peterson continued. "We can start then with the names of those three you do remember, if you please. Who was there?"

"Let's see..." Faith's brother-in-law muttered. "It were Private Fowler...and I think Sergeant Graves. Oh, and the other feller, the boss out to the fort. Um...I think his name is Robert or Roberts. Cain't be all so sure."

"Were they frequent visitors at the cabin?"

The silence stretched as Theo sat with his eyes shut tight. As the minutes crawled by, a titter broke out in a corner of the room. Then another from a different quarter. After another bit, the hiss of whispers swished louder and louder from one end to the other of the saloon.

"Captain!" Theo exploded. "It were that Captain Roberts feller what was there that night. They're all upstanding soldiers, not killers like her."

Someone let out a loud "Harrumph!"

Nervous laughter burst out.

Chairs squeaked.

Mr. Peterson removed his spectacles, wiped the lenses with his white handkerchief, and then gestured toward Theo with the spectacles. "Tell me, if you will, Mr. Nolan. How did three military men come to be so friendly with a simple store-keeper? Were they there to do business? It would seem it was fairly late in the day—well into the night, it would seem—too late, perhaps, for any regular kind of shopping."

Theo shifted in his chair and his cheeks reddened. Faith wondered how he would handle explaining how the soldiers had spent time drinking vast quantities of liquor with him and Roger on more than one occasion.

"Ah...sure!" he cried. "They bought...um...things. That's it, things for that there post of theirs a coupl'a times."

"How late did they leave that night?"

Theo's eyes opened wider. "How'm I s'posed to know? I weren't busy watching a clock the whole time. They left. It were nighttime. You cain't be saying nothing bad 'bout 'em. They're fine, decent fighting men, you know."

Perhaps they were, but Faith knew they were also military men who'd left their post more than one time to drink into the wee hours of the night with the Nolan brothers. And perhaps they placed an order or two while they were at it.

"How long after these upstanding soldiers left did *you* leave?"

"Um...er...well, I dunno. A while. I maybe could've slept a spell."

"So you were there, with your brother and Mrs. Nolan. The three of you. Otherwise alone."

"Nothing new there. Did it all the time."

"But this time, when it was all over, your brother was dead, the store in flames, and your sister-in-law had a wound on her head. You're the only one who walked off perfectly fine."

"Fine!" he yelled. "I ain't fine. The store's gone, and I ain't got no home. That ain't fine, mister. Oh, and Roger's still dead."

"We all know something happened. What we need to show is exactly what." Mr. Peterson came within inches of Theo. "Did you and your brother have a falling out that particular night?"

"Falling out? We didn't fall outta nothing. I lay down on the sofa, and Roger, why, he stayed in his chair."

The audience laughed again.

"Whut?" he asked. "It's true."

"Ah!" Mr. Peterson exclaimed, turning toward the audience. "I see you've referred to the truth, Mr. Nolan. So where is the truth of that night? Did you and your brother have words? Did you argue? Did you say something...well, untoward about Mrs. Nolan? Did you and Roger fight?"

Theo shrugged. "We never did talk about her none, but

we always were fighting. We're brothers. Brothers fight each other all the time. Nothing to it never."

"Did you fight that night?"

"Sure. We fought purty near every night."

"What did you fight about that night?"

Another shrug. "Don't rightly recollect. Something, I suppose."

"I *suppose* you have to do some better recollecting," Mr. Peterson said, then turned to the judge. "I suggest, Your Honor, that in light of the number of strangers in the house that night, and in light of Mr. Nolan's admission of a falling out with his brother, that there is sufficient evidence to leave our esteemed jury with reasonable doubt as to the accused's culpability. I move the case against my client be dismissed."

Theo leaped up and, with many gestures and much venom, launched into his usual litany of accusations.

The other men inside the impromptu court offered encouraging cheers. Murmurs of "Agitator," "Dangerous," and "Inciting riot" echoed around the room.

While the judge denied Mr. Peterson's motion, he did dismiss Theo from the stand, and allowed the trial to proceed. Mr. Parham was called to testify next. He added nothing new to what was generally known about the incident, although Faith appreciated his insistence that he hadn't seen her do anything to his food, and that yes, they'd both eaten of the entire meal.

He, too, was dismissed.

Reverend Alton took his place in the witness chair. Although he answered all the questions about his suspicions, he couldn't offer a single piece of solid, incriminating evidence against Faith aside from her presence in the church at the time when the cash box disappeared. Like the previous witnesses who had been unable to fully explain the events, he couldn't explain the disappearance of the collection box, and no one but Faith had seen the dog. On the other hand, no one could deny the knot on her head. She had been hurt. The main question remained—how had it happened?

When done, the reverend followed Theo and Mr. Parham down the center aisle formed by the rag-tag assembly of chairs in the saloon.

Then Nathan was called.

As he approached the chair, he met Faith's gaze. She couldn't quite read the odd look he gave her, but she saw no anger or accusation there. And he offered none as he was questioned.

Judge Hess put him through a series of questions much like the ones he'd asked the other witnesses. He then called Mr. Peterson, had him go into his examination.

"How long have you known Mrs. Nolan?" Mr. Peterson asked.

"About three years now."

"What has your contact been like during that time?"

He raised a shoulder. "She usually tended the general store when I went to place an order for the camp or when I needed something we'd used up. She was always busy, keeping things tidy and clean, and taking good care of her customers."

"How often has she delivered your purchases to the camp?"

"Just the one time."

The lawyer arched a brow. "Hm...only once. So you would say this was an extraordinary circumstance, right?"

"Yes."

"What brought about that extraordinary circumstance?"

Nathan glanced sideways at Faith then shifted in his chair. "Something went wrong with my last order. It seemed to have...vanished."

"Vanished? Could you please explain?"

"When it became clear that my order was late, that it should already have arrived but Roger hadn't brought it up to the camp, I went down to the store to see what had gone wrong. He wouldn't say, but told me he didn't have my supplies. He assured me he'd make sure we would have them before the trail became impassable."

"Did he follow through?"

The logger shifted in the chair again. "He did get the supplies, but he wasn't the one who delivered them. It surprised me to see Mrs. Nolan lead the loaded mules into the clearing at the camp."

"Did you ask her what happened?"

His gaze skipped over to her, and then away. "Of course, but she didn't explain much. My men and I helped her unload so that she could be on her way back down before it grew too late in the afternoon. It turns mighty dark quite early this time of year in the forest."

The lawyer paced in front of Nathan, back and forth, thinking, his expression one of deep concentration. Without warning, he spun to face the witness. "Did you follow her down the trail?"

Everyone gasped.

Even Faith.

Nathan jolted up out of the chair. "No! Of course, I didn't. What are you trying to say, sir? Are you accusing me in order to set her free?"

The audience erupted into a blathering din.

The judge banged his gavel on the table. "Order! Order in the court."

Someone chuckled from deep within the crowd, and Faith heard more than one person voice the word "saloon."

The judge hammered away again. "I'll clear the room if this continues. We need order, ladies and gentlemen." He turned to Mr. Peterson as soon as Nathan sat back down. "Carry on, please."

Faith's lawyer nodded. To Nathan, he said, "No accusation, Mr. Bartlett, but rather a reasonable question that must be asked. When did you next see Mrs. Nolan?"

Nathan told how the men saw the smoke rise above the trees, and how they hurried down the mountain to fight the blaze. He also described finding Faith in a quiet, densely wooded spot off to one side of the trail.

At that, Theo leaped to his feet. "Don't ya forget about my mules! She was stealing my mules." He pointed a stubby finger at Faith. "She's a dirty, guilty horse thief!"

Like a hammer against steel, his indictment rang out and struck home in her heart.

"Guilty," he hollered again. "Guilty, guilty, guilty!"

The judge called a recess in the proceedings, a wise move, seeing as how no one could have made sense of any further testimony in the uproar Theo's words unleashed. The women hurried to Faith's side during the brief break, and the men clustered together. Theo was left alone in his far corner of the room.

"How are you holding up, dear?" Mrs. Alton asked.

Faith couldn't speak around the knot in her throat so she only shrugged.

"Just you wait until I get hold of Eli tonight." Fire sizzled in Olivia's expression. "I'll be giving him a piece of my mind, all right. I can't fathom what's gotten into that man. *All* the men should have put their heads together and found a way to silence Theo's wild accusations by now. I can't believe they've let it go this far...even if Eli did humor me when I insisted you needed a lawyer."

Addie snorted. "Must be the same thing as what's got hold of my Joshua. On the one hand, he did what I insisted was right by Faith, but then on the other...he hasn't stopped this stupidity any more than Eli has. It's certainly not smart to give a lick of credence to anything that comes from Theo Nolan's mouth. These men have lost their senses, that's what. And I don't cotton to being patronized, I'll have you know." She shook her head, setting the pretty red curls to bouncing.

Mrs. O'Dell, the middle-aged owner of Bountiful's bakery, *tsk-tsked*. "I don't understand what would make that vile Theo think you, his brother's own wife, would ever hurt a soul, never mind kill Roger. I haven't thought of him as bright, but I honestly never thought him quite this dim."

Faith sighed. "All I want is to find out who did all these things. That would free me from the dark cloud that's hung over me since the night Roger died."

"I'm sure you do, indeed, want to know," Mrs. Myers, the

butcher's wife, said. "I'm right sorry I didn't see who it was running away from the horse that day out on Main Street. I reckon we wouldn't be here if I had." She placed a hand on Faith's shoulder. "I'm so sorry, Mrs. Nolan."

She smiled. "Call me Faith, and please don't fret over that, Mrs. Myers. You couldn't have known what had come before, much less what would happen next."

The lady's furrowed brow smoothed. "Thank you for your kindness, but I'll never forget I could've helped you. I can assure you I'll be keeping a closer eye on what goes on outside the shop from now on. Not a thing's going to get past me, no sirree!"

The ladies chuckled.

Mrs. Myers blushed, then, in a clear effort to divert attention from her gleeful nosiness, she went on. "What I want to know is if anyone's ever talked to any of them soldier fellas. Did you, Mrs. Nolan? Do you know if Marshal Blair did? Did that lawyer of yours over there ask 'em anything about that night?"

"Not that I know of. I wonder how long it would take to fetch them…"

None of the women knew how far the post was from town.

"The Army men out to the post generally keep to themselves," Mrs. Metcalf said. "They only come to Bountiful for business matters, mostly the bank and so on. They used to come to the mercantile more, but since your man and his brother opened themselves up that general store, they don't come so much."

How odd. Faith didn't remember the soldiers coming to

the store all that often. But before she could give that new scrap of information much thought, Mrs. Metcalf went on. "They do come to town for special events, like the box lunch auction over to the church a couple weeks ago. But not much more."

"I believe Theo's the only one who could know anything about that night," Faith said. "But he likely won't say more than he's already said. He's too stubborn, and doesn't often change his mind."

The women stood in silence until Judge Hess clapped his gavel against the table again. "Order in the court!" *Thump, thump, thump!* "The court will come to order now, please."

All those who'd stood subsided. The men returned to their seats. The women, Faith now noticed, gathered together on one side of the room. Anticipation hung thick in the air. No one knew who the judge would call next, and no one wanted to miss a moment of the proceedings. A tight ache began at Faith's temples. The trial wouldn't be over too soon for her.

No matter what the outcome.

In swift succession, the judge called Nathan's loggers to the witness chair. One by one, they attested how she'd only gone to the camp that one time with the replacement order. The logger who had been with Theo also described the scene in the forest when they found her calling to the three mules. He went on to describe how they found the animals shortly after, untethered and placidly grazing nearby.

Whenever someone mentioned Maisie, Daisy, and Lazy, pain seared through Faith. She missed their company, and as their gentle, protective natures were discussed, she feared for them in the future. She couldn't bear the thought of them left in Theo's possession. He didn't care about them. She doubted he'd spare them a minute's thought beyond whatever they could provide in the way of making money.

Those animals had always counted on her. In whatever way possible, and with the help she was sure the ladies would give her, she would see to it that they were cared for and safe if...if she were sentenced to hang.

She couldn't deny she'd been glad to see them when they'd followed her into the forest the night of the fire. And, yes, she hadn't spared a thought to going back. If one were scrupulously honest, then she had stolen the mules. Or had instinct moved her to free them from the abuse she knew they'd receive once Theo took over?

She had to pray some more and trust God for the answer.

Just as she prayed He'd guide the court to the right solution.

Right around the same time the discomfort in her head turned into a pounding headache, the judge dismissed the last one of Nathan's loggers. She tried to focus on Mr. Peterson's closing argument, and he seemed to do as good a job as he could, laying out the facts and the lack of actual evidence. When he was through, the judge set down his gavel and rubbed his bald head with both hands. His silence continued, turning more awkward by the second, before he finally glanced at Marshal Blair.

Faith couldn't miss the marshal's grim expression.

The dapper judge looked at Faith, kindness in his expression.

He then turned toward Nathan and gave a minimal shake of his hairless head.

Terror struck Faith, but there was nothing she could, or dared, do.

Nathan leaned forward, his eyes narrowed, his brow lined. His shoulders looked tight, and his face displayed fear. She thought he might spring up, but he didn't. He stayed put, his eyes never moving from the judge's face.

She began to shake.

Judge Hess shrugged. Faith wasn't certain, but she thought she could read regret in his gesture. Finally, he stood. With much ceremony, he faced the jury of six men to give them his instructions.

"I hope you understand the seriousness of the job before you now," he said. "You hold this woman's fate in your hands. Be sober, thoughtful, and if you need to ask more questions, send someone after me. I'll see you get all the answers you need. You also should not rush. You have all the time you need."

Faith thought she might have heard a butterfly's wings flap inside that saloon, so silent as the judge spoke. Gone were all the whispers from the ladies, as were the arguments and cheers from the men. Even Theo had the decency to keep quiet. She bowed her head to pray.

"Missus Nolan?" the marshal said at her side. "The judge asked me to bring you back to the jail while the jury does this part. I'm sorry, ma'am, but we need to head on out now."

Faith stood unsteadily, and, under the pretext of helping her with the gray wool cloak Addie had loaned her, the marshal offered her his considerable support. As he escorted her from the room, she caught Nathan's gaze. He looked distressed, and why not? It had been the most distressing day

Faith had ever lived—except for maybe the day her parents were killed. With all the dignity she could muster, in the midst of the greatest indignity she could imagine, she nodded in acknowledgment as she stepped past him. That's when she noticed the baker's dozen of women's eyes that also stared at her. Those thirteen bodies sat tense as fiddle strings, hands folded on laps or clutching purses, feet shifting around with each step Faith took so that each of her supporters could follow her progress to the door.

At the same time, twice if not thrice as many men watched her departure, too, their necks craning bit by bit to let them study her every step. Eyebrows beetled together over disapproving stares, and, unless she was much mistaken, Faith saw a handful of smirks behind a variety of mustache styles.

Silence reigned over all.

She held her head high, her shoulders firm, kept her steps steady. When she finally walked out, however, her brave façade crumbled. Had it not been for the kind marshal's clasp, she might have crumpled to the dusty boardwalk. Her wrists were shackled again, and she wouldn't have been able to do much to stop her fall.

When she heard footsteps behind her, she turned. Nathan Bartlett had followed them outside.

She stiffened her spine and drew back her shoulders, calling on the last bit of dignity she still had.

In the time she'd spent indoors for the trial, the weather had turned. Instead of the wintry sun that had fought valiantly to illuminate and warm the air earlier, a pervasive blanket of gray hovered overhead. The wind had picked up, and swooped down Main Street, cold and merciless and howling through town. It looked as though a storm was on its way in.

A chill shook Faith, threatening her balance again. She rocked on the heels of her boots. Although she'd been mortified to need the marshal's assistance, she once again was only grateful for his and Nathan's presence at her side. The icy air stung on its way into her lungs.

"Wouldn't surprise me none if it snowed tonight," the lawman said in a conversational tone. "Surprised we haven't had none so far yet."

At her other side, Nathan shrugged. "I could do with it waiting until this trial is over. The trip up the mountain won't be easy if it snows. That trail freezes right quick, soon as the temperatures drop. All my men are here, as you saw, and I don't want to risk anyone's safety."

A wave of dismay caught Faith by surprise. "I'm so sorry, Nathan. You shouldn't be here. You or your men. Go ahead. Go back to the camp. I'm sure the judge is done with you."

Nathan scowled. "Only a snake crawls away from his duty. You wouldn't be in this predicament if you hadn't brought those supplies to my camp. Roger lost his temper after you got back from seeing to my men's survival through the winter. That's why he argued with you. You fell in the scuffle, you said, although I suspect what happened is that Roger pushed you hard for bringing us our supplies. If you hadn't acted on your conscience, that particular scuffle wouldn't have taken place. Whatever led to him dying, it happened while you were unconscious. The least I can do is stand by you during this farce of a trial. Whether you did what Theo says you did or not is between you and God—"

"And that jury," she cut in with more spunk than she'd felt in days.

His nod conceded the point. "You're right. But it's between me and God, too. It's only right for me to stay through to the end."

Faith caught her bottom lip between her teeth. Those words bore the weight of finality as they echoed through her thoughts. The end...the end...the end.

Fine. Nathan would stay out of a sense of duty, just as he'd offered marriage right after she was jailed. Faith knew her duty, too. As a believer in Christ, the least she could do was go to her own figurative cross, keeping the valor and honor He showed before those who wrongly crucified Him as an example. To do that, she would have to trust God's provision.

*Sweet Father in heaven, where is that strength you promised?*

# Chapter 18

Nathan couldn't help but be impressed by Faith's quiet strength. She'd held herself with such courage as she'd walked down the aisle in the saloon that he'd been powerless to keep from putting one foot before the other and following her outside.

The chill of the wind hit him as deeply as did the shaky state of her future.

He still didn't understand the connection between the Army men and the Nolan brothers. It was the most unlikely friendship, and he couldn't see them as drinking partners, certainly not in the way Theo and Hector Swope were.

Had it been about the liquor? They could always take their supplies of spirits to the post and do their drinking there. What else had bound them? What had they been up to?

Nothing good, he feared. His dear mother had always held to the notion that things done under cover of darkness and during the hidden hours of the night were rarely those that put a body in a good light before the Lord. Not that Theo or Roger ever bothered to place themselves in any but the worst light before Nathan, so the brothers likely didn't worry about the Almighty's eyes.

At the jail, Nathan bid Faith farewell. Her nod was her only response. With that mantle of nobility about her, she sailed into the prison, and for some odd reason, he felt as though a bit of the light in his world had just gone out.

He scolded himself for the rare, fanciful thought.

As he turned to leave, he heard a man call his name. When he turned, he saw Mr. Peterson hurrying after him, a fist clutching his brown wool coat tight against his neck, his leather satchel clamped tight in his other hand.

"Blasted wind!" the older man groused. "This street is nothing but a huge funnel, hurling these gusts right through your town." He shuddered. "If you'll indulge me a bit, Mr. Bartlett, I'd like to beg a few minutes of your time. It's about Mrs. Nolan's trial."

Unease pooled in Nathan's gut, but he couldn't see how he could avoid the conversation. He nodded. "Where would you suggest we talk?"

"My room at the hotel," Mr. Peterson answered. "I don't know that we'd have enough privacy anywhere else."

The man's desire for privacy alarmed Nathan further, but at all times, the lawyer had struck him as a straightforward, sincere man. While curiosity and concern reared their heads, it stood to reason that he wouldn't learn any more until they reached Mr. Peterson's room. He didn't know if he found himself walking faster because of his impatience or because of the biting wind.

In the hotel, the lawyer led him to a small, neat room at the end of the second-floor hall. "It's rather plain, but it suits me. It provides a bed, a thick, warm quilt, a small wardrobe, and a table and chair. All a man needs to get his work done, and then rest. Please take the chair."

Although he would rather not sit, Nathan felt he didn't have a choice. Still, he hoped his natural tendency to pace and fidget when something weighed heavy on his heart wouldn't rise up and embarrass him. Once settled, he gave Mr. Peterson time to gather his thoughts.

The lawyer set his briefcase at the center of the table, slipped off his gloves and tucked them into the pocket of his coat, then hung the coat from a hook on the wall by the door. Only then did he face Nathan.

"I won't lie to you, sir. I'm worried. I sometimes can tell where the jury stands, but this time . . . I'm not certain what they're thinking."

Nathan stiffened. "Are you saying you've given up?"

"No, no. I haven't given up yet, and I've asked Marshal Blair to bring the three soldiers to town—"

"Marshal Blair and I have spoken with them. We didn't find anything of interest when we did. Besides, the judge already told the jury to go deliberate the case. Will he call them back? And if he does, then what? He told them to take their time, but I'm sure he won't want them to delay a decision. Isn't it too late to bring the soldiers before the jury?"

"The marshal insists he'll have them here in the morning. We doubt the jury will be done that soon. And I want to buy us some time. Something . . . something's missing, not quite right, even though I can't quite tell you what."

In spite of his better judgment, a spark of hope sprang to life in a tender corner of Nathan's heart. "Let's hope the jury's not fast at all. You've put into words the same odd feeling I've had."

"I'm glad we're agreed." Mr. Peterson crossed to the small window, and, while gazing out, continued. "I don't want to rely on the obvious, since I—and you—have that sense that we've missed something. Don't give up thinking back on all that's happened, on every conversation you've had about the crimes, anything you might have seen and given no importance. The answer usually hides in plain sight."

Although the lawyer's words gave him a measure of hope, Nathan felt mounting frustration. What *had* they all missed? He shook his head. "Here I thought we had little time to try to find the culprit while we waited for the judge's arrival. We truly have no time now. And yet... I can't give up."

Mr. Peterson smiled. "Neither can I. I wouldn't be much of an advocate if I did, now would I?"

Good to know he didn't stand alone in his determination to help Faith. Still... "What can we do that hasn't been done?" he asked.

Mr. Peterson gave Nathan a speculative look. "Well..." he said, drawing out each letter as he continued to stare. "There is something we should consider, since it stands a chance of succeeding."

"And that would be...?"

"We agree I wouldn't serve Mrs. Nolan particularly well if I didn't explore all the legal avenues available, right?"

"That seems obvious."

"Even though the ideas we consider might appear extreme, right, Mr. Bartlett—"

"Call me Nathan, please."

"Very well, Nathan."

He crossed his arms. "Could you explain what you mean by extreme?"

"Unusual, I suppose. Unusual situations sometimes call for unusual solutions."

Unease began to grow in Nathan's gut. "How unusual is it for someone to be accused of a crime they didn't commit?"

"That's not unusual at all. But we're dealing with a lady, a *lady*, Nathan, accused of killing her husband then setting their home on fire to hide what she has done. Not only that, but also the husband's heir accusing her of stealing the last bit of his inheritance, leaving him destitute as a result of her crimes."

The unease approached a sickly sensation. "But ... you don't think she did it, do you? All of it? Even poisoning Lewis Parham? And stealing the cash box at the church?"

"I don't think she's guilty of any of it, and I encourage you to rest at ease in that regard. It's just that I can't reassure the whole town of her innocence."

"I suppose you have an unusual solution to Faith's unusual situation in mind. What would that solution be?"

"Remember," the lawyer said, "what's most important for me is to protect Mrs. Nolan. There is something you can do that might ensure her safety and her future." He took a deep breath. "You can propose and take on her debts as your own. That might satisfy Theo's greedy nature. He might be persuaded to drop the charges against her, which would prevent a hanging sentence. When you make restitution to Theo, she will be out of danger."

Nathan laughed without much humor. "You're a bit late

with your suggestion, sir. I already tried to marry her. She wasn't having any of it."

"Really! And why not? It would seem the most sensible solution."

Nathan shook his head. "It would, wouldn't it? But Faith Nolan is made of sterner stuff than most. She already married out of need rather than want once before. She insisted she would never marry again for any but the right reason. She wants abiding love and affection, and neither one of us knows the other well enough for that."

The lawyer slapped his thigh. "The lady is quite something, isn't she? The more I get to know her, the more I like her."

Nathan realized that, even though she'd refused his proposal, he found himself in the same position as Mr. Peterson. The thought of a future with her grew stronger inside him. Had he tried hard enough that time to persuade her? Had he taken her refusal much too easily? Should he try again?

Before he could think the notion through, the lawyer continued. "Well, then, if she won't wed you, we'll have to find the one who did kill Roger Nolan. And why he did it."

"How do you suggest we go about it?"

Mr. Peterson made a face, then turned to his satchel. He withdrew the notebook Nathan had seen him use more than once and flipped through the pages in silence. As the silence drew out, Nathan began to grow uncomfortable, but he was reluctant to break the other man's concentration. The lawyer faced him again when he was about to burst from the wait.

"I don't have much here about that Indian raid you

and your men stopped," he said. "What can you tell me about it?"

Nathan shrugged. "There's not much to tell. The Indians left around these parts have been hiding from the soldiers, whose job it is to get them to Idaho. Can't say as I blame them for wanting to stay on their people's lands, but the government does have its rules. These men looked hungry, had no money, and winter was coming. I persuaded them to take food and some cash I could spare back then. I doubted the Nolan brothers would feel generous, seeing as it wasn't in their nature. I negotiated with the Indians, and they left with what I offered. The store was safe."

"I thought I heard say that Roger did business from time to time with the Indians."

Nathan shrugged. "He wasn't reliable. A couple of times, Roger only delivered part of the orders I paid for in advance for my logging camp at the time we'd agreed. I had to wait to receive the rest until..." He thought back. "The first time it happened, I waited until Roger got around to bringing the supplies up the trail—a month, maybe two. The most important time, the time that involves Faith, it took her taking it upon herself for us to get the critical part of our order. Who knows when Roger would have delivered our food."

"Did he regularly sell food to the Indians?"

"I don't think it was regular. He likely sold to the Indians any time they could pay his prices. Other times, I doubt he gave a thought to what might happen if he said 'no' after he said 'yes.'" Something Nathan had heard the day he and Adam rode to the fort came to mind. "I wonder...From what I hear, Roger sold quite a bit of liquor to all comers. It seems likely he was selling spirits to the Indians rather than food."

The lawyer arched a brow. "That's against—"

"The law. I know. I doubt that would have stopped Roger for one minute. If it meant money in his pocket, he would have broken every law the government passed. It wouldn't surprise me to learn that's what caused the trouble in the first place that one time I lent a hand to calm things down."

"Amazing what the lust for liquor can do to a man."

"And for cash."

They fell silent, and Nathan thought about all that had gone wrong on account of Roger's less-than-upright nature. After a bit, he said, "A man has to wonder what part Roger played in his own death."

The lawyer raised a shoulder. "We won't know until we find the one who killed him. Which brings me back to what I mentioned a while back. Have you given up on marrying Faith Nolan? The more I learn about the Nolan brothers, the more I think we might stand a chance of changing Theo's mind about that trial if you get Faith to go along with our plan."

He hadn't given the notion much thought after Faith had turned him down. He had been relieved in a way, seeing as how his life would have become even more complicated than it already was had she taken him up on his offer. He had no time for a new bride, no money for Faith's debts as well as his business. Although he admired her, and in spite of his growing attraction, he still didn't know her well enough to assure her of any kind of devotion.

"I haven't much thought along those lines since the day she said no," he said. "But there's not much to lose by asking again—aside from another chip off my pride."

The lawyer smiled and proceeded to encourage Nathan to try. As he listened to the man's arguments, he couldn't stop the anticipation that sparked to life inside him. Marrying Faith wouldn't be the worst thing that could happen to him. And marrying him was far from the worst that would surely happen to her if...well, if Theo had his way.

He stood. "It makes sense for me to think on it a mite, pray some more, seek the Lord again."

"Talk to Faith, too, don't you think?"

"That, too." He headed for the door. "I'd best be on my way. I've a few things to do, and time's passing fast. I agreed to meet Eli, and he does hate to be left to wait."

They said their good-byes, and Mr. Peterson walked Nathan to the hotel room door. "Don't spend too long chewing on this notion," the lawyer said. "Try and have an answer by morning, please. You don't have the luxury of time. I suspect that jury will come back with their verdict fairly fast, even if one takes into account the time it'll take to question the soldiers. And then...unless we have the culprit in hand, it might be too late to strike a deal with Theo."

As Nathan strode down Main Street toward the Bank of Bountiful, he couldn't ignore his milling emotions. He'd never been one to jump into anything without a great deal of thought, planning, and consideration from all possible angles.

"What should I do, Lord? I need time to think, to weigh all the problems that might arise. But Peterson wants me to act by morning. I don't know if I can bring her around to our way of thinking that fast. She's not one to rush into something like this any more than I am."

He couldn't believe he was contemplating marriage again. Marriage.

To Faith Nolan.

Once again, a reasonable man had urged him to marry her. Was God using these men to bring to Nathan the wisdom he wished for?

He'd tried to win a yes from her once before. It hadn't worked. Would he succeed this time?

Respect, admiration, and the normal appeal the pretty lady held for him had by now melded into true attraction. He had to be honest, before God and with himself. He could—would—no longer deny it, not after all the hours he'd spent face to face with God.

He cared for Faith, for the woman, even more than for the victim.

Yes, he would do everything in his power to make Faith Nolan his bride.

No matter what it might take.


It had been years since Faith had slept through a whole night in peace. The night before had been no different. And how could it have been otherwise? The jury had been sent to decide her fate. None of those six men had looked at her with anything that even resembled mercy.

No matter how strong her faith, no matter how much at peace she might be with her place in eternity, the fact remained that she didn't want to die. Not for someone else's crimes. Someone somewhere knew who had killed Roger and burned the store, who had poisoned the banker, who had set a horse loose on Main Street, who had stolen the cash box from the church.

But, who?

Who had taken the time to make it look as though she'd been the one? Who wanted her gone? Or at the least, locked up for the rest of her life?

She thought back over the scant years of her life. There was so much she hadn't done...so much she'd missed.

Like freedom, something she'd lost when the Indians killed her folks. Longing filled her heart. She'd never realized how lovely, how joy-filled, how free her years growing up had been. Mama had nearly died, laboring to birth a baby brother that never drew his first breath. The Lord hadn't blessed the family with another child, so her parents had treasured everything about Faith. She never could have imagined what she would one day face...what her marriage to Roger held in stock.

She knew marriage wasn't like that. She'd seen it at home, she'd read about it in Scripture, she'd held the dream in her heart.

Men weren't all like Roger. She knew.

She knew Papa, Reverend Alton...and Nathan, as well.

Faith remembered Nathan's proposal. How could she not? It embodied what she'd always wanted. It spoke to her of the future and hope.

She longed for the safety and security she felt when Nathan carried her in his arms, close to his chest. Faith wished his proposal had been real, not something inspired by his sense of duty. While she didn't know him well enough to feel the kind of love her parents had shared, she wished she'd known herself loved that much. By a man like Nathan Bartlett. He'd come to represent everything she'd ever dreamed of.

To be fair, she didn't know quite what she felt for him. Her life had been in such turmoil, she didn't rightly know if she could even name those feelings right then. She knew there was gratitude, but gratitude wasn't all she felt for the handsome logger. Still, until she knew love existed between her and a man, one like Nathan, she wouldn't let the need for safety and protection send her into another marriage for practical reasons alone.

Although the future she faced was one of uncertainty, she knew she wanted whatever God had in store for someone like her, the plans He had for her life. She knew if she married Nathan, he'd make sure she had everything she would ever need.

Everything, that was, but the kind of love her parents had shared.

"How are you?"

Faith stiffened at the unexpected greeting. She turned and to her surprise, Nathan stood outside her cell, Adam Blair at his back. The logger stood aside while her jailer unlocked the iron-bar door and let him in.

"I don't know when the judge will be sending after Missus Nolan," the marshal said. "But I reckon you'll have some time for your visit."

"Thanks, Adam," Nathan said. He waited until Marshal Blair left before turning to Faith. "How are you?" he asked again, more softly this time.

She shrugged. "I've been better, but it's been years since that."

"You do know there is a chance to make things, if not as good as they were back then, at least some better than they are right now."

For a moment, a spark of hope burst to life inside her. "Oh. You still think marriage is the solution."

"It might not be *the* solution, but it could be *one* solution. And I'm not the only one who thinks so."

"You're not the only one?"

"No. Eli and Mr. Peterson both think it's worth a try. A proper marriage, and then paying off your debts. They both believe they can talk Theo into dropping the charges against you once we've made restitution, and you're not likely to appear a threat to his finances. I care...I—I care what happens to you, and I'd be honored if you would take my name and all the protection that could bring you."

Tears burned behind her eyelids. Why would the Lord let this happen again, when she'd been longing for all that Nathan represented? "I haven't changed my mind," she said, her voice little more than a murmur. "And I know circumstances haven't changed, you can't say you now feel...love."

"I can't say anything to make you reconsider."

"No." She smiled. "Your kindness is endearing, and I appreciate all you've done for me. You do need a wife, and you should consider finding one. I confess I envy the lady who'll be so blessed as to win your heart."

He looked up, and, with a thoughtful expression on his handsome face, he studied her for a minute...two. A slow smile widened his mouth. "You could take the chance I offer and be the one to win my heart. There's no one else who has set her cap for me, you know."

She smiled wider and shook her head. "You can be persuasive, can't you?"

He crossed his arms and his smile broadened even more. "I've a mind to show you how persuasive I can be. And just so you know. I don't give up easily."

"It never occurred to me to think otherwise."

"So we're agreed. I've offered, you've said no, I'm decided to change your mind, and…well, from what you've said, you're accepting the challenge."

Alarm made her open her eyes wide. "I said no such thing. I acknowledged your dogged nature. That's not accepting a challenge."

"You've acknowledged I'm persistent." He chuckled. "I'm setting up to show you how persistent I can be. You're not done with me yet, Faith Nolan. Not by a long shot."

She had no idea what to say to that, so she kept her peace. A moment later, he stepped up to mere inches away, and looked steadily into her eyes. Slowly, with heartrending tenderness, he ran a finger down her cheek. It had been so long since anyone had touched her with such gentle kindness, with such delicate warmth, with such honorable admiration, that tears pooled in her eyes. She couldn't keep them from spilling, and with that same soft touch, Nathan wiped them away.

"You're not alone," he whispered. "I'm here. Whenever you need me. Remember that."

Remember? Oh, indeed. She would remember. As long as she lived. And that was where she found the greatest problem with his words, his actions. It would be best if she could find a way to forget. What good would it do her to hold the memory of something she dearly wanted but never could have?

What good would it do her to constantly wonder what it might have been like, if only she'd said yes?

# Chapter 19

A short hour after Nathan left, the marshal came to fetch Faith to court again. "Are you ready?" he asked.

She nodded, not trusting her riotous emotions to even try to speak. She couldn't deny the feminine part of her heart that had woken up after Nathan's latest proposal. Thoughts of a future filled with more of those sweet caresses coursed her mind, and even the notion of a kiss or two taunted her with what she'd refused.

How was she going to react when she next saw him?

How was she going to greet him amid the judgmental eyes of Bountiful's men?

How would she feel when the verdict came down, and she looked into his eyes?

Once they arrived at the saloon, Faith was relieved to learn she'd been granted a minor reprieve. The jury was called back from their deliberations, since the soldiers had been called in to testify. She sat in her chair again, laced her hands in her lap, and settled back to listen, a silent prayer running over and over in her mind.

To her dismay, however, the military men had nothing to

add to what had already been presented to the court. Captain Roberts, Sergeant Graves, and Private Fowler, the men she'd seen in the cabin the night of Roger's death, confessed that they'd spent the evening drinking far too much in the company of the Nolan brothers. They also conceded it hadn't been the first time they'd made the same questionable choice in evening entertainment.

More important, none of them had any knowledge of the fire, or Roger's murder, much less any of the other crimes of which Faith stood accused. At the very least, she couldn't fault Mr. Peterson's performance or his persistent efforts to extract any scrap of information that might be of help.

"Thank you kindly, gentlemen," Judge Hess said when the last soldier finished his testimony. "You've borne up well under Mr. Peterson's vigorous questioning, but I'll be dismissing you now. The court won't be needing you further." He turned to the six men seated to his right. "Gentlemen of the jury, remember your responsibility. A woman's life hangs in the balance. Be fair, be diligent, stick to the facts and not your feelings as you deliberate the matter."

He waited for each man to nod. "In the spirit of compassion, don't draw this out unnecessarily, either. Have compassion on Mrs. Nolan's need to know her fate. Again, a woman's life is at stake. Please go do your job, as I said before, with diligence and deliberate attention. We'll be waiting for your verdict."

The jury trooped out to the future saloon's storage room, which the judge had deemed suitable for deliberations. As they walked by, Faith forced herself to look each one in the face. Not a one was willing to meet her gaze.

Dread made her wonder again about the wisdom of rejecting Nathan's offer.

His proposals.

An odd hitch in her heart caught her off guard. It was wondrous in its own way. Nathan Bartlett wanted to marry her, never mind the reason why. He'd offered to make her his wife. To be at her side, to support her, encourage her, comfort her, and even to...care for her. She couldn't keep her gaze from straying toward him. She caught her breath when she realized his eyes were fixed on her.

What if they married, and then reason prevailed and the jury found her innocent? Would the kind of marriage Nathan offered be enough? Years and years down the road?

Time seemed to stop. The sounds of the crowd faded. The sights around her didn't register. For long moments they stared at each other. Finally, that slow smile appeared again on Nathan's face. Faith couldn't tear her gaze away.

A warm flush rose up from her neck, to her cheeks, all the way to her ears. Oh, my.

Nathan Bartlett was indeed, as she'd thought a number of times before, a splendid figure of a man. And he wanted to marry her. Her heart kicked up a fast little beat. She'd never been on the receiving end of a smile like that—intimate, private, full of meaning for only the two of them. She shivered and allowed herself to respond with a tiny mirror image of his grin.

Bolstered by the silent exchange, Faith settled in to await the jury's return. She needed the verdict, no matter whether it favored her or not. The waiting was the hardest thing.

Harder still than turning down the most splendid man she'd ever known had been.

As it turned out, she didn't have more than an hour to wait. The judge resumed his place behind his table, gavel in hand. When the audience noticed and took their seats, he clapped the hammer down, and looked over the crowd.

"The court will come to order again. Marshal Blair tells me the jury has their verdict. They're about to come back in here, and let us know. Mind you"—he glowered at those in attendance—"I *will* have order, understood? Even after we hear that verdict."

Not a breath disturbed the silence. Faith's pulse beat in a breath-stealing pace, so loud it rivaled the judge's heavy gavel strikes. Then, in that deep hush, the six men marched in, led by the grim-faced marshal. Faith's shivers turned to shudders.

Maybe she should have told Nathan yes and perhaps managed to avoid this horror.

And yet...and yet, a glance at him told her another marriage arrangement wouldn't do. Certainly not with Nathan Bartlett. Both she and Nathan deserved a marriage like the one her parents had shared, a deep affection that showed in all their conversations, their every laugh, their every moment together.

Determined certainty set in.

The men sat.

Judge Hess banged his gavel.

Marshal Blair approached the judge's table. The judge looked up at the lawman. "You have the verdict?"

"I do indeed."

"Then let the court hear it loud and clear."

Marshal Blair nodded and swallowed hard. "Guilty, your honor. The jury finds Mrs. Faith Nolan guilty of murder, attempted murder, and theft."

Gasps broke out across the room.

At the sound of the dreaded words, Faith felt as though she floated high above her body, still seated to the right of the judge. She watched those in the audience turn to their neighbors, whisper, and stare. Some shook their heads, most smirked.

Out of the corners of her eyes, she saw Nathan continue to stare at Theo, powerful emotion seeming to harden the lines of his face.

Judge Hess clapped his gavel again. "Order, folks. Remember? Order in the court." He gave the crowd a moment to settle down, which it did, in view of the stern expression he displayed. When all fell silent again, he nodded toward the jury. "We will recess again while the six of you take on the matter of the defendant's sentence. Once again, I plead with you for your serious deliberation, your conscientious consideration of Mrs. Nolan's actions, of the evidence—evidence, gentlemen—as well as the lack of evidence presented, as you come to your decision."

He waited for his words to sink in. Then, "Please present this court with the lady's sentence—"

"Sentence?" Theo roared, bolting to his feet as though shot up by a spring. "What sentence do ya want, Judge? They say she's guilty, and we hang horse thieves and murderers in these parts. That's all ya need ta know."

• • •

A numb feeling settled over Nathan as Adam Blair revealed the verdict. Buzzing rang in his ears when Theo burst out with his demand for Faith to pay the ultimate price.

The jury didn't take more than ten minutes to decide her fate and return. Ice filled his veins when the sentence echoed Theo's words.

Hanging. They wanted to kill Faith. To hang her.

Only two thoughts found a place in his mind. First of all, the thought of actually losing her made him realize, without a doubt, that he *wanted* Faith Nolan to be his wife. And second, he had to know why. Why had it turned out like this? Why had the judge let it all come to this?

Mr. Peterson had asked to have the charges dismissed. With one smack of that little wooden hammer, Judge Hess could have brought it all to an end. He hadn't. Nathan needed to know why.

As though from miles away, he heard the swish of the ladies' skirts as they left the saloon, their faces drawn, tears in many eyes. He also heard the crack of the men's boot heels as they followed the women on their way outside. The men, however, weren't as thoughtful as the women. They slapped each other's backs, some whispered comments, others allowed themselves a smirk or even a chuckle here and there.

Anger bubbled up in Nathan. He fisted his hand, ground his teeth, leaned forward, and began to stand.

"Easy." Eli laid a hand on Nathan's shoulder. "Let them go. Don't do anything that might make matters worse."

Aware of the wisdom in his friend's words, he nonetheless glared as he forced himself to stay put. "This cannot be allowed to stand."

"I agree. But this is not the time or place to act. Let them go."

Nathan pulled away from Eli's grasp, and leaned back in his chair. He didn't say another word, but watched Adam lead Faith out of the saloon, the metal handcuffs large and unnatural on her delicate wrists. The jury left directly after her, and the last one in that wretched party, Judge Hess, followed behind them all.

Only then did Nathan stand. With singular focus, he matched his steps to those of the judge, keeping an even distance between the two of them. Once outside, he continued in his pursuit, growing aware of the destination of those who'd left before him. And of the judge.

They were all headed to Folsom's River Run Hotel, most likely to enjoy some lunch and raise a drink or two in celebration of a job they considered well done. Anger burned in his gut again, but Nathan fought to tamp it down, to ignore it.

Then he heard a familiar voice crow in triumph. "Toldja, dinnent I?" Theo bellowed, as he and Hector Swope marched to the hotel, smirks on their faces. "It weren't jist murder Roger they say she did. They said she did attempted murder—that bank fella, you know."

Hector nodded, his attention fixed on his pal.

Theo laughed. "They couldn't not find her guilty, what with the rat poison in that box lunch she fed 'im, and all. I tell ya, I never seen a woman like to kill rats as much as that

Faith. She spent half her time up to the store sprinkling that stuff like it was sugar or salt..."

Nathan halted in the middle of the street. He stared after the two ne'er-do-wells. Bits of information seemed to come together to form a new picture in his head. Had he missed it all along? Did he have all the parts of the puzzle now?

Try as he might, he couldn't make it all fit. Not yet. Still, some things had come into focus.

He shot a sideways look at his companion. "Eli...did you hear what Theo just said?"

"Sure. The same things he's been saying ever since the night his brother died."

"Yes, but that's not all. Did you know what it was that poisoned Parham?"

Eli nodded. "Doc told us at the church that day. He said it looked like rat poison—"

"Exactly! He said it that day, but I don't recollect him telling anyone but those who were left at the church at the end—you and Olivia, the Altons, Adam, Faith, and me. Theo wasn't there."

Eli's eyes widened. "Are you saying...?"

"I never said anything about it being rat poison to anyone. Did you?"

"Only when Olivia and I talked it over after we went home. And that was only once or twice."

"Right." Excitement began to build. "And you know Doc as well as I do. Adam, too. Do either one of them strike you as having flapping lips, to go talking about such things all over town?"

"Never."

He smiled. "Now, the ladies are different, but I doubt they talked about the rat poison with anyone."

"No. They only care about Faith. They've wanted the charges dropped all along, saying they're nothing more than the foolish ramblings of the town's drunk. They wouldn't have given any fuel to the rumors."

Nathan began to walk toward the hotel again. "He may be the town drunk, but he's looking like a whole lot more right about now."

"He knew about the rat poison."

"Who, besides a handful of us, would have known what sickened Parham? Especially, since Marshal Blair didn't want word of it spread. He wanted to keep it silent, to make sure only the few of us and the culprit would know it was there. He never believed Faith had anything to do with it."

"Yes, the one who put the poison in the food would know."

They picked up their pace, the hotel at the other end of town their goal. They had questions for Theo Nolan, questions he'd have no choice but to answer fully this time. In front of all the men from Bountiful.

And the judge.

"I didn't kill nobody, I tell ya!" Theo hollered. "Poison is poison. I reckon...rat poison, well, we always had plenty of it up to the store. Faith used it all the time. *She's* the guilty one. Jury said so. I jist...jist made a good guess. No, no! I heered it. I heered...um...the marshal! Yes, the marshal said it were rat poison what kilt my brother. That's it."

Adam's face looked like a granite statue, its lines hardened from the moment Nathan confronted Theo in the hotel. "I never said a thing about rat poison to you, Nolan."

Theo's eyes couldn't seem to find a spot to look at. He glanced from table to table, man to man. "Nah...not to me, you dinnent. Ah...I heered you talk to—to...Folsom! That's who. At supper one night."

"Me!" the hotel owner objected. "I never heard a word about rat poison. Weren't me he told."

Theo blanched, then seconds later turned the color of well-cooked beets. "Then it musta been...musta been Whitman. Sure. The banker fella's boss. And they're friends, too."

Adam glanced at Eli, who shook his head.

"Seems to me," Adam said in his lazy-sounding drawl, "you know a mite too much about Parham's poisoning. Looks like you'll be spending some more time as a guest down to my jail. Starting now."

As he led Theo out the door, his prisoner yelled one more time. "I tell ya, it weren't me! I dinnent do it. It were—"

He cut off his stream of defenses, cleared his throat, then seconds later, from outside the building, those inside heard him start it up again. "I mean to say, it musta been someone else, seein' as I dinnent come up with no notion of killing no one. I don't even like rat poison, it smells so sick and sweet and...and it kills..."

The silence in the room slowly ended, as the occupants began to talk among themselves. Eli turned to Nathan.

"What do you think?"

More pieces of the puzzle had begun to move around in his head. "I'm not sure. Do you think Theo's got the wits to figure all that? To plan to kill Parham for—"

He fell silent.

Eli waited. Then prompted, "For..."

"I don't know. Why would he want to kill Faith?"

"He thinks she killed his brother."

Nathan narrowed his gaze, staring at the door through which Theo had left. "Revenge? You think that's what the box lunch was all about? And he was willing to poison whatever poor soul bought her box lunch, too?"

"Maybe. Maybe not. I can't be sure, but it almost sounded as though he was about to put the blame on someone else. As though he caught himself before he blurted out a name."

"Could be." Nathan met his friend's gaze. "But who?"

"It would seem Theo Nolan has more talking to do."

He smiled. "And Adam Blair's the man to make sure he does."

After Eli left to return to his office at the bank, Nathan watched the judge make his way between the tables in the hotel dining room.

The men who'd watched the disgrace of a trial congratulated the judge. At least four promised to buy him a drink. One waved a bill to pay for his meal. The mood grew more and more raucous, more partylike, and Nathan felt he was about to get sick.

It seemed everyone but Nathan had forgotten what Theo had revealed.

He called again on his determination. The travesty that had taken place at the saloon—a saloon, for heaven's sake—could not be left to stand. Especially not now. Nathan waited for the judge to find a table before he stepped further into the restaurant.

When the judge took his seat, Nathan approached. "Are you waiting for someone to join you?"

The judge glanced up. "Not at all. I'd be honored if you did."

"Thank you." He slipped his coat onto the back of the scarred oak chair, and pulled up close to the worn table. Only then did he meet the older man's gaze. "I needed to talk to you about...well, about *that*."

"I figured you would."

Nathan was grateful to see sadness in the man's eyes. As he pondered his choice of words, the judge went on.

"I'd like you to know, and to let Mrs. Nolan know, how sorry I am about it all."

For a moment, Nathan sat silent, motionless, frozen in place by the man's unexpected words. "If that's the case, then, please answer the one question I have." He waited until the man's dark eyes met his. "Why? Why didn't you stop it when you had the chance?"

Judge Hess rubbed his bald head. Then he leaned his forearms on the table and laced his hands. He met Nathan's gaze full on. "It was out of my hands, son. You saw the mind-set of the men in the court, especially since they were listening to the dead man's brother."

"The dead man's brother..." He laced his fingers, studied the calluses built up by years of hard work. "Do you know what just happened here? Minutes before you arrived?"

"No. I can't say I do. Does it have to do with the trial?"

"I'm afraid it does." Nathan told the judge what he'd pieced together from Theo's careless words. "I think we can safely say that Faith Nolan's not guilty of attempted murder.

How can that be changed, now the jury's brought back a verdict on something they didn't know?"

They discussed options, and the judge assured Nathan he would make sure the change would take place. "It doesn't change the murder conviction. Just because Theo knows something about the box lunch doesn't mean she's been cleared of killing her husband."

"No, it doesn't. But you can't believe she's guilty of that, either."

The judge sighed. "It doesn't matter what I believe. Our legal practice is for the jury of her peers to decide. They did."

"But you're the judge. You were in charge. They would have had to listen to your decision if you'd dismissed the case when Mr. Peterson asked."

He shrugged. "It's not that simple. You're a smart fellow. You must know what would have happened if I had interfered with the natural course of the trial in any way. We would have had our hands full trying to quiet down a riot. When things get out of control like that . . . why, a man can't know what kind of violence can happen. I couldn't run the risk of them taking the law in their hands."

Nathan scoffed, the sound full of bitterness. "And you think that verdict's not a matter of them taking the law in their hands?"

"Are you appealing the verdict?"

"I suppose I am."

"Then I'll have to handle the matter as per the law. I'll see to it that it goes through the proper channels."

Nathan gestured around the hotel restaurant. "Will that

stop all of *them*? Won't they ignore the proper channels and the law and throw a rope over a branch and hang her?"

His harsh words brought about the reaction he'd wanted. The judge flinched.

"I'm sorry, Mr. Bartlett," the older man said, his expression sincere. "There wasn't anything I could do. I couldn't dismiss the case against Mrs. Nolan. If you're so distressed, I would suggest you take Marshal Blair's counsel about the only possible way out of this dreadful mess. He spoke to me about it, you know. If you approach Mr. Nolan, offer to pay off Mrs. Nolan's debts—"

"That won't change those guilty verdicts in the murder and the theft."

"No, but it may calm him enough to allow the appeal process to continue. And there's always the chance one of you will uncover the identity of the real culprit."

"The real culprit? Does that mean you have doubts about her guilt?"

"Her guilt?" The judge laughed and shook his head. "I doubt that lady's killed anything greater than a plump chicken for a Sunday supper."

Nathan felt another chink appear in the icy prison that had encased his heart when the verdict was announced. He looked around at the celebrating diners. "Do you think...?"

"Start with Mrs. Nolan, son. She seems a sensible lady. I'm sure she'll see the wisdom in the two of you wedding as soon as possible. The rest should fall into place with time."

"A body would think so, right?" Nathan laughed. "What would you say if I told you I'm ahead of you, sir? I already proposed. She turned me down. Twice."

The judge blinked. "You don't say! Well, well, well. She's a spunky one, too, isn't she? Try again, son. Don't give up. It's the only hope I see to stop the inevitable."

"I understand."

The judge chuckled. "And to wind up with a splendid woman at your side for the rest of your life. I'd say she's well worth the fight for her heart."

Nathan nodded slowly. He was coming to that conviction himself.

Now to persuade the lady to say yes.

And to make sure Theo backed down.


Reeling from all the notions buzzing in his mind, Nathan left the hotel and headed toward the Whitman home. While he'd started out opposed to courting Faith on account of all he already had on his plate back at the camp, by now he'd come around to the other side. It struck him as the only chance they had to keep Faith alive.

He only had to convince the stubborn lady of the validity of his plan. He had but a handful of weapons in his arsenal. One of the most powerful ones was the lady of the house where he was staying. He suspected Olivia Whitman would be more than happy to nudge her new friend toward the institution of marriage, since she'd hinted the notion buzzed in her own, very busy, mind.

He mulled over his options, especially how best to approach Olivia and win over the right amount of her help and none of her tendency to "solve problems," as she called her actions. One of the soldiers who'd testified at the trial, Sergeant Graves, walked past him outside the hotel, arms loaded with a stack of heavy woolen point blankets. The sight of the yellow, red, blue, and green stripes against the creamy white background sparked something to life in his memory, and he watched the fellow march inside.

For a moment he considered what he should do next. Should he follow the man and see what he was up to? Or should he first take a look at the wagon tied at the hitching post, an Army insignia clearly visible on one side. Instinct told him to start with the wagon.

As soon as he reached it, his suspicion was confirmed. The vehicle was loaded with a stack of items that looked mighty familiar to him. If he wasn't much mistaken, he'd found his missing supplies. Saws, tools not normally associated with the military but much needed by loggers and by the occasional construction crews that abounded in the fast-growing Bountiful, filled a corner of the wagon. The two massive iron cooking pots that Woody had asked for rolled loose between a crate of dried beef and a sack of beans. A barrel of nails, which the camp needed for repairs to the buildings on account of the continual damage caused by the strong winds, sat right behind the driver's seat, and Nathan now knew that if he toted up the number of blankets the sergeant had carried into the hotel, he'd find they matched up to the ones he'd ordered but never received. How had the Army men wound up with his supplies?

He turned to head back in the hotel to get his questions answered and noticed two large barrels on the wooden sidewalk next to the wagon. Whiskey, and lots of it. He wondered how that had come to be loaded up with the other things, especially since he never would order spirits. He didn't drink, and didn't allow any at his camp. He couldn't imagine Captain Roberts allowed it at the fort, either. So why would his sergeant have such a large supply of the stuff?

As he turned toward the hotel, Sergeant Graves walked out. When the man caught sight of him next to the wagon, he stopped, a hunted look on his pale face. With a sudden show of bravado, Sergeant Graves hitched up his trousers and swaggered close.

"What are you wanting with our wagon, there, Bartlett?"

"Not a thing," he answered, crossing his arms. "I am wanting an answer about my supplies." He gestured toward the wagon. "My *missing* supplies."

The sergeant blinked. "I don't know nothing about your supplies. You might could talk to Metcalf over to the mercantile about 'em."

"You can stop that foolishness, Graves." Nathan dropped his easy stance and voice. "You know I didn't order *and pay* for these things at the mercantile here in town. Because they were close, and because they had the mules to get most anything up the mountain, I always ordered from the Nolan brothers. That's where these supplies came from."

He shrugged with exaggerated indifference. "I know nothing about the Nolan brothers and their store."

"You know enough to have gone drinking with them. Could these barrels of spirits have come from them?"

The brown eyes bounced from the door to the hotel to the wagon, from the schoolhouse across the street to the new structure going up right next to it, to the dirt on the road, to the dusty boardwalk—anywhere but at Nathan.

"Dunno where it came from. Captain told me to load it

up, give Folsom his things, and get the money Folsom owes the captain. Fellow owes him a whole lot."

"*Folsom* owes your captain money."

Sergeant Graves nodded. "Sure thing. Folsom, the fella who owns the hotel."

"And the captain sent you to bring all this to *Folsom?*"

"Uh-huh."

"I reckon this isn't the first time you've brought him a wagonload."

Unease rolled off the man in waves. "No, sir."

"And he's promised to pay the captain...but hasn't?"

Graves laughed. "Yeah, he's hard to squeeze a penny from. He pays, but he's slow, you know?"

Nathan nodded. He was in the process of coming to know. "Tell you what. Let me give you a hand hauling some of the heaviest stuff inside. I'm sure you can appreciate some help."

Relief brightened the man's face. "Sure can appreciate the help. Here. Let's start with the barrel of nails. They're the worst of all."

Nathan narrowed his eyes. "I'll help you with the nails, but how about we start off with one of the barrels of drink."

For a long moment, Graves considered Nathan's words. He shrugged. "Fine by me."

The two of them picked up the first barrel of whiskey, and together they carried it into the hotel. Eyes fixed on the front desk, Nathan saw the moment Folsom took note of who was coming in with Graves, a heavy barrel of whiskey between the two of them. A moment of panic lingered in the hotel owner's gaze, but then he stormed out from behind the desk.

"What's the meaning of this, Bartlett?"

Nathan nodded to Graves. They set the sealed barrel down, its contents sloshing and slapping against the wooden sides. Graves scurried back outside.

"How about you tell me what it *really* is about? I know where these things are from, and I know where they were meant to go in the first place. Seems a whole lot of folks are handling supplies I ordered a while back. Tell me, Folsom. What's your part in this?"

"Well, for one thing, that whiskey ain't mine." He jutted his chin. "That there goes to the fort. Dunno why Graves woulda brought back in what he just hauled out."

Nathan had suspected as much. "And how is it you ended up with the exact blankets I ordered from the Nolans? Not to mention every other item that I paid for in advance that never arrived."

The hotel owner began to fidget, twisting his hands together, glancing around the entry hall of his establishment. "Well, it's like this . . . er . . . Metcalf don't stock the point blankets regular-like, on account of them costing too much and taking too long to get shipped into town. So I have an . . . arrangement with the captain out to the fort. He brings me blankets and other supplies I need at the hotel, and I trade 'em for . . . well, for cheap spirits that I can get easy."

"That's a lot of *cheap spirits* for a fort with only a handful of soldiers stationed there these days. They've mostly gone with the Indians to the reservations, haven't they?"

Folsom shrugged. "Not all of 'em. They're still rounding up the Indian stragglers. Some of them Indians are still burning down homes after they steal the folks blind, you know. 'Specially after they've had too much drink—"

When the hotel owner realized what he'd said, he fell silent and refused to speak another word. He didn't have to. Nathan thought immediately of Faith's parents, how they had died. Something dark and evil had been going on. It involved the Nolan brothers, the men at the Army post, and the hotel owner. Faith had clearly had no part in it, other than suffering the consequences, he thought grimly.

He spun on his heel and headed toward the table where he'd last seen the captain. It was time for a blunt talk with the man, preferably in front of Judge Hess, and better yet, with Adam Blair close by.

If that conversation didn't flow as easily as it should, seeing how much Nathan had learned, well, then, his fists had an itch to help the words come out. The urge shocked him.

And here he'd thought himself so far above violence.

"Lord," he said under his breath as he strode between tables to the farthest corner of the room. "I gave you my word I wouldn't again take part in hurting another soul, but I don't know if I can stop myself today. Help me, Father, to do your will."

As he approached the captain, his gaze locked on the military man's face. His prey rose out of his chair, knocking it over in his rush. The clatter brought all conversations in the room to a close.

Nathan didn't slow down.

When he was only inches away from the crooked wretch, he broke the heavy silence. "I saw your wagon outside. I also had an interesting talk with Mr. Folsom and Sergeant Graves. How about you explain your scheme to the folks here today?

Won't do you much good to try and hide all what you've done."

The judge walked up to Nathan's right side. "What's this all about?"

"Nathan?" Adam stopped at his left.

"I have a wagonload of evidence outside, every item I paid Nolan for that never arrived. I also have two witnesses." Nathan nodded to where Folsom stood beside the sergeant. "I believe we're looking at our killer, arsonist, maybe even petty thief. Oh, and attempted killer, too. Seems he tried more than he succeeded, by the grace of God, seeing as Faith is still among us, and Lewis Parham, as well."

The plump judge's mild expression was no more, and in its place a thunderous frown lined his hairless brow. "I suggest you best start talking. And someone here needs to get word to the fort near Pendleton, too. We need the Army, and quick."

The captain looked to Folsom, but from the hotel owner's expression it was clear he wasn't about to help. Faced with clear, concrete evidence and the unyielding power of the law, Captain Roberts folded back into his chair, a look of devastation on his face. "I'm sorry," he said, his voice shaking. "I didn't mean for it to turn out like this."

"How did you expect things to turn out when you broke the law?" Nathan shook his head. "A lot of laws?"

"There's only five of us out to the fort," he said, lending more strength to his words. "The Indians ... well, there's not many, but the ones left, they have no intention of going easy to the reservation. We don't have the force to deal with many of them ..."

"What does that have to do with the whiskey and my sup-plies?" He wanted more answers, all of them, but Nathan knew it would go better for him if he went one at a time. The captain looked like a broken man.

"They like to drink. When they do enough, they don't fight back so much."

The judge glared. "The Army condones breaking the law, and selling liquor to Indians?"

Shame colored Captain Roberts's face. "They don't know. That's why we'd always bought spirits from Nolan...or Fol-som here."

That made a twisted kind of sense, trying to keep their lawless behavior hidden from the Army's eyes. More of the pieces of the puzzle fell into place. "You traded my order to Folsom as partial payment for the whiskey you felt you needed."

The captain nodded, an apologetic expression on his thin features as he glanced at the owner of the hotel. "Nolan didn't have my whiskey that day. When I met up with my men at the Nolans' store, I knew I had to talk to him about the delay. The time before, I'd taken the blankets and tools and things, but they weren't going to help us with the men we had to move to Idaho. We needed the whiskey."

"And Roger didn't have it."

Roberts shook his head.

"So he gave you my supplies instead, things to trade with Folsom that he needed more than the whiskey he bought...where?"

With a wave of his hand, the captain gestured to where Folsom still stood.

"I...uh...I go so far as Lillybelle's Palace down by Pendleton. I know the owner. She gives me a good price, and...well, I'm always needing to serve my customers, you know."

"You don't order through Metcalf?"

"Metcalf won't deal in drink of any kind. I ordered mainly from Roger, until...*you* know."

"Roger," Adam said at Nathan's elbow. "It all comes back to Roger. What did happen to the man?"

Captain Roberts lost all color in his cheeks. "My men and I saddled up and started down the trail for the fort. But I swung back. I wanted to push Roger to get our whiskey in. I needed it. When I got there, Mrs. Nolan...well, she was laid out on the floor by the hearth. Looked to me like she'd died. Roger insisted she'd be fine, that she'd fallen before, she was awkward. We...argued, and he swung an iron poker at me. I grabbed it, twisted it from his hand. I didn't intend to have him use it on me, and...and...well, I..."

As his voice died off, he moved his hands into a helpless spread.

Adam stepped closer. "You turned the poker on him. And then you set fire to the place to cover the murder."

"I didn't mean to. I didn't mean to kill him. It was an accident. He came at me...he stumbled, and..."

"What about Faith?" Nathan asked. "You left her there to burn alive."

"I thought she was dead already. I thought he was lying, that he'd finally killed her. She never moved the whole time. I never would have—"

"You were going to let her hang for what you had done."

That did it. The man broke down, admitted guilt had been eating him inside. The horror at the thought of leaving a woman, an innocent woman, to die like that. And then to learn she had survived only to pay the price for his crime. Torn between the need to save himself for his wife's sake, and knowing what awaited Faith, he'd been wrestling with his conscience all morning long.

But he'd failed to act.

He continued to talk, to tell all the dreadful details, how he'd paid Theo to sprinkle rat poison on the box lunch; how he'd spurred the horse on Main Street; how he'd sent Theo to do away with Faith at the church, since he'd feared she'd seen or heard him while she lay bleeding on the floor the night Roger died; how Theo had struck her but instead of killing her, he'd gone after the easy cash in the reverend's desk. He didn't stop until he'd confessed to it all.

Joy crept into Nathan's heart.

Faith was innocent.

She was safe.

Bitter tears poured down Faith's face. When would she be led, like a lamb to the slaughter, to that rope that was to end her life?

In the dark, stark cell, she prayed for courage, since she didn't want to flinch before the crowd that had found her guilty, even though she was certain, more so each day that went by, that she hadn't killed Roger. And she'd certainly not done any of the other things.

"Father...I don't want to die. There's so much I've

missed in life—I've missed life, for the most part. If there's a way to avoid this..."

She let her words die off. She had been offered a way that presented her with the promise of a future. And she'd turned Nathan down. Now, in the silence of her cell, she admitted what she'd tried to avoid. She was a coward, indeed. She feared marrying Nathan, falling in love with him, and then having to watch him from the distance created by a lack of love on his part.

Did she fear death at the end of a rope enough to take back her rejection? Or was she willing to spend the rest of her life, however long or short that might be, at the side of yet another man who didn't love her?

"Hey, there."

She looked up and blushed. The man who'd held her thoughts captive stood on the other side of the bars. "Hello, Nathan. I'm surprised to see you here."

He smiled, and then he did the most outlandish thing. He shook Marshal Blair's mass of keys right in front of his face. "I'm about to break you out of jail."

She gasped. "Oh, no! I could never do that. It wouldn't be right. The court...the judge—wait. Where is the marshal? What have you done with the poor man?"

Nathan jerked a thumb over his shoulder. "He's in his office. In fact, he's the one who gave me his keys."

"I don't understand."

His grin widened. "Ah, but you will. As soon as we get you out of here, and back to the parsonage. Mrs. Alton will be one mighty happy lady tonight. Only a mite less happy than you."

Ginny Aiken

"I'm going back to the Altons' house? Why? What's happened?"

He shot a glance up. "Looks like the Lord's not done with you down here yet. He's blessed us with the identity of the killer. You're no longer to even give a thought to that trial or worry about the sentence. You're a free woman, Faith Nolan. You're free to go."

He unlocked the cell door, and after pausing in disbelief, Faith stumbled out. A moment later, she spun and snagged the Bible from the bed, and then hurried back out again.

"You have a great deal of explaining to do," she said, "but I'm happy to have you do that explaining anywhere but here."

He caught her by the shoulder. "Don't hurry out yet. I need you to understand one thing. My proposal? It still stands."

"But—"

"Now, don't go speaking so fast yet. I have my reasons, and I want to lay them down before we go anywhere. I think we would make a great match, especially seeing as how you're still alone and with nowhere to go. I'm alone, too, but I have a camp, a solid cabin, food on the table, and warm clothes to wear. I've never met another woman as smart, hardworking, decent, and downright good as you. If I'm ever to marry, you're the sort I want by my side. Give it some thought. You don't have to answer right away—"

"I don't have to answer right away, but I can," Faith said, chin held high. "I already said I won't ever marry again on account of my basic needs. I already made one marriage bargain, and you saw how that turned out. I won't do that again."

• 344 •

"I heard you when you first said it, when you said it again, and now a third time. But I don't think you heard what I said. I'm persistent."

"I'm sure of myself."

"I don't give up."

"I've given in too much."

"This time is different. I'm different."

"Ah . . ." she said. "But you see, Nathan. I'm not."

He leaned back, the grin still on his face. "We shall have to see, then, Faith. We shall have to see."

# *Epilogue*

"The sack of coffee is right behind the barrel of pickles to the right of the bolts of gray wool," Faith said from behind the counter at the logging camp's company store. "You see it, Woody?"

"No, ma'am," the logger said. "Cain't say I can find anything the way you keep things in this place, especially these last few months. I don't know as I see any order in here—ah! There it is. What's coffee got to do with pickles and wool?"

Faith laughed. "Not much. That's where Nathan and the newest fellow he hired set it when they unloaded this last wagonload."

"It were easier before we got that road put in, when all we had was what those three mules could bring up. Speaking of, I think all three of them are getting lazy now that they spend so much time grazing in that pasture."

"They earned their rest. Which reminds me, there should be a barrel of apples around here and I promised them each one." Faith looked around until she spotted the barrel. "I know I haven't kept things so well these last few months, but

*Ginny Aiken*

I wasn't about to risk Nathan's wrath by wrestling fifty-pound sacks, you know."

"How right you are," Nathan said, surprising Faith as he walked into the store. "You're not touching those heavy sacks. Not these days, you're not."

She spun to face her husband and smiled, as he placed a tender hand on her swollen middle. She laced her fingers through his. "I didn't know you were back. I thought you'd gone with the rest of the men to the new stand of trees you're taking down."

He shrugged. "Got them started, and then, well..."

"I'd best be heading back to my stove." Woody shook his head. "Who'd'a thought the two of you..."

"Yes," Nathan said, smiling. "Who'd'a thought the two of us...?"

"You did."

"You're right, Mrs. Bartlett."

She chuckled. "Hm...you might want to remember that, Mr. Bartlett."

"When it comes to the store...that's always the case." He wrapped his arms around her waist, laced his hands at the base of her back, and leaned away to meet her gaze. "You have a gift for business, Faith."

She placed her hands on his muscular forearms, relishing the power there, and even more, the gentleness of the man. "Numbers are simple. It's not hard to keep track of them."

"Only numbers I'm interested in these days," her husband of one year countered, "are one plus one plus one."

Faith reached up to cup his cheek in her palm, tears of joy, so quick to rise these days, filling her eyes. "That, my love, is no group of numbers. That, Nathan, is a family—ours."

"Ours..."

She felt the smile on his lips when he covered hers with yet another of the million kisses they would share in the years to come. As husband and wife.

In a marriage full of love, more wonderful than any dream.

# Reading Group Guide

1. Read 1 Samuel 25:14–42. How is Faith's story similar to that of Abigail? How are they different?

2. At the beginning of the book, Faith feels hopeless in her marriage, worse than right after her parents' murders. When in your life have you felt like there was no hope? How did you respond? How did God answer?

3. Although Roger is a fictional character, based on a biblical one, spousal abuse is only too real a crime in our society. Have you learned to identify the signs? How do you, as a believer, respond to it? Have you ever reached out to a victim? Have you ever volunteered at a women's shelter? If not, what's held you back?

4. Nathan was determined to focus all his attention and energy on his logging operation. God, on the other hand, had different plans for him: Faith. When have your plans been foiled by God's much better ones? How long did it

take you to recognize God's loving hand in the circumstances?

5. Do you think Faith's pride hurt her? Have you ever been in a situation where you sacrificed for the sake of pride?

6. The women of Bountiful saw Faith's true nature. What societal biases clouded the men's reason? Have you ever faced a similar situation? How have you handled it?

7. Captain Roberts assumed Faith was dead when his fight with Roger turned deadly. Instead of checking on her, he tried to hide his crime by burning the cabin, and then ran away. Starting with Adam, we've all tried that at some point in our lives. When did you try to run away from accountability to God? What brought you up short? What happened after you finally faced Him?

8. Nathan was willing to give up his freedom to save Faith. When have you given up something major for another's sake? In the end, God blessed him richly for his sacrifice. How did God bless your love and sacrifice?

9. Faith, as Abigail in Scripture, felt convicted to do the right thing by Nathan. Have you ever had to stick your neck out like that? If so, when? What was the outcome?

10. In our lives, a "happily ever after" is hard to identify, since our days continue to go on. Author Ginny Aiken

keeps a prayer journal so that she can see how God answers her prayers. Do you recognize any "happily ever
afters" in your life? How do you keep track of God's
blessings? How would it impact your life if you did track
His mercies?

Read Olivia and Eli's story in

# *For Such a Time as This*

"The Biblical story of Queen Esther meets the West in an engaging historical romance."
—Vickie McDonough, award-winning author

*Hope County, Oregon—1879* When drought and plagues of insects put her family in a dire financial situation, eldest daughter Olivia Moore takes a live-in position as a nanny in the home of widower banker Eli Whitman. Gossip in the small town of Bountiful about their relationship, however, soon leads Eli to propose marriage as a business arrangement. Olivia accepts, and Eli is generous in providing for her. His one condition is that she never interfere in his business. But when Eli's bank forecloses on her parents' farm, Olivia is torn between her promise to her husband and her duty to her family.

Look for the next Women of Hope novel

## *She Shall Be Praised*

Inspired by Proverbs 31

Coming from FaithWords in 2014